Be
Becka, Elizabeth

FM

c l W9-BSL-549

Unknown means

UNKNOWN MEANS

Also by Elizabeth Becka

TRACE EVIDENCE

UNKNOWN MEANS

ELIZABETH BECKA

NEW YORK

Printed in the United States of America.

For information address Hyperion, 77 West 66th
Street, New York, New York 10023-6298.

Library of Congress Cataloging-in-Publication Data

Becka, Elizabeth
    Unknown means / Elizabeth Becka. — 1st ed.
        p.   cm.
    ISBN: 978-1-4013-0175-0
    1. Medical examiners (Law)—Fiction.   2.
· Women forensic scientists—Fiction.   3. Di-
vorced mothers—Fiction.   4. Police—Ohio—
Cleveland—Fiction.   5. Cleveland
(Ohio)—Fiction.   I. Title.
    PS3602.E283U55   2007
    813'.6—dc22   2007037425

Hyperion books are available for special
promotions, premiums, or corporate training.
For details contact Michael Rentas, Proprietary
Markets, Hyperion, 77 West 66th Street,
12th floor, New York, New York 10023, or call
212-456-0133.

Design by Karen Minster

FIRST EDITION

10   9   8   7   6   5   4   3   2   1

For my sisters,

Mary and Susan,

my friends,

my support

UNKNOWN MEANS

THE WOMAN'S BODY HAD BEEN POSED, SOMETHING Evelyn had read about but never seen. Twenty-eight, white, dead Grace Markham sat upright at her kitchen table, silky black hair skimming her cheeks. Mesh straps held her shoulders and waist to the high-backed wooden chair. One of the same straps had been used to strangle her, to judge from the width and pattern of the indentations in her skin. Her arms lay on the table in front of her, stretched forward far enough to keep them from slipping back off. She might have been sitting at a meal, were it not for the bulging eyes and tongue, and her head lolling to her chest. Perhaps the killer had not had time to fix that detail, or couldn't figure out how.

Evelyn James turned off the filtered vacuum that she had been using to pick up any loose hairs, fibers, or trace evidence on the floor's surface. Thunder rattled the windows, extra loud in the sudden quiet. "Is it *ever* going to stop raining?"

"It's the lake effect. Besides, April showers bring May flowers," Detective Riley told her.

"They also bring flash floods and backed-up sewers."

She leaned toward the body, close enough to catch the scent of fresh death. Grace Markham had tried to save herself, to judge from the scratches along her jugular and the broken fingernails, the red slash of constriction etched deeply into her neck. Part of a gold necklace had been caught against her skin so that the diamond pendant hung awry. Evelyn shifted the gem with one finger. "This has to be two carats, at least."

Homicide Detective David Milaski spoke for the first time since Evelyn had arrived, twenty minutes earlier. "I'll pick up one for you to wear to Marissa's wedding. Oh, that's right, I'm a cop. I can't even afford cubic zirconium."

An olive branch, an attempt to get past their argument that morning. She tried to reciprocate. "I'd just sell it to pay for Angel's college anyway. I don't know how else I'm going to afford tuition."

"Of course."

Wrong choice of subject. Evelyn held his blue-eyed gaze for another moment to tell him so.

"You two arguing again?" Riley asked. David's partner, the rumpled Detective Bruce Riley, had been a cop for thirty-two years and could pluck a tense tone out of the air like a sonic baseball. "If this has to do with Freedman's bachelor party, I want it on the record that I told him not to go."

"That was a great party," a uniformed cop, the contamination officer for the scene, murmured from the foyer.

Evelyn removed the filter from the vacuum and sealed it in a brown paper bag before she picked up her camera. The viewfinder framed Grace Markham's preternaturally still form like a bizarre piece of modern art.

Evelyn had seen death by strangulation before, more times than she cared to tally. The Medical Examiner's Office dealt with two or three homicides per week, and each one had to be examined by a forensic scientist—meaning her, until the Trace Evidence Department budget could allow for more staff. But this particular murder broke new ground.

Instead of in a violent back alley, Grace Markham rested at her own kitchen table, and in one of the most expensive high-rise suites on the Lake Erie shore. The Markham suite spanned the entire tenth floor, with four bedrooms, three baths, two offices, a TV room, and a sauna. At the main entrance, where the contamination officer stood to keep unwanted personnel out of the scene, the elevator opened directly onto the foyer's granite squares—rich people did not fumble with keys. The kitchen and open eating area flowed into a living room filled with leather furniture, a plasma flat-screen, and artfully lit photographs, the white walls and carpeting as clean as an unused operating room.

This was new. And not in a good way.

Most murders occurred on the spur of the moment, impulsive acts of rage or desperation that the killers tried to cover up or escape as quickly as possible. There should have been some sign of struggle or disturbed items to indicate the killer's process, his agenda, his desires. This guy had left them nothing but one very dead body.

Evelyn twisted the camera's lens, focusing on Grace Markham. "Where was the husband?"

"At work," David said. "He's an architect, currently designing the new Rhodes office complex in the Flats. No children. Miller and Sanchez are with him right now, finishing up his statement. He last saw Grace when he left for work this morning, around six. Grace had a nail appointment at ten and a doctor's appointment at eleven—prenatal visit. She is—was—two months pregnant."

Evelyn looked up. "Damn."

"Yeah. She didn't make either of her appointments, to judge from the messages on the answering machine. Meanwhile, the husband's been showing a proposal to a client all day, in full view of at least five people at any given moment. When's time of death?"

"Four A.M. to ten A.M., at a guess. The husband could have killed her before he left. We'll know more after the doctor does a liver temp at the lab."

"Why tie her up like that?" David asked.

"I don't know, babe." She gave him a weary smile. "I just got here."

"Do you think there's been a sexual assault?"

"The clothes are a little messy—sweater pulled out of the skirt, a run in the stockings—but that could have happened in the struggle." Evelyn used a ruler in her photographs of the straps, the scratches, a slight bruise on the left bicep, and the indentation in the woman's neck. "If I find anything, I'll have Marissa run the DNA as soon as she can. If I can tear her away from *Cleveland Bride*."

"Going to be a lot of young men upset about Marissa getting married," Riley said as he went through the victim's purse, which had been left on the counter.

"They had their chance."

"You going to be a bridesmaid, Evie?"

"There are things I won't do even for my best friend, and wearing a poufy dress is definitely one of them. Hey, don't walk on the other side of the table yet," she warned David as he leaned in to get a closer look at the body. "I'm going to dust the floor tiles in a little bit."

He remained next to her, hovering, as if hoping for insight. Unlike Riley, he had less than a year in the homicide unit, and Evelyn knew he felt the pressure of being the new guy. She smelled the cologne she'd given him for his birthday. He said, "I'm used to gangbangers, domestics, and liquor store robberies. But who does something like *this*? Think maybe it was a home invasion gone bad?"

She snapped a close-up photo of the dead woman's hand. "He wouldn't have left this rock around her neck. Are there any signs of burglary in the other rooms?"

Riley spoke up. "Nope. The whole floor is Howard Hughes clean. There's a few rings left on her dresser and a safe in her closet. Apparently untouched."

"I didn't think she'd keep a piece of jewelry like that in a little wooden box with a ballerina that turns when you open the lid. Crap—I'm going to have to fingerprint the pendant, and carrying around a necklace worth as much as this is makes me very nervous."

"Why?"

"Family members just love to believe that the Medical Examiner's staff are not only necrophiliac ghouls but thieving magpies as well."

Riley strolled the living room, viewing the framed photos. "Not that you're bitter or anything. Truth be told, places like this make me a little nervous too. Do you know where that table came from, the one our corpse is leaning on?"

"Value City?" Evelyn joked.

"No, that would be *my* kitchen table. It's a custom job. The mahogany was imported from Malaysia and costs more than I make in three months, or so says the building manager. He wanted to be sure that we would, quote, respect the quality furnishings, unquote."

"Maybe I should escort Ms. James and the jewelry to the ME's office," the contamination officer suggested. "Like a Brinks job."

"Carl—" Riley had his hand out to adjust a crooked frame, but before Evelyn could protest, he apparently thought better of altering a crime scene in even the most minuscule way. Ten years in Homicide and two ex-wives had trained him to observe without attempting to alter. "Why don't you go down to the lobby and bring up the ITS guy? He can collect the computer drives now that the vacuuming is done."

Carl reluctantly pushed the button, and after a few minutes he disappeared into an exquisitely paneled elevator car.

Riley sighed as the doors closed. "Sometimes the eager ones drive me crazier than the lazy ones."

"Don't we have to have a perimeter officer?" Evelyn asked.

"Doesn't matter." Riley scribbled a note on a battered pad of paper, then used the pen to scratch the middle of his back. "The elevator can only visit one penthouse per trip, and no one can get here from the lobby without the code."

"Quite a setup."

"The best money can buy. I bet the doorman has to walk a block downwind just to have a smoke. The insulation is something to crow about too. If there are any other tenants in this building, I haven't heard a thump or a scrape or someone's TV yet. It's like we're hermetically sealed."

Evelyn photographed the woman's hands, trying to work and absorb information at the same time. "Architecture pays that well, huh?"

"Hubby's only a fraction of the story," Riley went on, in his role as a repository of local information. "This is Grace Markham, born Carruthers. Daddy Carruthers has tons of money from the steel mills, from before they all went belly-up. Grace married William Markham a few years ago, and they moved in here. She can afford this place. She can afford the whole building."

"Huh," Evelyn said. "My dad worked at Republic for thirty-three years and didn't make squat."

"Mine walked a beat in Ohio City," Riley said, "and made even less."

David, relatively new to the city and without family there, said nothing.

"It's got quite a view," Evelyn noted. From ten floors up, the panoramic windows presented both banks of the Cuyahoga River, which had been a grimy, industrial valley only thirty short years before. Then renewal took hold in Cleveland, and warehouses up and down the Cuyahoga were converted to fashionable, and exorbitantly expensive, lofts for young professionals in designer suits looking for an urban existence and a ten-minute commute. Evelyn wondered if their lifestyle lived up to the magazine ads.

She turned back to the detectives. "Who found her?"

David flipped through his notes. "The maid, Josiela Ramos, found her at three this afternoon. Ramos is still downstairs."

Evelyn got closer to the straps holding the woman to the chair. Inch-and-a-half-wide fabric mesh, stiff weave. The killer had strong hands to tie something like that in a tight knot. "Why is the maid just getting here at three?"

"Because she had two other clients to get to this morning. She only comes in twice a week—more of a cleaning lady, I guess," David added. "Do rich people have cleaning ladies?"

"Do I look like I hang out with rich people? Did she touch anything?"

"She says no. She came off the elevator, saw the body at the table as soon as she stepped into the living room, and turned right around. By the time she got to the lobby, the hysterics kicked in and it took her ten minutes to make the doorman understand enough to call us."

"She didn't touch the victim, check for a pulse?"

"She's from Guatemala, and says she knows a dead body when she sees one."

"How long has she worked for them?"

"Three years."

"She deserves a raise. This place is so freakin' clean. . . ." Evelyn began to photograph the rest of the apartment, using the lull before the storm of body snatchers, other detectives, prosecutors, family, and media descended. She needed to record the scene exactly as she had found it. At least the vacuuming—something she loathed, since too much evidence could be as frustrating as too little—had been completed. But since the penthouse had obviously been cleaned often and well, the chances were good that she would find something the killer left behind, even though the maid, the building manager, EMS, and Evelyn and the officers had already brought in their own contaminations.

She knew cops found the beginning of a case invigorating. It jazzed them, facing a new situation, not knowing what would turn up. But in an out-of-the-ordinary setup like this, with no discernible method or motive, Evelyn felt overwhelmed. The penthouse contained the accoutrements of two lifetimes, and a clue could lie anywhere in any of the thirteen rooms. A diary entry about a disturbing stranger, the tape of a threatening phone call, a check written to an extortionist, a disputed family heirloom . . . any innocuous-looking item could hold the story that led to this murder.

On the other hand, the killer might not have intersected with Grace Markham's life until that morning. Grace might have been as surprised and confused at the time as they were now.

Evelyn paused in the kitchen, noting that even rich people keep cute magnets on their refrigerator doors. A child's wavering landscape in fluorescent pink and green rested underneath, remarkably, a dollar-off coupon for delivery pizza. The marble countertops held only two ceramic mugs, the remains of morning coffee solidified at their bottoms. The sink was dry. If anything had been cooked in this kitchen in the past week, no odor remained.

Evelyn put the camera away and pulled out her fingerprinting kit. As she brushed black powder over the glossy floor, a small, barefoot pattern—probably Grace's, though now she wore high-heeled Rochas—showed here and there. Two treaded shoes appeared, including one clear heel mark of a man-size boot. She stroked clear fingerprint tape over the pattern and transferred it to two five-by-seven glossy white cards placed end to end. "Any ex-husbands or ex-boyfriends in the picture?"

"Don't know yet." David held a piece of mail up to the light. "You'd think people who could afford this rent would pay their cable bill on time."

Riley consulted his battered notepad. "According to Sanchez, Grace is an only child and her parents are dead. No ex-husbands and she's been married for three years—kind of late for a former boyfriend to freak out. But the victim spent four years as a photojournalist for *U.S. News and World Report,* mostly in South America, with a special interest in human rights abuses."

David replaced the envelopes on the counter. "Really. A connection to the maid?"

"The husband didn't say anything about Ramos, apparently. But he said Grace couldn't possibly have an enemy in the world, except for, quote, those drug-dealing fascist spics she was always taking pictures of, unquote. I asked for details, but apparently he seems to think South America is one big country. I guess he doesn't find international politics particularly fascinating. I don't either," Riley admitted. "But I'd take a crash course if I thought my wife might be in danger."

"But she quit when she got married," David pointed out.

"Old-fashioned girl," Evelyn said. Now that she could step on the tile immediately surrounding the table, she pulled out a set of ten tiny glassine paper folds. Normally she would secure the victim's hands in paper bags for the trip to the morgue and scrape the fingernails there, but in this case she did not want to risk losing even the most minuscule trace of what might be evidence. She held each finger one by one over its labeled fold and dug underneath the nail with a clean wooden toothpick. Then she folded up the toothpick and the scrapings together.

Riley went on. "According to the husband, Grace planned to get pregnant the minute the honeymoon ended. She hasn't been out of the country, except for a few vacations in Europe, for three years. Now she divides her time between charity boards and committees and whatnot, raising money for the children's hospital and the Downtown Festival. She is, in his words, angelic."

Evelyn placed the paper folds in a manila envelope and sealed it with red tape. "Three years to get pregnant. That could put a strain on a relationship."

"Maybe it took her enemies this long to find her," David said.

Riley snorted. "Anybody with Google could find her. She's in the Arts and Living section every other week."

"You read the Arts and Living section?" Evelyn asked.

"Sometimes. You know who else does? The police chief, that's who. He's already called me three times for 'updates'—which means I'd better not think about eating, sleeping, or catching an Indians game until I have sweet Grace's killer locked up tight. And if I don't sleep, that means you don't either, partner. No canoodling, you two."

David ignored him. Evelyn frowned.

"Uh-oh. There wasn't going to be any canoodling anyway, was there? Come on, tell Doctor Bruce about it."

Now David frowned. "Riley—"

"Okay, okay, I'll mind my own business. Who am I, anyway? Just the guy who introduced you."

His partner ignored him and turned to the victim, who waited with the infinite patience of the dead. "How did the guy get in here? That's what I want to know."

Evelyn looked more closely at the bruise on Grace's left forearm, which had a slight sheen to it—not normal for a bruise. After a careful photograph, she broke a clean cotton swab out of its sterile packaging and rubbed. The dark smear came off. "Our killer isn't as particular about hygiene as Grace was. He left some dirt or oil on her arm. Maybe he picked it up prying the door?"

"No evidence of it," Riley told her. "The back door to the stairwell is dead-bolted with no sign of jimmying. He could have used her key to lock it behind him, but a key ring is still in her purse. I'll double-check after you fingerprint to make sure the dead-bolt key is still there. The only other way in is through the lobby, past the twenty-four-hour doorman and a video camera. One of our guys is going over the tape with the building manager now, looking for anyone who doesn't live here."

"You might also call Sanchez back to find out if the husband has his stairwell key," David suggested.

"Because if he loaned it to a hired killer, said killer might not have had time to return it to him yet?"

"Or the husband could have made a copy," David pointed out.

"Spoilsport," Riley said. "A key should be the only way in. To arrive by elevator, you need to punch in your code on the number pad, which will bring it to this floor and this floor only. The maid, the mister, and the missus knew the code."

David examined the back fire door. "Josiela swears she's never told a soul."

"That's what Markham told Sanchez. He was peeved that the maid told us the code, didn't see why she couldn't just let us in. No one knows the code—not the building manager, not the doorman, nobody."

"Is that legal?" Evelyn asked. "I thought landlords always had the right to passkeys."

"Rules are for commoners. All twenty-seven people who live in this building have serious money, and they want serious security."

"What if a pipe breaks, or the building's on fire?"

"I guess the firemen just have to break the door down. That's why they carry those axes. Of course, this doesn't mean that any of the three people with the code didn't secretly give it to a fourth."

"Say Grace had a boyfriend while her husband was at work." David shifted around a collection of coffee-table books, using the end of his pen. "If he calls up and she takes the elevator down to meet him, they might be noticed. She gives him the code, and he can stroll right in."

Riley considered this. "In that case, he'll be on the surveillance video in the lobby."

"Why couldn't she have let him in from the back staircase?" Evelyn asked.

"It sets off a light in the building manager's office—no alarm bell or anything, just a light. The manager would then call the tenant and ask what's up. That didn't happen."

"Maybe he didn't notice."

"The light stays on until he resets it. It didn't happen."

"What about a fire escape?" Evelyn slid the swab into a plastic microtube and snapped the top closed.

"There's one up the back, but the window there is latched from the inside, with a very light but consistent coating of dust on the windowsill."

Her hand on Grace Markham's arm, Evelyn turned to the two men. "So what we have here is a locked-room mystery."

"A what?"

"It's impossible for anyone else to have gotten into and out of this room undetected. Yet she obviously didn't kill herself. A locked-room mystery. I used to love those when I was a kid."

"Good," David said. "Solve this one."

A MERENGUE BEAT SPLIT THE AIR, TRILLING FROM THE
Nextel on her hip. The trace evidence lab's number glowed
from the screen.

"Evie?" Marissa asked. "How's it going, *chica*? Tony wants to
know if you're done there."

"Not yet."

"There's another disaster for you to visit. And I'm being literal."

Evelyn's nose itched, and she rubbed it with her forearm since
her gloves were covered with black powder. Next to her, Riley
flipped through the Markhams' address book. "I have three more
rooms to fingerprint, and I want to fume the table with superglue."

"Sorry, but there's been an explosion at the salt mine."

Evelyn held the talk button on the radio–wireless phone she had
been issued by the county, resisting the urge to bang it on the table.
"Excuse me?"

"The Alexander salt mine, the one under Lake Erie. The building is about a two-minute walk from where you are right now."

Tony expected her to go into a *mine*? Beads of sweat burst from
the pores on her forehead. "Wouldn't that be an Occupational
Safety and Health matter?"

Marissa's sympathetic sigh floated from the walkie-talkie. "I know it's the last place you want to go, Evie, but there's five guys dead of nonnatural causes. That makes it an ME case. Tony says all you have to do is photograph and supervise getting the bodies out. OSHA will do the rest. Hang tough. You can do it."

"I have my reservations about that." Evelyn snapped the phone shut.

"Salt mine, huh?" Riley asked.

Grace Markham's apartment suddenly felt unbearably stuffy. Evelyn buried her face in the sleeve of her lab coat.

"Ever been down there? It's pretty neat." He dropped the book back on the victim's desk and glanced at her. "You have a black smudge on your nose."

THE FIVE-STORY BUILDING perched on the corner of Lake Erie and the Cuyahoga River, a gleaming construction of fresh brick. Evelyn hated it instantly.

The Flats, the banks along the mouth of the river, had been an industrial depot before developers in the go-go eighties converted it to trendy bars. As the nineties went bust, the area began to go back to its roots, and the new salt mine building had been built over the rubble of the landmark Fagan's Pub. Evelyn had been to Fagan's only twice in her life (at seventeen, too young to drink but pretty enough to get past the bouncer, and at twenty-six, plenty old enough to drink but sufficiently young-looking to get carded), but that didn't matter. Fagan's had watched over both the lake and the city for generations, and she mourned it.

The parking lot attendant checked her ID, and a hefty man in a hard hat emerged from the structure to guide her in. It did not comfort her that he appeared even more harried than she felt.

"I'm Phil Giardino, plant manager. You can come this way. I don't know exactly why the ME's office needs to be here," he added without apparent malice. "OSHA will be out in full force any second now."

"Any industrial accident is an ME's office case. I won't take too much time." Believe me, I'll set a record getting back to the surface. "Where are we going?"

He held open a heavy glass door, and they entered the lobby—not one designed for public use but a small area with a time clock, lockers, and a secretary. Giardino moved with such a quick pace that she had to trot to keep up with him. He tossed information back over his shoulder. "We're opening a new vein. This whole building is new, an expansion of Alexander's main operation, at East Eighty-eighth. This morning's blast went wrong, somehow." He stopped at a heavy metal door and slid a magnetic-stripe key card through a reader to open it, leading her into a large room with file cabinets, two elevators, and three men sitting at a table covered in papers. A fourth man in a green uniform crouched in front of the elevator doors, tools spread across the floor.

Evelyn struggled to picture the situation she was going to have to analyze. "It caved in?"

"No!" Giardino snorted, as if that were funny. "Salt mines don't cave in, never have. For every room we excavate—that's a square area about sixty by sixty feet—we leave one room untouched. You get a sort of checkerboard effect, and it's plenty secure. No, it seems the dynamite charge had about twice the power it should have, knocked a front-end loader off its wheels and onto a group of guys. It killed three men right away, and two more died on the way to the hospital. I've got six wounded too."

He recited these facts as concisely as possible, his jaw muscles tight. Then he paused only long enough to push the button for the elevator. She hoped that didn't mean what she thought it meant.

She swallowed the lump in her throat and asked. "We're going down?"

"Yep."

"How far down is it?"

"About eighteen hundred feet."

She tried to frame that image in her mind, and the idea of it made her step back, knocking into the uniformed man's gear on the floor. "Sorry," she murmured, righting a bottle before it could drip more than a few spots of oil onto the floor. "Is the elevator working? It's not broken, is it?"

The man grinned at her, without the benefit of his right front tooth. "Just routine cleaning—oiling the cable and wiping up the dust from the carbon brushes. You're not claustrophobic, are you?"

Yes, she wanted to say. Yes, I am, and eighteen hundred feet down into the earth is about the last place I want to go. Why the hell do I have to investigate an industrial accident anyway? It's not like I'm going to know what I'm looking at.

But she already knew the answer. A bad industrial accident like this one could wind up in lawsuits for everyone from the company and the dynamite supplier to the workers' union. While OSHA would complete the official investigation, her first-on-the-scene photographs and notes would be used by all the parties. She wiped her hand on the hem of her lab coat.

"Come on," Giardino said and stepped into the elevator.

Its plain, metal-paneled interior looked normal enough, except for the rust spots that covered every visible inch. Eighteen hundred feet. The elevator rode smoothly, but could the floor, underneath the tile, be as rusty as the rest of it looked? Enough simply to collapse under their weight? Giardino had to weigh 250 if he was a pound.

"This seems a little rusted." Her voice creaked from her dry throat.

He grinned without mirth. "Everything rusts like crazy down there because of the salt. But it's secure, don't worry."

"What about fire?" She became aware of each breath. Was there sufficient oxygen in the mine? "Did the explosion cause a fire?"

"Just the initial burst. It burned the guys pretty bad, but then it died out. There's not much down there to burn, other than the seats off the machines and some jackets and stuff that they had thought were in the safe zone."

Nothing that a couple million gallons of lake water wouldn't put out, anyway. She grasped a handrail, and the gritty, flaking surface bit into her palm. "What about the lake? Did the explosion crack any walls, cause any leaks?"

Her persistent questioning finally penetrated his worry. "You don't have to be nervous. I've been in this mine five days a week for the past twenty-five years, and a few smashed fingertips is the worst I've ever suffered. We've mined salt from under Lake Erie since 1933. There's fifty miles of roads stemming from the original mine. They'll be mining salt here for the next three centuries." The car began to slow. "Besides, there's at least sixteen hundred feet of limestone between us and the bottom of the lake."

The *bottom* of the lake! Evelyn began to pray. Then the door slid open.

Instead of a cramped, coal black tunnel, the salt mine "room" stretched wide enough to accommodate two backhoes, a handful of men, and a coffee machine station. Anything metal showed the effects of the salty atmosphere. Plenty of lighting ran across the high ceiling. Every surface gleamed a muted white, like quartz. The air felt only mildly stuffy and the temperature pleasantly cool. It looked like a large parking garage made of salt.

"So this is where salt comes from," she said, relieved.

"Industrial salt," Giardino said. "Stuff used in chemical processes, for refrigeration, and for snow removal. You'll never be sprinkling any of this stuff on your eggs. The site is this way."

She followed him onto a large golf cart, nodding toward the curious stares of a group of men. They perched on the backhoe, dwarfed by its size. One of the men had a few smears of blood on his pant leg.

This isn't too bad, she told herself as the car took off with a jerk, bumping over the rough floor. Just don't think about being eighteen hundred feet down, connected to life and air by only a rusty elevator shaft. Or having an entire lake full of water on top of you, possibly beginning to snake its way downward after an overpowered explosion . . .

"You have to wear this." Her guide handed her a yellow hard hat. "We moved everyone out of the area, once the fires were out and . . . and we could see there was nothing more to be done for these guys."

A yellow, rust-flecked front-end loader lay on its side like a fallen dragon. Pipes and black soot streaked the white walls and ceiling. Smaller carts and trucks sat scattered as if hastily abandoned. Portable lights on stands filled the room unevenly, brilliance alternating with shadow.

She pulled out her camera, adjusted the flash. She put the viewfinder to her eye and instantly felt calm. Absorbing the area through the camera lens detached her from her surroundings, made her feel as if she were watching it on TV and wasn't actually eighteen hundred feet below the surface of the earth.

What appeared to be bloodied rags protruding from underneath the loader turned out to have human arms still in them. One man had been crushed only from midchest down, his head and arms unhurt. The two others were almost entirely buried. The metallic smell of blood wafted around the odors of oil and smoke.

Giardino stood to one side, allowing her to photograph the scene. "We're going to have to take this apart to right it, we don't have anything large enough to pull it up. We had to disassemble it to get it down here in the first place. It's going to take a while. This whole thing is going to take a while, set us back months."

She glanced at him before zooming in on one victim's upturned palm. She always did close-ups of hands, back and front, no matter the cause of death. Defensive wounds, discolorations, dirt smears could give a clue to what people had done immediately before they died.

Giardino, meanwhile, read censure in her look. "I don't mean to sound callous. That guy there, he lived on my street. We've been friends"—he broke off, his voice choking, and fished a bandanna from his back pocket—"for ten years. I don't know what his wife's going to do when she finds out."

Evelyn turned back to the distance of the camera lens, safely removing herself from the tremor in the large man's voice. She finished with the photos, then asked: "Can I see where the explosion took place? If it's safe."

He led her farther into the mine, without using the golf cart this time. The soot here came in more than streaks; every surface had been blackened by the explosion. It also held boulders of salt, some two and three times taller than Evelyn.

"We place the dynamite in predrilled holes. It will bring down eight or nine hundred tons of salt in boulders; we break those up into smaller pieces that get loaded onto trucks and go to the primary crusher."

She tried to picture the process, the hugeness of the undertaking, both frightening and impressive. What sorts of people come up with ideas like this? Let's excavate huge salt rooms sixteen hundred feet below one of the Great Lakes. Let's dig a canal across a Central American continent. Let's walk on the moon.

"The crusher's back past where we came in," he continued. "That breaks the boulders up into football-size pieces that go to the surface."

She wandered in and out of the salt mountains, photographing scraps of red paper from the dynamite sticks. She did not touch them; that would be OSHA's job. She would collect only evidence adhering to the victims themselves. "What do you think went wrong?"

"Hell, I don't know. I'd like to think the dynamite was mislabeled. I might know more when I can talk to the wounded guys. Most had plenty of experience, but we did have a few newbies in the bunch."

"I noticed the building seemed brand-new," she said as they re-turned to the room with the overturned loader.

"Alexander Mining sank a lot of money into this new vein. I in-vested part of my pension money in it. If OSHA shuts production down too long, a lot of people stand to lose a lot of money."

"So you had a number of new employees here?"

"I can't believe Duane—that's the foreman—would have let them near the dynamite, but who knows?"

"Was Duane wounded?"

Giardino's eyes grew wet, and he gestured at the floor, where the foreman's arm stretched out from under the heavy machine, fingers stretching upward in mute appeal.

T
HE TELEPHONE SHATTERED THE DARKNESS, SNAP-
ping Evelyn to attention with a painful jerk. 2:16 A.M.

Angel!

No, Angel was in the next room, in bed. She'd come home from her date hours earlier.

Mom! "Hello?"

"Is this Evelyn James?"

"Yes."

"This is Doctor Bailey at Metro General Hospital ER."

"How did she get there without calling me?" Her mother wouldn't have—

"Ma'am? Do you know a Marissa Gonzalez?"

THIRTY MINUTES LATER, with wrecked hair, no makeup, and clothes dampened by a cloudburst, Evelyn stumbled through the automatic doors of the hospital emergency room. The lights blinded her. White-coated staff moved with purpose. The results of assorted dramas waited in plastic chairs—a hugely pregnant teenager stared at the ceiling with a steely gaze of resignation, an odiferous older man moaned in the agony of delirium tremens, three men seated together had blunt-force injuries to various limbs. Through eyes like slits, she saw a young black man in a dark blue uniform approaching.

"Hey, Evelyn."

"Billy. Is she all right?"

He paused. "She's still alive."

Her voice ridiculously desperate, Evelyn asked again, "Is she going to be all right?"

"She's still alive."

They stepped to one side as a badly mangled young man went by on a gurney; for a moment Evelyn felt surprised to see him move, then she remembered that this was a hospital and not the ME's office. "What happened?"

"I was first on scene, a little after one. The doorman in the apartment building told 911 that she stumbled in from the parking garage, clutching her throat and trying to scream. Then she collapsed. They had to intubate her to keep the swelling from closing off her air."

"Someone attacked her?" Evelyn tried not to picture her friend with a tube in her throat, but the image sprang to her mind and stayed there. "Any description of the guy?"

The young patrolman took her elbow and guided her down the hallway. "The doorman didn't even look. He's not the intrepid type, I guess. My partner cleared the garage while the ambulance loaded her up, but he didn't find anything. The guy was long gone."

She had to force herself to ask the next question. "Did he rape her?"

"No. She had all her clothes on and no other injuries."

Evelyn let out the breath she'd held. "Where was her fiancé?"

"Working."

"At one in the morning? Where?"

"Here. He's on call tonight up in pediatrics."

"Of course. I wasn't thinking." Marissa had been complaining about her boyfriend's irregular hours since she'd moved in with him.

"He was waiting for us when the ambulance arrived. I guess the doorman called him—one of the perks of high rent. They keep their tenants informed. Apparently they were getting married next month?"

"They *are* getting married." No past tense. Not yet.

"I know a lot of guys who are going to be mighty grieved over that. Do you think this is the same guy?" Cops never used the word *perp*—the guilty party was just *the guy*. "The one that killed that rich girl?"

"Who? Grace Markham?"

"Yeah."

"Why would it be the same guy?"

"Well, the strangling bit and all. And it's the same building—the Riviera."

She blinked at him. "You mean La Riviere?"

"Yeah."

"What was Marissa doing *there*?"

"She lives there. With her doctor boyfriend."

Evelyn absorbed this. Marissa had told her about the new apartment, but Evelyn hadn't visited yet. She and Marissa saw each other every day at work, but life as a single mother was just too busy to allow for many nights out with friends. If Marissa had mentioned the name of the building, she'd missed it. Then, by the time Evelyn had returned to the lab to log in the evidence from Grace Markham's scene, Marissa had left for the day; there had been no chance for the coincidence to surface.

She pressed herself to the wall to avoid getting run over by a patient and two nurses. "Is it always like this around here?"

"They're still behind after that bunch came in from the salt mine." Evelyn and Billy entered the elevator, and the doors closed, sealing them in blessed quiet.

"Oh, yeah. I had to go to that."

The young officer shuddered as he pushed the 4 button. "I don't envy you. My cousin worked there one summer, but he can't take enclosed spaces."

Evelyn wished she could sit down. She also wished she'd brushed her teeth before leaving a note for Angel and peeling out of the driveway. It would be a long night, and she would have liked to have felt as together as possible. The elevator doors slid open.

"You! Evelyn James."

A stormy-faced Mama Gonzalez sailed down the antiseptic hallway like a tall ship with sheets unfurled. Evelyn felt like letting the doors drift shut and riding the small box to another floor, one where she wouldn't have to confront her friend's anxious mother.

She stepped out into the hallway. "Mrs. Gonzalez."

"You will find out who did this to my Mareesa."

"I will." She didn't dare say anything else. Rotund as well as tall, Mama Gonzalez could have snapped her in half.

"You will bring him to me."

"I'll . . . do my best."

"You will bring him to me. I rip his arms from his sides. I will tear out his heart."

Anger, Evelyn knew, felt more comfortable than fear. "And I'll help you. How is she?"

Tears gathered in the woman's eyes.

Evelyn hugged her, gently. "There's nothing worse than seeing your child in pain. I know. But the doctors here will help her. She'll be healthy again."

"This would never have happened if she'd stayed on our *prada*." The old woman snuffled against her shoulder. "If she'd stayed with her family, instead of moving out without the grace of marriage to live with that man."

"She loves him. And violence can happen anywhere." Evelyn patted her shoulder before stepping back.

Mama Gonzalez pressed a clean handkerchief to her nose. "We've lived on the same street all her life, and never did anyone touch her, not with her brothers around. You must find this man. She thinks you are so smart, she tells me so. Be smart now."

Evelyn did not make promises. She considered them risky. But no sort of qualification would do in this case. "I'll find him."

"Come on, Mrs. Gonzalez," Billy said. "Your son is in with the intake counselor, and they'll need you. She's in there," he added to Evelyn, pointing at the last room on the left as he led Marissa's mother away.

With a deep breath, Evelyn walked into the hospital room. It took conscious effort. She didn't want to see her friend—fiery, outspoken Marissa—laid out, scratched and bruised, with a tube in her agonized throat because some *son of a bitch*—

A whistling sound came and went in the clear plastic tube protruding from Marissa's perfect lips. Ice packs covered her neck. Her clothing had been replaced by a gown, and she had a scratch on her forehead. Long eyelashes rested on her cheeks. A doctor stood on one side of the bed; Evelyn approached on the other.

This drained form bore no resemblance to her friend. She had never seen Marissa function at less than 100 percent, somehow expending more energy than she took in, as if she culled it from the air.

Evelyn felt the red rush of pure fury start at the back of her scalp and work its way down, until her nose tingled and her heart thudded with hate. She would find who did this. And they would pay.

She grabbed the young woman's hand as if one of them were drowning. She wasn't sure which.

The doctor spoke. "Evelyn."

She saw now who he was. She had noticed only the white coat at first. "Robert. How are you?"

Dumb question. Despite being clean-shaven, wide awake, and neatly dressed in Dockers and a polo shirt under his lab coat, he looked like hell. His eyes glittered with unshed tears. "I hope you get this guy."

She nodded, unable to speak about their pain. Instead she gestured at the ice packs. "Okay if I take a look?"

"Anything, if it will help."

The ice bag felt subzero to her flushed palm. Marissa's entire neck had turned bright red, from either the cold or the irritation, and seemed double its normal size. A dark red line ran through the middle of it, developing the purplish hue of nascent bruises. Evelyn bit her lip and looked closer.

The ligature had left an inch-and-a-half-wide, uniform indentation, without dipping significantly in the middle. This indicated a flat shape, as opposed to a round type of rope or wire. The pattern had established itself in the front but wavered a bit on the sides, consistent with someone crossing the ends and pulling from the rear. It seemed to have a slight checked aspect. Like a weave. Like mesh fabric.

Like Grace Markham.

Damn.

She replaced the ice, caught Robert's eye, and jerked her head toward the door. They moved into the hall and conversed in low murmurs. "What is her condition?"

"They intubated to keep her from suffocating. It was either that or a tracheotomy, and you know how Marissa would feel about a scar."

"I know how she'd feel about dying," she snapped, stung that he would consider his fiancée's beauty in any medical decision.

"A trach is too risky, anyway," he hastened to add. "Of course, intubating means she has to be heavily sedated or she might pull the tube out. She won't be conscious to answer any questions for a while."

For a doctor, he seemed to be thinking like a cop. "Is she on a respirator?"

"No. The tube is there to keep her trachea from swelling to the point it cuts off her air. There's nothing wrong with her lungs. But now we have to make sure she doesn't stop breathing from the heavy sedation. If she does, then we will have to use a respirator, and that brings another host of dangers. We might have to paralyze the muscles with curare, and then she'd have to be weaned off that—"

Now he sounded like a doctor. "Did the lack of oxygen have any . . . effect?"

"Her EEG is normal. No brain damage. Her body is in shock from what has happened to it, but she should recuperate. She'll be fine." He repeated this, as if convincing himself. "She'll be fine."

"There's something else you should know." Evelyn gave him the basic information regarding Grace Markham's death.

"And this woman lived in our building?"

"Tenth floor. You didn't know her?"

"No, but I never have the time to meet my neighbors."

"Marissa moved in with you, what, three months ago? Did she ever mention the name Grace Markham?"

"No. You think this guy could live in the building?"

"It's a possibility." Evelyn moved out of the way of a nurse with a meds cart. Marissa and Grace Markham vaguely resembled each other—in their twenties, pretty, long dark hair. The killer could have an obsession with those characteristics. "Any odd incidents come to mind? Weird phone calls or letters? Someone following either of you? Any ex-boyfriends of Marissa's coming out of the woodwork?"

She could see the gears in his battered mind dutifully turn. "Nothing. We've had tons of calls lately, but all about the wedding. We just want to get married, and my mother is trying to turn it into the social event of the season, so there's a lot of back-and-forth with caterers and the ballroom. But nothing odd."

"Where was she tonight?"

"Out with the entourage—the bridesmaids. They had a dress fitting tonight and were going to get dinner afterward."

"Has Marissa seemed worried lately?"

He managed a grin for a split second before reality returned and erased it. "Just about my mother. And her mother. And then my mother again."

Evelyn asked herself the same question and got the same answer.

She saw Marissa five days a week at a stressful, demanding job, and lately the girl had been nothing but radiant. Evelyn leaned closer, trying not to breathe on the young man through her unbrushed teeth. "What about you? Any old girlfriends, a past flame who can't let go?"

A brief, modest smile, which didn't reach his eyes. "Nope. My girlfriends bid me adieu with shocking ease. Hell, the last woman I dated before Marissa is coming to the wedding and bringing her husband." He paused. "What about Marissa's job? You guys must come in contact with scumbags every day."

"Yes and no." Marissa's DNA analyses had sent a lot of people to jail, but forensic testimony represented only part of the overall prosecution. Defendants were more likely to resent the cops who arrested them, the juries who convicted them, or the judges who sentenced them as opposed to one lone lab tech. But one never knew. If Marissa's testimony had been the prosecution's entire case, a violent offender might have secretly vowed revenge. Evelyn would direct the cops to Marissa's past cases, ask them to check who might have been recently released.

And whose trials were approaching. A criminal might just be stupid enough to believe he could prevent the DNA results from being presented in court by killing the analyst, unaware that another analyst, such as Evelyn, could read them into the record.

The next time Evelyn testified, would a stranger tail her red Tempo all the way to Strongsville? Where her mother and daughter lived?

Such melodrama. There must be a more mundane explanation.

"We'll be sure to go over all Marissa's cases, carefully," she promised Robert. "Have there been any problems here at the hospital? Any parents—" She stopped, unsure how to word the question she needed to ask. The man had obviously had a hard few hours. "Have any parents been unhappy with you? Perhaps one of your patients suffered an unexpected tragedy?"

"Have I killed any kids lately, is that what you're asking?" He did not seem offended. "I lost one to pneumonia last week, but if that kid had any family, I never saw them. Parents are— Well, parents are usually the worst part of pediatric medicine. They're never happy, no matter what I do, but I've never had one angry enough even to refuse to pay the bill, much less—"

Try to kill my fiancée, he must have been about to say but couldn't make himself form the words. Evelyn patted his arm. "I'm going to need her clothing."

They slipped back into the room, both tiptoeing as if Marissa could be awakened by mere footfalls. Robert pulled a plastic bag with the blue hospital logo on it from the wardrobe cabinet and handed it to her. With a last, pained look at her friend, Evelyn returned to the hallway and motioned for Robert to follow.

He wiped his forehead with the sleeve of his lab coat. "Is there anything else? I want to stay with her."

She pulled a form from her camera bag. "I need to give you an evidence receipt for the clothing."

"Oh, hell, I don't care. I trust you."

"No, Robert, it's important. It's to maintain the chain of custody, so that if it becomes an exhibit at trial, I can document exactly when and where I collected it." She fumbled for a pen. "Of course, EMS and ER staff have already handled it, cut it and jumbled it all together here in plastic, but—" She glanced up at Robert and broke off. He looked ghastly, and impossibly young, as if the cold routine of procedure had finally brought it home to him: His love had been felled not by an accident or an illness but by a depraved and violent human being.

EXCEPT FOR a nice coat of paint, the parking garage of the Riviere did not share in the luxury of the building it adjoined. Nor did it enjoy its tight security.

"There's a million ways into this place," Evelyn griped. "Open spots all over."

"It's a parking garage, ma'am. It has to be airy. Otherwise the carbon monoxide kills people," Frank, the building manager, explained in what he probably thought was a patient tone. He had several things to be unhappy about and had listed them earlier: getting dragged out of bed in the middle of the night, how upset the rest of the tenants would be about a second attack on the property in twenty-four hours, how upset he, personally, felt over what had happened to poor Miss Gonzalez, and that an article in the *Plain Dealer* had already dubbed Grace Markham's killer "the Riviera Rapist." He could only hope the public would prove unable to discern the obvious difference between the names Riviera—a cheap motel on Pearl Road—and Riviere.

"I thought security was the selling point of this place."

"It is."

"Then why isn't our attacker on the video?" They stood in front of the ground-floor entrance from the parking garage to the lobby. Overhead, a camera recorded the span of flawless automobiles. If the man had attacked Marissa at her car, his grainy black-and-white image would have been recorded. But he had waited until she stepped just underneath the camera itself, a dead zone along the interior wall. The video caught part of his shoe, and that was all. "He had to know about your camera."

"Maybe he just got lucky," Frank suggested.

"Nobody's that lucky."

"You can have the video. Maybe you can blow that shoe up and get a brand or a size."

"Thank you. We'll try, but almost certainly we'll be left with the dark shape of a shoe. Video enhancement isn't like you see on TV shows. If we magnify, all we'll get is blobs of pixels." She didn't bother adding that his system, state-of-the-art only five years before, used an average-quality recorder taping average-quality VHS tapes, rerecording on the same ten cassettes over and over. She wouldn't have recognized Marissa, strolling toward the lobby after parking her car, if the time stamp hadn't directed them to the right sequence.

"Isn't there some program that can take each pixel and fill in around it? I saw that on the Discovery Channel."

"There is, but we don't have it, and it's more for film that has been damaged. It can't create resolution that wasn't there to begin with." She opened the door to the lobby, which gave her an unencumbered view of the front desk. "He did take a risk, right next to the lobby like this. You have a twenty-four-hour doorman."

"Exactly!"

"But once he got that strap around her throat good and tight, she wouldn't be able to scream. If he outweighed her and he could keep her from moving, she wouldn't be able to reach the door to kick it and attract attention. And at one A.M. on a weeknight, he had a slim chance of interruption."

She let the door close and traced the guy's escape route, skulking along the wall to the open, carbon-monoxide-releasing space at the street, the southwest corner of the garage. A piece of loose chain-link mesh had been pushed aside.

The building manager followed miserably. "Do you think it's the same person who killed Mrs. Markham?"

"I'm not sure yet," she lied. She did not know what the police did or did not want released, or how chatty Frank might prove if asked the same question. She used a flashlight to examine the open edge of the mesh, noting some dark fibers caught in one loop of metal. Behind her, she heard the lobby door open.

"Evelyn!"

She turned, and David's arms were around her. For a moment she forgot camera angles and fibers and questions about their future together and let herself melt into his strength, smell the damp leather of his coat, feel his fingers on the nape of her neck.

"Is she all right?"

Evelyn cleared her throat. "So far."

He turned to Frank. "Excuse us a minute, okay?" When the building manager had gone, he asked, "Is it the same guy?"

"I think so." She told him why as she collected the dark fibers from the wire loop in a small manila envelope. Then she brushed the low concrete wall with black powder, hoping for a shoeprint made as the man pushed past the mesh, but nothing showed up.

"So we have some kind of homicidal maniac at work in this building." He sighed. "And we have no idea what he wants, who he's after, or how he gets in and out. He probably knows the place, maybe lives here. I can imagine how the high-tax-paying citizens of La Riviere are going to react to that."

"They have to be warned."

"Oh, I know. At first light, Riley and I are going to visit every person on every floor, find out anything they might know. They'll feel plenty warned by the time we get done. Hell, for all I know, there could be someone else up there strapped to their kitchen chair."

"I hope not. You know, it bothers me that Marissa and Grace Markham look a lot alike. At first glance, I mean."

David thought on that for a moment. "You think Marissa was his original target? He got the wrong floor?"

"I don't know. It doesn't make much sense. He's smart enough to get into Grace Markham's airtight apartment, so we have to assume he's smart enough to pick the right target."

"Why didn't he attack Marissa in *her* apartment? Why the parking garage?"

Evelyn thought out loud. "Because he didn't know which apartment is hers? She hasn't lived here that long, and it's under Robert's name. Plus, Robert works irregular hours—who knows when he might come home?—and the parking garage has multiple escape routes in case he's surprised. The apartment doesn't." She sat on the edge of the concrete wall, weariness flooding her body. "But these are just guesses, and we need answers. And I know where to get some."

"Hey."

She looked up. He took her face in both hands. "You're not going to say, 'To the Batcave, Robin!' are you?"

She laughed, its sound echoing weakly from the concrete walls.

HER WORKPLACE HAD BEEN TITLED THE TRACE EVI-
dence Department for a reason. A single fiber or drop of liquid could provide the most important clue, assuming that a
scientist could translate an item's analyses into facts, after being
lucky enough to find it in the first place. Sometimes, though, a tiny
piece of debris turned out to be a tiny piece of debris, with no significance at all. Evelyn hoped her collection from Grace Markham's
apartment would yield more of the former than the latter.

She dropped her purse into the bottom drawer of her desk, a
battered hand-me-down from Records, and pushed aside the case reports piled on the calendar blotter to check the day and make sure
she hadn't forgotten about a scheduled court case or deposition.
These were canceled or postponed so often that they were easy to
forget, risking a contempt of court charge.

Her desk decor consisted of a black kitten Beanie Baby, a picture of Angel from her most recent school dance, and the framed
words "News flash—life ain't fair!"

The clock read 6:30. She hadn't bothered going back to bed.
She had called her boss, Tony, from the hospital but saw no need to
wait for him. She knew what had to be done and wanted to get

started before Tony, the ME, the cops, and one or two assistant county prosecutors massed in the conference room.

She poured liquid nitrogen through a funnel into the infrared spectrometer with great care. Evelyn couldn't help but feel uneasy around the stuff, as if her fingers might freeze to a shatterable brittleness if they got too close. Closing the lid, she let the computer warm up while the detector cooled down. She pulled out her sealed envelope containing a swab of the smudge on Grace Markham's arm and opened the pasted bottom of the envelope, preserving the original red seal.

Only the hum of the lab equipment kept her company; the sensible people of the world were still in bed or at the breakfast table. She would need some caffeine soon, preferably intravenously.

She rubbed the tip of the swab onto a gold-plated microscope slide. Infrared radiation, just like visible light, travels in waves, with specific frequencies and wavelengths. The beam of infrared light from the Fourier transform infrared spectrometer pierced the sample material, bounced off the gold plate underneath, and returned to the detector. The molecules of the sample interacted with the light, absorbing particular frequencies depending on which groups of elements it contained—a COOH bond would absorb radiation at a different frequency than an OH bond. The computer charted all these frequencies as a spectrum, which appeared as a jagged line above a ruled scale of absorption versus wavelength. Each spectrum glowed in its own specific color—the reason she had the only color printer in the lab.

A wide peak at 1000 probably meant silicone, but since silicone was the most common metal on earth, she didn't read too much into it. She saw a small amount of barium, found in most gunshot primers. The main ingredient, by far, was petroleum. Grease.

What had Grace Markham's killer been doing before he murdered her? He certainly hadn't accumulated any grease in her penthouse . . . unless he had picked the dead-bolt lock, getting himself oily in the process but without leaving a scratch on the lock and without setting off the warning light in the building manager's office? No. That left the elevator. He could have touched the doors—perhaps forced them open.

Tony's substantial bulk materialized between her and the window, blotting out the light. "How long is she going to be out?"

"I don't know."

"How long do you think?"

Evelyn glared at her boss. "I don't know. Hell, Tony, we don't even know if she's going to live."

"Stop crying."

"I'm not crying."

Tony didn't handle emotions well, especially other people's. With his eyes firmly fixed elsewhere, he insisted, "I hate to break it to you, but yes, you are. And stop using the Kimwipes as Kleenex. Those things are five dollars a box."

She sniffled into a microscope lens wipe, thinner than facial tissue but always available in the lab. "The worst part will be listening to the ME tell me how determined he is to bring Marissa's attacker to justice, when the only thing he's ever noticed about Marissa is her breasts."

"Stone's not that bad a guy." Tony collapsed onto a tall bench chair, spilling a few drops of coffee as the chair's wheels slid underneath him. Outside, the morning's rush-hour traffic slowly began to mass under a dark sky, and the reflection of her boss in the window made Evelyn pause. One Tony was more than enough. "And the prosecutor's office will do anything to keep him happy, including leaning on the police department to put every available guy on it. Which they'll probably do anyway. Her breasts have a lot of fans there too."

"Please don't make me have to hurt you."

"Relax. There will be a meeting at nine to map out the investigation and what we're going to tell the press—not only about

Marissa but about the Markham murder. Did you see the news last night? Grace Markham led on every channel. There's nothing that gets ratings like a rich dead chick. So let's get hopping, missy. With Marissa out, you're going to have to take over DNA."

"I don't think so! I have Grace Markham's clothes to examine, two bags of vacuumings, and then Marissa's clothes. Besides, I'm not DNA-certified anymore, remember? You made us choose a specialty a few years back. It's written in the SOP. I'm not even supposed to enter the DNA lab according to you."

"The SOPs are guidelines, not rules." He scowled at her. It had no effect. "We wouldn't be in this jam if Sayid hadn't left to join a terrorist cell."

Evelyn rested her chin on her fist, afraid that if she sat still for even a moment she'd fall asleep. "He's teaching at A&M, as you very well know. And Sayid's family has been in Ohio longer than yours! They have a farm outside Westerville."

"Then he shouldn't be so damn snooty. All right, I'll run your DNA. I do still remember how, you know."

She had her doubts, but kept them to herself and threw him a carrot. "That's great, Tony. I'm sure the ME will notice your extra effort."

That cheered him. "Yeah. So what was that rich broad's apartment like?"

"Beautiful. Great view of the Flats, and so high up she probably couldn't hear the partiers . . . if there are any these days. The glow of the Flats faded with this new millennium."

"Must be nice to have money." He began to walk away, stirring his coffee with a wood stick; they used to use the sticks for PGM enzyme electrophoresis and continued to order the small items just for coffee. At the door he turned and added, too casually, "She'll be all right."

Evelyn saw the worry etched into his round pate. Tony might have been selfish, tyrannical, and moody, but underneath that he wasn't a bad person. Or so she occasionally reminded herself. "We've got to get this guy."

"I know."

Evelyn got back to work.

Marissa had been wearing a black microfiber miniskirt, panties, tights, a 36D bra, short black leather boots, and a bright red sweater, and had probably left a trail of whiplash victims in her wake from all the turned heads. The EMTs and their happy scissors had reduced the outfit to rags, but under a stereomicroscope, Evelyn found no ripping, semen, or blood. She taped the items for loose hair and fibers and photographed them against the standard gray backdrop. Seeing Marissa's clothes labeled with a case number, stapled together, and hanging askew on wire hangers sickened her.

"You okay?" Zoe, the staff photographer, asked.

"Yeah." Evelyn retrieved the clothing with a trembling hand.

She submitted the fibers found on the mesh grate to the infrared beam and determined that they consisted of blue nylon 6,6. A very common synthetic fiber. She mounted them to note the diameter and cross-sectional shape. A blue fiber on Marissa's sweater came up consistent with the grate fibers in all characteristics, indicating that her attacker had left via the southwest corner of the garage. Hooray. It hardly seemed a helpful fact.

Reluctant to snoop, she had saved Marissa's purse for last. Besides, she doubted it would hold any clues—this guy hadn't been after her purse. A shiny black bag with a long handle, it contained the minimum items required for daily life—ChapStick, brush, money, credit cards, driver's license, Clinique Red Drama lipstick, and a date book with a myriad of wedding-related activities but no mysterious notations. The only other items were a gas receipt and a newspaper article.

Evelyn unfolded the small piece of paper, recognizing the typeface of the *Plain Dealer*. The column discussed a substantial donation made by a Frances Duarte to Butterfly Babies & Children's

Hospital for a new wing. Evelyn did not recognize the woman's face or name. Perhaps Robert planned to take his pediatric talents elsewhere, or perhaps they'd considered making a contribution themselves. Evelyn refolded the paper and placed all the items back in Marissa's purse, wishing she could put everything in her friend's life back together as easily.

"SO WHAT'S UP between you and Evie?"

"None of your business," David told his partner as he drained his fourth cup of the building manager's coffee in as many hours. He had five minutes to get another one before the next tenant came in. So far, the tenants interviewed had included a contractor, a pair of married surgeons, a banker, and a retired Hollywood agent who had moved home to be closer to his mother. The cops had learned exactly nothing; the other occupants of the building were quite alive but generally unacquainted with Grace and William. No one had any idea who could have done the killing, or when, or how. No one could shed light on Marissa's attack either.

Riley drummed long fingers on the stack of tenant contracts. "The path of true love does not run smooth."

"And what would you know about true love? You've been married twice and divorced twice. I call that not learning from experience."

"Ouch. You don't have to get nasty about it."

David poured a fifth cup. He didn't blame Evelyn for hesitating—finding her husband in bed with another woman had made her gun-shy. He could get that. But hell, he'd dived into a freezing river to save her. If that didn't prove his love, what would?

Patience, his father would say. David wished he'd inherited that trait along with the dark hair.

The door to the building manager's office—now their temporary interview room—flew open with drywall-cracking force, even as David heard Frank pleading, "But, ma'am—"

Saying the woman seemed agitated would be like describing Niagara Falls as a slow leak. David expected to see bolts of energy fly from her fingertips. Fashionably thin, with swinging hair to distract from the acne scars on her cheeks, she appeared to fill the doorway despite the fact that her head would not have reached his chin.

"Are you the cops?"

Riley looked at the invader with interest. "That we are."

"Are you going to find out who killed Grace?"

How could they possibly answer that? "Yes, ma'am," David intoned. "We will."

The building manager stammered, "I told her you were busy—"

"It's all right, Frank. We're not hoity-toity here. We can handle unannounced guests. Please sit down, Ms.—"

"Eames." She slammed the door in Frank's face and threw herself into the nearest chair. It skidded four inches over the thin carpet before coming to a stop. "Joey Eames. I was Grace's best friend. Sometimes I think her only friend."

David glanced at Riley, sat down, and crossed his legs. He had a strong hunch this woman knew something interesting. Not necessary helpful, but definitely interesting. "Tell us about her."

"She was a doll. Very generous. Her parents were kind of standoffish, so she was drawn to people like me, who express their emotions. I always express my emotions. It's so hard not to be phony in this world, you know what I mean?"

"I—"

"Grace believed that she'd been blessed and it was her duty to give back to the world. Her charity work was important to her, not just a photo op like most of these rich bit—. And she was very intelligent too. Did you know she was a photojournalist? Her work is all around the penthouse. She was brilliant, really. We used to hit every art gallery in town at least once a month, just to see if they had anything new. She was instrumental in getting funds for the art museum to do that big expansion they're doing. We've been inseparable for two years, after we served on the Downtown Festival committee. There was a picture of us at Tower City in *Cleveland* magazine, and that's what it said. Inseparable."

Joey Eames had no difficulty referring to her best friend in the past tense, David noted. For most people, that usually took some time. But Joey did seem to do everything faster than most people.

"We're sure she was a very sweet person, Ms. Eames." Riley reached into his jacket as if for his cigarettes, looked around for an ashtray, which didn't materialize, and withdrew his hand. "But—"

"That's what I mean! Who would kill a person like that? And in a place like this? It's like Fort Knox. Only her scumbucket husband, that's who. He's the only one with motive, method, and opportunity, right?" She hitched her chair a few inches closer to the desk.

"William?"

"Of course, William! He never loved her! He only married her for her money. He had been engaged to some rich girl before, but she managed to see through him in time and threw him out. Three months later, he and Grace are walking down the aisle. She told me that one time, as if it proved that their marriage had been destined by the stars, instead of the obvious wife shopping it was. Poor kid." She paused, her face falling into repose for only a split second, just long enough to show genuine pain.

"Do you live around here, Ms. Eames?" David asked.

"Lakewood."

"What's Joey short for?"

Her mouth twisted, and he had the feeling she'd rather not answer. She scooted her chair an inch closer to him. "Jolene."

"What makes you think William killed his wife?" He did not mention Markham's alibi.

"Because he's a scum-sucking opportunist, that's why. The money was all Grace's, and they had a prenup in case of divorce— but not death, get it? William doesn't like me," she added in an apparent non sequitur.

"Really?" Riley asked. "I can't imagine why."

His neutral tone didn't fool her. She paused for a moment; the silence swept through the room like a slap.

David made his voice friendly and warm. "Had they been talking about divorce?"

"He was cheating on her."

"Cheating on Grace."

She raked her hair with long nails, rocking in her seat. "Of course, on Grace! Who do you think I mean?"

"I'm sorry, that's just a big chunk of information. Who was the other woman?"

"Grace didn't know. But she had been worried about it for months. She added up the little things—coming home in a different tie than he went to work in, putting in all these late nights but not mentioning any big projects or rush jobs that might account for it. She thought it might be someone at work—and really, isn't it always?"

"Did she confront him?"

"Oh, yeah. More than once. He kept denying it. She asked me about hiring a private detective." She hitched the chair forward again. She'd be sitting in his lap in the next five minutes if he didn't move back.

"You've had experience with private detectives?" Riley put in.

She glared at him again, as if examining the question for some sort of insult. "Not personally, no, but who else could she trust? And my girlfriend's sister got one to follow her second husband, and she got great photos. That was a long time ago, but I told her I'd ask around."

"Did you recommend someone?"

"No, I hadn't come up with anyone. It was just last week she asked."

"Did she tell William she would hire a private detective?"

"Well, duh! That would defeat the purpose, wouldn't it? He just might have had the sense to get careful and the guy wouldn't get any pictures."

David threw in a curveball to keep her off balance but kept the warm tone. "Did you know the code to their penthouse?"

She picked at a loose thread in the seam of her slacks. "No. What would I need it for?"

"Any reason—to drop something off when she wasn't home, to feed her fish when they went on vacation."

"They didn't vacation much. The only thing she wanted to do was travel, and that was the last thing he ever wanted to do. But it makes sense, if you think about it. He didn't want to leave his girl-friend. Besides, he'd rather spend money on toys. He always wanted a new car, a new computer, something for his office."

"Did they argue about money?"

"All the time. He'd have gone through every cent if she didn't hold him down. So"—she slapped her palms on her thighs with the air of summarizing—"he kills Grace, gets all her money, and doesn't have to give up the girlfriend."

"How long had this affair been going on?"

"Two months. Maybe three, I mean, since she started noticing how all his little inconsistencies added up to a ton of bullshit."

"About as long as she'd been pregnant, then? Did she think his cheating had something to do with the baby?"

"Baby?"

Joey Eames sat, for the first time, perfectly still. She stared at David wide-eyed, every red blood cell draining from her face. "What baby?"

David felt a little ill himself. Only rookies made the mistake of revealing confidential information to a potential witness. But he couldn't take the words back, so he might as well see where they led. "Grace was two months pregnant."

After a pause, the woman spoke. "No, she wasn't."

"How do you know?"

"Because she would have told me."

"Maybe she didn't want to announce it yet."

She slapped her hand down on the armrest so hard it must have hurt. "It's not a damned *announcement*! She would have told me! We told each other everything!"

"Apparently not this," Riley said.

E VELYN TOOK OVER A PARKING SPACE FROM A DE-
parting Channel 15 van and hurried into the lobby of Grace's
and Marissa's building before the overhanging clouds could drop
their rain. Sometimes she thought clouds viewed the city of Cleveland
the way pigeons saw people's heads, as an attractive target.

"Morning, Justin," she said to the doorman—or deskman, since
he spent most of the time behind the front desk. He seemed to leave
it only to dart out like a gunshot to open the door for any tenant,
whether young, old, male, or female, carrying a heavy package or
nothing more burdensome than a stock report, like the nicely
dressed man she'd passed on the way in.

"Hi, Mrs. James."

It amazed her when people remembered her name, a trick she
couldn't pull off to save her life. She knew his face, of course, but
got the name only because it had been embroidered onto his shirt.
He marked his place in a pharmacology textbook on the counter and
gave her his full attention.

"Are you in college, Justin?"

"Graduate school. The detectives are in there." He nodded toward the closed office door behind him. She heard a woman's raised
voice.

"I won't disturb them, then. I just need to collect samples from around the building and then get one more from the Markham apartment."

"Sure." Unlike the building manager, Frank, Justin didn't care if she referred to the suites as apartments rather than penthouses. "I think there's a cop up there guarding the place. If you call up, he'll come down. He's the keeper of the code."

"The what?"

The younger man flushed a bit. "I guess Mr. Markham raised a stink about the cops knowing his code. He said they have to keep it to a minimum, so they only tell the guy who's the sentry or whatever that day."

"The contamination officer? He's the one who notes everybody that goes in and out of the scene."

"I guess. I don't know why he bothers."

"As long as we might have to examine something else or collect more evidence from it, we have to keep it under our constant custody, so to speak. Otherwise, if we wanted to come back later, we'd have to get a search warrant or a second consent from the owner."

"No, I mean I don't know why Mr. Markham bothers. He's going to move out in a week or two anyway. I guess he just wants his stuff safe in the meantime."

Evelyn leaned her arms on the marble countertop, feeling the weariness flow through her body. "Had they been planning to move?"

"No, it's just because of the murder. He told Frank not to renew the lease—it's up at the end of the month—because he never wants to come back to where Grace was killed. Can't blame him, really. It would make my skin crawl."

Evelyn pictured Grace's body at their kitchen table. "I don't blame him either. Do the officers know about that?"

"I guess so. Frank probably told them. It's lucky for Mr. Markham that the lease is almost up—we rent in five-year increments, so he'd lose a bundle if he moved out prior to that without at least a six-month notice."

Enough about Grace. Evelyn wanted to learn more about Marissa's attack. "How long has Robert Tenneyson lived here?"

"He was here when I started, and that was two years ago. I can look it up for you if you like." When she deferred, he went on to tell her that the doctor seemed like a nice guy, worked irregular hours, and always gave him a Christmas bonus. The phone rang, cutting him off, and Evelyn stayed quiet while he took the call.

The woman's voice still filtered, nonstop, out of the manager's office. Justin transferred the phone call. Evelyn zoned out for a moment, lulled by the warm lobby, trying to remember the last time she'd seen her daughter. She hadn't been home for dinner and had collapsed in bed by the time Angel entered the house, giggling after her date. The late-night phone call had dragged her out long before Angel had to get up for school, so it had been about thirty hours. No problem, really . . . Angel had school all day, and Evelyn's mother lived next door, always ready to stuff her granddaughter with more calories than any teenage *Cosmopolitan* reader wanted to encounter.

"Justin," she asked when he hung up the phone, "how many people work in this building?"

"There's me, Terry, and Leroy on the desk. We rotate. There's Frank, of course. Our maintenance guy is Gerard. He's got an office off the garage. That's it, really."

"No cleaning staff?"

"Gerard takes care of the lobby and the stairwell and maintains the heating and air-conditioning. The tenants hire their own staff and make their own arrangements for them to come in and out, so that's got nothing to do with us," he clarified with something like relief. "That includes home improvements like paint or appliance installations—of course, that has to be approved by Erie Realty first, but on the whole the tenants are free to do anything they want as long as it doesn't make too much noise."

The building did seem pretty streamlined. Not a potted plant or even a piece of carpet took up space on the lobby's white marble floor. Ditto for the sidewalk out front. "No valet parking?"

"Nope. That adds a lot of liability, I guess, so Erie just doesn't do it. Besides, there's only fourteen suites in the entire building. The garage has three floors, and that's plenty."

"No way from the garage into the building?"

"Only that door right there."

"Such wealthy people don't mind parking their own cars and carrying their own groceries?"

"Well, there's me to carry stuff." He grinned. "But our tenants are kind of more interested in being left alone than they are in being pampered. That's why there's no fitness center, no party room, no rooftop deck—just residences. It's a quiet place. And they don't have to haul too many groceries, they have people to do that. There are only three floors with children, and not even those families are into home cooking, I don't think. There's an elderly couple on four—he made piles of money in munitions during the Korean War—and they eat every single meal out. Breakfast, lunch, and dinner."

Her stomach rumbled. "I can't decide if that would be good or bad."

"Oh, bad. Definitely bad. All the preservatives and additives in food these days, not to mention the sodium level in most prepared dishes." He patted his textbook. "It's amazing that stuff hasn't given them four heart attacks apiece by now. Which would be a pity, 'cause they're nice."

"Are most of the residents nice?"

He thought. "Most are just in and out. We don't interact enough for me to know."

The door to the office remained closed. "What's Erie Realty?"

"The owners' group. That's where Frank and Gerard send their reports. They pay our checks and manage our benefits. That's why I took this job—dental." He tapped his two front teeth for her, apparently demonstrating some recent work. "That, and it gives me plenty of time to study, especially on weekdays, when it's quiet."

"Do they own any other buildings?"

"Sure, a bunch. They have the Crown Point place on Ninth, the Guarley Towers next to Jacobs Field, two office buildings side by side across the river, the Harrity in Euclid, a big complex out in Lakewood . . . and more than that, but I don't know them all."

"And here there's just you and the other guys you mentioned?"

"Yep. Why, though? I mean, you don't think—"

"At the moment I don't know what to think, Justin. Could you show me where Gerard's office is?"

He plunked a small "Be right back" sign on the counter and came around to the front. She cringed a bit when he plunged through the door to the parking lot, half-expecting the hovering monster that had attacked Marissa to be waiting, but the garage held only cars and the echoes of passing traffic. Justin led her to an unlabeled metal door in the southeast corner of the garage. She had left it covered in black fingerprint powder the night before.

A trim man with a graying beard and a uniform crouched in the doorway, backlit by the lights of his cluttered office. He tossed a blackened paper towel into a garbage can and tore another off the roll, then looked up at her. "I have you to thank for this, don't I?"

"Sorry." Don't apologize, she scolded herself. You were doing your job.

"He couldn't have gotten in here, anyway," the maintenance man insisted. "I lock it when I leave. Did you find anything on it?"

"No."

He straightened, then leaned over a set of three streaks, darker in color than the background. "What about these?"

"Those are smudges. They could have been left there by fingers, but they're not distinct enough to be of any use to us. The paint has oxidized—it's exposed to at least some of the elements—so it's not a very good surface for prints." Most of the powder had wiped away, but some had worked its way into the porous paint. The door would have to be repainted if he wanted it to be clean.

"Then why did you have to stain my entire door if there was no chance of finding a fingerprint?"

"There's always a chance."

He rolled his eyes, then cleaned the smudges as best he could. "Have you caught the guy who killed Mrs. Markham? Or grabbed that other girl?"

"Not yet."

"Nothing like that has ever happened here before—at least that I know of, and I've been here seven years. You think the same guy attacked that girl out there last night?"

"We're not sure yet."

He threw away the paper towel and replaced the bottle of cleaner next to similar items. "Well, what *do* you know?"

"We're investigating," she said through gritted teeth. "And I need your help. I'm collecting oils."

He blinked, his exasperation temporarily turning to confusion, and gestured at his overflowing shelves. "Well, I have WD-40—"

"Not right out of the bottles, because any contaminants—dirt or debris from the building—could be distinctive as well."

The exasperation returned. "Then what?"

"I need to collect from places around the building, particularly entry and exit points. Lock mechanisms, hinges, that sort of thing. Could you show me around?"

"I got a choice?"

"No," she lied.

"Might as well. Not going to get any work done today anyway with you guys swarming around like mosquitoes."

He didn't seem like the type to volunteer information, so she made her questions specific. "I know there's a side door to the alley at the end of the hallway behind Frank's office. Aside from that door, the lobby door, and the door to the garage here, are there any other doors into or out of the building?"

"Nope."

"Is there a freight elevator?"

"Yeah, at the other end of the building." He crossed his arms, gave another puffing sigh. "We use it to deliver large items like furniture. It opens into the stairwell at each floor."

"And there's only the one stairwell."

"Yep."

"Can I see that, please?"

"Sure." He locked his door behind them, and they entered the lobby, where Justin had returned to his post. "But he couldn't have gotten into the Markhams' apartment that way. It would have set off the indicator light in the building manager's office. I already showed the cops that, but I don't know if they understood it."

"What if Frank had gone to lunch when it lit up?"

"Doesn't matter. The light stays on until you reset it." He paused before a steel door labeled "Fire Use Only," near the exterior door leading to the alley. A flight of small but clean stairs stretched upward, seemingly without end. The freight elevator doors sat to her right. "You really want to walk up ten stories?"

"Not particularly, no. I'm going to think of it as my exercise for the day."

"Suit yourself."

He began to climb, and she followed. Her knees let out squeaks of protest, beginning with the first step. "The door isn't locked?"

"Of course not, in case of fire. And you can't get into the penthouses from the stairwell anyway—each penthouse door is steel with huge dead bolts. You'd need a stick of dynamite to get through them."

Gerard, she noticed as they approached the fourth floor, did not seem put out by the exertion. His breath did not come heavy, and his pace did not slack. I need to work out more, she told herself. "Do the tenants ever use the stairwell?"

"Only Mrs. Cameron on six. She's kind of a health nut—she'll walk up, set off the light in Frank's office, and then call to tell him there's no fire. It never occurs to her to let him know in advance. So then he frets, thinking maybe there *is* a fire and her smoke detectors aren't working." He snorted, passed another landing. "Frank worries a lot."

"Is there a camera in here? In this stairwell?"

"One, on the first floor. We passed it when we came in. It's motion-activated, since the stairs are hardly ever used."

"So tenants could move around from floor to floor up here without being on camera."

"And there have been tenants who have taken advantage of that little fact, believe me. Spouses often work conveniently long hours around here," Gerard said—still not breathing heavily, damn him.

"Like who?"

"Geesh, don't quote me. I don't need to get fired here. Besides, I'm exaggerating—there was only one, and I only know about them because both couples divorced and moved out, a year ago. Besides, the camera idea was to protect from outside criminals—I imagine the designers figured there was no reason to be afraid of anyone rich enough to live here."

She paused on the eighth-floor landing to take a breath, unable to keep up appearances for two more floors. "They may have been wrong about that."

THE OFFICERS HAD ALREADY INVESTIGATED THE
stairwell, and she did not notice anything they might have
missed. No debris. No dirt, save for a light coating of dust in
the corners. The freight elevator doors sat closed and silent at each
floor. All the apartment doors, including Grace's, appeared undam-
aged. The fingerprint powder she had left there the day before had
been removed.

"I washed that off. Did you have to cover the whole door in that
stuff? Took me a half hour to clean off," Gerard complained. He
peered at a nearly invisible smudge remaining next to a hinge. "And
I still couldn't get it all."

A man with a neat streak. Normally she would wonder where
he'd been all her life, but under his fierce glare she hoped that, wher-
ever Gerard had been, he would stay there.

The Markham crime scene had been surgical-suite clean. Was
that a clue, or merely the joint result of Josiela's talents and a very
quick murder?

"So did you get any vitally important clues after ruining my
door?" he asked.

She didn't point out that, if the killer had entered this way, either he had a key or someone had let him in. "I see what you mean

about the dead bolts. He'd have to use a bazooka to get it open without a key."

"There's always *Dial M for Murder.*"

She grinned in surprise. Perhaps she and Gerard had something in common besides a bent for cleaning. "The husband gives the killer his key and gets it back afterward?"

"Or the husband gave the killer Grace's key and he put it back in her purse before he left."

"But he'd have shown up on the stairwell surveillance tape." She didn't add that the stairwell door had been locked behind him—impossible if the killer had left Grace's key—because she did not know which facts the police might want to hold back. Instead she turned her face to the ascending steps. "Okay. Onward and upward."

"You're going farther?"

"I need to see all of it. There's only five more floors, right?"

The stairwell ended at a door, heavy with a bank-vault-quality dead bolt. Gerard pulled a set of keys from a deep pocket, and they emerged onto the roof.

There are worse places to be than fifteen floors up on a temperate day. They had even hit a dry-weather moment, a lucky break during a Cleveland spring. Water pooled across the asphalt expanse. In the distance, through a short forest of air vents and other ductwork, the hazy blue lake spread into nothingness. Traffic below melded into a low hum, and the Terminal Tower gleamed in the distance, stolidly holding its own against the upstart BP and Marriott structures. She took a deep breath, tasting the rain, lake water, fish and oil scents in the air, then headed for the edge. Gingerly. Heights could be scary, but she loved the view.

A large doorless structure sat in the center of the roof, separate from the stairway booth. "What's that?"

"Elevator machine room," Gerard said.

A wall ran around the perimeter of the roof, but it stood only calf-high, not high enough to prevent anyone from falling—no doubt why they kept the door securely locked. She looked down on the dizzying panorama of freighters along the Cuyahoga riverbank for a few minutes, then got back to work. The cops, she knew, had been up here as well, but she wanted to see for herself. Crisscrossing the roof garnered no clues save for a Snickers wrapper and an empty Marlboro box, both of which she collected. The few cigarette butts present looked as if they'd been there since the turn of the millennium. The next roof over belonged to a warehouse; the two buildings were the same height but separated by an alley. The killer could have moved from one to the other if he were an Olympic long-jump medal holder, and extremely brave. On the other side ran the full expanse of St. Clair Avenue.

Her Nextel began to speak. "Where are you? Are you there?"

She pulled it off her belt, cursing Medical Examiner Stone for having thrust the modern convenience on his staff. "I'm here."

"Where have you been?" Tony complained. "I've been calling."

"Inside a concrete stairwell."

"Where are you now?"

"On a roof, fifteen stories up."

"Don't fall off."

"Good thing you said something, I never would have thought of that. What's up?"

"Do we have more proteinase K?"

"I don't know. What are you doing?"

"I'm doing the DNA analysis." The electronic transmission couldn't remove the stiffness from his voice. "What do you think I'm doing? Since you're too damn *busy*, of course. And where's the positive control? The 9477A?"

She told him what she could and hung up with a sigh. The most high-profile cases since last fall, and Tony had to do the DNA. No wonder he sounded harried. She felt pretty harried herself.

"Are you done?" Gerard called after ten minutes. He hadn't

moved from just outside the door. Perhaps he didn't care for heights or great views.

"No. Can we go in there?" She pointed at the boxy room.

He shrugged, turned, and held the roof door for her. She followed him down half a flight of concrete steps, across the landing, and up to a door labeled "Machine Room—Authorized Personnel Only." He opened the door with a key. The well-lit, roomy area held an elevator, several large machines, and one man. A flight of stairs led to a sort of loft, where a huge, complicated piece of what looked like hundred-year-old iron with a wheel on one side jerked into motion as she watched. She jumped a foot.

"Jack, this woman's from the police," Gerard said.

"I didn't do it," the other man said and laughed, holding out his wrists as if held by invisible handcuffs.

Evelyn didn't bother to correct his assumption that she was an officer, but inwardly she groaned. Like she hadn't heard *that* one before.

The machinery made enough noise to drown out a low-flying plane. A four-foot-square steel box on her left revealed rows of switches, which clicked on and off. Next to that stood a computer-monitor stand, almost like a self-check kiosk at the airport. But the thing in the loft dominated the room.

"That's the motor," the elevator repairman said, following her gaze. He wore his sandy hair in a shaggy seventies cut and held a blackened tool in his hands. Embroidered patches on his green shirt read "E-tech" on one side and "Jack" on the other. "It's turning the cable. The motor for the freight elevator is there."

She glanced at a twin of the loft machine standing off to her right, quiet and unmoving, then looked back at the one she'd first seen. "Is that very old?" A dumb question, but she wouldn't have been surprised if the engine dated back to the turn of the last century, to a time before cost dictated quality, when things were built to last.

"The motor? No. I think this place was built in the mid-eighties."

"And it winds up the rope? And that pulls up the elevator?"

He grinned. "No, the cable is looped over the top of the driver—the wheel. On the other side is the counterweight. When the elevator goes up, the counterweight goes down. Here, I'll show you. You're here about that murder, huh? And that girl in the garage?"

He did something at the computer kiosk. Then, using a rodlike key in a tiny hole at the top of the elevator doors, he opened the door, revealing the moving cables. She had to force herself to go within five feet of it. Heavy machinery terrified her, always had, and she had no idea why. As a child, she had turned her face away from the exposed areas of amusement park rides to pretend they weren't there. She still opened a car hood with trepidation, sure that doing so involved great physical risk.

The two men waited while she thought, listening to the hum of the metal gears. The top of the elevator appeared at the floor level, and the motor stopped. The room grew quieter. She inched forward. There were only two ways into Grace Markham's apartment—the fire door and the elevator.

The top of the elevator was surprisingly crowded, with more machinery she didn't want to see. A heavy beam held the car like the handle on a bucket, and the main cable—actually a bundle of six cables—attached to its middle. Three buttons on the center beam were labeled Up, Down, and Stop. A squarish, flat shape seemed to glow at its edges, and she realized what it must be. "There's a hatch in the elevator roof, right?"

"Yep. And before you ask, no."

"No what?"

"No, someone couldn't have climbed out of the elevator through the hatch and waited for Grace Markham to stop at her floor. The hatch doesn't open from the inside. That's only in movies. Besides, he'd run the risk that someone else would call it first and he'd be riding up and down the shaft on the car top."

Evelyn tried to picture standing on top of a moving piston in a dark shaft, and then tried not to. "What if he lived above her? If she stopped at her floor, could he have opened the doors to the shaft on his floor and gotten into the elevator and then into her apartment?"

"No. Besides, a seventy-five-year-old widow lives above the Markhams."

"Well, any floor. Could he climb down the ladder—"

"There is no ladder in an elevator shaft. That's another only-in-the-movies thing. And the hall doors won't open if the elevator isn't there, no matter what. It's a safety feature."

"But you can open it."

"Well, yeah—but only on the top floor and the bottom floor." He pointed to the round keyhole at the top of the door. "Every building is like that. So who killed the woman? You don't think the husband did it?"

"We don't know. But thanks for the help—and Erie Realty hired you?"

"Yep."

She wondered why Justin hadn't listed him as an employee. As if reading her mind, Gerard spoke up. "He's only here on Tuesdays."

"Sometimes not even then, depending on what else is going on. I might be here tomorrow too, if I can't get this software patch to work."

Evelyn perked up. "Is something wrong with the elevator? Like stopping at the wrong floors?"

He seemed almost sorry to have to shoot down another one of her theories. "It tends to run with the doors open on car top inspection. It's got nothing to do with stopping at floors. I already told those two detectives all this just an hour or two ago."

"Sorry. Actually, I came up here to collect oil samples." She pulled a small packet from her bag.

"Oil?"

She broke a sterile swab out of its packaging. "Grease, whatever."

"From the elevator?"

"And the dead-bolt locks, and the Markhams' exercise equipment—any source of oil in the building."

Behind her, Gerard's sigh could be heard over the clacking. "Our tax dollars at work."

"Be my guest." The elevator repairman stepped to the side, holding the door firmly open.

She moved gingerly forward. Every inch of the car top seemed covered with oil, or dirt, or some sort of heavy black coating. She extended the swab toward a mechanism at the closest edge.

"That's the door operator," Jack told her, not that she really wanted to know.

She slid the swab into its microtube with trembling hands.

"Anything else?"

She gave up the brave front and held out a fresh swab. "Can you reach that hatch with this?"

"Sure." He slid a screwdriver into the door as a stop and stepped into the darkness. "Just anywhere on the hatch?"

"Around the edges."

He returned with a blackened swab. "There you go. You really think he was fooling around in the shaft? Sheesh, that's all I need, to come in and find someone flattened on top of the car."

She tucked the labeled swabs away in her kit. "He got into Grace Markham's apartment somehow. He avoided the camera in the garage. He's someone who knows this building like the back of his hand."

"Like us," Gerard said. "More like me, since I'm here all week long. I think I'd better get a lawyer."

Evelyn didn't know what to say. Usually cops interviewed potential witnesses. She stuck with dead people and inanimate objects for a reason.

Luckily, her Nextel beeped. She hit the green phone button.

"Mom? I'm going . . . project . . . Steve."

"Angel, you're breaking up. I'll call you right back." Evelyn clipped the phone to her belt. "Sorry about that. My daughter. She must be home from school already. The high school has— Oh, crap."

"What?" Jack asked, wiping his hands on a rag, though they didn't seem dirty.

"It's Meet the Teachers at the high school today. That's why she's out early." She looked at her watch. "Well, I'm going to stand up Mrs. Evans—again. The woman is going to think I don't exist and report Angel to Children and Families as an orphan."

Jack grinned again. "Nothing like squirming around in those little desks while every teacher in the school tells you why you're a lousy parent. My son raised so much hell that, by the time I showed up, they wanted to give *me* a detention."

Evelyn laughed. Gerard sighed.

"One more thing. Could anyone—tenants or staff—take the elevator from one floor to another floor without going to the lobby first?"

"Nope."

He seemed as sure of that as he had been of everything else. "Can you tell how many trips went to Grace Markham's apartment that day?"

"Nope."

She gestured at the computer. "That information isn't recorded?"

"Not unless we're doing some kind of traffic study or something, but otherwise, no. Sorry." He opened the door of a large, white rectangle, nearly the size of a refrigerator. Behind it sat what seemed like a mile of wires, running in short loops from one small bar to another. She recognized the kind of green electronic panel found in computers, sticking out from between them. "This is the controller. To override the automatic system and make the elevator go to a certain floor, you'd have to jump out the circuits manually."

"Could someone get in at the lobby and come up here?"

"It's coded, like the floors. Only me, Gerard, and Frank have the code."

"See?" Gerard said. "We're going to wind up screwed, mark my words. You think one of these rich guys will go down for this? I'm calling my lawyer."

Virtually anyone could have attacked Marissa. Suspects in Grace Markham's murder included Gerard, Jack, and Frank, who had means of entry—at least to the elevator shaft and controls—and opportunity but no apparent motive; William Markham, who had means and motive but no apparent opportunity; and some unknown person with apparent motive and opportunity but no means of entry. Even if he could get to the roof, he still wouldn't have a way to get into Grace Markham's penthouse without the code. Evelyn wondered if the young couple had made their elevator code an easy number, like their address or their wedding date, because it was beginning to look as if either the killer had guessed it or Grace Markham had invited him in.

SHE FOUND RAFE JOHNSON IN HIS OFFICE, A FORMER
supply closet outfitted with an overwhelming number of
computers, monitors, TVs, VCRs, and one lone laptop, all
connected to one another by yards of cable. It made her claustrophobic. "Hey, Rafe."

The video analyst didn't turn. "Figured you'd be by."

"Got the tape from evidence lockup?"

"You left a big, obnoxious note on my door, didn't you?" For
that of a very young, slight man, his voice struck notes like a string
bass. He paused to tilt his head back and slide a long candy string
into his mouth. "Despite a public education, I *can* read."

"Thanks." She squeezed past a protruding Magnavox and
perched carefully on a stool that had once had four legs. A vintage
Chicago CD played softly in the corner. "You're the best. What are
you eating? I smell cherry."

"I ain't touching that one with a ten-foot pole. It's Twizzlers Pull-
n-Peel, and no, you can't have none. Now listen up." The TV in front
of him displayed the familiar grainy image of the La Riviere parking
garage. "I've gone over the two hours before Marissa drives in. At least
it's not multiplexed, none of that jumping between fifteen cameras
per second crap, so I still have some feeling left in my retinas."

"You can feel your retinas? That don't sound right, son."

"I'm glad you're so funny this morning. Just a bucket o' joy. Problem is, there's no one. No one comes in, no one leaves. Don't no one in this building ever go nowhere?"

"It was late, on a weeknight. These are rich people."

"If I was rich, I'd go everywhere. Weeknight, weekend. The desk clerk ran out once to get himself some dinner. Nothing else."

"How do you know it's the desk clerk?"

"Because the second videotape covers the lobby. He leaves a little sign on the desk, walks out through the parking garage, don't know why, maybe to save himself a couple of steps on the way to the deli. He comes back in fifteen minutes with a white bag, and then nothing happens for hours. Then Marissa walks right up to the camera. Look at this." He tapped a button on the remote, advancing the tape frame by frame, twirling a dreadlock with his free hand.

Evelyn felt herself tense, as if the attack were happening again right in front of her and she couldn't do anything about it. Her muscles gathered, ready to strike out.

"You see this patch of dark here—it looks like a hand, or an elbow. Something. Maybe a gloved hand." He froze the picture. "And that's it. That's as much as we see of the guy." He turned to the computer monitor. "I captured the image, deinterlaced, and brightened it. Now it looks like a slightly lighter blob."

She squinted, as if that might help. "It still could be a glove, or an arm."

"Or even Marissa's hair."

"What about the shoe? That dark thing that appears in the lower left corner—"

"I brightened that too." He changed images. "See? But it's still a blob. What was Marissa wearing?"

"High heels. The hospital gave me her clothes."

"That's too square to be a high heel. I bet that's his shoe, just not much we can do with it."

"Looks like a tennis shoe. A dark one."

He considered the photo. "Maybe with a lighter stripe on the side. Maybe a Nike, or an Adidas."

"You can see that? You really *are* the best."

"Tell Marissa that. When she's up and around again, remind her that she still has time to call off that wedding." He hit the Print button. "How is she?"

"She should make it. That's all I've gotten from the hospital so far."

"You think this guy was some old boyfriend of hers, killed the Markham woman by mistake? I heard Marissa dated some gangbanger in her wild days and the guy still follows her around."

"Who said that? Besides, how would the guy get into the Markham apartment? It's like Fort Knox."

"It's a rumor. It's not supposed to be logical."

"It's a lie."

"Don't shoot the messenger, lady. I just thought you ought to know what the busy little bees are buzzing about around here."

Evelyn sighed. "I can't say I'm surprised. Marissa's gorgeous, and she speaks her mind. There's plenty of staff here who would love to blame her for her own misfortunes."

"Just thought you ought to know," he repeated.

"I appreciate it. Look, the video of the lobby— Is that the entire day on there?"

"Yep. Those two from Homicide are going to come by later."

"David and Riley?"

"No, the two chicks. The cute one, Sanchez, and her partner. They left me a big, obnoxious note too. They want me to pick out the Markham dude leaving for work and then see who comes and goes after that. I already checked it out—you can see who comes and goes by way of the garage, but there's no way to tell where someone goes once they get in the elevator. If your guy lives in the building, you're screwed."

"Can you keep an eye out for anyone carrying a bag or a case? And about those cherry Pull-n-Peels . . ."

"No."

"I haven't had breakfast yet."

"That ain't good. It's the most important meal of the day, you know. What kind of bag?"

"Don't know. It's just a guess, that he'd carry his straps in something, maybe even some gloves. My blood sugar is probably dropping."

He pulled the vaguely shoelike image out of the printer and handed it to her. "There's your shoe."

"Not much chance of getting a size from that," she said. She had compared the shoeprints lifted from the kitchen floor with her unofficial database of ME staff shoeprints and figured it for a size 10. William Markham, she knew from inspecting his closet, wore size 10, so the prints might belong to him. "Don't forget to print a picture of everyone who left the building as well as entered."

"If I give you a Twizzler, will you go away and stop thinking of work for me?"

She received her cherry prize without making any promises.

"I bet your guy's *still* there," Rafe added.

Evelyn shuddered. "Deciding on his next victim."

THE RHODES Business and Living Center in the Flats consisted, at the moment, of a haphazard array of ironwork that still managed to imply a sweeping design. David took a moment to follow the beams from the arching tower down to where they met the choppy Cuyahoga. Whatever else William Markham might be—adulterer, murderer—he was one hell of an architect.

Riley finished his smoke, and they entered the construction site through a rusting chain-link fence. A steady drizzle turned the earth to one big mud puddle, through which men carrying impossibly heavy loads splashed in random patterns. For once, David felt it was just as well he couldn't afford expensive shoes. Past the mud, a pile driver took steel rods larger around than a man and pounded them into the earth. The steady pounding dug into his cerebellum, carrying the promise of a deadly headache. He should have passed on that fifth cup of coffee at the Riviere, but he'd needed it to keep going.

"At least we don't have to tote buckets of grease and rivets for a living," Riley pointed out, but he seemed almost cheerful. Perhaps, despite his habits, his lungs perked up at the prospect of breathing air that wasn't either recirculated or filled with nicotine. "This has got to be hell in the winter, one street off the river like this."

After five steps, David's trousers were speckled with mud up to the knee, and he was damn tired of getting wet. "I can't wait to have my own washing machine, with the amount of laundry I create—"

"You want to move in with Evie so she can do your laundry?"

"That's not what I said." His partner was the closest thing David had to a friend in his entire adopted city, and he couldn't even talk to him, knowing that Riley would take Evelyn's side in all matters. David suspected the older detective had been half in love with her for years. He changed the subject. "This is an interesting location for Markham's job, right here in the Flats."

"Because these lucky guys can spend their lunch hour staring at girls in Christie's?"

"Because the Riviere is on the other side of the river. You can see it from here."

"So William could easily have snuck out of the site, gone home, killed his wife, and been back before anyone realized he was gone?"

"Exactly."

"Good thinking, son. I really like to see you taking initiative, theorizing about our potential murderer using the facts at hand."

"All right." David took advantage of a dropped wooden plank to step out of the sucking mud for five feet. "What's wrong with it?"

"William Markham wasn't here the day Grace died. He spent

the day at his office on East Thirtieth, presenting plans to a client for a mall out in Beachwood—like they need another mall. So he's seventeen blocks away and not missing from the powwow for more than a bathroom break, all day long."

"You neglected to mention that yesterday, when you said his alibi checked out."

"We haven't had time for details."

"Isn't God in the details? Okay, so he hired someone."

Riley eyed a welder. "I see from that guy's tattoos that he's been inside more than once. If William wanted a tough guy, he might not have had to look too far."

They approached the construction trailer. "But this guy isn't a tough guy," David argued. "He's a sick guy. It seems personal, trussing her up like that. And a hired hood would have lifted the cash from her purse at the very least."

"I know." Riley sighed. "But so far, hubby's all we've got."

They entered the trailer without knocking, to find William Markham and two quite hefty men leaning over a set of blueprints held down by coffee cups. After introductions, the construction manager told them to use the trailer for as long as they needed and threw Markham a sympathetic glance as he left with his partner. The murdered woman's husband sank into a battered leather desk chair. "Good morning, Officers. What can I help you with?"

Riley straddled a stool, shrugging off his blazer. Once they were out of the spring breeze, the temperature seemed warm. "Nice-looking building, so far."

Markham rubbed a palm over his receding hairline. Well-cut pants hid the baby fat he'd never lost, and he had managed to get into the trailer in them without accumulating one-tenth the mud that David had. "They've already sold the ground floor to two restaurants and a gym."

"With a generous tax break from the Lakefront Development Plan, no doubt."

"The Flats started out as factories and sleazy bars, and grew into a cultural mecca. We can't let one bad decade push it back into the sludge."

"Very civic-minded of you. You're a strong guy, coming to work the day after your wife and baby get offed."

"You've locked me out of my own home. Where am I supposed to go?"

"We're going to release the scene later today. Besides, you've already worked that out, haven't you?"

Markham looked up at Riley from the shade of his fingers. "What do you mean?"

"Frank told us you're moving out—"

"Can you blame me?"

"No, not at all. He also gave us your forwarding address."

Markham remained still as stone. The pile driver, David noticed, managed to reverberate right through the thin trailer walls as if they were still outside.

"I wonder how you're going to move into that address at the Quay 55—gorgeous place, by the way, love the view—when there's already someone living there. A young lady. A really nice-looking young lady, as a matter of fact, named Barbara Quinn. A young lady who used to work at Markham and Johnson, until four months ago. What happened? You had to find her other employment because you were afraid that one of your staff would tell Grace?"

Markham straightened up but didn't respond. Nor did he look particularly shocked.

"Was that when Grace started to have you followed?"

"Followed?"

"According to a friend, she planned to hire a private detective."

Markham rolled his eyes to the ceiling. "Let me guess. Jolene Eames."

"You're acquainted with Miss Joey?"

"Joey's a hanger-on. She hasn't got squat and doesn't want to work to get it, so her best plan is to hang around with someone who has. Grace picked up the lunch tab, the bar tab, the concert tickets, you name it. She gave her money to make her rent now and then. Joey used Grace to meet eligible men, guys she didn't have a chance in hell with anyway. Joey never met a person she didn't use. Grace was too sweet to call her on it."

"Or call you on it."

He sighed. "Or me. Yes, everything you suspect about Barbara is true. I am moving in with her, and we'll be married as soon as we get the license."

"And Grace knew?"

"Grace suspected. And she didn't hire some PI, at least not that I know of—that's Joey Eames's flight of fancy. Grace would ask if I was seeing someone, and I'd convince her I wasn't. Look, I know I'm a snake, but I couldn't make myself tell her the truth. I couldn't hurt her. If she'd been one of those cold trust-fund babies, I could have just said sayonara, and she'd have waved me on with the prenup as I walked out the door. But Grace was too soft. I didn't know how to tell her."

"Now you don't have to," David pointed out. "And the prenup doesn't apply. You have to admit, you have two of the oldest motives in the world. Money and sex."

"I didn't kill her," he said without anger.

"And now Barb doesn't have to worry about being a stepmommy."

"I didn't kill her! I had even decided to tell her the truth. I thought if Grace had someone of her own, a baby, she wouldn't mind me leaving."

"Oh yeah." Riley put a cigarette to his lips, striking the match so hard it didn't light. "Women just love being left to raise a kid all by themselves."

"Grace didn't need my help, she could afford to hire a live-in. Maybe Joey killed her—Grace had been getting tired of her lately."

"Is that why she didn't tell Joey she was pregnant?"

"I guess so. She didn't want to tell anyone, for fear something would go wrong. Her mother had had a lot of miscarriages. There's something else you guys should look at—maybe Grace found out something shady about one of those charities she spent so much time with. They're always throwing millions of dollars around. I'm not the best husband in the world, but I wouldn't hurt Grace. I have no idea who killed her. But"—the muscles of his jaw tightened, smoothing out the baby fat to look older, harder—"I hope you catch him. And I hope you kill him."

David found himself believing the man but still refused to be sidetracked. "How long has Barbara had the elevator code to your apartment?"

"Penthouse. And she doesn't. She's never needed it."

"And why did Barbara quit your firm?"

"Like you said. A few people on my staff had gotten a little too interested in our relationship."

"It had nothing to do with her father kicking off and leaving her about a million and a half in real estate?"

Marblelike eyes widened. Money is wasted on the rich, David thought, like youth on the young.

"Yeah, we know more than you think. For future reference, Markham, when we talk, we'll always know more than you think. So you've picked up another wealthy babe. How *do* you do it? You're not Hollywood material, you're not baby-sweet, you don't seem like a sparkling conversationalist. What do they see in you?"

The man seemed incapable of taking offense. He considered the question, somberly. "I listen to them."

"That's it?"

"That's all they really want."

Riley got to his feet. "Thanks for your time."

Outside, the rain had paused but the mud still ran. The workers began to open lunch pails or line up at the hot dog stand parked on the sidewalk. An ironworker descended from the heights and unlocked his safety harness. David detoured across the site to step over exposed spikes of rebar. "Look at this."

The stained khaki harness consisted of mesh fabric straps, an inch and a half wide, and heavy metal buckles. Velcro closures kept the harness from shifting around on a moving body. The attached cable disappeared into the heights above. "What do we know about the guys that work here?"

"We'll go back, ask for a roster." Riley pushed his cigarette into the mud with his toes. "We could run all the names for past records. If Markham doesn't want to give us the roster, we'll try to get a judge who's easy on search warrants. There's nothing to indicate this job has anything to do with the crime. Little Willie wasn't even here that day, and there could be three other sites just like this that he's also involved in."

David let go of the harness, watching it swing gently in space. "We're looking for a strap of mesh in a haystack of rebar."

"Sort of."

"Hey!"

They turned. One of the guys who had been looking at blueprints with Markham stood there, and all three hundred pounds of him glowered. "What are you two doing in there?"

"Just—"

"Get out of there!"

"We're the—"

"This is a hard-hat area! You want to get brained?"

Since they didn't, David and Riley filed out to the mud-filled expanse. They located the construction manager, asked for a roster of employees, and received a polite refusal. The manager was very sorry for what had happened to Grace Markham, but it had nothing to do with them and cops made his guys nervous. They had not, he admitted, always been angels.

"Let's get the hell out of here," David said. "I'm going to have to go home and change clothes."

"Too bad you don't live right across the river, like Markham. Oh, that's right, he doesn't live there anymore. So what do you think of his theory of bagging women, Milaski? Do you *listen* to Evie? Really listen?"

David unlocked the car. He tried to listen. He tried like hell to hang on her every word.

Then maybe you should listen to what she's telling you now. She's saying no by not saying yes.

No. She just wasn't sure yet.

Then when?

She's got Angel to think about.

And she always will. Convenient, isn't it?

David knew he couldn't respect a woman who would put her boyfriend above her child. Problem was, he wasn't sure he could love a woman who didn't put him above everything.

Selfish, yes, but human beings were a selfish lot.

"Well?" Riley demanded.

"Sorry. I wasn't listening." He threw himself into the driver's seat and started the car.

EVELYN TRIED TO REACH ANGEL AT HOME, BUT NO ONE picked up. She tried Angel at her grandmother's next door. No answer. Perhaps she should have bought her daughter a cell phone for her last birthday, as she'd asked, but the way Angel could talk, the first bill would have taken out the entire household budget. Evelyn's ex, Rick, refused to buy one on the same grounds, despite pulling down twice her salary. Evelyn had suggested a pager, but Angel had balked. Pagers were *so* last millennium. Evelyn put the phone back in her purse and returned to the old teaching amphitheater she now used as a work space.

At first glance, Grace Markham's clothing didn't tell her much. The victim had been wealthy enough to afford designers whose names Evelyn didn't even recognize, and slender enough to wear said designers in a size 4—the more enviable of the two conditions, in Evelyn's opinion. She spread the items, one by one, on an examination table covered with fresh brown paper.

Under an alternative light source, the sweater showed no signs of semen or other bodily fluids. She did notice some odd, gleaming streaks on the skirt—not semen but thin lines of some reflective substance. She cut an inch-square swatch and placed it in a manila envelope before she taped the skirt, pressing clear packaging tape to the surface. She then smoothed the tape onto a sheet of clear acetate, to examine later for hairs and fibers.

The bra showed nothing. Either Grace had not worn nylons or the killer, for some reason known only to himself, had taken them away with him. The panties glowed brightly, indicating the presence of semen. Evelyn wet a piece of sterile filter paper with distilled water and pressed it to the inside of the crotch, holding it flat with a firm, gloved hand, while in the other she thawed a microtube full of frozen acid phosphatase reagent. She had a few minutes to kill while waiting for the filter paper to absorb any bodily fluids present, and used them to make mental notes: buy cat food and stop by the hospital to see Marissa on her way home. Then she flipped the filter paper over onto the clean brown paper that covered the table. She shook the tube of reagent—this motion had become so ingrained that she now shook everything before use, from lip gloss to milk, with sometimes disastrous consequences—and used a disposable pipette to drop the reagent onto the filter paper. The light brown liquid immediately turned to a deep purple as it reacted to the acid phosphatase found in semen. She excised a piece of the panties' crotch for Tony to analyze.

The killer had—thank God—not had time to leave any DNA on Marissa. Only the pattern on her neck could tie the two crimes together, and pattern comparison could be iffy. A mark in skin wasn't like a rigid tool mark left on a piece of metal. Evelyn had photographed it as best she could, snapping pictures of Marissa's skin as her fiancé held the ruler. By the time a trial rolled around, only the photographs would remain. Grace's flesh would have decomposed, and Marissa's neck would have healed.

And Marissa *would* heal, Evelyn told herself. Marissa was stronger than she was, smarter, better. Able to outfox Tony with a single word, to ease Evelyn's workday with just a grin. Evelyn needed her.

She broke down and called the hospital to find out if Marissa's condition had changed, only to be told that she remained intubated, under heavy sedation.

She hung up the phone and got back to work.

The two straps holding Grace Markham to her kitchen chair had been cut rather than untied, to preserve the knots—though they were simple square knots, the kind any schoolchild could tie. Evelyn pulled a few loose fibers out from the cut end and mounted them on a glass slide with a drop of Permount. The circular green tubes appeared too uniform to be natural fibers like cotton or linen. Under a polarizing microscope, they gave off the rainbow hues of nylon.

The fibers appeared dirty, with dark blobs clinging to their sides. A drop of xylene washed them off and quickly evaporated, leaving an irregular film on the glass slide. The microscope provided a close-up look but no more clues as to what it might be. Probably inorganic, since it did not appear to have cells.

With superfine tweezers and a stereomicroscope at its highest setting, she put a fresh fiber on the gold FTIR plate and mashed it around until some of the contaminant smeared off onto the gold. Then she made another trip to the tank of liquid nitrogen.

A voice interrupted her analyses. "I did it."

Tony stood in the doorway, holding a sheaf of paper with colored charts.

"What?"

"I ran the DNA from the Markham vaginal swabs."

Despite the fact that Marissa did the same thing every day without expecting a medal for it, Evelyn summoned up a congratulatory smile. Her boss seemed so damn pleased with himself, and perhaps with some positive reinforcement he'd consider similar tasks—tasks other than drinking coffee and berating his staff—in the future. "That's great. Really great."

"Don't you want to know what I found?"

"What did you find?"

He actually threw his arms out, as if appearing in the finale of a Hollywood musical. "She had semen in her!"

"Wow." Evelyn didn't know what else to say.

"Even one with a tail, so it was pretty fresh. And it's not her husband's."

She stopped smiling. She had figured as much after finding the acid phosphatase in the panties and the mysterious streaks on the skirt. Unlike most sex killers, he had taken the time to re-dress his victim—creating the death pose had been that important to him. "That poor woman. At least she was probably already unconscious or dead, or she'd have some sort of defense wounds or bruising."

"Unless he was her boyfriend," Tony pointed out. "It would explain how he got in."

"Or she had a boyfriend visit earlier, and the killer arrived afterward. But why wouldn't the boyfriend come forward now?"

"Because he'd be the obvious suspect. Or maybe he's married too."

"But I didn't find any unknown fingerprints. A boyfriend wouldn't be that careful."

"I sent the semen results to CODIS." Tony referred to the national Combined DNA Index System database of DNA profiles. "Maybe it will hit there. If it is the killer, that's kind of odd—to have a guy who's careful enough to use gloves but not a condom."

"A lot of them don't like condoms."

Tony gave her a skeptical glance. "You just don't want Grace Markham to have had a hand in her own destruction."

Evelyn tapped the computer keyboard in front of her, sending a beam of light through the contaminant from the fibers. "You scare me when you're insightful like that. I hate blaming the victim."

"Sometimes it's justified."

"A lot of the time it's justified. But this is a medical examiner's office—we're all about the victim. I can give Grace Markham the benefit of the doubt and assume she didn't invite this guy in. At least if we find him, we've got him. DNA tells all."

Tony swayed a bit, balancing on the balls of his feet. "Do you want to call your boyfriend and tell him, or should I?"

"No, you call him." She had to smile as he bustled off. Sharing a forensic find with law enforcement was one of the satisfactions of the job. Otherwise, all the facts and figures they established were written into a report, put in a file, and stored in a cabinet. A great deal of their work never helped, never made a difference, because it didn't find its corresponding unknown on the other side of the investigative equation. It just passed through and kept on going, into a vacuum.

As this DNA evidence might, if they never found the guy.

EVELYN MOVED through the self-opening doors at Metro General Hospital, promising herself she would stay only ten minutes. It would not help Marissa for Evelyn to sit and stare at her, and Evelyn had a daughter at home waiting for their traditional Tuesday taco night.

She entered the elevator, lost in thought, not noticing the other occupants until one with a small notebook and very high heels stepped closer.

"Hi!" the woman said brightly. "Clio Helms, *Plain Dealer*. Aren't you Evelyn James?"

"Um, yes."

Clio Helms had toasted-almond skin, dimples, and way more energy than Evelyn felt like coping with at the moment. "Are you here to visit Marissa?"

"Yes." And it's Ms. Gonzalez to you, honey.

"Was she attacked by the same man who killed Grace Markham?"

Evelyn forced her features to relax and spoke calmly. "All questions should be directed to the medical examiner, Elliott Stone. The office will be open in the morning."

"But you're investigating the case. How about an update?"

"The case is being investigated by Homicide Detectives Riley and Milaski. I'm sure the Cleveland PD spokesperson can assist you."

"Marissa Gonzalez's future mother-in-law isn't too crazy about the upcoming nuptials, is she?"

Evelyn looked at the woman now, with narrowed eyes. "I'm not sure what you're implying, but it sounds pretty absurd so far."

The reporter gave a ladylike snort. "Hey, my sister was knifed by one of her bridesmaids—nothing gets emotions going like a wedding."

Evelyn shook her head. "Sorry, but I can't see it. Is this four? Could you push four, please?"

"Don't police have a duty to let the tenants of the Riviere know that they are under attack?"

I think having cops there all day probably tipped them off, Evelyn thought. The doors parted, at last, letting in a puff of antiseptic air. "Excuse me."

The reporter stood between Evelyn and the hallway. "Do you have a suspect? Why does he attack rich women?"

"*Excuse* me."

"Come on, Evelyn, help out a fellow working woman here. It's tough being in print media. I'm up against the talking heads on Channel Fifteen."

Any shred of patience Evelyn had left evanesced like fog in sunlight. "You ain't my sister, honey, and I'm not the spokesperson for the Medical Examiner's Office. I'm a working mom who hasn't slept or seen her kid in two days, so how about helping *me* out?"

"Does the suspect work at the Riviere?"

Words, obviously, were useless. Evelyn pushed forward to sweep past Clio and her notebook into the fourth-floor hallway. She did not look back until she had reached Marissa's room. A phalanx of nurses had stopped Clio Helms at the border of Intensive Care.

Inside the room, Mama Gonzalez kept an exhausted watch over her child. The setting sun crept around the edges of the draperies, casting a rose tone onto Marissa's pallor; her chest moved up and down and the EKG monitor reported a steady heartbeat, but the patient's skin seemed to have sunk onto her bones until her cheekbones stood out, stark and cold.

Evelyn turned to the older woman. "I'm going to sit with her for a few minutes. Why don't you go home and get some dinner?"

"*Sí*, I was about to. The boys will be hungry." No matter that the boys, Marissa's brothers, were in their twenties. Mrs. Gonzalez pulled herself up by the metal pole of the monitor that recorded her daughter's pulse and blood pressure. A glowing green line showed the reassuring jagged activity of a heartbeat. "Have you found the man yet?"

She had no good way to put it. "No."

The portly mother regarded Evelyn for a moment, wrinkles etching deeper into her face by the minute. "Are you going to?"

"Yes," Evelyn lied. "I'm sure of it."

Another long moment. Then Mrs. Gonzalez turned and left without another word.

Evelyn took her friend's hand, watching her breathe, the crisp white sheet over her chest rising and falling, shallow but steady, wondering why, except for her mother and daughter, she noticed other human beings in her life only when they were about to leave her. "Don't think you're going to die on me. Who am I going to talk to, without you?" she said. After a moment, she added: "And I'll be one of your bridesmaids if you want me to."

The sheet continued to rise and fall.

"Seriously. I'll wear the poufy dress and everything." Evelyn's voice caught in her throat. "Just don't freakin' die on me."

Still no response, of course. Evelyn hooked a chair's leg with her foot, dragged it closer, and sat down without letting go of Marissa's hand.

Ten minutes, she told herself.

She woke after what felt like thirty seconds to the clear voice of a male: "X-ray coming through." But the voice and the machine rumbled right past Marissa's door and kept going, toward other voices discussing arterial blood and a second carotid line. A patient down the hall must have been in distress, the staff rushing to respond. Evelyn didn't move—best to stay out of their way.

It's cold in here. How do they expect people to get well inside a refrigerator? Her eyes opened, sighting along her left arm, now serving as a pillow. The room had grown dark—how long had it been?—and no one had turned on Marissa's light. Even the green glow of the monitors had died. Oddly, Marissa no longer seemed to be in her own bed.

But I'm still holding her fingers. In fact she's squeezing mine a bit, so she has to be here.

Her body is, but her face seems to have disappeared, replaced by one large hand.

And we're not alone.

Evelyn's head flew up, her subconscious cottoning on to current events long before her conscious mind. A man stood over Marissa, one hand covering the end of the breathing tube, the other balancing a pillow over the unconscious woman's head.

Evelyn shot to her feet, but instead of the attacker's face she saw only his approaching fist. The knuckles of an oversize hand caught her jaw before her brain could register the sight. The force knocked her onto her back, with her head caught against the wall at a painful angle. For a moment she saw only heavy black work boots thudding out of the room.

Evelyn pulled herself up on the bed rails and bent over Marissa. She did not seem to be breathing.

Evelyn didn't bother with the call button, assuming "Help!" at the top of her lungs might get more immediate action. Marissa's neck remained bandaged, so Evelyn laid her head on the patient's chest, listening for a heartbeat, which she could feel, and a breath, which she could not.

Evelyn was looking about frantically, about a hairsbreadth from total panic, when a rasping sound came from Marissa's breathing tube and a young, stolid nurse appeared at the foot of the bed.

"Help her!" Evelyn pointed, as if the nurse might not be sure who "her" referred to. "Someone just tried to smother her. Did you see him?"

"See who?"

Evelyn sprinted from the room. This guy had attacked Marissa once and gotten away. He wouldn't do so again.

The hallway stood deserted, stretching a hundred feet in either direction, but only ten paces away a door slowly closed. Evelyn thrust the metal door open, hitting the wall with a bone-jarring *clang*. The stairwell. She looked up, then down, saw no one, and stopped to listen for footsteps.

Nothing. Not even the sound of a door closing.

She moved, tripping down the steps so quickly that only one hand on the banister kept her from falling, and even that couldn't last. After two more landings, she slipped on the edge of the bottom step and knocked her left kneecap so hard she thought she'd dislocated it. With her footsteps temporarily quieted, she heard the smallest sound of movement, like the footstep of a cat or the brush of a shirtsleeve against a doorjamb. He had slipped through a door, away from the stairs.

Then she was up and moving again. On the second floor, she checked the hallway for her assailant, nearly flinging the stairwell door into a man in scrubs with a cart full of medications.

"Watch where you're going!"

"Sorry."

She flew down another flight, rails slapping against her right hip, and entered the lobby next to the emergency room. A nurse sat behind the counter, listening to a rail-thin and obviously inebriated woman talk about stomach pains. She looked only slightly more interested when Evelyn ran up, panting. "Did a man just run through here?"

"That's about the only thing that hasn't happened tonight. Nobody's been here but me and Miss Wilson for the past half hour."

"Yeah," confirmed Miss Wilson. "When'm I goin' to see a doctor?"

Evelyn returned to the stairwell. Another flight took her to the basement. She plunged through the final door and knocked her shins into the front fender of a cherry red BMW.

Both hands on the hood steadied her enough to look around. A parking garage. Considering the average sticker price represented here, a parking area for doctors.

You would have thought doctors would have demanded better lighting. Weak fluorescents hung over the main driving aisles, and the corners of the garage disappeared into shadows. It smelled like stale exhaust and leather upholstery. And it was silent. And she was unarmed.

She heard a noise from behind the door, the perfect spot for a predator to sit and wait—the slight swish of cloth on cloth, like a man's legs when he walked, or two arms skimming the body as they raised a strap overhead.

Too late, she began to turn, her hands instinctively coming up. He slipped the noose over her, dropping it around her neck, and tightened. She felt his body pressed up against her back, his breath in her hair. He smelled of oil and stale Doritos.

Her right hand and two of her left fingers were caught in the strap, and she used them to push it away from her neck. The mesh fabric bit into her palms. She wouldn't make it—her windpipe still sucked air, but eventually her arms would tire, and then her fingers would simply be crushed along with her throat.

A piece of advice came back to her. When throttled, she had read somewhere, breathe through your nose. You will always get enough air through your nose, no matter what happens to your throat. It hadn't made sense to her at the time, and it didn't now, and in any case she lacked the discipline to try it. Her mouth struggled to bring in air, no matter what her brain said. She needed to *breathe*! *Now!*

She kicked at his shins, to no effect. Her foot glanced off its target and hit the BMW's passenger door. The car's alarm began to peal, a deafening sound in the enclosed space.

She braced her elbows against his chest, using his own body as leverage to hold the strap away from her throat. A flash of light appeared to her right. Her brain had begun to shut down, to let unconsciousness seize the moment. Her view narrowed until she saw nothing but weakly shooting stars.

A
S IF FROM A DISTANCE, SHE HEARD A VOICE: "DAMN car alarms! Hey! What are you—"

The strap slid from her neck so quickly it burned her palm. She slumped to the ground, her face protected from the beeping car only by her still-raised arms. The attacker's footsteps receded into the distance.

Hands eased her onto her back, holding an eyelid open to receive a bright light. Fingers felt her neck for a pulse. She looked up at a handsome young man in a white coat. An angel, she decided.

"What the crap happened here?" the angel demanded, shouting over the pealing alarm. "Was he trying to strangle you? I've been telling them we need more security down here. Did he take your purse?"

"I can breathe."

"I see you're breathing. Open your mouth, let me see. Doesn't look too swollen. Did you get a look at the guy? I just saw a dark jacket."

She listened to him for another moment or two, because doing so meant she could keep her head in his lap, but then wondered if Marissa had come through her near-smothering. "I think I'm okay. I'm going to get up."

"Do you have any other injuries? Did he hit you? No, don't—" he added, as she reached for the door handle of the Lexus in the next space to pull herself up on. Its alarm joined the first's, a cacophony of chaos. "Aw, man! I hate those things."

She located the elevator, unwilling to take the stairs in her present condition. Her breathing remained unencumbered, but her heart raced at a stroke-risking speed. On top of that, her hip ached and her knee had begun to stiffen. She pushed the button for ICU and motioned for her rescuer to follow. The killer might have run out of the garage; he might have had a car there and driven out—impossible to hear an engine over the alarms; he might still be there. She was in no condition to give chase, and she didn't want this excitable but handy young man left alone with him. When the closed doors had muffled the car alarms, she told him, "Thanks for your help."

"Any time. I don't get to ride to the rescue too often. You'd better get some ice on that throat."

"The cops will be here soon," Evelyn said, hoping the ICU nurse had called them. "I'm sure they'll need to get your statement."

The eager flush faded from his cheeks. "Okay, but I don't have all night. I'm meeting some nurses at John Q's."

She found the ICU floor as quiet as she'd left it, the silence falling hard on her numbed ears. The stolid nurse emerged from Marissa's room just as she reached it, with the young doctor in tow.

"How is she?"

"Someone unplugged her monitor, and now it's giving me these." The nurse waved a printout under Evelyn's nose, then absently thrust it upon the doctor. "Her pulse spiked and O-two saturation dropped. What happened?"

Behind her, the clock on the wall read nearly six. Evelyn had slept for an hour. "Call the police."

"ONE HOUR. I try to leave for one hour, and what happens? Again, he almost kills my Mareesa." In the hallway outside her daughter's room, Mama Gonzalez stood in front of Evelyn with hands on hips, smelling of fried tortillas and fury. "And then he almost kills you. You, who are supposed to be so smart. What are you people *doing*?"

"I'm sorry, Mama Gonzalez."

"Don't be sorry. She's still alive because of you. But this is a bad man, and he's going to get you both if you don't be more careful! Running all over the city with who knows who and—" From there she broke into a tirade of Spanish, only a few words of which Evelyn could translate. *Family* and *reasonable* cropped up more than once.

David dropped to the bench beside her, his face chalky and lined.

Marissa's mother briefly focused on him. "You, another one. Why these girls have no sense in who they—" Her words trailed off into Spanish again as she returned to her daughter's side in the ICU room.

"You okay?" David's tone belied the simplicity of the question.

"Yeah."

"Six P.M. is meal break time for half of the nurses on the floor. The other half were down the hall losing a patient to cardiac arrest. I have to wonder if he watched for a while, waited until no one was at the desk to notice the alarm when he switched off the monitors. He may not have known that you'd be there, but either way he couldn't count on getting another opportunity. He must have decided to risk it."

Evelyn removed the ice bag from her throat and added it to the one on her left knee, holding them with one hand. "If I hadn't woken up, it would have been even better. Who would suspect murder when I was sitting next to her the whole time?"

"But you did wake up." He reached out an arm, and she leaned against his shoulder, feeling muscles like steel belts under her cheek. "Then he knocked you down and ran out?"

"Yes."

He picked up her right palm to examine the burn from the strap. "Why did you chase him?"

"Because I wanted to see who he was, where he went. What should I have done?"

"*Not* chased him." He pressed the injured palm to his lips, and the fear in his eyes prodded her with guilt. "Don't chase bad men, Evelyn. He could have killed you. He could so easily have killed you."

"I know." Only by the sheerest luck had she gotten her hands under the ligature; otherwise she would have stopped breathing by the time the doctor appeared. If he had lingered over a patient's chart a moment longer, chatted up a student nurse, stopped in the men's room, she would have died. "Believe me, I know."

"I don't know how I'd do without you, but I know it wouldn't be good."

Guiltily averting her eyes from his pain, she asked, "Why did he end up in the doctors' parking lot? Did he just follow the stairwell to the end, assuming I'd get out at the lobby? Did the parking attendant see him leave the garage?"

"The doctors all have magnetic cards to get in and out of the lot. No attendant, and the machine does not record activation times. But three nurses having a smoke around the corner did not see a car go by, and he probably would have been driving noticeably fast, his adrenaline pumping."

"Is there another way out of that garage?"

"There's a hallway that leads to some maintenance areas. He could have gotten to the sidewalk outside from those and turned away from the smoking kiosk, so that the nurses didn't see him. He could have waited there until you two left and then taken the stairs or the elevator to another floor. He didn't go through the lobby. Nobody there but a nurse and some drunk lady." He pinched the bridge of his nose. "If he knows when the nurses would be busy, he probably knows every inch of this hospital too. And Marissa's boyfriend is a doctor. I'm starting to feel a little suspicious about that."

"A doctor could provide a much more sophisticated murder

weapon than a rope or a pillow." With so many—their mothers, their coworkers, the media—expressing reservations about Marissa and Robert's marriage, she felt obligated to defend them. "This guy covered the breathing tube, but he also held a pillow over her face. Intubation cuts off any flow of air to the nasal cavity, so he didn't need the pillow—she couldn't breathe through her nose anyway."

"And a doctor would have known that. I'm not saying it's Robert, but it could be someone he knows, who also works here, an obsessed ex-girlfriend—"

"This was a man. That, I'm sure of."

"You didn't get a good look at him?"

"No," she said miserably. "The room was dark and no one had turned on the light—"

"Or he turned it off."

The hallway began to shift in front of her eyes. The killer had sneaked in and prepared to murder Marissa while Evelyn slumbered, vulnerable, only a foot or two away. . . .

"Come on." David gave her a little shake. "Don't zone out on me. It's over. Marissa's no worse for wear, the nurse said. Her vital signs are all decent, and brain activity has not changed."

"Yeah."

"And he won't get near you again." He squeezed her shoulders for emphasis. "You're not to go off investigating on your own this time. Right? Promise?"

"And Marissa?"

"Twenty-four-hour guard. I know, if we'd had one from the start, this wouldn't have happened. But officially, Marissa's attack is a random attempted rape. There was no reason to think, until now, that he had targeted her specifically. I certainly never thought he'd follow her here."

"Neither did I."

"So starting now, we function with extreme caution. Right?"

"If he planned to kill me, he could have. He could have . . . strangled me first, then moved on to Marissa. Even if I struggled a bit, she wouldn't have woken up."

"Maybe he didn't know that."

She considered this. "Then he took a hell of a chance, smothering a conscious adult with me sleeping right there. He wasn't clamping the pillow down hard, which suggests that he was trying to avoid leaving an impression of her teeth in her upper lip. Her death would look like a result of the unsolved strangling instead of a new attempt at murder."

"About how tall?"

"I don't have the slightest idea," she admitted. "I was peering up at him, so my perspective was skewed. I thought he was about your height, that's the best I can do. You know how crappy I am at estimating measurements."

"Hair?"

"It seemed close to the scalp. Medium brown, I guess, but the light wasn't good."

"What about his skin? Black? White?"

"White. I'm pretty sure, anyway." Her forehead slumped into her palm.

David's arm tightened around her. "Don't feel bad. Now you know why eyewitness testimony is one of the most unreliable forms of evidence. It's hard to take in every detail in two or three seconds' time."

"Boots."

"What?"

"He wore heavy work boots. Black, I think, though everything about his clothing looked black against the light from the hallway, like a silhouette."

David made a note, though she knew a great many men in the area wore boots, and it didn't have to be for work purposes. The constant examination of victims' clothing kept her up on fashion trends. Most of the victims she saw wore Nike athletic shoes, but Timberland boots ran a close second.

"We searched floor to floor, but we didn't find anyone who didn't have a good reason for being here. That doesn't mean much, since he had plenty of time to leave before we got here. Security got right on the ball, but this building has a million exits. And maybe he's someone who *does* have a good reason for being here."

David tucked his notebook into a jacket pocket, then paused, hands clasped between his knees. "This guy saw you, Evelyn, and you saw him. He's brutally murdered one woman and seems determined to murder another. I'm not trying to push you, but maybe I should stay at your house. Just temporarily."

"I live thirty miles away from the crime scenes."

"It would give Angel a chance to get used to me being there before the arrangement becomes permanent."

As he obviously expected it would. Her voice sounded more harsh than her injured throat could justify. "I'll think about it. He didn't want to kill me, David. He tried to smother Marissa without even waking me up. He socked me just to get me out of the way— he didn't try to strangle me until I followed him. I promise, I'll lock all my doors and windows and stay aware of my surroundings."

"A locked door didn't keep him from Grace Markham."

David was right, which didn't make her feel any better. But she wouldn't be pushed to a decision, not even by some homicidal stranger. "I know."

"And he's twice attacked Marissa in public places."

Evelyn raised herself, favoring the swelling knee. "Why *is* he so damn determined to kill her?"

"Maybe she can tell us, if she wakes up."

If.

HOLDING A BAG OF ICE TO HER THROAT, EVELYN sized up the boy now standing in her kitchen. Black hair, gelled into discrete spikes. A stud in one nostril. Baggy jeans. Scuffed athletic shoes, which should have been discarded months ago. Slouching shoulders above an oversize T-shirt that advertised ACDelco spark plugs. Evelyn appreciated the T-shirt, the most normal item in his ensemble.

"This is Steve." Angel squeezed his arm, smiling into his face with entirely too much zeal. Where had her daughter—the sarcastic, feminist, unyielding girl who disputed everyone's ideas from what to have for dinner to the president's foreign policy, who thought dating overrated and boys hopelessly backward—gone, and who was this fawning creature who had been left in her place?

"Hi," Steve said. The boy made eye contact with Evelyn, indicating either honesty or cleverness. It did give her the opportunity to see that the whites of his eyes were fairly clear and the pupils did not jump. He seemed to be drug-free at the moment. That was something, at least.

"What's wrong with your neck?" Angel asked.

"Long story. Where have you been?"

Her daughter's eyes slid to the clock, which read 10:15. She was supposed to be in by 9:30 on school nights. "At the library, working on our project."

"The library closes at nine."

"We went to get ice cream."

"Dairy Queen also closes at nine."

"We went to Cold Stone."

"You hate Cold Stone."

"But it doesn't close at nine." Her daughter's voice was a few degrees cooler than the ice cream. "What's the difference? You weren't home anyway. We saw you pull in just before we did."

Evelyn's stomach fluttered, in either anger or fear—anger at her daughter for pretending that not coming straight home from work equaled neglect, and fear that she might be right. Evelyn didn't have the energy to deal with either emotion.

Steve looked uncomfortable, which made Evelyn like him just a little. She tried to make her damaged throat relax. "Okay. What's your project about?"

"Mrs. Evans is really into this Roman Empire stuff. We have to make a scale model of the Colosseum, like we're in fourth grade. She wondered why you weren't at Meet the Teachers today," Angel added coolly. "You usually have so many questions for them."

Steve said that he had to go and gave Evelyn a halfhearted wave before opening the door to the garage. "Good night, Gellie." He pronounced it with a soft *G*, as in Jell-O.

He has his own name *for her?*

Angel, so starved for her mother's attention, promptly went upstairs for her nightly half-hour toilette. Evelyn replaced the ice bag on her throat.

When it came to boys, Evelyn had had it easy for too many years. Angel had raven hair and a strong frame, but her male classmates had never seemed to notice her for any length of time, and Angel had never seemed to care.

Then this Steve had come along, and suddenly the phone rang every night, and Fridays and Saturdays found Angel anywhere but home. And this was normal. Angel was seventeen and lively. Her first serious boyfriend was not a life experience to avoid.

But that didn't mean Evelyn had to be enthusiastic about it. Not when she saw the results of disastrous relationships arrayed on gurneys every morning.

It also made her wonder how Angel would react if Evelyn suddenly moved David into their household.

She threw the ice into the sink and turned off the lights.

A BUZZING NOISE woke her to the night-filled room. It couldn't be time to get up already. She could swear she had been lying there for only an hour.

The buzzing, apparently, came from the phone. No, no, *no*!

She read the clock through bleary eyes. One-thirty, so she had been lying there for *two* hours. She should have felt positively rejuvenated. "Hello?"

"Evelyn? We have another one."

Who was this, and what were they talking about? "Another what?"

"Another body," David's voice told her.

She sat upright. "What? Who? Is Marissa all right? Where?"

"It's not Marissa. It's not even in Marissa's building. We're in Lakewood."

"Lakewood?" That was across the river and a generation or two of old money away from the Riviere.

"You'd better come out. I'll give you directions."

She let her forehead rest for a moment on pulled-up knees. I can't do this, she thought. Not even with all the caffeine in the world. I'm not twenty friggin' years old anymore.

"Let me get a pen," she said.

· · ·

LAKEWOOD'S GOLD COAST had consisted of luxury high-rises when the Flats were still an industrial wasteland. Evelyn had been inside one of them exactly once, when a prom date took her to Pier W for dinner. All she could remember of the place were the cloth napkins and how each stall in the ladies' room had its own tampon dispenser.

Riley greeted her, his face glowing red and blue as the lights on the nearby patrol car turned. "Your throat okay? How are you feeling?"

"Like Ford has been using me for a crash-test dummy. If Tony doesn't hire more staff soon, I'm going to mutiny."

"Want a hand with that equipment?"

She shifted her camera bag and fingerprint kit to her left hand. "No, I got it."

"David's inside with the Lakewood detective, Womack. He's the lead on this. They called us because they knew about Grace and figured it's got to be the same guy. Then I think he called Channel Fifteen, because they got here before I did."

"Why does he think it's the same guy? Who's dead?"

"You awake?" He cocked his head at her.

"I'm walking and talking. I can't guarantee that's the same thing."

"Your shirt's on inside out."

"Who's dead?"

"A woman named Frances Duarte. Forty-five, single. Same MO—strangled, strapped . . . You okay? You look faint."

"No." She steadied herself against a stone pillar to the right of the double doors, the pebbled surface rough against her palm. "Not faint, just surprised. Marissa had a newspaper article about a Frances Duarte in her purse when the guy tried to kill her."

She would not have thought it possible to surprise the jaded detective, but this did. "No shit!"

"Nope."

He lit a cigarette and puffed before he spoke again. "You think it really is some crazed gangbanger ex-boyfriend of Marissa's?"

"Who said that?"

"One of our traffic investigators, who got it from one of your body snatchers, who said he got it from one of the pathologists."

"Why would an ex-boyfriend of Marissa's kill Grace and now this other woman?"

"You want logic from a rumor? What the hell does it mean, then?"

"That these attacks aren't random. There's a thread between this new victim and Marissa. Only location seems to link Marissa and Grace, but we can't be sure of that until we can ask Marissa. Is there a connection between Frances Duarte and Grace Markham?"

"Just the MO. Strapped to a chair, no sign of forced entry." He stubbed out his cigarette in a large, sand-filled pot and guided her through the lobby, all marble and mirrors. "She lived alone, with tons of bucks and a cat."

"Is this building owned by Erie Realty?"

"Is it what? Oh, I see— No, Baylor Group. I asked the staff— the desk clerk and the superintendent—and they've never heard of the Riviere."

"Who found the body?"

"The super. Or building manager, as the plaque on his office door says. He lives here, gets the apartment for free for running the building. He says the people downstairs have been complaining about a smell coming from Frances's place."

"I see." The elevator opened.

"No, you'll smell. She's probably been like this at least a week. I hope you have a mask in that kit, and not one of those little paper ones." He pushed the button for the seventh floor. "The manager thought Frances had gone out of town, he says, but he always watches *America's Most Wanted* before bed, and suddenly the idea of a bad smell started to worry him. So he checked."

"He's got a key to her apartment?"

"He's got a passkey to every apartment. Unlike the other place, this building is about old money, not high security. Tenants have regular old keys, the elevator stops at every floor, and people use the fire escape as a patio. But the rent's probably higher. Go figure."

The doors opened to spill them into a richly carpeted hallway. Two uniformed Lakewood officers and a man in plainclothes exchanged a joke, cutting it off when they saw her. Perhaps they took her for a grieving family member. She must have looked even worse than she felt.

"I'm Evelyn James," she announced to the group. "Medical Examiner's Office." She ran a hand through her hair, wishing she'd taken a few minutes to put on some makeup.

One of the uniformed guys wrote her name on a clipboard. The officer in plainclothes, a wiry type with thin, graying hair cut short, extended his arm.

"I'm Ian Womack, Lakewood Homicide. Thanks for coming out."

I don't have a choice, she always wanted to say when officers thanked her. This is what they pay me for. This time, however, she didn't feel that way. "Thanks for picking up on the MO. This same guy attacked a friend of mine, and I really want to get him."

"That's what Riley said." He walked with her to the doorway of Frances Duarte's apartment, then paused to let her get an overview. And adjust to the smell.

Unlike the clean white lines of the Markham apartment, Frances's home seemed to be composed entirely of wood. Hardwood floors, walnut furniture, two walls of built-in shelves, all polished to a soft gleam. Oriental rugs and velvety upholstery blended together with the heavy draperies and the massive ironwork fireplace. Then Evelyn's eye went to the souvenirs, the statues, African masks, displayed jewelry, and ancient books that Frances Duarte must have spent a lifetime traveling the world to collect.

But the most arresting item in the room was now Frances

Duarte's body, tied to a deeply cushioned armchair as if she'd been watching the lifeless TV set.

"I can't help but wish he'd stayed in Cleveland," Womack told her, though he didn't sound too regretful. His eyes sparkled with points of adrenaline, and he seemed ridiculously awake for the middle of the night. The beginning of an investigation, she thought. He's jazzed.

I, on the other hand, want to curl up and die. Who the hell is this maniac? And how are we going to catch him?

David emerged from the kitchen. "I hope you have a mask. Your throat hurt?"

"Hardly at all. My knee is worse. How are you doing?"

"All the windows, including the one over the fire escape, are locked from the inside. There's no sign of damage to the door—"

"No. I meant how are *you* doing? You look worse than I feel."

A dimple appeared but didn't stay. "I'm trying to convince my-self that sleep is overrated."

"Any success?"

"No."

Womack went on. "We've got her friend coming over—a guy she listed as next of kin on her lease. Apparently she doesn't have any fam-ily, but they've been friends forever, he says. I don't know what that means, maybe a boyfriend, maybe not. He's the only other one with a key, and it's still in his possession. Obviously we'll take a real good look at him, even though he says he's never heard of Grace Markham."

David stirred. "You asked him that?"

"Yeah."

"Wouldn't it be better to do that in person? When you can ob-serve his reaction? Maybe it could give us a clue." His voice grew more strident with every word.

"So we'll ask him again." Womack's thin chest seemed to expand.

"I'm going to get started," Evelyn said, not to interrupt the growing conflict but because she didn't care about the growing con-flict. David would have to sort out the investigative approach; she had work to do. She left them in the doorway and moved into the apartment.

With another glance at what had been Frances Duarte, she pulled out her secret weapon—a pair of swimmer's noseclips. They kept her nostrils closed to the heavy scent of decomposing flesh; over her now-open mouth she stretched a paper mask. Latex gloves covered her sore hands. Then she switched on the heavy Olympus and began to photograph the scene before the investigators moved in and began to examine things. None of them would touch the body, so it could wait.

The apartment spanned half the floor, with six bedrooms, three baths, and a formal living room in addition to the more casual space Frances now rested in. The temperature in each area hovered around seventy-one degrees. Her vast collection of items seemed undisturbed. Evelyn observed the area through the camera lens, her mind overflowing with questions. The apartment, though cluttered, seemed as clean as Grace's. No signs of another person's presence—one used cup in the sink, one toothbrush next to the medicine cabinet, no clothing that wouldn't belong to a forty-five-year-old woman. An automatic food and water dispenser and a self-cleaning litter box in one of the bathrooms took care of the cat. In her roomy office, old newspapers lay neatly in a recycling bin, and her mail had been sorted at a rolltop desk.

"Didn't her mail accumulate at the door?" she asked David.

"In her box downstairs, but she had mentioned going up to the lake, so the manager didn't think anything of it."

She turned to the shelves. "Who dusts all this?"

"She does. Did." He poked at a carved, stylized elephant. "She didn't go for the highfalutin lifestyle, according to the building manager. She didn't have a maid or a cook. She drove a low-end Cadillac. To judge from her clothes, she shopped at JCPenney. His words."

"Where's Womack?"

"Downstairs with Riley, waiting for this friend to show up,

probably bouncing up and down with excitement. I couldn't deal with him anymore. We'd end up with two strangled bodies in this place."

"Hey, we might be excited too if we weren't about to die from lack of sleep."

"We would have had the sense not to let our entire unit troop through the place so they could get a good look." He ran a palm over his face. "You might as well not bother vacuuming. I'm not sure we'll ever know how many people have been in or out of here to-night."

"I notice the carpet is dirtier from the door to the chair. Did we do that, or is it just a high-traffic area?" She lowered herself to one knee, the injured one protesting with stiff creaks, and clipped carpet fibers into a manila envelope.

"Don't know. Why did our guy move to Lakewood from the Flats?"

Evelyn turned to the corpse. Decomposed bodies were the ab-solute worst. To get through them, she had to focus on what needed to be done, and then work quickly and efficiently until she could turn away and strip off the gloves and mask and breathe normally again. No room remained for revulsion, or sympathy.

The woman's body had turned completely black, the skin of the shoulders and waist bulging past the mesh fabric straps. The skin had peeled off in places, and the fingertips had begun to shrink. Fat cells had broken down, oozing a lemon yellow oil. The clothes—what had been a sky blue knit shirt and navy polyester slacks—were soaked by decomposition fluid to a uniform bluish black. Her head hung forward, its blond curls now lank and matted. "I'd guess she's been dead about a week, so she beats Grace by four or five days. The question becomes why did he move to the Flats from Lakewood, not vice versa. When was the last time anyone saw her?"

"The desk clerk said last Thursday, six days ago. But she often took the staircase down to the parking lot, so he didn't think that too odd. I don't know what the friend's going to say. I guess Womack was too eager to tell him about Grace Markham to ask that."

Evelyn moved in closer, photographing the woman's body in sections—knees to shoes, thighs and hips. "It's the sixty-four-thousand-dollar question, isn't it? What ties Grace Markham to Frances Duarte?"

"They're both rich. That's all I've got."

"Odd that there aren't any maggots. This place doesn't look it, but it must be as clean and well-sealed as Grace's. Did the killer rob the place?"

David stood beside her as she photographed, pale, as if the camera flash had washed him out. "Not that we can tell. Her jewelry box seems undisturbed, and there's no wall safe. We haven't looked in that purse next to her yet. We found her closet door open. The rest of the place is neat and buttoned down, but a lot of people get lazy about closet doors. Do you always shut yours?"

She clicked the shutter at a large diamond ring on Frances Duarte's right hand. "Always."

"You're kind of strict about that sort of thing, aren't you? I guess I'll have to shape up if we're ever going to cohabit."

She took another picture.

"*Are* we ever going to cohabit?" He dropped to a crouch, lowering his voice to keep it from carrying into the hallway, where the two patrol officers kept moving farther away from the smell. The Lakewood crime scene officer had disappeared into the bedroom. "Look, I know whispering across a decaying woman's shins is not the right place to have this conversation, but it's late and I'm really tired and it seems like we've been debating this for two months. Do you want me to move in with you, or not?"

Suddenly she was very, very awake. So awake that her blood pounded through her veins like a flash flood, making her head ache and stars appear in front of her eyes. "David, I love you. I'm crazy about you. But I have a daughter and a mother and a household. It just isn't that simple for me."

"And you think, what, they don't know we're sleeping together?"

"Knowing and living with are two different things. My mother's very old-fashioned. Little things like marriage are important to her." Her voice sounded nasally harsh, perhaps from the noseclips. "But it's Angel, really. I don't want her thinking that because something is okay for a mature divorceé, it's okay for her."

"You think she's still a—"

"Don't," she ordered, and for a moment her voice didn't sound weary at all. "Don't even go there. What I think is that I'm the mom. If I have to give up something I want because I think it's best for my daughter, I'll do it."

"Give up me?"

"No. That's not what I mean— I don't even know what the hell I mean. I just need more time to think about it, and I can barely remember my own name at the moment. It's different for you. It's just a matter of packing your suitcase and your dog and hopping in the car."

"So you're assuming the bigger risk, is that it?"

She examined that while taking a picture of Frances's purse, a small clutch bag resting under her right hand. "Yes, that's it. I *am* assuming the larger risk."

"And it's not a risk to give up my space and let the whole world know how I feel about you when you could up and change your mind one day and toss me into the middle of the street?"

She would not back down. "The worst thing that could happen to you would be a little humiliation. The worst thing that could happen to me is seeing my daughter drop out of school to have a baby because she was trying to keep up with Mom. It's *not* the same thing. I don't care if I'm being overprotective and reactionary. Guess what, I'm a parent. I'm allowed to be."

"Angel is a convenient reason, Evelyn, but I'm not buying it. You have your house to yourself now and you don't want to share it, that's all. I'm good enough to sleep with, but after that I should be careful not to let the door hit me in the ass on the way out."

"That's not true." Or was it? Had she gotten so good at keeping her feelings at arm's length that she automatically kept the rest of the world there too? "I am not saying no to you, David, I am not. I am saying, for the moment, that you're right—over some decaying woman's shins is not the place for this conversation. You're just going to have to wait."

Then he spoke as if he were biting his lip at the same time. "All right. I'll wait."

"Thank you." The harshness in her voice had nothing to do with the noseclips.

"But not forever."

"I wouldn't expect you to."

He stood up without another word and left the apartment. She straightened. The Lakewood crime scene officer stood next to the kitchen table, Asian-shaped eyes large over his mask. "Um . . . find anything interesting?" he asked.

Only that I'm old and tired and suddenly want to kill everyone in the entire world. Especially the guy who did this.

THE ARMCHAIR IN WHICH SHE RESTED HAD ABSORBED most of the fluid oozing from Frances Duarte's body, so that the floor around her remained clean. Evelyn and the Lakewood tech, Bobby Ito, sat on their legs like students at a teacher's feet.

Evelyn slid the purse from under Frances Duarte's hand, and they skimmed its contents—money, credit cards, a pocket calendar, coupons, et cetera. It seemed as tightly packed as the apartment.

The straps around the corpse had been tied with firm square knots, which Evelyn left in place. Once the straps came off, the body would collapse. She tilted the head back. Swelling from the fluids gave Frances Duarte's face a badly beaten appearance, but in fact, no injuries appeared. Evelyn found no lacerations or large bruising on the head at all.

The indentation around the neck had bloated and shifted like the rest of her epidermis, but in two drier patches toward the back of the neck—the fluids under the skin had answered the call of gravity and moved forward—the mesh fabric pattern appeared.

The victim wore a bra and panties underneath her clothing. Swollen feet strained against tightly laced Rockport walking shoes.

"Kind of strange. There's no sign of a struggle." Evelyn glanced toward the door. "She has a peephole, a chain, and a dead bolt that would still be here after a nuclear attack. The guy didn't break in. He had a key, or she let him in, or maybe he attacked her at the door and dragged her in."

Ito nodded. "All this stuff she had, but nothing's knocked over. It's almost like she was sitting here watching TV and he came up behind her."

"It takes a while to strangle somebody. She would have struggled."

"There's nothing to hit here if she kicked out with her feet. We can ask the neighbors if they heard any thuds or stomping."

"That would mean he got into the apartment earlier, and waited for her." She felt a chill, not from the cool air or the late hour. She pictured Frances Duarte sitting at leisure in her own cozy home, surrounded by things she loved, items that represented a life of interests and energy. The last place in the world she should feel afraid. Then a sound behind her, a scrape of a shoe, and something around her neck, closing off her breath. Did she see him, turn at the last moment? Look into her killer's eyes?

Did she ask *why*? Why her?

Evelyn moved into the kitchen, gazed back at the TV to see her own reflection appearing as a silhouette against the overhead light. But the light might have been out, and depending on what had been on the TV at the time, a dark scene or a bright one, Frances might not have seen a reflection. She could have been dozing in her chair as he approached but would have woken up pretty damn fast once she felt that strap around her neck.

She might not have been watching TV—and why turn it off if she had? In Evelyn's experience, criminals didn't usually tidy up a scene afterward, locking doors or turning out lights. But this guy was not usual. In such close spaces, surely something had been moved in the few minutes Frances would have had to fight for her life. By now a week's coating of dust had covered the tracks of any item that had been moved so that no clue would remain to tell them where the killer had first encountered his victim. Without that information, she could not guess how he got inside.

"Are you going to scrape under her nails?" the tech asked.

"Yeah. I don't have much confidence, since she probably scratched her own neck trying to get air, and her nails are soaked with her own juices, but maybe we'll get lucky."

"Let's hope so."

They cut the straps and released the body, and called in the ambulance crew to load her onto a gurney. The back of the body and the armchair were consistently soaked with decomp fluid. Evelyn taped the chair, though the damp surface tended to cling to its fibers rather than yield them to the adhesive.

"I'm going to start printing," Ito told her. Officially, it was his scene, and she remained there only by invitation.

"Need any help?"

"Sure." He sighed. "Look at this place—no clue where the guy was or what he did while he was here. We're going to have to do every inch unless the cops come up with some ideas. And if it turns out to be someone she knew, any prints we find aren't going to mean a thing anyway."

"Why don't we stick to this room, the kitchen, and the master bedroom suite?" she suggested. "There's no reason to think he touched the rest of the place—unless he's brilliant at covering his tracks, he didn't seem to have any goal here other than to kill Frances Duarte. I'm going to walk through again anyway, take another look."

"Have a ball."

Three of the six bedrooms were used for storage, stack after stack of cardboard boxes, all labeled and arranged alphabetically. The remaining two were guest rooms, neither of which appeared to have hosted a recent visitor. Frances had stocked the guest bath with soap and shampoo, but no personal items rested there, no water rings or rumpled towels.

Frances's office consisted of a full wall of filing cabinets and an elaborate cherry computer desk arrangement, of which Evelyn felt particularly envious. She pulled on gloves and slid into the leather desk chair, bumping her sore knee, to thumb through the desk calendar and the in-box. The room seemed undisturbed, utterly normal except for that preternatural stillness that affects crime scenes, as if the inanimate objects knew their owner would not return.

A fat tabby sprawled on a futon. It fastened one eye on Evelyn, calculated her threat level as minimal, and went back to sleep. Evelyn wondered if it had come into contact with the corpse, but its paws seemed clean. A photo of the same tabby with a woman sat on the desk. This, Evelyn assumed, was Frances Duarte. She held herself with a classic elegance; she might not have had Grace Markham's glamour or size 4 clothes, but her skin had remained smooth into her forties, and the dark blond hair fell to her shoulders in thick waves.

The pinching caused by the noseclips finally got to be too much, and Evelyn pulled them off. Away from the family room, the odor permeated but did not overpower.

"That friend of hers, Aimes, hasn't seen her since last Thursday, March twenty-seventh." David stepped into the room, rubbing one eye. Either he had decided to shelve their conflict until they finished the crime scene or he was too tired to think about it. "That's nearly a week. He said she mentioned her cabin on Johnson's Island, so when she didn't answer her phone, he assumed she'd gone to the lake for a few days."

"In April?"

"He says she didn't mind the chill. The cabin doesn't have a phone—probably the main attraction, if she's got this guy dialing her up all the time. He left four of the ten messages on her machine."

"A boyfriend?"

"I don't think so. I get the feeling he worked on that for a lot of years, then finally gave up and settled for 'friend.' I think he's one of those, like how Markham described Joey—a hanger-on. He liked being around Frances, rich and too nice to tell him to get lost. Or she was lonely, who the hell knows? She's got one sister, never married, no kids."

"There's a box of toys in the closet there."

"She has two small great-nieces in Tucson. They visit once in a while. No kids of her own."

Evelyn turned the desk calendar so he could see it. "She had plenty of appointments. Things to do, places to go at least every other day. She missed a dentist appointment and—look, here. 'Butterfly Com Bd,' eight o'clock yesterday. Butterfly Babies and Children's."

"That clipping that Marissa had in her purse."

"Exactly. Frances Duarte made a large donation to help open a wing. How that would be related to her death, I can't begin to guess."

"It involves money, and that's always a good start. Apparently Frances gives out plenty of it—the *Cod* submarine museum, Case Western Reserve, the Rock and Roll Hall. Her parents left her an estate simply bulging with cash and a case of noblesse oblige."

"Grace did a lot of charity and community work."

"True. But they all do, in this set—it seems to come with being rich. According to the friend, Aimes. Beldon Aimes."

"Sounds pretty old-money himself."

"Yeah, well, his driver's license says Buford, so I'm taking Beldon with a grain of salt."

"He called four times but never came over here?"

David shrugged. "He figured she was out of town."

"No enemies? No disputes?"

"A few."

She dropped a bundle of letters, apparently from a pen pal in Africa. "You're kidding. *This* woman had enemies?"

"Believe it or don't. Apparently Frances, though sweet and loving and terribly generous, et cetera et cetera, had no qualms about speaking her mind, and she watched Daddy's money—that's what she called it, Daddy's, never hers—as closely as he would have wanted her to. Her estate makes a substantial donation to the art museum every year but always finds out what they want to do with it first. This year one of the directors is pushing for a small auditorium for performance art."

"Frances doesn't care for performance art?"

"She loathes it. Described it—to the director's face—as charades by people who desperately want to be artists but have no talent whatsoever. She planned to withhold her contribution. She and the director had a fight about it last week."

"A fight meaning—"

"A verbal argument. Right in the lobby of the BP building, no less, next to the piano player."

"So Frances wasn't the pushover Grace seemed to be."

"Even Beldon/Buford thinks she went a little overboard with that one."

"What about Butterfly?"

"Never mentioned it, according to him. He's not surprised she made the donation, though."

Evelyn mused over that for a moment. "I meant to ask Marissa's fiancé about Butterfly Babies, but I didn't see him at the hospital. Butterfly is a stone's throw from the ME's back door—"

"Evelyn. Don't even think about investigating on your own, not this case. I'll check it out, I promise."

She smiled but committed to nothing. "Did the neighbors hear anything?"

"We'll check the floors above and below tomorrow morning. She had this floor to herself."

"This place isn't *that* big."

"Her place spans half the floor. The other half, across the hall, is divided into two suites. One has been empty since the owner died four months ago, and the couple in the other have been in Europe for six weeks."

"How'd the owner die?"

"In a hospital, from a laundry list of illnesses. The kids are squabbling over the apartment, that's why it's still empty. Find anything in here?"

"No threatening letters. I can't find a PDA, a Rolodex, or even an old-fashioned address book. It might be on the computer, and I'll leave that for the experts."

"Unless the killer took the address book with him, though why he'd want that—"

Her heart gave a peculiar skip. "To get Grace's address. I doubt she's in the white pages."

"We don't know that these two women even knew each other," David pointed out, but his young wrinkles flexed with worry. "Still, I'd like to know who else might be listed."

She stood up, straightening her stiff knee. "Me too. I'm going to start with the processing—I've put it off long enough. I hope he didn't wear gloves."

They returned to the family room. The body had taken some of the more pungent odors with it but not all. Evelyn retrieved her fingerprint kit and put on a fresh cloth mask.

"I'll take the kitchen," she told Bobby Ito.

"Help yourself."

Kitchens were not areas conducive to fingerprints. The highly refined carbon stuck to the water and oils left by the ridges of human skin to develop a latent print, but it also stuck to any other source of oil or water, and cooking areas tended to retain both. Greasy vapors coated ranges and walls, refrigerators gave off too much moisture. But it seemed that Frances used her kitchen only as a convenient place to keep the phone and her very healthy collection of wine. The refrigerator held condiments, some wilting fruit, and little else. A layer of dust topped the cans in the cupboard. Take-out menus cluttered the bulletin board under a child's drawing—probably done by one of her great-nieces. The stick figures had been sketched with the same fluorescent pink and green as the drawing in Grace's kitchen, but with some matte primary shades as well. Evelyn wondered if Grace ever had children around, perhaps used her friends' kids as practice for her own future clan. She also wondered if Frances ate any ethnic cuisine except Chinese—she must have had a menu from every Chinese restaurant on the West Side.

"David."

He swayed slightly, as if he'd fallen asleep on his feet. "Yeah?"

"The Markhams ate out a lot. I wonder if they ordered in a lot too."

He followed her gaze to the menus. "We can get phone records for both places, that should lead us to the most recent deliveries. But at this building someone without a key has to come through the lobby—they can't get in through the parking lot door. I'll get with the clerk."

"All he'd have to do is wait until a tenant opened the outside door, then grab it before it closed. Or if he had his hands full, they might have held it for him."

"Riley and I can ask when we interview the tenants tomorrow. Later today, I mean. It wouldn't explain Grace, though. A delivery person couldn't have gotten to her penthouse unless she came down and got him, and the doorman would have had to call up to her. Besides, there were no delivery people on the video."

She brushed black powder over the range, producing a few smudges along the edge. "Anyone with a package?"

"I think so. One or two, maybe. But Grace didn't give the code to her personal friends, so she certainly wouldn't have handed it out to a kid with pizza."

Evelyn sneezed black powder into her sleeve. "What did Beldon say about Frances? Would she have opened her door to someone she didn't know?"

"He said she's a friendly person and not particularly security-conscious. She would forget to lock her car half the time because she didn't think it important."

"So she might have opened up to any stranger with a good excuse. The door was locked when the manager found her?"

"Just the knob, so the killer only had to turn the latch and pull it shut when he left."

Evelyn gazed again at the chair, now missing its occupant. "I can't help feeling that she had been sitting in that chair while he came up behind her, as if he had waited inside the apartment for her. Did anyone see her after Thursday morning?"

"The doorman says no. She came back after lunch—apparently the one she had with friend Buford—and no one recalls seeing her after that."

"He could have been waiting for her then."

"If he had a key. Or if he's a hell of a locksmith and could pick both the knob and the dead bolt without leaving a single scratch on either."

Evelyn rubbed her face with a forearm, avoiding the dirty gloves.

"Now you have a black streak on your forehead, you know."

"I'll have more before I'm through. Grace Markham, Marissa, and Frances Duarte have to have a point of convergence. The circles have to intersect at some point."

"I know," he said and yawned. "But if I don't get some sleep, I'm not going to be able to find a point on a pencil."

VELYN DID NOT BOTHER GOING HOME. THE ONE, PER-
haps two hours of sleep she might have been able to grab—if
she could have gotten her mind to shut off that long—
wouldn't have helped. Angel could get her own breakfast. She was,
as David often felt the need to point out, seventeen years old.

So Evelyn chugged a Diet Coke and arrived at the lab a few
minutes before Tony, then presented him with the new set of DNA
samples.

He swore.

For once, she felt a touch of sympathy for her boss. "I know
what you mean."

"How much longer is Marissa going to be on her back?"

The sympathy evaporated. "She's unconscious, Tony."

"Tell her nobody likes a crybaby. You think her future mother-
in-law had her whacked?" he went on. "Or it was her ex-boyfriend's
gang buddies?"

"Where are these rumors coming from?"

"Nowhere," he said. "And everywhere. But more important,
there's a pile of messages on your desk, OSHA needs to get with you
about the salt mine, and viewing starts in two minutes. You'd better
get down there."

"Isn't viewing the supervisor's—"

"I'll make coffee."

"Okay."

The pathologists—the doctors who performed autopsies—and the heads of Trace and Toxicology met each morning to "view" the deceased parties who had arrived since the previous day. Each victim was seen and his or her history read aloud by the deskman on duty, so that the doctors could decide which postmortems they wanted to volunteer for, or if a complete postmortem needed to be done at all. The lab staff, for their part, could see what they could add to their task lists for the day. The scene always felt surreal, especially under the too-bright fluorescent lights, especially so early in the day, especially when one had gone without sleep.

Evelyn would have to test the hands of the suicide-by-gunshot victim for primer residue before the autopsy could be performed. For a homicide victim, beaten to death by her now-confessed spouse, she would have to call the hospital and get the sample of blood that (they hoped) had been collected before the victim had been transfused, before her blood had been mixed with someone else's DNA, so that a comparison with blood found on the suspect's shirt would be accurate. Evelyn would also have to tape the clothing, photograph and store it, scrape the woman's fingernails, and examine her hands. In the case of an accidental fall from a scaffold, she wasn't sure what she'd have to do—probably nothing except write a brief description of the clothing and have it photographed. And all this work would feel very real indeed.

She turned to one of the toxicologists, Ed Durant, his face moist and pasty. "Did you draw the short straw this morning?"

"No. Our peerless leader can't get his butt out of bed in time, so it falls to me to do his job for him. Not exactly a first. I'm always at my station long before anyone else in the department punches the time clock."

Evelyn suspected that Ed arrived to work early because, like

Tony, he had no real life outside the brick walls of the ME's office, but to say so wouldn't be prudent. She needed him. "I have this case—"

"No," he said, either to stop her from asking the inevitable favor or because the two letters made up his favorite word.

"You heard the same guy has now killed two women and nearly killed Marissa in the past week?"

He said nothing, but his scowl ebbed a bit. Even Ed had a touch of empathy somewhere beneath the ponytail and the extra hundred pounds. "I heard this guy likes dark-haired women who drive Volvos."

"Marissa doesn't drive a Volvo, and Frances Duarte was blond. I've got this strange grease on Grace Markham's arm, and also on the threads that I think Marissa's attacker left behind in the parking garage, but I can't figure out what it is. It's petroleum-based, but it doesn't match any lubricant in the FTIR library."

"First case," the deskman boomed, giving her a firm look. Evelyn shut up as he wheeled in a seventy-five-year-old victim of cancer who had died at home. Even those dead by natural causes had to come to the ME's office if they had not seen a doctor in the prior three months. The assistant ME decided a full postmortem would not be necessary. No one disagreed. They waited for the next gurney.

"Female, thirty-three, MVA, unrestrained passenger versus truck." This shorthand meant that the victim had been riding in the passenger seat, without a seat belt, when her vehicle collided with a truck. During the ten seconds while one gurney was wheeled away and another took its place inside the circle of white-coated people, Evelyn whispered at Ed.

"And I got samples from the elevator mechanisms because it's the only way into the apartment, but neither of them match. They all contain mostly petroleum, but the amounts of the other components are different."

"Sucks to be you, doesn't it?"

"Can you run it on the GC/mass spec?" The gas chromatograph/mass spectrometer combined two of the most helpful analytical instruments in a lab's arsenal, a gas chromatograph to separate organic compounds and a mass spectrometer to separate those compounds further by splitting them into charged molecules.

"Since you already know what it is—that would be grease—I can't see how that furthers your knowledge significantly."

"I had hoped your libraries would be more extensive than mine."

A pause, while Ed appeared to study the fifty-year-old who died of a heart attack halfway through the entrée at his favorite restaurant. Evelyn let the hook set.

"They are quite thorough for each category of samples," he admitted, after they heard about the housepainter who fell while painting shutters on a four-story condominium.

"I'll sign it in with Jenny later today," she promised. Ed insisted that any sample be officially submitted via Toxicology's administrative assistant, both to maintain the chain of custody and because it made him feel like he had his own personal secretary.

Frances Duarte was the last victim for the day. Her bright white body bag rested on a gurney in the second autopsy room, the one set up for decomposed bodies, and the group of doctors now moved into it to finish up the viewing process. The room had two sets of glass doors with an air-lock corridor between them and a door to the outside, which could be fitted with a screen door should the staff need fresh air more than air-conditioning or heat. The plan had been to keep the odors from creeping through the rest of the building. It didn't work. On a list of requirements for the new building, air-flow control sat at the top.

The deskman looked around for a pair of gloves. Not used regularly, the room tended to be understocked, mostly with cast-off supplies. Evelyn pulled a pair from her pocket, too small for him, but he used them like rags to unzip the bag and pull the edges down over the gurney like the corners of a fitted sheet. Then he gave a summary of the case and added that Evelyn had been at the scene. All eyes swiveled toward her.

She summed up—very briefly—the circumstances surrounding Grace Markham, Marissa, and Frances Duarte. She hated to bring Marissa up and knew that Marissa would hate it as well. Working waist-deep in dead bodies every day could make one paranoid, and eager to feel a boundary between the staff and the victims. Us and them—us were alive, them were dead. If one of us crossed the line, others could follow.

She shuddered, maybe just because of her fatigue. Maybe not.

No one wanted to think of Marissa as a victim, Marissa least of all. But if Evelyn tried to avoid the topic, people would assume there had to be more to the story. Nothing beat a good drama like a terrific conspiracy. So she told them all she knew.

To her relief, Evelyn's friend Jonathan Tyler elected to do the postmortem on Frances. The youngest pathologist on the staff, as well as the only African American, he would devote his full attention to the murder victim despite the uncomfortable working conditions. A less dedicated doctor might rush a bit. The decomp autopsy room smelled grotesque when unoccupied, and certainly no better now.

But the pathologist had become as accustomed to the smell as she was, and he leaned on the counter with a newspaper and a cup of coffee while he waited for the autopsy assistant to label the specimen jars. Technically, food and drink should not have been present in the autopsy suite, but familiarity bred contempt, and they had all become very familiar with the common pathogens.

Meanwhile, Evelyn removed Frances's clothes, layer by layer, and spread them on a gurney covered with brown paper. Zoe, the photographer, snapped a picture at each stage, though they would not produce the most salacious slide show in the world. Under the blue knit shirt and navy polyester slacks, Frances wore a 34C bra, cotton panties, and knee socks. No necklace, only gold stud earrings and the diamond ring, which required soap to remove. Despite taking care, Evelyn also removed a good deal of skin.

Only the bra caught her attention. Possibly white at one time, each cup showed abrupt lines along the outside where the decomposition fluid had not been uniformly absorbed. This could have been due to some irregular design, a flaw in the fabric, but she cut a section for further analysis.

"How is Marissa doing?" Jonathan asked her.

"The same."

"Don't worry, Evelyn. She strikes me as pretty tough. There's an article on her in the Metro section," the young doctor added. "By a Clio Helms."

"Let me guess. Marissa used to be an international jewel thief, and her ex-partner tried to kill her because she wouldn't share the booty. It's about the only theory I haven't heard."

"She talked to Mrs. Gonzalez."

"I'll kill her." Evelyn darted to his side and clutched one edge of the paper.

"Hey! Gloves!"

Her blue-latex-covered hands were coated in decomp fluid, leaving brown smears on the edge of the newsprint. She pulled them off without taking her eyes from the paper. "Sorry. I can't believe that girl weaseled her way up to Mama Gonzalez. Did she have the nerve to print the gangbanger ex-boyfriend story?"

"Actually, it's kind of nice. I never knew Marissa had been her high school valedictorian."

"Me neither." Evelyn read over his shoulder, or rather next to it. Jonathan's height overshot hers by nearly a foot.

"Here, take it. We get any closer and you'll be sitting in my lap. I don't mind, but people will talk."

"I will," the autopsy assistant said, lining up the specimen jars. "I'll tell everyone. Man, it stinks in here."

Evelyn barely heard them; she was too busy reading Clio Helms's crisp account of Marissa—a brave Latina who had worked her way out of poverty only to be struck down two months before her fairy-tale wedding. All true, though Marissa would certainly snort when she read it, and threaten the reporter's life in two languages.

Clio ended without making any loose allegations, adding only that police were investigating. She did, however, include an account of the second attack in the hospital on both Marissa and Evelyn. No wonder Ms. Helms and four other reporters had left messages for Evelyn. She abandoned the newspaper and joined Jonathan at the autopsy table.

"What do you think?" she asked.

"Just a guess." He tilted the woman's head gently to one side. "But I think she's dead."

"Everybody's a comic."

"A bit cranky today, are we?"

"No, we're not, I am, and that's because I've had about four hours' sleep in the past two days and I think I'm going to die. Can one die from lack of sleep?"

"Can't say I've ever seen it. What ailed this lady, however, I'm familiar with."

"He strangled her?"

"Yep. From the back, I'd say, with something wide."

"This?" She pulled out the strap that had held Frances Duarte's shoulders to the armchair.

He compared the fabric mesh to the slightly desiccated imprint on her neck. "That could be it."

"No way to tell for sure, huh?"

"Not with her skin this decomposed. But I'll excise the section in case you can analyze it on the SEM or EDX. Otherwise, all I can say is the injury is consistent with the mesh strap."

"Any other signs of violence?"

He began to wash the woman's face, trying to see past the discolored, slipping skin. "Looks like she's got some tiny abrasions here, next to where the strap was. Probably her own fingernails, trying to free herself. I don't see anything else. No bruises, no cuts. Nothing on the hands."

"So he got her from behind. She couldn't reach him to fight him, and instead spent the last of her energy trying to loosen the strap just enough to get one more breath of air. I scraped her fingernails at the scene, but it was almost certainly a waste of time." Even if Frances Duarte had scratched the killer as well as herself, his skin cells would be lost in the swell of decomposition fluid.

She hung the victim's clothing up, piece by piece, and scraped it with a clean plastic Popsicle stick. Hairs, fibers, and other debris—and with luck, some of it from the killer—landed on the brown paper underneath. She picked up the paper, made a fold, and tapped the scrapings into a clear plastic petri dish. The clothes were too damp to be taped. She hung them in a corner of the room to finish drying. Tomorrow she would come back and seal them up in brown paper bags.

Then she went to the vending machine, returned, and sat on a stool to watch Jonathan from a distance, sipping her Diet Coke in direct violation of departmental SOPs. She needed the caffeine.

"Her neck didn't break," Jonathan said at last, pulling off his gloves. "He crushed her larynx and shut off her air. I took swabs, but even if they're positive for semen, I can't tell if she's been raped. Decomposition might be masking any tiny vaginal tears. I don't find any defense wounds on her hands or arms."

"Grace Markham had no signs of injury either. She was dead or unconscious at the time of the rape, and Frances's death probably followed the same MO," Evelyn said.

"Or they weren't raped and the semen is from a boyfriend. Or maybe the same boyfriend."

"It's possible, but so far there's been no sign of any boyfriend in either woman's life. Assuming we find semen in Frances Duarte's swabs, and still no boyfriend turns up, we have two cases of sex occurring in conjunction with murder. In light of that, it strains credibility to think the sex part is consensual. I have that feeling about this guy. He's one sick puppy."

"Maybe we'll get lucky and his DNA hasn't completely decomposed. I don't find any other injuries besides her neck."

"So they didn't have a long struggle. He just slipped the strap over her head and that was that."

"And you think this is the same guy that got Marissa."

"Yes, for two reasons: the marks on her neck and the threads, probably from his jacket, caught by his escape route through a mesh fence. The marks match the straps on Grace and Frances. The threads match the fibers on Marissa's clothing, and the oil on the threads matches the grease on Grace's arm. Obviously I can't tell if he left a smear of grease on Frances. It's the same guy in all three cases, I'd bet my paycheck on that."

"I don't think I'll take that bet. But why didn't he attack Marissa in her apartment, like the other two?"

The idea made Evelyn's skin crawl. "Frances lived alone, and Grace's husband worked a steady schedule. Marissa's fiancé is in and out at all hours. The killer could never be sure he'd find her alone."

Jonathan nodded as he sectioned Frances Duarte's liver on a polypropylene cutting board, dropping pieces into a liquid-filled jar. The autopsy assistant sealed each plastic jar and attached a printed label with the victim's name and six-digit case number. Each biological specimen the doctor collected—hair, blood, gastric contents, as well as tissue samples in a quart container of formalin—would be labeled. "Meanwhile, why don't you get some sleep tonight?"

"Is that a polite way of telling me I look like crap?"

"It would be impossible for you to look like crap, Evelyn—"

"You gallant child, you."

"—but you're getting there."

CAN'T BELIEVE I'M DOING THIS, EVELYN THOUGHT. NOT again.

The salt-mine elevator shaft made its badly lit, rusted-out way into the depths with reluctant shudders of movement. It carried Evelyn and the OSHA inspector, a rounded older woman wearing work boots and a nylon vest with enough pockets to satisfy a fly fisherman. She stood about four-ten including a hard hat with a photo ID clipped to it, a boon to Evelyn, who couldn't remember names when well-rested and under present circumstances could barely recall her own. The tag read "Margery Murphy."

"There's no stairs here," Evelyn noted, unable to keep her mind off the rusted elevator.

"You've got tougher thighs than me if you want to walk down eighteen hundred feet. Or back up."

"But what if the elevator breaks and there's guys in the mine?"

"Then they're screwed."

"Doesn't seem safe."

"It's not a ride at Disney World, honey," Margery Murphy said kindly. "It's a mine."

Evelyn tried to smile. "You're used to salt mines, I take it."

"Me? I'm practically the damn *expert* on salt mines, at least in the Northeast area—exciting, huh?"

"Um, yeah."

"I meant that as a joke, honey. What's the matter? You'll trot right up to dismembered corpses and a little salt mine makes you nervous?"

Surely the elevator car had slowed, its single light dimmed. "There's the part about being sixteen hundred feet under the lake."

The inspector's head bobbed in a chuckle, swaying a few curls that had escaped from the hard hat. "Relax. They never cave in. Coal mines, though—two hundred years and we still can't make those safe."

The car stopped. Evelyn hoped that meant that the doors would open and not that they were stuck halfway down the shaft. "Why is there such a large difference between the two?"

"The type of soil around them. The pH, minerals in it. Mostly the structure—coal deposits tend to meander, but salt deposits are very large and geometrically sound. They've been mining salt out of this one since the early sixties, and there's still enough to last a hundred years from now."

"So what happened here then?"

Margery Murphy's boots slapped their way off the elevator and onto the carved salt floor of the first mine room. She gazed around, from the rough white floor to the pipes running along the wall. "That's what we're here to find out. This is very interesting. Very interesting."

To Evelyn, it all looked the same as it had two days before, with one exception. Today the mine was empty except for the two of them. Two women. In a series of sixty-by-sixty rooms. Buried underneath Lake Erie. Where there had recently been an explosion.

What the hell am I doing here?

"Well, let's see the spot," Margery said, hefting her toolbox onto her shoulder and looking like one of the Seven Dwarfs. "You lead the way."

Evelyn walked this time; she didn't know how the golf cart worked and didn't want to take the time to learn. She put her flashlight to use even though the ground seemed level and the area well-lit. What if the power went out, left them encased in a large salt box far below the earth with no lights . . .

"This look like anything has been changed since you were here?" Margery asked. "Equipment still here? Was that piping installed before?"

Evelyn glanced up at the cables and four-inch pipe mounted high on the salt wall. It turned into another room shortly, but the cables kept going toward the damaged area. "Yeah."

"Well, they should have told me about that." As they walked, the OSHA investigator fiddled with a small black box inside a nylon carrying case.

"Why? What is it?"

"This the loader?"

The front-end loader waited for them, retaining enough material from its victims to fill the room with the odor of seared, rotting flesh. "That's it. They turned it upright to get the bodies out. Otherwise it doesn't seem to have moved."

Now Margery seemed more interested in her black box. "Hmm."

"What's that?"

"Air-quality monitor."

"Looking for carbon monoxide?"

"That's not usually a problem in salt mines." The reading must have satisfied Margery, because she put the box away, took copious photographs of the grisly loader, and moved into the room where the explosion had happened. "Whew! Quite a fire in here. And fast."

She took more photographs while Evelyn kept her mind off her claustrophobia by following the burn marks back to the point of origin. She arrived at the area of most damage—a blackened, jagged crater in the salt—but couldn't pinpoint the source more precisely than that. "You think there was something wrong with the dynamite?"

"Don't think so." Margery had her air monitor out again, taking reading after reading around the explosion site. Finally she stopped and sighed. "Yeah. They should have told me about that."

"About what?"

"The natural gas they're storing down here."

The lights going out no longer seemed like the worst thing that could happen. The entire chamber igniting into a fireball before Evelyn even had time to think about running to the elevator, that would be worse. "Gas?"

"Yeah. One of the extra uses of salt mines—once you've got all this space cleared out down here, it's a great place to store stuff." Margery took out a small rock hammer and cheerfully broke off pieces of charred salt, which she placed in a manila envelope. "Toxic waste, garbage. For gas, they pump water into a deposit. And what does salt do in water?"

"Dissolve?"

"Exactly. Dissolve a good chunk of it and then suck all the solution back out, and you're left with a bubble in the salt deposit—a nice, inexpensive, closed container. Pump in some gas, and it will stay there until the gas company needs it, usually in winter, when demand peaks and people start complaining about high prices."

"The gas exploded?"

"No, no!" Margery stored her envelopes in one of the many pockets in her nylon vest. "If a room full of gas had gone up, we wouldn't be standing here and the body count would be a hell of a lot higher than seven. The fish would be reclaiming this space right now."

Evelyn wanted to sit down. "The East Ohio Gas Company leaked gas into the sewers and killed a hundred and thirty people—"

"In 1944, I know. But that was liquid natural gas, and this is just the compressed form." Margery thought on that a moment. "At least I hope to hell it is."

"Are you done?" Evelyn asked. "Can we go now?"

"Don't worry. The air monitor says we're fine. Gas has been

stored in salt mines for forty or fifty years, and it's never exploded or even leaked, that I know of. The pipes used to pump it in and out, however, can. All it takes is a hairline break and the gas seeps out over time, moving upward through gaps in the strata. Even that won't hurt anything, usually, unless it finds someplace to pool, like in the Hutchinson, Kansas, explosion. I'm betting it found a little pocket right around here, and still didn't become a problem until someone poked a stick of dynamite into it."

"And there's no gas here now?"

Margery put on a pair of scratched reading glasses and checked the monitor readings again. "Well—"

"Can we go now?"

And to Evelyn's everlasting horror, the OSHA inspector said, "That might be a good idea."

Evelyn scooped up the inspector's toolbox and turned. It was all she could do to keep from breaking into a run.

Margery trotted to keep up with her. "Nothing to panic about, honey. There's just enough gas present to register, so we have to leave as a precaution until I can come back with proper breathing equipment and trained personnel. Then we can trace the leak, if there is one."

"You'll come back," Evelyn panted. "I won't."

"Now that you've officially turned the scene over to me, you don't have to. Slow down, missy. There's the elevator."

"What if it causes a spark? What if it ignites—"

"It won't." Margery pressed the button, and the world did *not* detonate into a mass of flame. "So, where's a good place to eat around here?"

"The mine is at fault, then? You said they're in trouble—because they were storing natural gas?"

"Nothing wrong with storing natural gas, that's what I'm trying to tell you. It's usually as safe as T-bills. The wrong part was not telling anybody about it, especially us. Alexander Mining apparently bypassed all the permitting and licensing aspects of this little side job, since I didn't find word one about it in their paperwork. I'm guessing they needed the money."

The elevator stopped inside its long, thin tube with a rumbling *clang,* and the doors opened. Still, the air did not catch fire. Evelyn stepped gingerly inside and did not speak until they were making their way upward. "Apparently it will be a while until this new mine begins to pay for itself."

"Usually is. So they diversified their services, to get some cash coming in." Margery watched Evelyn glance at the ceiling for the fourth time. "I think we're almost there."

"Sorry. I don't like being underground."

Margery shifted her black box to one hand and patted Evelyn on the shoulder with the other. "Don't feel bad. No shame in admitting that some places are plain scary. Like there was this—here, I'll take that toolbox back—this mine in a little town way outside of Great Rock Bluff, Kentucky. You could spit from one side of the city limits to the other, that kind of place? We were there on a routine inspection of an anthracite vein—" She paused to stuff the nylon case into a vest pocket.

"The mine was scary?"

The elevator stopped, and the doors opened. Margery Murphy held one with the palm of her free hand. "No, the mine was fine, nothing wrong there. The bar across the street from the entrance, though— I still wake up in a cold sweat dreamin' about that place. Come on, help me find that Giardino character. I have some questions for him."

14

FRANCES DUARTE HAD ONLY ONE LIVING IMMEDIATE relative, her sister in Tucson. To David fell the unenviable task of informing the woman that her sibling had been brutally murdered. She had been understandably distressed but could not shed any light on who might have done it. To her knowledge, Frances had neither lovers nor enemies.

David yawned, reached for his foam cup, and felt surprised to find it empty. He tossed it in the overflowing wastebasket next to his desk. The Cleveland Police Department Homicide Unit fell in the middle of how police departments were usually depicted on TV—neither as dirtily cluttered as in the gritty dramas nor as spiffy as in the lighter series. Large windows lining one wall kept the room bright and airy, allowing the men and women working there a great view of Ontario Street and the Marriott Center, with the blue expanse of Lake Erie off to the far left. Desks stretched across the linoleum floor. It was a functional room, with no concessions whatsoever to decoration or style.

Riley shifted in his chair. Their desks faced each other in the typical partnering arrangement. Both blotters were littered with the statements of Frances's neighbors, collected early that morning. Several people had noticed the smell, but the last suspicious sound noted had been a month earlier, when a squirrel had gotten loose in the air duct and it took the manager and a pest control serviceman two days to catch it. David's partner nodded at the trash can and said, "Why don't you bring a ceramic mug in so you don't have to use those Styrofoam things?"

"I will. I keep forgetting."

"Maybe you have settlement issues."

"Come again?"

Riley clasped both hands behind his head, dispensing wisdom like a skinny Buddha. "You don't have a single personal item on your desk, not a picture, or a plaque, or a damn coffee cup. You toss away money in rent every month instead of buying a place and building some equity. You even lease your car. Sort of the reverse of the nesting instinct—more like the 'ready to fly the coop at a moment's notice' instinct. No wonder Evie doesn't want to let you move in."

"Did I miss something? Did you get a mail-order doctorate in psychology without telling me?"

"Just stating the facts. Sometimes it helps to hear things from a disinterested party."

"Sometimes it helps for people to mind their own business." David began to stack manila folders, snapping each one down in a precise arrangement. He'd have walked out, taken an early lunch, except that he and Riley had an appointment to talk to Buford Aimes again.

"You want the woman to open her home to you, you're going to have to make her think you're in it for more than laundry privileges."

"And you got all this from a coffee cup?"

"It's the little things that tell on us, partner. Always. Like when we interview a suspect—he looks up at the ceiling every time he lies, or he taps his foot when we ask about the drugs. It's the things we don't even know we do."

Riley's low opinion of him came as no surprise to David. "Have you been sharing these theories with Evelyn? Is that why she's balking at living with me?"

Swooping an *X* over his chest with one finger, his partner swore: "Not a word."

"I have an idea. Why don't you start dating again, so you can worry about your own love life and stay the hell out of mine?"

Riley gazed at him with the exaggerated expression of a sad puppy. "I'm trying to help the two people closest to me, and this is the thanks I get. Harsh, man. Real harsh."

"I—" The phone cut David off, and he snatched at the receiver. "Milaski, Homicide."

"I'm calling about Frances Duarte."

"Yes, sir?"

"I think there's a few things about her that you need to know."

David had taken several such calls that morning, from a woman who had dreamt about the dead woman to a college student who called from the art museum to say that Frances had left her umbrella there, as well as two TV stations who had fibbed their way past the police department switchboard. But this guy sounded both sensible and serious, and besides, David would grasp at any straw to avoid discussing romantic entanglements with his partner. "Okay. Where are you?"

EVELYN SAT in her well-lit lab, cluttered but roomy and blissfully aboveground, and analyzed evidence from the two crime scenes. The dirt on the carpeting in Frances Duarte's apartment turned out to be powdered carbon, with a few additives. She or Bobby Ito must have been careless with the fingerprinting process . . . No, she'd collected the carpet fibers before they began processing for prints. She added the carbon to her mental list of puzzling facts.

"Good night, Evelyn," Tony called from his office. "Turn the lights out when you leave."

She looked at her watch: 4:25. "You're going home?"

"Yes, home. You know, that place that's not work? That has food and TV sets and my dog?" He detoured through the lab, peering at her over the top of the FTIR. "Don't pull another all-nighter. The ME said to put Marissa's case first, but he's still not approving any overtime."

"I won't stay too late. It's just that the lines on Grace Markham's skirt and Frances's bra seem to be some sort of waxy substance. I'm trying to break it down. Have you heard anything back from CODIS?"

"Heck, no. That will be weeks yet. But the swabs from Duarte came up positive for semen, and the DNA says it's the same guy. I guess that's not really a surprise, is it?"

"No, but it's good to know. If we had two different guys with the same murder weapon, that would be confusing. On the other hand, we wouldn't have a serial killer. I don't know which is worse."

"You're sure the two women didn't have the same boyfriend? It could be what connects them."

"David and Riley have asked everyone who knew these women. If either one of them had a man in the wings, it's the best-kept secret since Roswell."

"You call *that* well-kept?" He glanced toward the window. "I'm getting out of here before that rain breaks. Have a nice evening, and remember one thing."

"What?"

"Working late without approval is not overtime. It comes from the goodness of your heart and you can't put a dollar value on that. Or even comp time."

"Thanks for the tip," she said, but he had already left. She knew she should follow his example or Angel would eat Pop-Tarts for dinner—again. But Grace Markham's skirt caught her eye.

With a fresh disposable scalpel, she scraped along the waxy line just until a few flakes appeared on the glass slide beneath the fabric. Then she made a dry mount by placing a coverslip on top and moved the whole thing carefully to the microscope stage. After all that, the flakes appeared to be just that, flakes, of a consistently pink color. She still had no idea what they were.

She transferred one of the flakes to the tiny, round salt window for FTIR analysis and flattened it to the surface with a small metal roller. The resultant spectrum told her that the sample contained mostly paraffin, with a number of pigments.

Crayons?

She analyzed the lines on Frances's bra, listening to the last few members of the Toxicology Department file to the stairwell. Even Ed—the only staff member who bothered to wait for the slow elevator—had left.

Same result—not exactly the same pigments in the same proportions, but similar enough. The killer had crayoned on Grace's skirt and Frances's bra. Why?

Crayons meant children to Evelyn. Neither of the two dead women had children, though Grace had been pregnant and Frances had her great-nieces. Had they gone to the same ob-gyn? Had Frances been struggling with the last few ticks of that biological clock, thinking about having a baby at forty-five? What about Marissa? Were her clothes intentionally omitted from the killer's crayoning schedule, or did he run out of time when the doorman appeared?

They could have had a number of connections to children, but Evelyn simply didn't know enough about the two dead victims to guess.

Or maybe they had nothing to do with children at all, and the wavy marks were the work of an artist who used victims as canvases. The loops formed no picture or letters that she could see, just heavy-handed scribbles.

She moved into Tony's office. He had the only computer with Internet access and, as usual, had been too lazy to shut it down since he could never remember his password. She put "crayon" in the search engine subject line and hit Search, hoping to find a chemical formula—an idle hope, of course. No manufacturer would post their product's formula on the Internet unless they wanted to go out of business. She did turn up more brands besides Crayola, and more types besides paraffin—crayons now came from soybean oil, all-natural beeswax, and washable materials. Too bad she hadn't known of those when two-year-old Angel decided to practice her art on the new wallpaper.

Angel would be home from school by now. Evelyn picked up the phone and dialed her own number, listening to it ring four times before the machine picked up. Perhaps she'd gone somewhere after school. *Perhaps I should rethink that cell phone idea.*

Evelyn left a message, telling her daughter to go next door for dinner. Evelyn hadn't discussed this plan with her mother, but Dorothy never minded an opportunity to feed people, and Angel would heed any order relating to her softhearted grandmother. It might distract her from the fact that she hadn't seen her own mother in two days. Then again, it might not.

The crayoning made no sense that Evelyn could see, and it did suggest children. Grace had been trying to get pregnant for years. Marissa's fiancé was a pediatrician.

Suddenly Evelyn thought of the children's *hospital.* Grace and Frances both worked for its fund-raising effort, and the article in Marissa's purse had mentioned the hospital as well as Frances Duarte. Evelyn had a few minutes, and Angel wasn't home anyway . . .

She typed "Cleveland charity children's fund-raising" into the search engine. This produced an overwhelming number of sites, but most dealt with either the organizations seeking the funds or individual philanthropic foundations. In either event, she couldn't find a list of fund-raising committee members before growing impatient. She could call David and ask him to find out, but David and Riley were busy with interviews, and besides, the main Butterfly Babies hospital building sat not four hundred feet from the back door of the Medical Examiner's Office. Why not just walk over there?

Evelyn chose the cleanest lab coat from the community closet. It hung on her like a tent, but it had no loose threads or faded bloodstains. She stepped into the ladies' room to blot her face and brush her hair. Butterfly Babies took a dim view of law enforcement and would be more cooperative with a fellow science professional. A touch of sheer lipstick, and she looked . . . She looked like a civil servant who hadn't slept in a week.

Oh well.

The soaring atrium at the University Hospital's facility always made Evelyn wonder what the designers had been thinking. Did they assume that the beauty and elegance would reassure parents, make them believe their children were in the most competent hands possible?

If my kid came here, I'd look at this glassed-in beauty and start worrying about the bill. Obviously the people here make way too much money.

The development office sat on the fourth floor, behind huge oak doors with gold lettering. A frizzy-haired woman about Evelyn's age stood at the reception desk, a cell phone propped on one shoulder, placing items one by one into an oversize handbag. Her name tag identified her as an administrative assistant. Down a silent hallway to the left, one office remained lit. With a sinking feeling, Evelyn realized how late in the day it was. Surely everyone had gone home for the night.

"The six-quart pan, Jimmy. Look at the bottom of it, the size will be engraved right in the metal. Spaghetti is not that hard." The woman looked up at Evelyn without enthusiasm. "Can I help you?"

"I'm Evelyn James, from next door. I need some information about your fund-raising committee."

"Which one?" To her shoulder, she added, "She's six, Jimmy. She can't tell the canned stuff from the jar. Just pick a flavor."

"You have more than one?"

The woman motioned with her right ear, without losing the phone wedged under her left. "Mark Sargeant might still be back there, the third door on the right. If he's gone, there's some brochures on the end table that explain the committee's work— Jimmy? Don't forget the garlic bread."

Evelyn picked a color brochure from a Lucite rack. Behind her, she heard "Take it out of the freezer, that's all. I'll take care of—" And the door clicked shut. She turned. The woman had left.

Holding the brochure, Evelyn explored the hallway. Besides one small conference room, she found four offices. A brass name plaque on each desk identified the occupants, from capital campaign director to special events director. Except for the woman at the front desk, there did not seem to be any staff under the level of director. Spotting the file room, Evelyn wondered if there was a filing director.

The lights still shone in the capital campaign director's office. A collection of promotional items, from tiny stuffed bears to tricolor highlighters, cluttered the top of the desk. Wilting balloons drifted against one wall. A framed picture of a handsome man with former mayor Mike White rested on a shelf. Papers lay on the desk, tempting her.

Well, weren't charitable contributions public records? And if they weren't, they should be.

She peeked at the top of the stack. A balance sheet for a recent charity auction detailed costs, which were astronomical, and the intake, even more so. A profit glowed at the bottom, in bold. How could a hospital be considered a charity anyway, now that nearly all of them were for-profit concerns—signaling the end of reasonably priced health care in America, in Evelyn's opinion.

Names of the seven members of the Butterfly Babies Capital Campaign Committee edged the paper. Grace Markham was third from the bottom.

"Can I help you?"

Evelyn jerked to attention. The man in the doorway had dark hair, narrowed eyes, and very broad shoulders. He had a pleasant expression and a friendly smile, and yet every cell in her body wanted to run like hell. "Are you Mark?"

"The one and only. Something fascinating about my desk?" But he didn't come closer to see what she had been looking at, merely stayed in the doorway with the same amused look her cat got when he spied a mouse away from its hole.

"Sorry, didn't mean to be nosy. I wanted to ask about your fund-raising committee. Is Frances Duarte still a member?"

He did not flinch at the name; either he did not yet know she had died or he had some talent as an actor. "Yes. Lovely woman. She's in our Campaign Cabinet, which I chair. Our current focus is adding a new wing to the neonatal unit. Perhaps you would be interested in our pledge program? Gifts usually start at one million."

Evelyn tensed her jaw to keep it from dropping. "Um. Tax-deductible?"

His shoulders brushed the doorjamb on either side, effectively trapping her. "Of course not. As a for-profit hospital, we're not a 501(c)(3). Are you a friend of Frannie's?"

"No, not really. I was also wondering about Grace Markham."

His voice dropped in both tone and warmth. "What about her?"

"Is she still active in Butterfly Babies fund-raising?"

"Why? Who are you?"

She moved toward the door, closer to him. "I'm sorry, I didn't introduce myself. I'm from next door—the ME's office. I'm working on Mrs. Markham's death, and I have some questions."

He nodded, bouncing on the balls of his feet with his head cocked slightly and his hands in his pockets. The relaxed pose did not reassure her, did not make up for the intensity of his gaze. "I didn't know you were allowed to do that."

"Why wouldn't I be?" Evelyn existed in a gray area so far as authority went. As a scientist working to resolve a case, she could ask questions of anyone she liked. Of course, she had no authority to make them answer.

He appraised her for another moment, leaning close enough for her to decide she didn't care for his aftershave. "Grace was a nice woman. She headed up a dance we had two years ago at Hornblower's, did a terrific job. I was sorry to hear about her death."

"Did she and Frances work together here?"

"I'm sure their paths crossed."

"Any problems with either of them?"

"What sorts of problems?"

"Any sort. We're investigating Grace's death. I want to know about her friends."

"Really. I'm afraid I have nothing to share. I didn't see much of her for the past few years."

"Thank you, then." Evelyn moved to leave, and he turned sideways and leaned on the door molding to let her brush past him into the hall.

"It's too bad, what happened to Marissa."

She froze. His features were masked by the dimness of the room, but the outline of his body stood sharp and tense.

"She works for you, doesn't she?"

Evelyn stopped trying to sound cool. "What would you know about it?"

He pushed off from the wall and came toward her. Away from the light in his office, he became a dark, hulking form in the dim hallway. But his voice remained light, as if he were playing a game he hadn't let her in on. "Just what I read in the paper this morning. She's such a beautiful girl—and about to be married, I understand."

"How do you know her?"

"Marissa did her undergraduate co-op in the pathology lab here. I headed up the lab at the time. Great student. Very . . . intense."

Evelyn hated the way he said it, hated the way her friend's name sounded rolling off this man's tongue. A thousand questions flooded her mind, and she didn't want to ask a single one of them. Instead, she stated, "And now you're in fund-raising."

"Better hours." He crossed in front of her and held the outer door open. "Be sure to let her know I wish her a speedy recovery."

Evelyn left. She bypassed the elevator and headed for the stairs, trotting downward as if the Riviere killer followed on her heels.

D AVID COULD HAVE INSISTED THAT FRANCES DUARTE'S accountant come to the station, but he felt like getting out of the cramped homicide unit—maybe he *did* have wanderlust, as Riley had accused—and figured an accountant with rich clients would have a much more comfortable office in which to meet.

He figured wrong. The firm of Merrill, Brandon and Steinberg rested on the fourth floor of the historic Cleveland Arcade, a hundred-plus-year-old structure of glass and brass and tile, officially the first indoor shopping mall in the young United States. But all the glass and brass did not absorb sound, and at quitting time, cacophony reigned.

And Patrick Merrill did not, to judge from his workplace, believe in spending his dollars on designers or in making clients so comfortable that they might overstay their welcome. David and Riley perched on hard metal chairs with their knees brushing the front of the accountant's desk.

"How long have you kept Miss Duarte's books?" David asked.

"I've managed her family's foundation accounts since she was a child."

David raised one eyebrow. "She was only forty-five, and you can't be more than ten years older than that."

The man smiled for the first time, his chubby cheeks lifting. "That's true. I meant since she was eighteen and came into her trust fund. Steinberg had handled the family's money for longer than that, but they were one of the families he handed over to me as I developed my career."

"Where did the money come from?"

"Steel, originally. Frances's grandfather owned the first steel mill in Cleveland back when men came by the boatload from eastern Europe to work here. He had the sense to diversify into shipping and real estate before steel took a turn for the worse. He'd roll over in his grave if he knew how Republic Steel—I mean LTV—died out."

"What did Frances's father do?" David asked.

"Took care of the businesses like a shepherd with sheep. Unlike most second generations, he didn't tear through it in a wild youth. And Frances inherited that sense."

David leaned forward, bumping his knee. "Did she have any recent or ongoing conflicts over the funds? Did she and her sister disagree over their shares? Any long-lost relatives coming out of the woodwork, an injured worker suing for a few billion dollars?"

Merrill shook his head with a slight smile. "Not at all."

"Then why did you call us?" Riley asked.

"Frances is—was—about to lose a great deal of money. It wouldn't have bankrupted her, of course, but it's still a substantial amount."

David flipped open his notepad. "How much? And why?"

"She made a bad investment on the advice of a friend. I *wish* I could stop clients from doing that. I tried to tell her—"

"What investment? What friend?"

Another slight smile. Apparently Merrill found the rashness of nonfinancial personnel amusing, or perhaps bemusing. "Frances invested in the Alexander salt mine company. She seemed to feel that the Flats area needed to reclaim its industrial heritage to bring this city out of its depression."

Riley nodded. David said, "The mine that just caved in?"

"Salt mines don't cave in. There was an explosion."

"So the investment is not going to work out?"

"For reasons that have nothing to do with the explosion. Don't get me wrong, gentlemen—the original portion of the Alexander salt mine company is rock solid. It's been, like the Duartes' money, in the family for several generations—probably why Frances trusted the girl. Alexander wanted to open a new mine on Front Street, and Frances went ahead with her investment even though I warned her that the price of salt couldn't support the massive overhead required to open a new mine. The new mine has been losing money since the first day; the accident is only the final nail in its coffin. Frances wouldn't have made a penny back, and the papers were written well. She couldn't have appealed to the main company for any retribution. I pointed that out to her as well, but—"

"What girl?"

"Hmm? Oh, Kelly Alexander, the owner's daughter. A friend of Frances's. I think they had several charity concerns in common, though they had been acquainted for years."

"How much money?"

"One point seven million."

David felt his jaw slacken.

The accountant nodded. "Yes. Not an inconsequential amount."

"That's like an entire year's salary for one of the Indians' second string," Riley said. "So Frances got pretty irate with this Kelly?"

"No, no. I had advised Frances against the investment, but she insisted that she knew the risk, and besides, Kelly Alexander stands to lose even more—of her own money, not the company's."

"Did Frances ask Kelly to help her make some of the money back?"

"No. She didn't seem to bear any ill will against Miss Alexander, and she would not have been destitute. The loss represents only seven percent of her entire estate."

"Then why did you call us?"

"Because it's still one point seven million dollars. I couldn't be sure it was not, well—"

"Significant."

"Exactly."

EVELYN MOVED SLOWLY across the parking lot behind the squat Medical Examiner's Office, despite the first few drops of a spring drizzle. She needed Marissa to wake up and explain some things. Who the hell was Mark Sargeant to her, and why did she have a clipping about a dead woman in her purse?

If Marissa had worked at Butterfly Babies when she was in undergraduate school, perhaps she'd met Grace and Frances at that time—but what would fund-raising have to do with pathology? Besides, Grace would have still been working as a photojournalist and presumably wouldn't have had much time for charity work.

Could Mark Sargeant have been the man in Marissa's hospital room, the one Evelyn had struggled with? Standing close to him in the hospital offices, she hadn't felt the slightest shred of recognition. But as David had pointed out, eyewitness testimony was notoriously unreliable. She wanted to believe, as all humans did, that her instincts were better than average, but wishful thinking might have been exactly that.

Maybe Sargeant hadn't meant to insinuate something slimy when he spoke of Marissa. Perhaps he'd thought he sounded charming, chatting in the dark.

But all that still wouldn't explain why someone had decided to try to execute the three women.

"Hi," said a voice to her left. A slight form in a raincoat moved to shelter her with an umbrella, nearly poking her eye out in the process. "Can you believe it's raining again? Must be lake effect."

The newspaper reporter. "Clio," Evelyn said.

"It's Greek, you know." The young woman fell into step beside her. "The name. It means 'the proclaimer, the woman who made known her opinion.' Appropriate, huh?"

"I thought reporters were supposed to deal in fact, not opinion."

"Good point. Are you okay? You seem to be limping."

"I'm fine."

"Have you made any progress in the Riviere cases? Or the Duarte case? It *is* the same guy, isn't it?"

"What makes you say that?"

"About six patrol officers, each of whom shall remain nameless."

"Great," Evelyn muttered, picking up her pace a bit.

"So what about it? I need official confirmation."

They reached the dock, and Evelyn trotted up the three steps to the back entrance. Unfortunately, the overhead door had been opened for a funeral home, now loading a gurney into the back of their hearse, and Clio Helms followed her right through it. "Talk to the homicide unit. It's their investigation."

"Detectives are boring. It's forensics that's the glamour job nowadays. How about a personal, slice-of-life story on you? Readers would love to hear about what it's really like."

Evelyn turned and faced the woman to keep her from moving any farther into the building. "Look around you."

Three gurneys sat at random in the loading area. Two of their occupants had been neatly zipped into white plastic body bags, but the single sheet over the third allowed an emaciated lower leg to poke free. Clio paled a bit but said, "So? I grew up on East Eighty-fifth and Quincy. I stumbled over a dead body in our stairwell while going to catch the bus. Mom had to write a note for my third-grade teacher to explain why I came in late."

"But does this seem glamorous to you?"

"Tell me what it's really like, then. My readers would love to know. I'd love to know."

A counterattack seemed in order. "How is your sister? The one that got stabbed by her bridesmaid."

The change of topics seemed to surprise the young reporter, but she promptly recovered. "She's fine. It took eighteen stitches and sure didn't do much for the white dress, though. Why?"

"I like to know the end of the story."

"So do I."

Evelyn sighed. "I wish I could help you, but I can't. All public statements issue from the medical examiner. His office is on the second floor. I'll show you to the lobby."

"I've already been there." Clio stuck her pen behind her ear, pushing back caramel-colored curls, but made no move to leave. "So why do you think this guy is on such a rampage?"

"Second floor. Let me show you—"

"Did you know Grace Markham and Frances Duarte were friends?"

Evelyn stopped. Clio waited. Behind her, the deskman had waved the hearse on its way and now stood in the open doorway, considering the young reporter's form with an appreciative eye. "I assumed they were acquainted. They must have traveled in the same social circles, had the same interests."

"They were more than acquainted. They served on the Downtown Festival committee and the children's hospital capital campaign."

"I know."

"They belonged to the same country club."

"Mmm-hmm. I'm sure it has quite a few members. Besides, if you have information to share, Ms. Helms, you should share it with the investigating detectives."

"I thought if I tipped you off, you could return the favor."

"Sorry. I can't help you."

"I'm not asking you to compromise the investigation. I mean after you catch the guy, give me the scoop. An insider's account of the process and the apprehension."

"I appreciate your confidence in us, and I'm sure that's a reasonable—"

"They were close friends."

"What?" Evelyn turned to accept three boxes of sterile cotton swabs from the purchasing secretary, who thrust them into her arms without explanation and kept going. An order must have come in. "How do you know that?"

"The *Plain Dealer* has a beautiful thing we like to call the Archive. Everything newsworthy that's ever happened in the city of Cleveland since the paper began, in 1841. Okay, maybe not everything. But it had society page blurbs about Grace Markham and Frances Duarte at dinners for Darryl Pierson, on backstage tours at the Rock and Roll Hall of Fame, heading to New York for shopping trips. Including, of course, what they were wearing. I think when it comes right down to it, there's not much to say about the rich except what they were wearing."

"When was that?"

"About four years ago. After that, not so much. They're still mentioned in tandem here and there—we ran a picture of them with a Sunday magazine article about a new restaurant that opened in Tower City just two months ago."

Not surprising that the women would be friends, Evelyn thought. Their lives must have been quite similar. Had they had a falling-out? And what could they possibly have had in common with Marissa?

Clio Helms seemed to read her mind. "But what's the connection with your DNA analyst?"

Evelyn opened her mouth to point out that the killer might simply frequent expensive apartment buildings, and the fact that two of the victims knew each other could be a not-too-surprising coincidence. If they had been close friends, surely Grace's husband or Beldon Aimes would have mentioned it.

Perhaps she should put Clio Helms on to Mark Sargeant . . . except that if some dark secret of Marissa's did lurk behind that murmuring voice, Marissa would hardly be grateful for its airing only two months before the wedding. And if he knew more about Grace and Frances than he professed, the journalist could wind up dead. So, for that matter, could Evelyn.

As Riley would say, she bunted. "What are you doing here, anyway? You can't be following me."

"That doesn't say much for your self-esteem, Evelyn. Why wouldn't I be following you? I said I came to see if your spokesperson could tell me anything new, which he couldn't. Neither can the cops. I think they're just rounding up the usual suspects."

The usual suspects . . . Outside the dock, a discreetly lettered ambulance backed up to the protruding concrete edge, piercing the air with a shrill *beep-beep-beep*. The deskman forgot about watching Clio and caught Evelyn's eye. "Traffic coming in. Three cars on I-71. Nasty."

"Time to go, Ms. Helms." Evelyn all but shoved the young woman out the back door and promised to call if and when she could talk.

Evelyn headed to her lab via the lobby. Their wizened receptionist, Mrs. Anderson, flagged her down with a lit cigarette. The "No Smoking by County Ordinance" sign on the wall behind her did not apply after quitting time, she explained. "Your peerless leader just toddled upstairs after he spent fifteen minutes telling me how hard he's worked. First time in twenty years, I'm sure. I'm surprised he hasn't put in for disability yet, having to get out of his chair more than twice during the day. How's Marissa?"

"The same, last I heard."

"She still going to marry that doctor boy?"

"Of course." She'll be fine. She'll be fine.

"Good for her."

Evelyn climbed the steps to the third floor, now nearly deserted, to survey the small room at the back of the building that housed the DNA equipment. Tony would hit the roof if he thought she had checked up on him, but she doubted he would notice.

First she emptied the biohazard container he'd left full and put away the instruction manuals he'd left on the counter, and she doubted he would notice that either. Then she moved over to the computer attached to the STR—short tandem repeat—DNA analysis system.

She found the printout for the semen sample from Grace Markham and compared it with the one from Frances Duarte—which had, miraculously, served up male DNA. They matched perfectly; not even Tony could screw that up. They had the DNA of the killer.

The thought made her pause. There could so easily have been a third set of samples, and a chart with Marissa's name at the top.

She moved the mouse, and the monitor sprang to life, courtesy of Tony's less-than-perfect lab techniques. He hadn't shut the computer down. She hit the Search History tab.

Tony said he'd sent the results to CODIS, but Marissa often ran fifteen samples of DNA a day and kept the results in her own database. Evelyn had been too tied up with crayons and grease at the time, but after her talk with Clio Helms, she wondered if Tony had run their samples against their own gang of usual suspects. As expected, he hadn't. Keyboard keys clacked under her fingertips as she followed the on-screen commands.

A box at the bottom of the screen glowered. "Searching."

"What are you doing?"

She could have sworn her heart physically left her chest. She looked around to see Tony in the doorway. "You scared the crap out of me."

"Why?" Tony considered their surroundings as safe and comfortable as the average kindergarten, and most of the time, so did Evelyn. Very few criminals broke into a morgue. "You think that guy who throttled you is going to come back?"

Yes, she wanted to say. I do. He might assume I saw his face. He might assume I can identify him. But she couldn't show weakness to Tony unless she wanted to hear about it every week for the next ten years. Besides, she had a more delicate confession to make. "I'm just checking searches."

His blue eyes darkened to storm cloud gray. "I said I put in for a CODIS search."

"I know."

"So?"

No way around it. "I'm searching our own database. Our past cases, the ones that Marissa had analyzed since we went to STRs from RFLP type analysis."

A pause while he considered what to do. He had simply forgotten, of course, or somehow assumed that the computer would do that automatically, but that would not be the explanation.

The computer beeped to get her attention. A results window had opened, listing things like match probability and percentages.

A lightning strike from Tony. "Why isn't running this search in Marissa's written SOP, then? I followed it carefully, and I'm sure—"

It took a moment for Evelyn to comprehend what the computer screen showed her. "Tony."

"I'm going to have to have a talk with the princess when she gets back to work—"

"Tony!"

"What?"

"Look at this." She stared at the screen, trying to absorb it.

Her boss stalked up behind her and read over her shoulder. Then he said, "Holy crap."

OUR KILLER IS THE UNKNOWN SUBJECT IN FIVE UN-
solved rapes," Evelyn breathed into her phone.

David, on the other end, did not seem to be breathing at
all. *"Five?"*

"Over the past, let me see, four years."

"Where? Who? What are their names?"

"You'll have to hang on a minute." She scribbled the evidence
item numbers on a piece of paper and hurried down the hall, with
Tony on her heels. "I need the daybooks."

"The what?"

Information regarding every item, every sample, every victim
the Trace Evidence Department had dealt with since 1968 had been
entered into tall red ledgers, with one page for each day. (The years
before that were detailed in students' composition notebooks.) The
six-digit case numbers assigned by the deskmen went in the left-
hand margin, and each sample or item of evidence got a distinct
three-part number. Someday, and sooner rather than later, a computer program would hold all this information, but Evelyn could
wait. Aside from an occasional case of writer's cramp, the ledgers
worked well. She could locate an item from a 1982 murder or a

1971 industrial accident in minutes, and no computer hacker in the world could reach information written only in ink. Besides, it gave her the sense of history in the making.

She pulled the books from 2003 to 2006, plunking them into Tony's arms.

It took, as usual, only seconds to find the entries. In all five cases they had received only the sexual assault kits, no other evidence, such as clothing or bedding. Each notation listed the submitting agency.

She read the information as she found it. Even Tony became caught up in her frenzied activity, holding the large books for her like a well-trained altar boy.

The first case had come from a wealthy suburb to the southeast of Cleveland named Solon; the second occurred in Parma, the largest suburb of the city, a working-class neighborhood to the southwest. In 2004, the evidence had been submitted by the Cleveland force. The Cleveland police lab, the state police crime lab, and other area facilities conducted DNA analysis, but when backlog held up results, the cops could come to the efficient ME's office.

In 2005, a case from Euclid, to the east of the city along the lake. "2006, Cleveland again," she told David.

"He gets around," Tony pointed out.

"He does indeed." Phone propped between ear and shoulder, she took the ledgers from her boss, steadying herself with their bulk. Their killer had expanded from rape to murder. What did he plan to do next? "Just when you think it can't get any worse—"

"I'll see where the past cases are, if they're still open or what. Then I'm going to pay another visit to the grieving Mr. Markham and find out more about his late wife. Maybe our guy not only got more violent, he got more specific. And, Evelyn—"

"What?"

"Be careful."

She promised she would and hung up as Tony appraised her with a knowing eye. "What?" she demanded.

"I'd take that advice, if I were you. Obviously this guy doesn't mind getting out of the city now and then."

A tremor ran through her, chilling her from her toes to the pulp of her teeth. Their killer had eluded capture many times. He'd gotten good at it.

And at finding his targets.

A HALF HOUR LATER, David flipped his phone shut. Riley had already left, after informing his partner that the Indians were back and raring to go, and a night baseball game should be regarded as a thing of beauty. Even in the rain.

Five unsolved rape cases. He'd called each department involved, but in every one the Records Department had closed and the case investigator had gone home. Stymied by the workday.

He called Joey Eames, without success. Her weary-sounding roommate told him to check out the bar at the Marriott. After she picked up a new pair of black pumps, Joey planned to anesthetize her pain before Grace Markham's funeral tomorrow.

David stood up and grabbed his blazer. The Marriott stood on the next block, catty-corner to the police department. All he had to do was cross the street.

DESPITE HER STATED INTENTION, Joey Eames seemed completely sober as she chatted up a gray-haired gentleman in the Marriott hotel's subdued maroon interior. The gentleman left as soon as David flashed his badge, peeving Joey Eames.

"What did you do that for? He's in pharmaceuticals and seemed . . . nice. He knows a du Pont." She sipped her cosmopolitan while hitching her skirt another inch up her calf. The new shoes rested in a Nine West bag under her stool.

David ordered a beer. What the hell, his shift had officially ended. "Sorry. It's just habit, announcing myself that way. I thought you might not remember my face."

"I remember everyone's face." She made it sound like a curse. "Have you caught the guy who killed Grace yet?"

"No, and that's what I wanted to ask you about. Do you know Frances Duarte?"

"That woman that was killed in Lakewood? No, wh— Shit! You think it was the same guy that killed Grace?" Three other bar patrons looked up as if deciding to go the way of the pharmaceuticals man. A fourth continued to chase an olive around his martini glass.

"Could you keep your voice down?"

She couldn't. "This is some kind of serial killer psycho dude who kills rich women? Are we all at risk?"

"Joey, please—this is a confidential investigation. I'm exploring all available roads, that's all. Do you know Frances Duarte?"

"All available roads, my ass. Do they teach you phrases like that at a cop seminar?"

"No," he lied. "Frances Duarte?"

"Never met her. I saw her at a party once, on the Franklins' yacht. Kind of a boring little thing. No fashion sense."

"Were she and Grace friends?"

"Grace never mentioned her, though I'm sure they knew each other. Cleveland's a small town, really."

"Did Grace know a Marissa Gonzalez?"

"Doesn't sound familiar."

"I'm sorry, but when did you meet Grace again? I forgot."

"About two, two and a half years ago. In the owner's box at Jacobs Field. A guy I dated at the time knew William, so we started to chat. That rich crowd—I'm not one of them, you know."

David didn't respond. Evelyn had said the reporter had said that Grace and Frances took shopping trips together, but that had stopped before Joey arrived on the social scene. Perhaps Grace had never mentioned Frances. But then, she had never mentioned her pregnancy either to her "inseparable" friend.

Joey fingered her glass, twirling the stem between her thumb and index finger. "I'm sure William told you that I'm some kind of groupie, hanging on to Grace just to get an invite to good parties so I can meet rich men. You're a working guy, right, being a cop?"

"Just a cop. No trust funds out there with my name on them."

"Then you understand."

"Sure." Understand what?

"I'll level with you—William is right. But what else should I do? I've got no family, no education, no talents except friendliness. I can schlep along trying to support myself on minimum wage, or I can marry well. Why shouldn't I give it my best shot?"

"That sounds reasonable." And it did, when she put it that way.

"It's not like I'm some kind of slut. I'm not interested in a quick lay. I'm after a marriage . . . a commitment, kids, a house, all of it."

"That's what I want." Where the hell did that come from, on one-third of a beer? I want to settle down, and no one believes me. Minus the kids part. Evelyn and I are a little past that stage.

Joey didn't pursue his confession. She remained lost in her own history, not even commenting when David had her glass refilled. "If I don't get it, I'll go back to getting by on what I can make waiting tables, but what's so bad about a little proactivity? Hell, William did the same thing. He comes from only a rung or two above me on the social ladder. Grace carried both of us, is the truth."

"Did Grace seem to resent that?"

"Nah. Never. I think she thought carrying people came along with the money. Like cocaine to rock stars, a given."

"Had anything strange happened to Grace lately? A weird phone call, a letter? When you two went clubbing, did anyone pay more attention to her than she wanted?"

Joey snorted. "Clubbing with the beautiful people isn't like hanging with the college students at Shooters. Grace didn't even drink. She quit a few months ago, said it gave her a headache."

When she became pregnant, David thought, wondering again why she hadn't chosen to share that particular piece of information.

"We didn't have to fend off drunk losers. Everyone in our groups belonged there."

"Okay, how about someone who *did* belong? Did Grace have any admirers? Even a sympathetic ear, a friend who didn't care for how William treated her?"

"William came with us sometimes. He wants to see and be seen as much as anybody. But I don't remember Grace ever having a problem like that, ever saying that this guy gave her the creeps or she wished that guy would get lost. She didn't have a care in the world—except for William's piece on the side, of course, and half the time she'd convince herself that the bimbo didn't exist." Joey's eyes grew wet. "A rotten way to treat a woman."

"Yes, it is. Can you go back a week or so, tell me everywhere you two went?" It took a while to note. Joey had a prodigious memory for the places they went, the people they met, even what she and Grace wore. David jotted that information as well; it would help the restaurant and bar staff members recall the two women. If Joey and Grace had had an argument . . . The killer had to be a man, but Joey could have hired someone. And if anyone had ample opportunity to observe Grace's elevator code, Joey had.

A half hour later, with an empty beer glass and a full notebook, he said, "Thanks for your time."

"Mmm." Now on her third drink, she swept him with a look. "Just a government salary, huh?"

"Nothing but."

"Well. Have a nice evening." She turned to scan the room for the pharmaceuticals man.

THE LOBBY INTERCOM AT THE QUAY 55 BUILDING HAD been made with sufficient quality to convey the irritation in William Markham's voice loud and clear. "What the hell are you bothering me at home for?"

"I'm investigating the murder of your wife, sir," David said, clearly and distinctly, noting with satisfaction the way the four tenants passing him in the air lock stopped to listen. It wouldn't take any skin off his nose if they figured out what a first-class bastard they now had for a neighbor. "I didn't think it would be such a bother. If you'd prefer, you can come down to the station in the morning—"

"All right, all right." The buzzer sounded, though David simply followed the other tenants through the heavy glass doors. Quay 55 did not have Riviere-level security, only glossy hardwood floors throughout and a view of Lake Erie from both sides of the building. The other tenants gave him plenty of space during the elevator ride upward, darting glances at one another while avoiding his.

A redhead opened the door, a striking woman with high cheekbones and an eagle's glare. She took a moment to size him up, but not as Joey Eames had. A debate took place behind her eyes, as if she were trying to decide how much of a threat he represented. Without any obvious conclusion, she stood back to let him in.

"I'm Barbara Quinn. I'm sure you've heard about me."

"Yes. You're the piece on the side." Let's get her on the defensive, see what she does.

"To Grace's friends, that would be me, yes," she stated with neither relish nor shame. He followed her into an airy, modern space with a huge flat-screen TV and a fireplace. Tall, abstract wood sculptures placed here and there accented the floor, almost like in Frances Duarte's apartment, though these seemed more like artwork than travel souvenirs. Barbara Quinn planted her slim body in its flowing pantsuit in an armchair and motioned for him to have a seat. "To William's friends, I have saved him from a life of misery. I'm the woman he's *not* marrying for the money."

David kept his voice neutral, matching her frankness. "But he doesn't need to now, does he? He has Grace's estate."

"He already knows he doesn't need it, and it's not worth the price. Grace was a nice person, and we're sorry she's dead. William married her for her money, but she married him to have a baby. It was not a happy marriage."

"Perhaps so, but Grace didn't want it to end. Did you know she planned to hire a private investigator?"

"But she didn't, did she?" Barbara pointed out, crossing one long leg over the other. "Grace didn't really want to know. You forget, this is a woman who covered wars in the Middle East. If she wanted proof, she could have simply followed William to work in her own car with her own collection of telephoto lenses. But no, she ignored all the signs, then got agitated enough to confront him. A child could tell he lied, but she chose not to see it. As I said, I'm sorry she's dead, but beyond that I don't have a lot of sympathy for her. She made her own decisions."

"Why didn't William tell her the truth, then?"

"Ask him yourself."

The man in question appeared, dressed in a thick terry-cloth bathrobe, which seemed a strange way to attend an interrogation.

Apparently Markham truly did *not* care what people thought of him. Of course, David thought, now he can afford not to.

"I married Grace for her money," William Markham admitted without a shred of self-consciousness as he threw himself into the leather upholstery. "I'm going to marry Barbara for her strength. Believe it or not, I really do want the people around me to be happy. I get uncomfortable when they're not. I planned to keep Grace as happy as possible until after the baby came, and then tell her. I didn't kill her, though only Barbara and I seem to know that. The papers are acting like I'm the next Sam Sheppard."

"So she did not know for sure that Barbara existed?"

"No."

"Or her name, address, nothing like that so far as you knew?"

"Of course not. That's what I just said."

"As Ms. Quinn pointed out, Grace was a resourceful woman." David looked at the redhead, now sipping an amber-colored liquid from a snifter. "She never contacted you?"

She shook her head, framing her face with curls. "Never."

David tried to recall the surveillance video, if a woman matching Barbara Quinn's description had entered the elevator with a man. She could easily have gotten the code from Markham, and she had the second-best motive after his. But David would have noticed a woman like her on the video. She looked something like Evelyn, but skinnier and much harder.

She could have hired a killer, of course. He wondered if he could get a warrant for her financial records and check for large, recent withdrawals. Probably not. Motive, no matter how blatant, did not by itself constitute probable cause. Not in this legal age.

"Did Grace babysit?" He mixed around his questions to keep both of them off guard—if Barbara Quinn ever got off guard.

Markham seemed baffled. "Babysit? Like, children?"

"Yes. Her friends' children, that sort of thing."

"Never. Lots of our friends have kids, of course, but they're not usually at the types of events we go to, and I couldn't have stood little kids running around my penthouse." He gave a tiny shudder.

David pictured the white walls, white carpeting, and glass coffee table. "I just ask because you have a child's drawing hanging on the refrigerator. I wondered where it came from."

Barbara drummed long fingers on the side of her glass while Markham looked blank. "I have no idea. I never noticed it."

"It's a picture, done in crayon on buff paper. Do you know how long it's been hanging there?"

"No. It could have been there for the past two months for all I know. Grace never kept much in the refrigerator, so I sort of ignored it."

"Yeah." David wondered if William Markham knew anything about his wife other than her society connections and her bank account. "We noticed your fridge didn't seem too stocked. Did you and Grace eat out a lot?"

"Just about every night. Grace didn't cook."

"Did you get food delivered often?"

"Yeah, all the time."

"How did the delivery person get to your apartment? Did you give them your code?"

"Hardly. Barbara doesn't even know our code—I mean, she didn't need it."

Her eyes skewered him over the rim of her glass. "I know what you meant, dear."

"We'd meet the kid in the lobby."

"They wouldn't come up to the apartment?"

"Penthouse. No."

"It doesn't matter if it's an apartment or a penthouse, dear," Barbara pointed out. To David, she explained, "Old habits die hard."

"They do indeed," he said, wondering how Barbara Quinn, whose father's wealth still meandered through probate, could afford a loft at Quay 55. Perhaps she had received a generous severance package from the firm of Markham & Johnson. "You were engaged before you married Grace, weren't you, Mr. Markham?"

"Yes."

"Who were you engaged to?"

"Girl named Kelly. A very wealthy girl named Kelly." He scowled a bit. Having reformed his gold-digger ways did not ease the sting of past failures. "Her family owns the salt mines."

"Kelly Alexander?"

"Yes. You've heard of her?"

Joey could have translated Markham's look—that an average schmo like David would never have had occasion to meet the rich salt mine heiress. "Yes. When were you engaged to Ms. Alexander?"

"About eight years ago. We were too young, only about twenty-one. We met at Princeton."

"And Kelly had a little more on the ball than Grace," Barbara said, swirling her liquor.

"Okay, Kelly figured my interest lay more in her portfolio than in her. Is that what you want me to say?"

"Honesty is our policy now, darling."

He let out a harsh breath of air, but his irritation dissipated with it. "Kelly tossed me like last week's milk, and about a year later I met Grace."

David made a casual note, wondering how to phrase his next questions, not even sure where they were headed. "You both move in the same social circles. It must have been awkward when you and Grace ran into her."

"No, not at all. Kelly and I parted on good terms, no hard feelings. She married a few years later, for love, apparently. At least on her part. The guy is this geeky little geologist who works at her dad's salt mine—tell me *he* didn't get a good deal."

"Grace didn't mind socializing with her after you two got together?"

"Mind? They were friends. Their families had known each other since they were kids—that's how Grace and I met, really. I'd still see Kelly now and then and ran into Grace at one of the Alexanders' soirees. Kelly threw us an engagement dinner."

"Did Grace invest with Kelly?"

"Invest?"

"When Kelly Alexander began her project to open the new salt mine, she had several investors. Did Grace buy any shares?"

"Oh, that. No way. Here I am trying to keep some semblance of nightlife in the Flats alive and Kelly puts a damn *factory* at the mouth of the river. I don't know who she bribed to get the permits, after the city spent years forcing out the stone and material-handling companies."

"You're sure Grace didn't buy in."

"Grace knew how I felt about it, and we always discussed the finances."

Barbara stirred. "As you might expect, that was the one aspect of the marriage William took a great interest in."

"I gave her the damn baby, didn't I?"

She sipped without expression.

He swallowed his anger quickly and, it seemed, easily. "I had to pay attention to the money. Grace had stocks and bonds and funds out the wazoo, and rarely kept up on what they were doing. I know she hadn't invested in anything new since the last millennium. We hardly ever saw Kelly anymore."

"Why not?"

"She's too much of a party girl, even after she married that geek. Grace didn't want much to do with that."

"Yet Grace went clubbing with Joey Eames."

"Yeah, but not often. They did more shopping and charity dinners and stuff like that. Kelly takes fifty of her closest friends to Aruba for the weekend, attends the Olympics, never misses Cannes."

"It's surprising Joey didn't angle for an invitation to Kelly's." David prodded the man's antagonism, hoping for an unguarded disclosure—but everything William Markham said seemed un-guarded. The imperturbable Barbara would have made a more interesting sparring partner.

"She has. But Kelly would cut Joey down to size with two words and a nod. She's not softhearted, like Grace."

"Did you or Grace know Frances Duarte?"

"Kind of a dowdy woman. I think she came to Grace's wedding shower, something like that."

Barbara perked up. "That woman that was killed in Lakewood?"

"You must move in the same circles," David said.

"You think the same man killed both Grace and this Frances Duarte?" Barbara seemed, in her elegant way, even more excited than Markham—and why not? It would clear her intended from any suspicion in Grace's murder. A wandering psycho with a resentment for rich women would be the answer to Barbara Quinn's prayers.

"We have to explore all possibilities. Would Frances and Grace visit each other?"

"Not that I recall." What had occurred immediately to Barbara came a bit more slowly to Markham. "She was murdered too? And you think it's the same guy?"

"We're going to find out."

William Markham settled back into his chair. "Man, that would be great."

David stared at him.

"What do you expect me to say? After all"—he beamed at his new fiancée—"honesty is our policy now."

"THE SWELLING'S GONE DOWN," ROBERT TOLD EVELYN as they stood outside Marissa's hospital room. The young woman's fiancé even had some color back in his face. "We're hoping to remove the breathing tube tomorrow."

Evelyn breathed a sigh of relief. Once the sedatives wore off and Marissa regained consciousness, maybe she could answer some questions. Evelyn doubted the girl would remember much about the attack, but perhaps she could shed some light on Mark Sargeant. Not that Evelyn would stop probing—she had no intention of waiting a whole day. "I'm glad. Robert, did she ever talk about doing an internship in pathology at Butterfly Babies and Children's?"

The relaxation flushed out of his body. "She mentioned it once or twice."

"What's the matter? She didn't like it?"

"She said the lab director was a creep. That's all she'd say, creep, quote unquote." The memory obviously troubled him, and he kept his voice low. Mama Gonzalez stood at the nurses' station, fifteen feet away, letting the sympathetic women ply her with coffee and cookies. Or perhaps he didn't want the sleeping Marissa to pick up his words.

"But you think there was more to it?"

"She didn't say. But we don't have secrets between us, so I'm sure she would have told me if it were important."

"Has she been planning to donate to the hospital? Or you? Were you thinking of taking a position there?"

"The idea crosses my mind now and then, usually when my bank account seems less than healthy. They're a great facility, but I'm happy here."

"Okay. I'm going to go hold her hand for a minute, then I have to go. The cop has been good about standing guard? Where is he now?"

"He's taking a bathroom break while I'm here."

"Just don't leave her on her own."

The young doctor gave her a dead-tired smile. "She'll never be on her own. But, Evelyn?"

"Yes."

"Don't fall asleep."

She chewed a fingernail. "Absolutely not."

TWENTY MINUTES LATER she crossed the parking lot in a driving rain. No secrets, Robert had said.

You sweet, naive boy. Everyone has secrets.

He'd also said Marissa would not be alone. According to David, neither would Evelyn, if she chose to have him move in. She stepped back from a passing car, avoiding the splash of rainwater from its tires.

Trouble was, she kind of liked it . . . running her home the way she wanted, paying the bills she chose to create, scheduling her time off without someone else's approval. Was this independent? Or self-ish, set in her ways? Did she really want to be alone for the rest of her life, with no one but the cat and the TV set and maybe pictures of grandchildren for company?

"Didn't your mother ever teach you to come in out of the rain?"

She turned. David stood there, getting wet.

"I figured you'd stop here on the way home from the lab. We need to talk."

"Yes," she admitted. "We do."

"Mind if we do it somewhere drier?"

"That sounds like a terrific idea." She moved up to meet him, sliding one arm around him, holding up the umbrella with the other, and they kissed as if they had not seen each other in eight weeks instead of eight hours. Rain soaked his hair, and the water made the decomp smell waft up from her lab coat. A laid-out SUV in a handicapped parking space began to beep at them to move out of the way, and still Evelyn felt it was the most romantic moment in her life to date. She wanted to collapse into his arms and never leave. She would have promised him anything.

"Actually," he said when they finally moved to let the car back out, "I meant we need to compare notes on Grace and Frances. But that can wait."

"It can, indeed."

THEY DID NOT discuss either Grace and Frances's killer or their future together. They did not discuss much of anything at all.

David's dog, Harry, woke her by licking her toes. She went from pleasant slumber to sweating panic in less than two seconds.

"What time is it?"

"Hmm?"

"It's almost ten—I have to go! Angel's going to wonder where the hell I am." She gathered her things so quickly that Harry began to bounce around, expecting a walk or at least some form of exercise. "I can't believe I fell asleep."

"Yeah, for two hours. You haven't slept in over two *days*, Evelyn, and neither have I."

"I know, but I still have to go home. As soon as you and Riley run down the reports on those five rapes, can you bring them by the office? We could sit down and talk over everything we have. Now I really have to go."

David sat up, rubbing one eye. "Okay, I'll drive you."

"What?"

"You left your car at the hospital, remember?"

"Crap!" She pulled her coat on, snagging a finger on the sleeve cuff. "Okay, then. Come on."

He stood up, wearily stretching. "Geesh, Evelyn, relax. She's seventeen years old."

After three days without sleep, she did not have the patience to keep a frigid tone from her words. "You don't have to tell me how old my daughter is."

"Okay," he grumbled. "Fine."

EVELYN HUNG UP her coat and emptied out her lunch bag, fed the cat, and folded the laundry. All the little things that held her life together. "You didn't have to follow me home."

"I didn't feel like being alone tonight," David said, drinking a beer at her kitchen table. "And I'm betting you don't either. So where is she?"

"She's supposed to be home by nine-thirty. It's a school night. She's usually good about it—beauty rest and all."

From the garage she heard the cat meow, and then the door burst open. Angel and Steve came in with their arms around each other, and Evelyn instantly saw the problem.

Angel staggered more than walked, and clung to the boy for support. Steve seemed steady, though damn startled to see David there. Evelyn did not introduce them.

"Hi, Mom!" her daughter said brightly. "Shorry we're—sorry we're late." She drew herself up to her full height, made direct eye contact albeit with reddened eyes, and enunciated her words with such care that it would have been funny under other circumstances. "I know it's a school night."

Not for the first time, Evelyn wondered what sort of fantasy world she had been living in when she named her daughter Angel. "You've been drinking."

"No! Um—I wasn't. It's just—"

Evelyn turned her attention to the young man with the baggy pants and that ridiculous nose stud. At least he had the grace to look sheepish, unless it had been planned along with the direct looks and the respectful tone. "On the way home from the library we stopped at Don McAfee's house. He had a spur-of-the-moment party because his parents, um, weren't around."

"Mmm-hmm." She did not recognize the name. Angel was making all sorts of new friends.

"He gave Angel a beer."

A beer, as in singular. And I'm sure he simply *forced* it on her. "Mmm-hmm."

"Then I figured I'd better drive her home."

Evelyn sorted through several scenarios. One, Steve knew exactly what his buddy Don had planned for the evening. Free beer, no supervision, partly empty house . . . and had plied her daughter with alcohol, preparatory to peeling off her clothes. Angel's clothing seemed in order, but the sober Steve would have had the presence of mind to see to that. Two, Angel, underweight and unused to drink, had gotten utterly silly on exactly one beer, and Steve had been enough of a gentleman to drive her home . . . if not enough of one to drive her home on time.

From the corner of her eye, she saw David open his mouth, so she preempted him. "It's time for you to go home, Steve."

Despite her cold tone, he grinned with palpable relief, and got while the getting was good.

Angel swayed slightly. "I didn't think you'd be home."

Evelyn deflected the guilt reflex and counterattacked. "Come off it, Angel. I miss two meals and I'm an absentee parent? You really think that's going to work?"

"It's been more than two."

"I know what you mean," David muttered from behind them.

Evelyn turned her head toward him. "It's time for you to go home too."

"This *is* my home. At least I thought that was the plan."

"That was *your* plan," she said before she could stop herself.

Angel turned, one hand on the wall. "I'm going to bed."

"Good idea. And by the way, you're grounded for the next month."

"A month! What about the spring formal?"

"Tough."

"You can't do that!"

"This way you'll think before you act next time. I'm supposed to do that. It's my job."

"You're job is working with dead people," Angel wailed. "And I'm not dead!"

"And I want you to stay that way. Don't you *get* that?"

"By locking me up?" Angel's wavering gaze swiveled around to David. "Isn't a month ridiculous? It's not like I'm freebasing crack."

"She's got a point," he said to Evelyn. "We did the same thing at her age."

She looked at him, feeling as though she'd never seen him before. "How would you know what I did at her age? And you," she added to her daughter, "go to bed."

Angel crossed her arms, wavering. "You are *not* grounding me."

"Want to bet?"

For a moment, Evelyn thought her daughter might walk out. She could; she had money, friends, and a father to go to. Evelyn would not have been able to stop it. Beads of cold sweat pricked her skin.

But weariness and perhaps an attack of self-reproach won out, and Angel whirled so fast she lost her balance and thudded up the stairs. Evelyn listened to the squeak of the bedsprings as Angel's dead weight collapsed across them. Only then did she turn to David. "Don't *ever* side with my daughter against me."

David slid his empty bottle to the center of the table, gently but pointedly. "We all tried beer in high school. They're drinking it in grade school these days."

"And what happened? We got in trouble. That's what happens when parents give a crap. I know you want to get in good with my daughter before moving in, but this is not the way to do it."

He stood, scraping the chair legs along the tile. "This isn't some power play, Evelyn. I just happen to think you're wrong. Kids respond better if you're truthful with them."

"You don't even have kids, David. What the hell do you know about raising them?"

He let that sink in on the way to the door. "Thanks. It's nice to feel valued."

"This has nothing to do with value. You can't expect to have an equal say in raising my child, David. You simply can't."

"In case you haven't noticed, you're a little past the raising stage. She's almost a woman. And you can't expect me to become part of this family and then sit quietly and keep my thoughts to myself. That's not going to happen."

But that was what she wanted, she realized. She wanted David close to her, inside her household, without disturbing one iota of its dynamics, and that would not be possible. In frustration she countered: "No one's holding a gun to your head."

"Hell." He pulled the door open. "No one's even leaving a light on."

The wall shook as the door slammed. Evelyn locked it and turned out the kitchen light, wishing she could disappear into the darkness like a wisp of fog. She had gone through a difficult divorce to get her autonomy back and could not share it with anyone. But without David she had nothing to look forward to but an ordered, dedicated existence with a pool of loneliness at its core.

Abruptly she realized her feet were cold and she needed to get an empty wastebasket to put beside Angel's bed in case of a nighttime emergency. Perhaps she could garner a few more details at the same time. The testimony of a person under the influence might be inadmissible according to the rules of law, but it wasn't according to the rules of parenting.

Upstairs, she found Angel gazing at the ceiling, the light still on, as if expecting her. Without turning her head she said, "David's moving in?"

Y OU'RE IN EARLY," MRS. ANDERSON SNAPPED AT her. "I haven't even had my first coffee yet and you're prancing through the lobby like a human alarm clock."

"I couldn't sleep." Evelyn slid her buff-colored time card into the slot to receive its stamp, feeling the thump vibrate through the piece of heavy paper. "I wound up talking to my daughter for half the night and staring into the darkness for the other half. I got an hour or two, so I should feel better."

"*Should* being the operative word?"

"I think my brain has stripped a gear—it keeps turning and turning without doing anything."

"It just needs oil," the older woman said. "I recommend Southern Comfort."

Evelyn walked up the three squat floors to the lab, turned on the lights, and started the coffee. Then she filled up the FTIR with liquid nitrogen and pulled out the four sets of crayons she had bought on her way to the hospital yesterday afternoon. Crayola dominated the market, but she had found other brands: Rose Art, Creative Crayons, and Bic, as in Bic pens.

These crayons consisted mostly of paraffin wax and pigment. She ignored the pigments, since such a range of colors existed, and discovered that the base substance varied only slightly. None was an exact match for the samples on Grace's and Frances's clothing.

Evelyn noted the results absently, her mind occupied. David would arrive after he and Riley had visited the various police departments to schmooze with the suburban detectives and ask for copies of their reports. She was so *not* ready to see him. This was why work relationships were a bad idea. She occupied herself with backed-up clothing examinations and the vacuumings from Grace's apartment for three hours until they arrived.

She and David greeted each other soberly, as if someone they knew had died. She would have preferred anger.

The Medical Examiner's Office building's single conference room had a large table, threadbare carpeting, and wooden, 1950s-style cabinets, but at least they could spread out. A line of chatter streamed from Records down the hall, and the fluorescent lights hummed.

"Let me guess," Evelyn said. "The victims were all wealthy and involved in charities."

Riley made an obnoxious sound, like a buzzer. "I hope you didn't place any bets on that, Evie, because you'd be busted. Not a rich girl among them."

Her jaw went slack for a moment. "You have to be kidding me."

"He not only moved up to murder but moved up to a higher brand of victim." David slid a report from the Solon PD across the table to her so that their fingers did not touch. "This first rape victim—at least the first that we know of—was a biology major sharing a duplex. A Tuesday night in April, four years ago. He grabbed her from behind as she used her key in the door after a late class. He wore a mask, so she never saw his face and was too traumatized to tell the detectives any more than that. The second happened in December of that same year, to a married schoolteacher, mother of three, single-family home in Parma."

"Not an apartment?" Parma had long been the suburb most

picked on for having a high tally of bowling alleys, white socks with loafers, and lawn ornaments, though not violent crime.

"Nope, a house. She went to the hospital and had the kit taken, but only after detectives promised never to contact her at home. She refused to tell her husband or her children, so if we get in touch with her, we'll have to be careful."

Evelyn shifted on the thinly cushioned chair as empathy shocked her out of her personal funk. "To go through that and then have to pretend, every day, that you're fine and everything's normal . . ."

"It's been three and a half years, so that might have changed, but we'll be careful anyway."

"He wore a mask in that one too," Riley put in. "She noticed he had duct tape around the neck, even."

Evelyn pondered that as David went on. "The next, July three years ago, occurred in the victim's apartment at East Fifty-fifth and Superior, a welfare mom whose kids were at school."

Riley took off his jacket. The spring weather made it too warm for heat and too cool for air-conditioning, and the room felt stuffy. "Definitely not an acquaintance of Grace Markham's."

"The door lock wouldn't catch half the time, so he got in that way and surprised her in a dark bedroom. She couldn't be sure if he wore a mask or not, but she didn't get a good look at him. She could only remember being terrified—her twelve-year-old daughter would be coming home from school any minute, and the idea that he might attack the little girl made her fight tooth and nail. Literally— she bit him, said he should have a scar on his shoulder."

"Good for her."

"Also good for us that the rape kit gave us DNA results, because it apparently didn't occur to the detective on the case to take the sheets with the guy's blood." A huff of breath made it clear what David thought about sloppy work. "The fourth victim, attacked in July two years ago, lived alone in a nice high-rise in Euclid, only a block from the lake. Not on a par with the Markham residence, but nice enough for a camera in the lobby, which didn't show any strangers. Of course, the side doors work on a buzzer, and our guy could have just followed a tenant in. She didn't even know he stood behind her when she opened the door."

Evelyn shuddered. "Hell."

"This is not the guy you should be chasing into dark parking garages."

She glared. It didn't help when Riley added, "He's got a point there, Evie."

"How come when men do something dangerous, they're brave, but when women do it, they're stupid?"

"I don't want you brave," David said, snapping out the words as if they pained him. "I want you alive."

It felt good to hear he wanted her at all.

"It's all hindsight," Riley said. "If you succeed, then you were brave. If you fail you were stupid."

She held up her right hand in weak protest. "All right. I promise not to chase this guy into dark parking garages . . . if I can help it. Go on."

"The fifth case, September of last year: victim came home to the near West Side from the night shift at the Ford plant. She passed her husband in the parking lot, they chatted, he headed off to work, and she went inside. She thinks the guy followed her from the stairwell and wished she'd listened to the little warning bell in the back of her mind, according to the report, but she was tired. He grabbed her before she even got her key in the lock, and that's all she could remember. He must have smashed her skull into the doorjamb, or else he brought a weapon with him, because she came to two hours later on her living room floor with one hell of a headache."

He stopped. The three people in the room mulled over these stark facts. Up the hall someone burst out with a harsh laugh.

"He got more violent with the last one," Evelyn observed. "Perhaps he escalated to murder even before Grace Markham—or Frances, I keep forgetting she died first. There could be bodies out there we haven't found, in wooded areas or landfills."

David shook his head. "I get the feeling he likes getting to them on their own turf. It turns him on."

"Let's not forget Marissa," Evelyn said. "He attacked her in the parking garage, so he's not always perfectly consistent. If he could get into Grace's apartment, why not Marissa's?"

Riley pulled out a cigarette and rolled it between his fingers without lighting it. "Maybe he thought the boyfriend would be home. The architect's a nine-to-five guy, but like you said before, the doc's hours are less regular."

"Do we know how he got into Frances's building?"

"No," David told her. "We canvassed every family there. No one admitted to holding the side door for a person who wasn't a tenant. One of them might have forgotten or is embarrassed to admit it, but that's what we're left with. The camera in the lobby didn't pick up any strangers."

"They're all in apartments except the teacher in Parma." Evelyn started to put the end of her pen in her mouth, then stopped herself. She could never keep her "dirty" pens—ones she'd used after touching bloody bodies or clothing—separate from the "clean" ones. "Did any of the last two victims mention a mask?"

"The fifth never saw him, obviously. The fourth—" David paged through the reports, now spread over the worn table. "Yes. Ski mask."

"Taped on?"

"Doesn't say."

"I wonder. That attack in Parma is the only one in a single-family home and the only one that mentions the mask being taped on—two factors that don't match the other incidents. He wanted to be extra-sure she didn't get a look at him." Evelyn shrugged.

"You think she knew him?" David asked.

"It's possible. Unless he taped on the mask in every case, and the victims just didn't have a chance to notice it. He could be a neighbor, or an acquaintance. What grade does she teach?"

"Doesn't say. You think it could be a student?"

"Or the father of a student, or another teacher. The victims were a college student and two mothers, one a teacher. Grace wanted a baby and worked with the children's hospital charity. Frances spent time with her great-nieces. But two of the victims had no children at all, and the college student wouldn't have been at the same school as the children of the other two. It's probably nothing."

"Nothing is about all we have to go on," Riley said. "That's why we can't make this information public yet. The city would panic."

Evelyn passed the reports back. "Maybe it should."

"Yeah, that's all we need. I'm going outside for a smoke."

David gathered his folders. "Marissa has no children or any connection to a school. Did you say she worked for the children's hospital charity?"

"No. The man who heads fund-raising now worked in pathology when she did her internship there. Maybe there is no connection between the women at all and we're chasing our tails. He might just follow them off the bus. Maybe he worked in their buildings."

"We could check. Seven buildings in four years—that's pretty short-lived employment. Other staff might remember him if he caused a problem, got fired. But the Parma one wasn't in a building but a private home. And the duplex wouldn't have had maintenance staff on the premises."

Evelyn rubbed the bridge of her nose. "There's got to be something. The problem is that whatever the connection is, it might be so bloody obscure that we'll never find it. We need to track him down another way, don't ask me how. We don't even have a general description, just a series of DNA amino acids."

"You get any sleep?"

"Not as much as I need. How about you?"

"The same." He studied her with a weary squint.

She wanted to say she was sorry, but she wasn't sure what for. This whole moving-in thing was a bad idea, she decided, bound to create one conflict after another—Angel, money, space. She should write him off. Say good-bye.

But she couldn't say good-bye. Not now, not ever. "I'm sorry."

"So am I." His resigned manner made the hairs on her arms stand up. Was it really over?

Riley strode back in. "You ready, partner? Indians at Twins tonight. I've got to be at Flanagan's by eight to place my bets."

David stood up. Evelyn asked what they planned to do.

"We're going to reinterview the five victims, try to find out what they had in common with Grace Markham and Frances Duarte. If we don't come out of that with a solid lead, then I want to talk to this Kelly Alexander."

"You think this could all be about money?"

David paused at the door. "Probably not. But we haven't got much else to go on. What about you?"

"I've got hairs, I've got fibers. I hope they have something interesting to say."

"Evelyn?"

"Yes?"

"Stay out of dark parking garages."

THE VACUUMINGS FROM GRACE MARKHAM'S APART-
ment consisted of fibers from her wool carpet, hairs, other
fibers, bits of popcorn, one dead fly, and a tiny rhinestone
button. Most of the hairs seemed consistent with Grace and her husband, but seven seemed inconsistent. Human hairs could be
"matched" only if they had attached skin cells, which could be analyzed for nuclear DNA. The hair shaft could be identified with mitochondrial DNA, but it would have to be sent to the FBI lab for
that more complicated analysis, and results could take months. No
two hairs were ever the same, but if the range of characteristics—
color, medulla, cortical fusi—in the questioned hair all fell into the
same range of characteristics of hairs from the known sample, then
Evelyn could say the questioned hair could have come from that person. She could not get more definite than "could have," an answer
that most cops and prosecutors did not care for, so hair comparisons
were a quickly dying art.

Four of the seven were short and dark—she could check if they
might be the cleaning woman's. Of the other three, only one had a
root, a dried-up anagen bulb, which meant that the hair had stopped
growing and probably fallen out of its own accord. The remaining
two, a dirty-blond color, could give up mitochondrial DNA, but

they already had DNA at the scene. Talking the FBI lab into mitochondrial analysis simply to find out if the hairs matched the semen made little sense.

The too-numerous fibers were no more help. They would be helpful only when compared with the killer's clothing, which of course they didn't have. She poked through them anyway, in case one seemed particularly unusual. At 40× magnification, one fiber, a thick, blackened thing, resembled a tree branch with the rough, irregular surface of a natural plant fiber. From the slide filing cabinet, a squat, unlovely metal box with skinny drawers to accommodate glass slides placed on their ends, she retrieved a few examples from her reference collection of mounted fibers. After a few minutes, she decided it must be hemp.

Hemp is a remarkably useful plant fiber, related to but markedly different from the marijuana plant. Hemp fibers can be found in items from rope to oil. Hemp jewelry had become increasingly popular in recent years. Grace Markham didn't seem to go for the surfer look, but supporting hemp allowed people to feel they were pro-marijuana mavericks without actually breaking the law, so doing so might appeal to wealthy types wanting to keep it real.

This hemp had been dirtied. Using a stereomicroscope, which functioned as a very powerful magnifying glass, Evelyn scraped a trace of the contaminant from the fiber onto the gold plate for FTIR analysis. In no time at all she found herself staring at a spectrum matching the oil on Grace Markham's arm. The grease that didn't match the elevator or the safe lock mechanism or the fire door lock mechanism. So the hemp fiber had come from the killer.

Their case consisted of crayons, grease, two dirty-blond hairs, hemp, blue fibers, and the DNA of a serial rapist, now murderer. And no apparent connection among the victims, except for Grace and Frances, and that could be a coincidence.

Each woman had been attacked in her own home, but not all lived alone. Perhaps the victims didn't know one another, but the killer knew them. He knew when there would be no one else at home. He knew that the schoolteacher's kids were elsewhere and that Frances Duarte's neighbors were out of town. He knew that, if they managed to cry out, no one would hear them. He had planned the attacks, at least for days.

But he had moved on to murder, choosing two women of more wealth than his past victims, attacking one in a virtual fortress of an apartment. Why? What had spurred him on to murder in the first place? Why strap the dead women up, when the rape victims hadn't been bound in any way? Why crayon on the clothing?

The rich women worked with the hospital charity. The first rape victim majored in biology. Perhaps she had done a rotation in a path lab, like Marissa? Evelyn would call David and ask him to find out. The other victims had children.

Lunchtime had arrived. If she wanted to wander through Butterfly Babies & Children's Hospital on her way to the food court at the medical school, what could be wrong with that?

The hospital was only one of Frances's and Grace's charities, and it might not have any significance in their deaths. But there *were* those damn crayon marks.

Only the primary colors on the walls and the cartoon-character draperies distinguished the children's wing from the rest of the hospital. Most of the beds were adult-size, which only called attention to the tiny forms between the sheets. A toddler lay preternaturally still, watching a television program with glazed eyes. A girl of about ten had one leg in traction and a restraining order posted on her door. Another talked gaily on the phone, the bandanna slipping off her bald head as she demanded to know where the D.A.R.E. dance would be held.

Evelyn said a prayer of thanksgiving as she walked that Angel had been born healthy and remained healthy. Now if they could only get through the early driving years. The busy nurses watched her curiously, warily. An unknown doctor on the floor could not be a good thing, but they did not question her.

At the end of the second-floor hall sat an activities room, occupied by a white boy sleeping on the couch and a black girl of about ten. The girl sat at a round table in a chair slightly too small for her, coloring. Crayons littered the table, on and around several dog-eared coloring books. Evelyn approached her as cautiously as she would have a pile of broken glass. Other people's children made her nervous. Hell, her *own* made her nervous.

She wedged her butt into an undersize chair and picked up a book. It featured Japanese cartoon characters she had never seen before, but she paged through it and picked up a red crayon, stopping at the picture of a dragon.

The little girl looked at her with a skeptical expression and a large scar down her left temple. An IV drip on a portable stand snaked down to her tiny forearm. "Who're you?"

"I work next door. I'm just taking a break for a while."

The girl couldn't have had any idea which "next door" Evelyn meant, but she nodded as if she did.

"What's your name?"

"Cadence."

"That's a cool name," Evelyn said truthfully. "Where'd you get that?"

"From my *parents.*" At least she refrained from adding *well, duh!*

Evelyn colored the dragon's eye, squirming with embarrassment.

Cadence relented after a moment, adding, "My father plays in a band when he's not doing his Army job. He's in Iraq right now."

"I see." Evelyn put down the red crayon, picked up a green. She had not seen the brand—Sander—before. "What are you doing here?"

"I have a brain tumor."

"Oh."

"They took part of it out. But part dug into my skull bone."

"Oh." What the hell else could she say to a ten-year-old who dealt with weightier problems in one day than Evelyn had in a lifetime? Her divorce seemed like the Electric Slide compared with this girl's daily dance. "Have you been here long?"

Cadence didn't answer, instead leaning forward to view Evelyn's work. "You're supposed to stay inside the lines."

"I know."

"What are you writing next to the dragon?"

"The brand and color names of the crayons."

The girl's eyebrows moved toward each other, making it clear that, while she had doubted Evelyn's intelligence before, now she had serious doubts about her mental stability.

"I'm interested in crayons," Evelyn added weakly.

"Oh."

They colored in silence for a while. The boy slumbered on the couch, deathly pale but wheezing just enough to keep Evelyn from hitting the nurse call button.

"They're going to build a new wing here, you know."

Cadence did not, apparently, find the topic fascinating. "Yeah."

"Does anyone here ever talk about that?" Great detective work here, girlfriend. You're pumping a ten-year-old in case she has time for philanthropic work between the chemo treatments.

"Yeah." Cadence viewed Evelyn's bizarre work again, permitting herself a small shake of the head. "I went to some fancy dinner last Christmas. I sat at a table on the stage, and some guy talked about me. The nurses said it was so people could see what they were donating money for. My mom said it was a dog and pony show, but there weren't any animals."

Evelyn suppressed a smile. "Do you remember any of the people who were there?"

"Nah. But we had ice cream for dessert. With cherries."

"I love that."

"So do I," said a new voice. Clio Helms, from the *Plain Dealer*, stood in the doorway. "Hello, Cadence. Mrs. James."

"Ms. Helms." Did the nurses let just anyone wander around this floor? Evelyn, at least, had the passport, a white lab coat. But then parents and family probably visited at all hours, and their personal contact had to be more important than security, and not too many kidnappers targeted gravely ill children.

The reporter asked, "What are you doing here?"

"She's taking a break," Cadence explained. "But she can't color very good."

"Really."

Evelyn watched the woman saunter over and join them, taking sadistic pleasure in seeing Clio wedge her twenty-something butt into one of the Lilliputian chairs. Which she did with much less effort than Evelyn had. "And what are you doing here?"

The reporter picked up a crayon. "Same as you. Trying to find a connection between Grace Markham and Frances Duarte. So far, only this children's hospital comes up. What about you?"

She doesn't know about the five rapes, Evelyn reminded herself. See that she doesn't learn of them from you. "I work right next door."

"And you hang out here?"

"I was on my way to lunch."

"Excellent idea! I'll buy. How about it, Cadence? We can pop over to Club Isabella's and have some fettuccine."

The girl giggled. "I can't. I have to stay here."

"We'll get it to go. Prime rib okay?"

The girl giggled again. Evelyn used the moment to pull, quietly, the page with the dragon picture from the book. She could not do it quietly enough.

Cadence frowned. "You're not supposed to tear the pages out."

"I'm sorry." Evelyn couldn't have felt worse if she'd yanked out the girl's IV. "I didn't know that."

"*Everyone* knows that."

"Don't be too hard on her," Clio said. "I think Evelyn really needs that picture."

Cadence just shook her head.

"Come on, Evelyn." Clio stood up, smoothed her skirt, and patted the little girl on the back. "Excuse us, Cadence. We need to talk."

The girl waved a desultory hand, without looking up. "Whatever."

Clio waited until they had entered the elevator before asking. "So what's on the coloring book page?"

"A dragon."

"Can I see it?"

"My artistic abilities are not for public viewing."

"I meant what I said about lunch. I'll buy. I get an expense account for such things."

Over her rumbling stomach, Evelyn declined. The elevator doors opened into the lobby.

"Can't be seen consorting with the enemy, huh?"

Evelyn paused to face her, next to the potted trees. "You're not the enemy. But people have died here, and I have to respect their memories and the grief of their families. I can't chat about the intimate details of their last moments just to see my name in print."

Golden brown eyes appraised her. "I can understand that. But we've got a psycho running around, and catching him before he kills another woman is more important than etiquette."

"I'm not going to be catching him. I'm a scientist, I analyze things. Detectives catch people."

"But you've got a friend in the mix, which gives you more incentive." Clio crossed her arms, wrinkling the lapels of her tailored suit. "My money's on you."

"Fine. Then tell me if you found out more about Grace and Frances." Evelyn continued her march toward the exit doors.

"They had stopped hanging out, apparently, but they were both on this hospital expansion campaign. The hospital needs seventy-five million, and so far they've got about fifty. Actually, the books say they have fifty. The auditors say they have thirty-five."

"How do you know all this?"

"A friend of mine is preparing a series on fraud in high-dollar charities. She's been chatting up every financial consultant in town and let me see her research."

They emerged from the building into yet another Cleveland spring drizzle. "You're saying fifteen million dollars are missing?"

"I'm saying there's a rumor going around that the auditors found some major discrepancies last month. Nothing is official yet."

"And what part did Grace and Frances play in this?"

"Frances pledged a cool million during a dinner that Grace organized, last Christmas."

Evelyn thought about this during the short walk across the ME's office parking lot, barely noticing when Clio hustled her past a man with a notepad and an ABC logo on his shirt and then accompanied her into the building. "Who supposedly has this money, then?"

"The campaign chair, a guy named Mark Sargeant."

"Mmm."

"You know him?"

"No."

"You seem to—" The reporter's roving eye suddenly fell on a mangled arm, half of its flesh stripped off, peeking from under a sheet. "What happened to *that* guy?"

"I don't know."

"He looks mangled." She patted her pockets and came up with a small notepad.

"Something probably mangled him, then. And you think, what, Mark had Grace killed because she found out about the embezzlement? Rumored embezzlement? Or was in it with him and he didn't want to share the proceeds?"

Clio forgot the skinned arm in a heartbeat. "Is that your theory?"

"No. It wouldn't explain Frances—she made one donation and had no other involvement, right?" She had to raise her voice as the overhead door began to inch its noisy way up, revealing the rear of an ambulance backing up to the dock. Rain pelted its roof with loud taps.

"But if you were Grace and your old friend had donated a boatload of money to your cause, which you then found out had been corrupted, wouldn't you give her a call? Say, Gee, I'm really sorry, but I might have steered you and your funds wrong?"

And Frances spoke her mind, guarded her parents' money as closely as she did their memory. She might have confronted Mark, demanded an explanation. "Possibly."

"Shit! What did that person die of?" Clio pointed as two strong deskmen pulled a gurney from the ambulance. A pale face in full rigor grinned at them; a stiff arm crooked a roguish finger.

"I don't know."

"But—he—"

"Clio, I can't tell just by looking at them. When will the auditors know for sure? Will they announce their findings?"

"They have to. It's public record. I should reiterate that it's just a rumor at the moment."

"Well, it's interesting. Good luck with your story. You can use that door there to get back into the parking lot."

"What about the unsolved rape cases that the two homicide detectives have been asking about?"

Evelyn stared.

Clio nodded without relish. "Now are you going to tell me what's up with the coloring book?"

DAVID AND RILEY SPENT THE MORNING TRACKING down four of the five earlier victims. They could not find the college student, who had taken a job in another state after graduation. The Euclid and near West Side victims had not been happy to revisit the horror but were willing to answer any questions put to them if doing so would help the cops catch the guy. The welfare mother's kids were now in high school; she had a job and one hell of a lock on her door. The schoolteacher lived in the same house and taught at the same school but had lost her family the year before, when her husband divorced her and took the children to Columbus. The detectives did not ask why.

Not one woman knew Grace Markham or Frances Duarte, or the buildings in which they had died. None was active in charity work.

The intervening years had not helped them to recall any more details about their attacker than they had originally told the police. Except, the schoolteacher added, she had become convinced that she knew the man, had met him at some previous point in her life. She could not explain this belief, whether she recognized a smell, a shape, the tread of his shoe. He had not spoken or given any overt indication of familiarity with either her or her house, but still her brain insisted that he knew her. Perhaps, she added, she simply quested for an explanation of why she had been targeted, so she could know it wasn't her fault.

But with such vague impressions, she could not be sure she would know him if she encountered him again.

With the chief threatening to bust them to Traffic if he didn't see the society strangler behind bars, and without any better ideas, they went to see Kelly Alexander. They didn't have far to go—only a few floors down to the holding cells. Kelly Alexander had been arrested on seven counts of manslaughter regarding the salt mine disaster.

They waited in a small room with scuffed gray cells and without so much as a chair while the corrections officer relayed their request for an interview. A desk officer sat behind reinforced glass and watched them without visible interest.

"I bet she's lawyered up," David said.

"With her money, she's probably got a panel of legal counsel. You think Markham figures he's getting the last laugh after she dumped him?"

"But now he's found love with the indomitable Miss Quinn."

"And another marriage. How about you?" Riley persisted. "You and Evie making any plans?"

"Maybe. And, no offense, they don't include you."

"But do they include *her*?"

David leaned against the grimy wall, avoiding his partner's eye. "I'd like to."

"Good. Does that mean I'll be getting a pretty ivory invitation in the mail one of these days?"

David snorted. "I just said we'll stay together. But marriage—not a chance."

"Not *any* chance?"

"No."

"Then you're a fool."

"Excuse me?"

Riley waited until a hefty guard guided a kid in an orange jump-suit through the waiting area and the desk officer buzzed them in through a heavy steel door. "I'm saying if you let her get away, you're a bigger fool than even I suspected."

David could feel his ears get pink. "It's none of your business."

"No."

The desk officer swiveled his gaze to David, who said, "She doesn't *want* to get married, anyway. Period."

"She tell you that?"

"Yes."

"Recently?" At David's silence, Riley added, "Because women sometimes pitch balls they *intend* to go foul."

"What's that mean?"

"That when women say they'll never get married, they usually mean that they don't want to get married until they decide they do. Or, in the case of my second wife, 'I don't want to have any more babies' meant until just after the wedding, when the biological clock started clanging like Big Ben."

The desk officer nodded in agreement, with all the gravitas of his twenty-odd years.

"Thanks for sharing," David said. "And you've been married how many times?"

"Two."

"And divorced?"

"Two. It should have been three, because I'd have divorced the first one twice if I could have, just to be sure."

"Uh-huh. And I should take advice from you?"

"He's got a point," the desk officer put in, before answering his phone with an *uh-huh*. "Ms. Alexander and her husband can see you now."

They followed their guide to one of the interrogation rooms, done in the same scuffed gray decor as the waiting area but with a flimsy table and four chairs. "This can't be much like her place in

Bratenahl," Riley said. "I'll bet Ms. Alexander is in a deep state of culture shock."

"You seem to have a love-hate relationship with the rich, partner. You'll notice I don't need a coffee cup to figure that out."

"Long story." Riley stood by the door, apparently fascinated by the wire mesh embedded in the glass of the small window. "I might tell you someday. Then again, I might not."

The guard opened the door for a young man in a suit, and the prisoner. Even in a baggy orange jumpsuit and no makeup, Kelly Alexander stunned. Her eyes were so blue David could see the color from across the room. Her blond hair stuck out at odd angles, as if her hairdresser had used gardening shears, a look that probably required a lot of cash to get.

Under normal circumstances, her complexion would have seemed flawless. Today it looked as if she hadn't slept in a week. "Has someone else died?"

David blinked. "I beg your pardon, ma'am?"

"From the mine. The death toll is up to seven. I thought the other two were going to be all right, but they were too badly burned."

"We're not here about the mine."

She halted. "You're not?" She turned to the man, as if to confirm this.

"Then why are you here?" he obligingly asked.

"We're here about Grace Markham and Frances Duarte."

Kelly Alexander's eyes filled with tears.

"Why don't you sit down, honey," the man said, "so the guard can take the cuffs off?"

She threw herself into one of the metal chairs and sniffled as the guard removed the handcuffs. "I haven't had a chance to even think about them, or send flowers or anything—I don't even know who I'd send them to. Frances didn't have any family in town, and that loser Grace married would probably throw them away."

The detectives sat across from her, and the guard retired to the hall. Riley coughed his smoker's hack. "I understand you were engaged to that loser before Grace was."

"And didn't I try to warn her! But Grace couldn't believe anything bad about anyone. She'd seen, not to mention photographed, the worst this world could hand out, but it didn't toughen her. Quite the contrary. It made her more determined to give everyone she met one chance after another."

Like Joey Eames, David thought. "We'd like to ask you some questions about them."

"Sure."

The young man said nothing until he noticed their curious looks. "I'm not Kelly's lawyer—I'm her husband, Adam Farley. She's not concerned about having her lawyer present, despite the fact that, as of this morning, we have twenty-five lawsuits pending."

"Twenty-six," his wife corrected. "And the equipment manufacturer wants the next payment on the front-end loader that got trashed. I know all about the legal situation, Adam. But I don't hide behind my money, and I'm not going to hide behind a lawyer."

"What happened at the mine?" David asked, purely out of curiosity.

"We still don't know," Adam Farley admitted. He had a slender frame and intelligent gray eyes. His nose seemed permanently wrinkled in response to the jail smell, a mixture of disinfectant and sweat. "I believe the dynamite was faulty, carried a stronger charge than it should have. But it's also possible that some of the natural gas stores leaked from a faulty pipe or crack in the salt and pooled. I checked for that when we put in the drill holes, but when the dynamite went off, it could have breached a pocket."

"You work at the mine?"

"I'm the geologist."

"That's where we met," Kelly put in, rubbing her husband's back with a few tender swipes. "Twelve hundred feet below the earth, in front of a bunch of spitting, swearing, tattooed guys that used to let me ride on their shoulders when I was a kid. It was terribly romantic."

He patted her knee as her smile faded.

"Decades ago, there were serious accidents in the mine maybe once every couple of years," she told the cops. "We haven't had a death since before I was born. Now this. I swear, if my father doesn't disown me, I'll disown myself."

"Every industry has accidents, Kelly," her husband consoled.

"I didn't get the clearances to store natural gas. That wasn't an accident."

David began to steer the conversation back to his case. "William Markham isn't happy about your mine being where it is."

"That's just his latest politically correct bandwagon." A spark returned to Kelly Alexander's eyes as she expressed her opinion of the late Grace's husband. "That the city would bounce back if we take the Flats back to their RiverFest, party-barge heyday, not thinking that no one's got the money to party if they don't have jobs. Heavy industry is what built this town, not overpriced drinks at Shooters."

Riley leaned back in his chair as if he were not particularly interested in either the recent murders or Kelly Alexander, but his eyes never left her face. "Frances Duarte invested in your mine, didn't she?"

Kelly nodded. "Poor kid, she must have worried when she saw the share values slipping and sliding. Don't get me wrong, it will come around. The world uses a lot of salt, and nobody's willing to stay home in a snowstorm anymore. The mine would have paid for itself in another five years. But they would have been lean years under any circumstances."

"And now, with this accident?" Riley pressed.

"Hell, I don't know. It depends how much the juries want to give the families. We'll be sued for every penny the mine will ever bring in and then some. We can only hope the appeals court will leave us enough to live on. At least that's what my lawyer says.

Maybe by then the press will stop camping on my lawn and I'll be able to answer my phone."

Her husband shifted on the cold metal chair. "I thought you weren't here about the mine."

"Frances Duarte had a lot of money. We have to consider the possibility that it might have a bearing on her death," Riley said. "Did she talk to you about the investment? Express any disappointment?"

Kelly raked her fingers through already tousled hair. "You think her investment in the mine could have something to do with her murder? Are you crazy?"

"As I said, we're covering bases."

She shook her head, sending her blond locks into a funnel cloud of curls. "We got together for dinner once or twice in the past few months and commiserated, but I think she felt worse for me than she did for herself. I asked if it put her in a bind or anything, but she said no, if she wanted to make it up to her estate accounts, she could still cancel the million dollars she'd pledged to Butterfly Babies. The paperwork hadn't gone through yet."

David didn't look at his partner, but he felt that spark cross between them, the sudden alertness that an unexpected fact can produce. "Had she told the hospital that she might want her money back?"

"I don't know."

"Mrs.—" David stopped, unsure which name to use.

"Farley," Kelly supplied.

"So you know the fund-raising director there—Mark Sargeant?"

Her husband spoke up. "The campaign chair."

"Yes. You know him?"

"Do I. He hits on every woman in sight," Kelly explained. "Young or old, married or single, doesn't matter to him. That's why they finally kicked him out of the Pathology Department, he couldn't keep his hands off the candy stripers. But even he knows to be discreet around the people making the donations. You think he killed her for *not* giving a million dollars to the hospital?"

"It's a lot of money. Had Frances mentioned him, or the fund-raising, in recent months?"

"Not that I recall."

"So the three of you were friends—you, Grace, and Frances."

"Sure."

"Anyone else in that circle?"

She leaned forward, seeming to welcome the change of topic. "Sure, about fifty. You know, the same names and faces you see at every event. We all know each other. Maybe I should clarify—Grace and Frances and I were friends, but not *best* friends. We only saw each other every couple of months."

"What about Grace and Frances? Were they close?"

"Not particularly."

Then what the hell did they have in common that made someone murder them? David chewed his lip. "You used to see more of Grace than you did recently?"

"Yeah, I guess you could say that."

"Any reason why? A falling-out?"

"No." For the first time her attention seemed to wander. She took in the unforgiving environment with a slight curl to her lip, not of disdain but of dismay. "Well, Grace apparently wanted to stream-line her life when she got on the mommy kick. The biological clock started ticking, a sound to which I've been blissfully deaf so far."

"So she stopped going out as much?" David pressed. Not according to Joey Eames, and Kelly seemed strangely reluctant about the whole subject.

"Sort of. And, well, we were driving home after a party one night and I had a little too much— I probably shouldn't be telling you guys this."

"We're not traffic cops," Riley assured her. "So you had a little too much to drink—"

"Yeah, and had an accident. It shook us all up. I'm way too old for that kind of irresponsibility."

"Was Grace hurt in the accident?"

"A scrape and a bruise. Same for me."

"And when was this?"

"About two years ago."

David thought that over. The spark had fled, leaving a deadening feeling, of having spent days asking questions without learning a single helpful answer. "Mrs. Farley, I'm going to show you a list of five names, and I'd like to know if you recognize any of them." He handed her his carefully printed list of the five rape victims. She read dutifully while he watched her face. She gave no reaction at all.

She handed the list back. "No. Should I? Who are they?"

He didn't answer. "Can you think of anyone who might want to kill Frances?"

Kelly Alexander cuddled her cheek to her husband's shoulder and avoided their eyes for a long silence. Someone is heavy on your mind, David thought. Give me a name. But then she straightened up and said, "Not a soul. That lounge lizard friend of hers probably wanted to at times. He's been trying to get her to marry him for years, but no go. Sometimes I thought Frances just wasn't interested in men, but maybe she had her heart broken at a young age. For whatever reason, he couldn't talk her into it."

"I don't think he would kill her, though," her husband said.

"No. He's too skinny. She'd have broken him in half."

Riley leaned forward, and the chair's thin metal legs squeaked in protest. "What about Grace?"

Again, the suspicious pause before she spoke. "I'd love to insist that waste of flesh she married did it, but I can't honestly believe it. He's not used to getting his hands dirty."

"What if he got someone to do it for him?"

She shook her head. "He hasn't got the guts. Once you get past his dimples, he hasn't got much of anything."

E VELYN WAS CONVERSING WITH THE AFOREMEN-
tioned waste of flesh at that very moment. "I saw it on your
refrigerator, Mr. Markham," she explained, remembering
Grace's refrigerator, with its attached pizza coupon. "A picture in
crayon on paper, like children draw."

"Oh, yeah." A blast of noise erupted in the background. "Excuse me if I shout, but I'm at the Flats project, and they're breaking
up the old slab here. That cop asked me about some kid's picture
too. I saw it last night when I packed up. Don't know where it came
from, though."

"Would you mind if I took that for analysis?" None of the
crayons from the children's hospital had matched those used on
Grace's and Frances's clothing. Evelyn did not know where it could
lead her, but she had to follow the trail. The only evidence of
crayons in either apartment had been the drawings.

"I don't know where it is."

"If you could have the building manager let me in—"

He paused for another spate of jackhammer noise. "Why didn't
you take it when you were there?"

"Because I didn't know it was important."

"*Is* it important?"

"I don't know."

"You don't know what's important, you don't know who killed Grace, you don't know how he got into my apartment . . . What *do* you guys know?"

"Look, Mr. Markham, it's a long shot, but if you could just have the manager let me in—"

"You can check, but the apartment should be empty. I had the movers get all my stuff yesterday. I was up all night packing it. I just wanted to get out of there, you know?"

Yeah, to join Barbara. "What did you do with the picture?"

"I probably threw it out."

"You did?"

He raised his voice, because of either the background noise or his frustration. "The cops said they were done with the place and I could do whatever I wanted. If you needed it, you should have taken it."

She couldn't argue with that. "Where did you throw it?"

"I put all the stuff in garbage bags. Then I had the door guy take them out to the Dumpster for me. Then I gave him the code and signed off on the lease and I was out of there. And I'm not going back. If you want to go looking for it, be my guest."

"Thanks so much," she said, too tired to keep the bitterness out of her voice.

"Hey, one more thing. That necklace that was on Grace when she was killed?"

"Yes?"

"When can I get that back?"

THE SMELL in Frances Duarte's apartment had not improved much.

"The crime-scene cleanup place is coming tomorrow," the building manager told her, unabashedly holding his nostrils closed with one hand. "You can't believe what they charge, either. Thank heavens the Phillipses are in Europe. I tried leaving the windows open one day, but then it drifted to some open windows upstairs and those people complained. Besides, it's been raining every hour on the hour."

"That's spring in Cleveland."

"I brought the reporter from the *Sun Star* papers in here too. He threw up."

Evelyn pulled the curtains back, turning what had been a dim cave into an apartment, albeit one with every single item moved out of place from their searching and a large stain on the floor under the armchair. The carved wooden animals on the long shelves seemed to have migrated under their own power, their original positions indicated by gaps in the dust. Motes of it floated in the air. Frances Duarte's apartment had at least one thing in common with Grace Markham's—so well soundproofed that it might have been hermetically sealed. To Evelyn's relief, the child's drawing still hung on the bulletin board.

"Do you need me for anything else?" the manager asked and seemed greatly relieved when she said no.

The drawing, on its stiff buff-colored background, clung to the bulletin board with a single pushpin. The pin matched others on the board. Evelyn had no compelling reason to believe the drawing related to the killer, but he had left her crayons as a clue, and she could not ignore that. Plus, Frances and Grace turned out to have less in common than Evelyn had expected, but they both had drawings.

The child had drawn a flat surface in fluorescent green, with a lemon yellow sun emitting rays. Pink scratches in the sky could, she supposed, be birds. Three stick figures of various sizes stood along the green road or lawn or whatever it was. An amorphous black spot below the line defied identification. The artist had not signed his or her work.

What the heck am I doing here? Evelyn thought. Marissa's in Intensive Care, OSHA is calling every half hour to come and see the clothing from the mine accident, and I don't have a single forensic clue to find this killer. And here I sit gazing at a child's idea of a Sunday stroll.

She slid the paper, without folding it, into a brown paper grocery bag and sealed the top with red tape. Technically she should have gotten a search warrant to return for more evidence, since the crime scene had been released, but the crime rate in Cleveland had spiked with the end of winter and no one, certainly not Riley or David, had time to get her one. The odds of the picture yielding any real information were slight. If it became relevant, she'd have to hope for a sympathetic judge to get it admitted.

Then she did another walk-through of the apartment, reluctant, as always, to leave the crime scene. She knew the nagging feeling would set in as soon as she turned her back on it—did she miss something?

Frances Duarte's office, unlike the rest of the apartment, did not remain as Evelyn had left it. File cabinet drawers stood open, and papers covered the desktop. Someone—perhaps her accountant?—had been reviewing her finances.

"Hello."

She jumped and turned. A wiry man, his gray hair too old for his face, stood in the doorway, holding a cardboard box in both hands.

He's older than I am and his hands are full, she thought. I can take him.

Then she realized that the killer wouldn't have given her warning. This must have been the hanger-on, the friend who'd worked for years to be more than a friend to Frances and now come up finally, irreversibly empty. "Are you Beldon Aimes?"

"The very same. Who are you?"

She explained herself, watching him carefully. "What are you doing here?"

"I brought Frances's ashes. I cremated her this morning."

It would have been hard under normal circumstances to feel

afraid of the slight, almost silly-looking Aimes, but that comment nearly did it. She had a mental image of him flicking the burn switch at the crematorium, or perhaps setting a torch to a pyre, as if Frances had been some kind of Viking warrior. "I'm sorry for your loss."

"Thank you."

"Did you have a service?"

His face grew more animated. "Oh yes. All the best and beautiful turned out, expressing plenty of sympathy for Frances and none for me. They hate it when one of their own dies, you see. It reminds them that, despite scientific advances, money still can't buy immortality."

He would have been one of their own, had Frances married him. Now that chance had been lost to him forever. Oddly enough, Evelyn found this very normal antipathy reassuring. "It was kind of you to bring, um, her here. Did the building manager let you in?"

"No, I have a key." He placed the box in a space at one end of a shelf. "And I'm her executor. Well, her sister is her executor, but she's not in town, so she asked me to take care of the details."

"Like her finances?" Evelyn gestured at the desktop.

"I had to take all the recent statements to her accountant. He handles all that. I have no access to Frances's money, if that's what you're thinking," he added with a prim set to his mouth. "Have you found the monster who did this?"

"Not yet. I know Frances was active in many charities. Did she do a lot with Butterfly Babies and Children's Hospital?"

"Probably. She worked with half the charities in town." His chin trembled, and he placed one hand on the small cardboard box. "She was so generous."

"Did she ever mention it to you? Have anything good to say, or bad to say?"

"Not in particular."

"Did she know a woman named Marissa Gonzalez?"

"No. Doesn't sound like someone she would know either."

Oh really, you sycophantic little pseudosnob? "What about Kelly Alexander?"

"That Alexander bitch! She didn't even come to the service!"

"She's in jail."

"Probably just as well, as I'm sure the media would have followed in droves. Now that Frances isn't here to lose any more money, I'm almost glad that explosion happened. I suppose that's a terrible thing to say."

"Seven people died." So yes, it is.

He stopped.

"Why don't you like Kelly Alexander?" she asked, though she could guess.

"Because she treated me like a lapdog. Her own husband was nobody too, wouldn't have two pennies to rub together if he hadn't married her, but *that's* okay. But me she talks to with contempt wrapped around every word."

"Frances lost a lot of money with her?"

"You better believe it."

"Did Frances get angry at Kelly about that?"

"No," he admitted. "I don't know why, really. Frances was always so careful with her parents' money and became upset if brokers mishandled it. But she didn't get upset with Kelly."

"Because they were friends?"

"I asked her once. Frances said she owed her."

"She owed Kelly?"

"Yeah."

"What for?"

He shrugged. "I have no idea."

"Is there anything else you can tell me about Frances and Kelly's relationship?"

"No. Why all these questions?" He sat across from her and leaned forward, somber and conspiratorial. "You think *Kelly* had her killed?"

"No, no. We're just trying to find connections between Frances and Grace, that's all."

"And Kelly's it." He warmed to the idea, reaching out and patting her knee in his enthusiasm. "And she's got the money to do it too."

"But no motive."

"Sure there is. Money is the oldest motive in the world."

"But wouldn't Frances have motive to kill Kelly? Not vice versa?"

"Maybe Frances demanded her money back."

"You just said she didn't seem upset about it, and there's nothing to show that the mine investment had anything to do with Frances's death. Look, since you're here, I'd like to ask you about this." She unsealed the brown paper bag and pulled out the drawing. "Do you recognize this?"

He studied the crude depiction. "No. Should I?"

"It hung on Frances's bulletin board. Have you seen it before?"

"Yesterday."

"I mean before her murder."

"No. But then I hadn't been here in a week or two. Why?"

"Do you know where it came from?"

"No idea. Probably one of her friends' little brats."

"Who? Can you give me their names?" She used Frances's notepad to jot down a list of seven sets of parents. Aimes didn't recall the names of the children, or even how many each couple had.

He waited until she finished writing before returning to the most interesting topic. "So you suspect that Alexander bitch, right?" He patted her knee again, and let two fingers rest there.

"You know," she said as she secreted the list of names in her camera bag, "when I processed this room, those shelves were completely full. With a gorgeous blue willow vase at one end, where the box is now."

He removed his hand and pulled at his lower lip.

"It seems some objects have been moved. And some of the

animal statues from the living room are missing. Have you been packing Frances's things?"

"Yes, actually. She had a number of rare first editions, and some of her carvings were one of a kind. Quite valuable."

"And?"

"I took them to my place for . . . safekeeping. After all, you can't trust anyone these days."

"No." She stood up, collecting her paper bag with the drawing in it. "Indeed."

THERE IT IS," JUSTIN TOLD HER. "YOU'RE IN LUCK.
Pickup is tomorrow."

Evelyn squinted at the rusting green Dumpster. "Yeah,
lucky me. Would you happen to remember what color William
Markham's garbage bags were?"

"White."

She climbed the stepladder Gerard had reluctantly retrieved for
her, to glimpse a sea of garbage bags. "They're all white."

"Yeah, a lot of them."

The sun had managed to burn off nearly all of the gray morning
clouds and now blazed against an azure sky. Cleveland office workers would emerge from their towers to find whatever patch of grass
they could locate downtown, in the northerners' eternal quest to
brown up that winter pallor.

It figured. The one day she would have welcomed a heavy cloud
cover to keep the heat off her back. Perhaps even rain—at least it
would have tamped down the smell. She hefted a few white bags out
of the Dumpster and climbed back out. The box had been filled too
high to be able to work inside it, and the back alley gave her a more
stable surface to spread out the material.

She might be working all by herself in a deserted alley next to the building their killer frequented, but she had no cause to worry—murders only happened at night. At least they did on TV.

Except for Grace.

And maybe Frances.

She looked around. No one. She got to work.

Most of the Riviere's residents, she quickly discovered, had the finger strength of trapeze artists when it came to tying knots in their garbage bags. She began to slash them open with a disposable scalpel. The tenants also tended to overstuff—whoever said Americans live in a disposable society had been right on the money. Instead of examining each item, she rummaged around for mail or other items to identify the bag as coming from the Markhams'. Sweat began to roll from between her shoulder blades. She could have taken off the lab coat, but that would have meant exposing her bare arms and a shirt she felt rather fond of.

After fifteen bags of garbage, and deciding to write a note to the people on eight to point out the importance of shredding one's credit card bills, she found not William Markham's garbage but Marissa's. A piece of junk mail with Robert's name on it sat on top, stuck to an empty RavioliOs can.

She felt the same sense of unease as she had when opening Marissa's purse. Surely parts of Marissa's life were not for public consumption, or even for a close friend's. Everyone, Evelyn reminded herself, has secrets.

But protecting Marissa's life by catching her attacker took priority over her sensibilities. Evelyn knelt uncomfortably on the grimy concrete and ripped a clean garbage bag off the roll she had brought along. Then she went through her best friend's trash, piece by piece.

After fifteen minutes she had discovered nothing except that one or both of the couple worried about plaque on their teeth and Robert had been living on TV dinners for the past few days. No newspaper clippings or any other papers mentioning Grace Markham or Frances Duarte turned up.

Robert tended to throw his junk mail away unopened. Marissa had the habit of opening most of hers, then tearing the solicitations in half before disposing of them. One, however, had been torn into several pieces, and the letterhead read "Butterfly Ba———"

It took another fifteen minutes to reassemble the letter, a standard solicitation for the capital campaign. The printed signature read Jenna Lawson, but at the bottom another hand had scrawled: "I hope you'll come to the Gala Night in June. I can't wait to see you again. Love, Mark."

To judge from the number of pieces to which she had reduced the letter, Marissa hadn't felt any enthusiasm for the idea. Or she hadn't wanted Robert to see it.

What had gone on here? A teacher-student affair? The note and Mark Sargeant's sexy drawl when he'd spoken of Marissa seemed to suggest it. Or perhaps Sargeant had tried for an affair and didn't comprehend the word *no* even now—though the letter was dated April and the note mentioned seeing her in June. Hardly a hot and heavy pursuit, and even if that were the case, the outspoken Marissa would have told her fiancé. Hell, she would have told the whole world.

Unless she didn't want the information to affect Robert's plans, in case he decided to take a position at Butterfly. Perhaps she'd contacted Sargeant, told him to leave her alone once and for all. The hospital sat right next door to her workplace—Marissa could have stormed into his office at any time.

Not for the first time, Evelyn wished her friend could be awake and healthy.

She put the letter in a brown paper bag, again pushing aside her qualms. At least she would not enter it at the lab unless necessary. The chain of custody had long been broken—meaning she didn't need a search warrant to do her Dumpster diving, and turning in the evidence later rather than sooner wouldn't make a difference.

She finally located Markham's bags, tucked neatly into a corner of the metal box. Bags and bags. The man had thrown out all of Grace's clothing.

The waste of it horrified Evelyn. He could at least have dumped the bags a few blocks away, at the Goodwill at East Fifty-fifth. For a haul like this, they probably would have come to pick it up. Evelyn's thrifty soul quailed, but while she might happily have shelled out cash for the items at a resale shop, she drew the line at taking a dead woman's clothing out of a Dumpster. Even a gorgeous Halston sweater like this one . . .

Markham had tossed away every single thing his wife owned except for her jewelry—her papers, photos, old bills, toothpaste, schoolbooks, a high school report card. Evelyn believed Markham to be a self-centered jerk of the highest caliber, but did this indicate a guilty conscience as well?

The skin on the back of her neck begin to burn as she skimmed the belongings. The cops had already searched the apartment from end to end, but that had occurred before they knew about Frances Duarte and the possible significance of the children's hospital. Nothing new, however, came to light.

The child's picture from the refrigerator turned up in a bag with granola bar wrappers and the remains of egg foo yong. Markham had wadded it into a ball, causing the brittle paper to break more than it wrinkled. Evelyn recovered as many pieces as she could and sealed them in a manila envelope. After speeding through the two last bags, she hefted the resealed garbage bags back into the Dumpster, returned the ladder to Gerard, and left, tired, thirsty, and smelling worse than the garbage had.

"I APOLOGIZE for my appearance," Evelyn began. "But I was already in the neighborhood, and I'm kind of pressed for time."

"Looks like you've had quite a morning."

"I smell like it too." She sipped ice-cold water from the Culligan cooler Henry Taylor kept in the corner of his office. Little more than a cubbyhole in the Cleveland Police Department Crime Lab, it afforded at least a skinny window with a glimpse of the lake. Paper covered the walls—technical bulletins, Midwestern Association of Forensic Scientists (MAFS) meeting notices, and cartoons—as seemed appropriate for the Questioned Document Examination Department. The department consisted, in its entirety, of Henry Taylor.

"Did I tell you I'm running for president?"

She didn't have to ask of what. Henry had been a vocal member of MAFS for all of the twenty-five years he had worked with the crime lab. "Yes, you did. Good luck."

"It's going to be quite an election. Ruby and Jillian are running against each other for treasurer, you know. I'm going to do them a favor and vote for someone else; if one wins over the other, the St. Louis lab will become a war zone. You're going to the conference, right?"

She shook her head. "Tony can't spare me. His words."

"But it's right in Parkersburg! Only four hours."

"I'll cast my vote by proxy. I promise. Now about this paper—"

He abandoned politics with obvious reluctance. "What do you have for me? A family disputing Daddy's will, in which he leaves his estate to his twenty-year-old wife? Forged prescription? Hold-up note?"

She opened the paper bag she had brought from Frances Duarte's apartment. "Art, actually. Here we have a lovely pastoral scene, depicting a summer stroll. Regrettably, unsigned by the artist."

Henry's salt-and-pepper eyebrows climbed an inch up his forehead.

"In this bag, we have a damaged product." She held up the crinkled picture, which dusted the outer edge of his desk with flakes of paper. "Sorry. A nice rendering of a house with a car out front. At least I think that's what it is. Note the artist's use of fluorescent color here, quite bold."

The questioned document examiner sat back in his chair. "I can't wait to hear the story behind this. Before you go any further, Evelyn, let me say—I've done children's handwriting and I've done documents in crayon. One time involved both. But I've never compared drawings. I couldn't—"

"I'm not asking about the drawings. It's what they're drawn on." Evelyn placed the more intact picture in front of him. "The paper—it's not from a coloring book or a sketch pad. It's torn, neatly, at both ends, almost as if it came from a roll or from some larger piece. It's brittle enough to rip off in a straight line if you fold it back and forth once."

He stared in horror. "You ripped it?"

"I experimented with a piece from this one, the one Markham wadded up."

Henry Taylor pulled on a pair of cloth gloves but still did not touch the picture, observing it from a distance of four or five inches. His neck must hurt at the end of the day, she thought, like mine when I'm at the comparison microscope too long.

"This is the Grace Markham case?"

She explained the similarities between Grace's murder scene and Frances Duarte's. "I need to know if the paper used could have a common origin."

"I can tell if they came off the same roll, perhaps even in sequence. Let's go into the lab. Bring the other one."

The rooms of the Cleveland Police Department lab, while as worn and cramped as the ME's office, had been built from the start for a larger staff with a larger case volume. Rows of lab benches with sinks and compressed-gas nozzles made it resemble a high school chemistry class. Evelyn greeted the drug analysts and DNA techs as Taylor snaked his way to a place in the back.

There, he wiped the black counter in front of a stereomicroscope with antibacterial spray and a disposable, lint-free cotton cloth. Then he placed the two pictures side by side.

For the first time, Evelyn could see how similar they were. The width of the paper from the non-torn ends seemed identical. The child liked to leave himself, or herself, an inch of margin all the way around. The colors varied, but the same shades of peach and magenta seemed to be used in both. It gave her a chill—a killer's calling card left in innocent loops of colored wax.

Don't jump to conclusions, she told herself. Grace and Frances knew each other and had friends in common. They might have been acquainted with the same child.

Though the police interviews had not turned up any such child, and also, what about the crayon on the victims' clothing?

Henry Taylor first used a handheld UV light—Evelyn had the same model—over the front and back of both pieces of paper. Nothing fluoresced, except the already fluorescent crayon marks. Then he busied himself with the stereomicroscope, placing the Duarte picture and the intact edges of the Markham picture close together, though not touching, under the lens. Then he tried the other two edges. Finally, he straightened.

"We don't have a jigsaw match. I can't say they came from the same roll. That's what makes me different from Fred Viancourt, by the way—I'm not afraid to say I don't know. Did you read his article in the newsletter last month?"

"Henry, about these pictures—"

"The paper appears consistent, and very unusual. It must be almost completely softwood."

"What does that mean?"

"Paper is made out of wood fibers. Specialty papers might have some synthetic elements, and fancy writing paper has cotton or linen, but most paper is originally wood. Hardwood fibers are short, so the paper is smoother but weaker. Softwood fibers are longer, so the paper is stronger but rougher—not paper at all, more or less."

That puzzled her. "What do you mean?"

"I mean it's paper, but it's not meant for writing. It's too thick and easily compressed—see how the crayon strokes sink in a little? And it's so brittle. You couldn't fold it and put it in an envelope, because that quickly weakens the surface until it breaks."

"So what is this stuff?"

"It could be specialty paper for some artistic or aesthetic purpose—say a company makes replicas of Egyptian papyrus. They start with this, then break it up and glue it back together to look more ancient, stamp the design on the top. But more likely, it has some industrial purpose."

"Such as?"

"I've only run into this once, but machinists use stuff like this to make gaskets and pads between connections. They call it fiche paper—you can use it between nonmoving machine parts when you need to shim them, because you can use more than one layer until they fit. You place the paper in the spot you need and knock the excess off with a knife—kind of like trimming a piecrust."

"But it's just paper. Wouldn't it disintegrate in a short time?"

"No, as long as it didn't get wet. Oil won't bother it."

Machinery. The killer had left a smear of oil. The bodies had been held with mesh straps.

She had gotten sidetracked with children and charities and now came full circle back to an industrial setting. Somewhere in that circle rested her killer.

William Markham had access to heavy industry, whereas Mark Sargeant, on the face of it, did not.

Henry Taylor watched her face. "Does that get you closer to your killer?"

"I'm not sure. But it's interesting, Henry. Thanks a lot."

He slid each picture back into its designated bag. "No problem. Just don't forget to vote."

W OO-EEE." TONY HELD HIS NOSE AS EVELYN deposited her bags on the large examination table. "You smell bad."

"At least I have an excuse," she muttered.

"What was that?"

"Nothing. I found both pictures, and Henry Taylor says the paper is consistent. Now I have to examine the crayons used in the drawings and see if their FTIR spectra coincide with what's on the victims' clothing."

"And then what?"

"Then I'm back to trying to find a particular set of crayons in a major metropolitan area."

"Good luck with that. Two OSHA guys are on their way over here—that cute little lady inspector and another guy. They need to see the photographs and the victims' clothing."

"Great." She moved the pictures to her FTIR table and filled the liquid nitrogen container.

Tony watched. Finally his silence made her suspicious enough to say: "What?"

"You have to show them the photos and the clothing."

"Yeah, no problem. I'll put it in the amphitheater for them, give them some gloves. Don't worry, I'll make nice."

"You're not getting it. You have to stay with them every second they are in this building. They are not ME personnel, which means they don't wander around here unescorted or view our evidence unsupervised."

"Why? It's their case, for all practical purposes."

"Because it's evidence in what could be a series of multimillion-dollar lawsuits. And because my lab doesn't leave evidence lying around for anyone to alter, pilfer, or contaminate."

Evelyn pulled the blood samples from the day's victims out of the dumbwaiter and set them on the table to be entered and labeled. "But I've got stuff to do!"

"Yeah. Crayons."

"Crayons from a serial killer who's gunning for Marissa."

"I know it's Marissa, believe me. If it's not you reminding me every ten minutes it's the ME. But Cleveland's finest are working on that, and besides, these guys are just as dead."

"But no one murdered them. It was an accident."

"Hitting a light pole when you're backing out of a space at Wal-Mart, that's an accident. Screwing up so bad that seven people die, that's a crime. And we investigate crimes." He yawned, sending a wisp of Dorito-scented breath her way. "You think I wouldn't prefer meeting with the cute OSHA lady to approving the air-flow setup for the new lab with the architects? If I can get out early, I'll even take over for you. She'll be here in twenty minutes. And change that lab coat."

She shoved the bloods into the refrigerator and used the twenty minutes to confirm that the crayons matched. She had tested every color used on the drawings and the victims' clothing. The pigments, of course, varied with the different crayons, but the base materials, the paraffin and its additives, were identical. The crayons had come from the same manufacturer, though not necessarily the same box.

Her brief moment of satisfaction faded almost instantly. She still had no idea who these crayons belonged to and what they had to do with Grace Markham or Frances Duarte. Neither woman had crayons in her apartment. David and Riley had not found a child in common through their interviews with friends.

Time, perhaps, to abandon crayons and move instead to the murder weapon.

"HOW YOU DOING, HONEY?" Margery Murphy said in greeting. "You look like you haven't slept in a week."

"It feels like that. Did you find the gas leak?"

"Doesn't seem to be one. I went down with a whole crew, and we couldn't even get a significant reading." She eyed the sealed brown bags, each resting in a seat in the old teaching amphitheater as if waiting for a lecture. "Is this the clothing from our dead guys? Good."

Evelyn opened the first bag and pulled out a work shirt, which had once been blue. She spread it on a fresh piece of brown paper. The young man with Margery asked, "Does it always smell like this?"

"Victims' clothing, or the building?" Evelyn asked.

He had close-cropped hair, dimples, and the beginnings of a beer gut. He had to be ten years her junior, but that did not stop him from being very friendly. "Both."

"Yes."

"Don't mind him, honey," Margery told her. "He's new. This belongs to the one found completely under the overturned loader?"

"Yes, with just his hand sticking out." The image came back to her in a sad, grainy picture of red blood against soot-blackened salt. Suddenly she regretted having tried to blow off this investigation because of Marissa's attack. Seven guys, just trying to bring home a paycheck . . . "Do you know what happened, if it wasn't a gas leak?"

"We're not sure."

"Some anomalies have turned up in the batch of dynamite," the younger one said, ignoring Margery's warning look. "The natural gas stores are all accounted for."

"We're not sure of that yet," Margery said, "so keep it under your hat."

"Yes, of course." Evelyn repackaged the shirt and brought out a pair of pants as Margery jotted notes on a pink notepad. "What about Kelly Alexander?"

"Out on bail," the young man told her. "She'll still be fined for not filing all the paperwork for the gas storage, but she might be off the hook for manslaughter. We don't know yet. How long have you worked here, by the way?"

"Eleven years. What—"

"How does your husband feel about you working with stiffs all day?"

"I'm divorced, and we call them victims here. Wh—"

"So you're single now."

"Leave her alone, kid," Margery said. "She's way out of your league. And take a picture of these jeans while you're at it."

"What was wrong with the dynamite?" Evelyn asked.

Margery held a paper bag open for her partner to replace the blood-crusted pair of pants. "We're doing tests now on the rest of the supply. The manufacturer's quality control is up-to-date. Either a batch wound up overpowered or a worker screwed up and used too much. But the survivors didn't see anything suspicious, unless they're lying. I'd lie too if I screwed up and got seven people killed."

"Maybe it was a bomb," the younger one suggested. "And not the dynamite at all. Maybe it's terrorists."

Evelyn slid off one latex glove to rub her eyes. "So they take out a salt mine?"

"They're terrorists. How bright can they be? Or maybe it's industrial sabotage."

"No motive," Margery scoffed. "The owners were losing their shirt anyway."

"Could closing it down improve their financial situation?" Evelyn asked. The odds of this disaster having any relation to the murders seemed nearly nonexistent, but it couldn't hurt to examine all possibilities.

"Maybe they did it themselves!" the younger one said. "For the insurance."

That seemed as likely to Margery as unintelligent terrorists. "You can't get insurance for something like that. Liability for injuries, yes, but not for simple failure to thrive. The mine will pay for itself eventually, though it will have to produce for years first, probably decades. But if it doesn't operate, there's no chance at all."

Evelyn had an idea. "I'm just going to run upstairs and get something I'd like you to look at, if that's okay."

Margery nodded. The young man perked up, as if she might return with doughnuts, or at least some candy.

She left the room, running up the back staircase to the creaking protest of her knees, and collected the children's drawings on their unique paper. Sure, evidence from a multideath incident had been left with unauthorized personnel. But if you couldn't trust the people charged with safeguarding the working conditions of the American labor force, then who could you trust? All the same, she raced back before Tony could catch her.

Margery confirmed what Henry Taylor had said, that the thick, brittle paper could be used as gasket material in heavy machinery. But what kind of machinery?

The young man rubbed a piece between his fingers. "Anything. Vehicles, lifts, conveyor belts, elevators, assembly lines, factory equipment. Virtually anything."

"A hospital?"

"Sure. Air conditioners, pump motors."

She put the drawings away and retrieved, from a storage room next door, the straps used to bind Grace Markham to her kitchen chair. They smelled considerably less than the ones used on Frances Duarte, and Margery's partner already looked a little green around the gills. "What about this? What would a strap like this be used for?"

The young man examined one end as his partner continued to photograph the miners' clothing. "Safety harness. Or a tow strap. Or tie-downs—those are ratcheting straps used to secure cargo loads. This width could be used to hold gas tanks in a box truck or pipes or boards to a flatbed. What did you find on it?"

"Find?"

"Traces of stuff," he went on, a slight impatience creeping into his voice—after all, didn't she work in the Trace Evidence Department? "If you find bits of wood, it could have been used to tie crates or planks. Flakes of metal could be pipes or even boxcars, but that would need heavier fabric. Plumbing supplies might leave bits of PVC."

"Oil."

"Oil, or grease?" Margery asked.

"All I know is it's petroleum-based. I don't usually work with inorganics."

"Then it could be either. Grease is oil with a ton of stuff in it. Additives are there to make the oil thick and sticky, to stay on whatever part it's supposed to be lubricating. Sometimes things that are oiled accumulate dust and junk, and these stick to and mix with the oil until it becomes grease."

"Lots of stuff contaminates oil," the younger one put in.

"Take boron." Margery warmed to her subject with the relish of a born lecturer. "If there's a cooling system involved, then boron usually works its way into the lubricants—but some engine oils use it for antiwear and as a detergent."

"How can you tell what's meant to be in the oil and what's a contaminant, then?"

"You can't, unless you know what the oil was originally intended for. It's like concrete. If you have a small sample of concrete with fiberglass particles in it, the fiberglass might have flaked off parts of the mixing truck when they poured the concrete. But it might have fiberglass purposely added for strength because the concrete is from a load-bearing floor. See what I mean?"

"I do. And it's a little overwhelming."

"Unfortunately, yes. If you have no idea where this strap came from, you're going to have a hard time distinguishing what is supposed to be on it and what isn't. Your only hope is to find something completely unique."

"Like what?"

"I wouldn't have the slightest idea, honey. And I'm ready for the fourth victim's clothing, if you don't mind."

YOU SEEM PRETTY PERKY FOR A GIRL WHO JUST cheated death."

Marissa could smile now that the breathing tube had been removed. She had been evicted from the ICU and freed from all the attendant devices, even the IV. A cop sat in the hall outside her room, but so far only reporters and minor political figures looking for a photo op had tried to approach. The precise outline of the mesh strap on Marissa's neck had smoothed out, but the skin now bloomed in shades of purple and black. Her body remained depleted and weak, but considering what had happened to her, she seemed downright, well, perky. She could even talk. "You know me," she rasped out in a whisper Evelyn had to strain to hear. "One tough chick. Just tell me this will all be gone for the wedding photos."

Evelyn had her doubts, but Marissa did not need to hear them at that particular moment. "You'll be the most beautiful bride ever."

"Ha." Oxycodone eased most of her pain, though swallowing took visible effort. "And who told that reporter that some nonexistent ex-con ex-boyfriend beat me up? At least Mama set her straight before Robert's mother could read that little tidbit with her coffee."

"I don't know. I've been wondering myself."

"I'll bet it's that bitch in Toxicology." Marissa's eyes closed, the better to plan a wholehearted spate of vengeance.

Evelyn let her rest, planning how to word the questions she needed to ask, whether or not Marissa would thank her for it. There had to be a logic here, even a twisted one, and her best chance of finding that elusive thread lay before her in a bundle of crisp white sheets.

But she couldn't wait for long. The cops wouldn't be able to justify keeping a uniformed officer off the streets to guard Marissa for more than another day or two. The killer had not, so far as they knew, tried to approach Marissa again, and Evelyn could not prove he would. Eventually, the protective detail would pull out and her friend would be left vulnerable. Unless Evelyn could find the guy first.

Marissa had given a statement, telling them what she could recall of the attack, but it did not provide any new information. The man had worn a ski mask, approached her from behind, and seemed completely unfamiliar.

"Marissa."

"Mmm?"

Evelyn explained about the clipping in Marissa's purse. To her relief, her friend did not seem angry about the violation of her privacy. But neither did she clear up the coincidence. "Robert keeps talking about moving his practice to Butterfly Babies. I cut out the article because it said they'll be expanding, and if he wants to work there, this would be a good time to pursue it."

"You don't know the woman mentioned? Frances Duarte?"

The patient frowned slightly. "No, I don't think so. Why?"

"It may all be connected with the attack on you." She didn't tell Marissa that the woman had been murdered, just as she didn't tell her about the killer attacking Marissa a second time. The girl had come back from the dead; she didn't need to know every horrific detail immediately. "Did you know a woman named Grace Markham? She lived in your building."

"No." As before, Marissa drew the vowel out in a note of uncertainty.

Evelyn held up Grace's picture. "This is her."

"Vaguely, maybe. I could have passed her in the lobby or something."

"You did a co-op at Butterfly Babies and Children's, didn't you?"

The oxycodone-induced peace seeped from Marissa's face. "Yes."

"Did you know a Mark Sargeant?"

"Why?"

"He's head of the capital campaign committee, and both women were involved with benefit work there. Have you and Robert contributed to the building fund or attended any events for Butterfly Babies?"

"Yeah." Marissa's weariness seemed to turn to wariness in a flash; the assertive woman's personality had not been choked out of her. "A dinner last Christmas, that's all. Why? What's Sargeant got to do with anything?"

"I don't know, maybe nothing." Evelyn hitched her chair closer and leaned in, smelling the pleasantly clean scent of hospital bedding. "What's he to you, Marissa? He acts like he has a secret."

"He doesn't."

"I'm not prying. I need to know."

"He was head of the Path Lab, that's all. He's a jerk. I haven't set eyes on him since I graduated, and I don't want to either." She turned her face away.

"I know you're not feeling well, but, Marissa, that's because someone tried to kill you, and there's no reason to think he won't do it again. Two women are dead already, and I'm out of time and out of information. I have to know everything. What did Sargeant do to you?"

A sigh. She turned her bruised face back to Evelyn. "Nothing I can put him in jail for. He arranged the schedule so I'd always be working alone, and then he'd put his hands in every nonprosecutable spot on my body every minute I was there. He held my grade over my head when I began to complain—after all, he didn't cop feels, he gave my shoulder a friendly pat. If I went to my professors, he'd have made me look like some hyper spic trying to get rich on an easy lawsuit."

She had been younger then. A man who tried that on the adult Marissa would have finished his day in the local ER. "He never tried to rape you?"

A tiny shake. "I've kept thinking about it over the years—I probably will until the day I die, damn the snake—and I don't think he wanted to. He never tried to see me outside the lab, never called me at home. He didn't want sex—he wanted control. He liked jerking me around. He liked watching the blood drain from my face every day I had to walk into that lab. He liked knowing he could take someone and make six months of her life miserable. It was control."

Evelyn reached over, stroked a stray lock out of Marissa's face. "Sorry to bring it up. Don't strain your voice."

"What I hate most is that I let him get away with it. I didn't do a thing."

"You were young, Marissa. Besides, somebody did something, because he's not head of the Pathology Lab anymore."

"It's not enough," the girl said grimly. "And who's dead?"

"What?"

"You said two women were dead. Who?"

Evelyn hesitated; then her Nextel trilled its little merengue beat. "Yo."

"Evelyn," David said. "You won't believe this."

Her heart sank. "No. I don't want to hear it."

"We've got another one."

I can't do it, she thought. I'm exhausted, I'm out of ideas, and I need to go home and make dinner. I can't catch this madman who is cutting a swath through our city like a smart bomb. Leave me alone. It's not my responsibility. "Where? Who?"

Marissa lifted her head. "What's up?"

"It's Kelly Alexander. We're at the salt mine."

"Kelly Alexander!"

"Now *that* name," Marissa whispered in a thoughtful rasp, "I do recognize."

THE BRICK BUILDING ON THE SITE OF THE DEFUNCT
Fagan's already had the forlorn look of long abandonment,
though work had ceased only three days before. No attendant
patrolled the lot, no workers bustled near the time clock, no employees at all except for the plant manager, Phil Giardino. He waited
on the ground floor with the two homicide detectives and a uniformed officer.

"I found her," he whispered to Evelyn. He sat in the secretary's
chair off the lobby, hands clasped between his knees. "I went up to
get the ADT sheets, and—she's—"

David held her gaze with eyes so bloodshot they could have been
diseased. Had he slept at all the past three nights? "She's in her office
on the second floor. She came here straight from the jail to approve
the payroll."

"The guys still have to get paid, you know?" Giardino explained.
"We don't know how long it will be before they see another paycheck. Kelly, she was concerned about that."

"Who else—"

"No one else in the entire building," David said. "Her husband
dropped her off about two P.M. and went to their lawyer's office to
draft a press release."

"She came here to work all alone?"

Giardino seemed to find it odd that Evelyn found that odd. "This is her building. She helped design it, she had it built, she owned it. Kelly's been around the mine since she was a little kid. I used to take her down the shaft to visit her old man. Such a cute kid."

Watching a six-foot, two-hundred-and-fifty-pound veteran miner dissolve into tears nearly undid her. Another second and she'd have been crying with him, picturing a blond toddler clinging to the fingers of a young Phil Giardino, descending into the black pit with a happy giggle. This same toddler grew into a smart entrepreneur who quit her safe haven to see to her employees' needs. "By the second floor, you mean upward, right? Not down?"

"Up, yes," Riley confirmed, to her relief. "I've got a team clearing each floor of the building. We can't enter the mine unless OSHA says it's safe."

"It wasn't safe before?" Evelyn asked, recalling her recent trip to the depths.

"It's routine," Giardino told her. "There's no gas—faulty dynamite caused the explosion—but they still have to go through an integrity checklist before the workers can come back. That's what the press release is going to explain."

"So Alexander mining is off the hook?" David asked.

The plant manager snorted. "Are you kidding? This is America, there's no such thing as an accident. We'll be sued by everyone from the families of the seven guys to men who weren't even at work that day to the labor union."

"I hope it's not the responsibility of the geologist," David said. "He's already going to have to deal with his wife's death."

"He inspects the dynamite, but there's no way he could have known that it was bad." Giardino stared at the floor, eyes unfocused. " 'The danger's so prevailin' that no one ever knows.' "

"What's that?" Evelyn asked.

"It's an old mining song. I used to sing it to—" He broke off in a nearly silent sob.

Over his shoulder, Riley said to her: "David can show you the crime scene. I'll stay here and finish Mr. Giardino's statement."

She hitched her camera bag over her shoulder and followed David to the elevator. A few more strands of gray had appeared in his black locks; somehow he had lost several pounds without her noticing. Had that happened only in the past few days? "How are you?"

"I feel like we're under siege."

"Marissa's going to leave the hospital soon, David, and head right back to the fortress that didn't protect Grace Markham. He got in there, he got in here. How?"

The elevator began to move. "The place is locked up tight, with monitored alarms on all the exits except the front. No one has a key to the front except for Giardino, Kelly, her husband, and her father, who is also at the lawyer's office. There's a camera on the front, but surveillance only shows her coming in, no one else. Husband dropped her off about two, got to the lawyer's at two-ten. Her dad was already there. Giardino came here from lunch at Pat Joyce's about three, and camera surveillance confirms it. We'll track down his lunchmates, but I bet they'll tell the same story. I can't see that guy killing this girl." The elevator doors opened, and they stepped into the hallway, turning to the right. Down the hall to their left, she heard footsteps.

"Another uniform," he explained. "Three of them are checking the other floors for things out of place, windows unlocked, that sort of thing.

"Giardino says Kelly called this morning and told him she would approve the payroll before going home and leave it on her desk for him to pick up and take over to ADT. He walked in and found this."

They stopped at the doorway. Kelly Alexander's modest office had been lovingly decorated with art deco flair and framed photographs showing the history of the original salt mine. Plush carpeting and leather armchairs filled the small space, leaving room only for the polished cherry desk behind which the victim now sat, strapped to her ergonomic chair. Her hands lay on the desktop, palms down. A trail of blood and the haphazard pile of items on the floor, apparently swept from the desktop, belied the sense of calm.

Evelyn flicked on the light, touching only the very edge of the switch. Clouds had once again gathered to block out the sun, turning the ambient light a misty gray. The single window faced the Terminal Tower instead of the lake, and did not have the soundproofing of an apartment. The blare of a horn sounded clearly from the street below. "These dark tracks in the carpeting, are they from Giardino? Or us?"

He turned up the bottoms of his shoes. "Mine seem clean. We can check his."

Evelyn turned her camera on, focused on the spots in the carpeting. "He drew blood this time. He's escalating again."

"Maybe not." David followed her into the room as she snapped photos. "We haven't checked under her clothes, but I see blood on her hand only, and no injuries."

"You think she got him?"

"There's a community development award under the desk with blood on it."

She knelt down. A clear blue crystal award in the shape of a star on a pedestal rested on the carpet, partially under the desk drawers. Crusted blood covered two points of the star. "Looks like Kelly here clocked him one. Good for her." The emotion faded before it had barely begun. Kelly's spunk hadn't saved her. Evelyn put the camera away and began her examination.

Forty-five minutes later she paused, sitting on her knees in the middle of the room. David leaned against the windowsill.

"It's hard to tell from the carpeting," she began, "but I think he grabbed her elsewhere in the building—maybe he got in because she let him in—and then they got into a fight. Or he made entry on his own somehow, she heard him and got up from the desk to see who it was. I found the payroll sheets in this pile of stuff, but there's no marks in pen or pencil anywhere. I don't know what 'doing payroll' looks like, but I'm willing to bet she didn't get to it. He caught her almost right away. What's that noise?"

David glanced out the window. "Two news vans and a bunch of reporters with microphones. That Clio Helms is right out in front. Just as well," he added with a sigh. "Maybe they'll leave her husband alone long enough for us to tell him his wife's dead."

"You feel sorry for him, don't you?"

"His wife loved him," he said simply. "Even though he didn't have much to offer her."

Evelyn caught her breath. A particularly heavy cloud dimmed the already weak daylight; the features of his face became indistinct.

"David—"

"What?"

A faint *ding* sounded from down the hallway. The elevator had arrived, and in another minute they would no longer be alone.

"I love you," she said. "I may be an overprotective mother, and that's my right. I may be intransigent about a lot of things, and that's my right too. But I love you."

His shoulders slipped downward as if he'd let out a deep breath. "Why do we keep having these conversations over dead people?"

She smiled for the first time that day. "Hazard of the job, I guess."

Riley appeared in the doorway. "The media is running with the idea that our culprit is one of the dead miner's family members, angry that Kelly here walked out of jail this morning. I'm going to let them round all four bases with that if they want. It will keep them out of our hair. So what went on in here, Evie?"

"Well," she said. "From the marks in the carpeting, that chair nearest the door is an inch out of place, as if they shoved it on their way in. She must have been struggling. They moved behind the desk, where Kelly grabbed the award from that filing cabinet in the corner." She pointed at the dust-free spot on its surface, the same diameter as the base of the award. "She whaled on him with it, probably either upward to the head or downward to the thigh. The little bit of blood spatter on the wall behind the desk would be about thigh high."

"Ouch," David said.

"But he strangled her, she dropped the award, and he positioned her at the desk. Some of this debris might have been pushed off the desk in a struggle, but I don't think so. It isn't thrown off and scattered—her folders, pens, clock are all in one pile right next to the desk, as if he moved them to clear the desktop because he wanted to place her hands like that. Or he wanted to wipe his prints off the top, because I don't find any. And on top of the pile of desk stuff, what do we find?"

She held up the picture.

David sighed again. "I didn't even see that there. This just gets better and better."

The child had sketched a car, with large round wheels and an antenna. Stick figures with sad faces stood next to it. The pavement had been colored magenta, and the headlights glowed lime green. Tall buildings with empty windows lined the street. "He likes street scenes, I guess—houses, people on a road."

Riley studied it. "And our guy did that?"

"Our killer's child. Or our killer himself, drawing like a child. Don't ask me, because I don't have a clue."

"Neither do I. All the doors and windows are locked, no signs of prying. The maintenance tower on the roof might have been used— the rain leaves dirty water marks all over the door, and the area around the handle looks disturbed. The bar latch sticks, so we can't be sure if he has a key or the door couldn't lock."

"How could he get up to the roof from outside? Is there a fire escape?"

"Yeah. Plus we're practically on top of the building next door—it would only be a ten-foot jump or so."

"Five stories up."

"Five stories up," he confirmed.

"This guy's a bloody Flying Wallenda," David said.

"I sent a uniform over there to check their roof, see if there's signs of disturbance. It's the Stadium office building, and they're pretty busy over there even in the off-season. Wouldn't be hard for our guy to slip in and out."

"He's good at that," Evelyn said.

"There's two maintenance guys on staff who might have a key to the tower. I'm going to check with them now." Riley pulled out his Nextel and a cigarette. "After I catch a smoke, if it hasn't started raining yet."

Evelyn slid the drawing into a brown bag and placed a sticker on the front, moving with the lethargy of exhaustion. "What are we going to do, David? You can't guard Marissa forever, and this guy isn't going to stop. Why should he? We've been on this case round the clock for over three days now, and we don't know anything more about him than the day we found Grace Markham."

"Come on." He sank to the floor next to her. "He's just a man. A crazy one, sure, but a man. We'll get him."

"We don't know why he's doing this or how he picks his victims or who he might go after next. We also don't know how he materializes into and out of locked buildings. All I do know is I'm tired and I want to go home and forget that I even do this for a living. And maybe even eat something for a change."

He tilted up her chin with one finger. "Remember one thing."

"What's that?"

"There's no such thing as magic. You told me that once—no magic. Either the victims let this guy in or he finds a way. He's flesh and blood. He leaves a trail."

She gazed at her collection of paper bags. "But how am I going to pick it up?"

AFTER TWENTY MINUTES ON THE PHONE WITH HER
mother, Evelyn had received a detailed update on the
progress of her niece's baby, learned of an anniversary party
at her cousin's in Pennsylvania, which they were expected to attend,
and found out that Angel had gone home after picking at dinner.

Dialing her own phone number gave a busy signal, which, she
hoped, meant that Angel was gathering information over their slow
Internet connection about the ancient Romans, and not simply chatting with Melissa or Steve about her unreasonably strict mother.
Once the county gave her that whopping annual cost-of-living in-
crease, she would spring for a DSL line.

The time clock read 4:25 P.M. With her arms full of evidence,
she blocked her boss's exit. "Tony, I need help."

He tucked his thumbs into his back pockets, eyeing her. "No,
you don't. You never need help."

"I do now. This guy is on a full-blown rampage, and Marissa is
going to be kicked free of both cops and doctors any minute now.
Here, take this." She thrust some of the evidence at him and guided
him away from the door.

"You don't have to push. I was only going next door for a

sandwich. It's not like the ME's going to let me go home on time with the media watching our every move."

"You know Kelly Alexander?"

He dumped the packages on the large examination table. "Duh. The one that owns the salt mine and walked out of jail after seven guys died, that Alexander. The one who just got murdered. Tell me there's no justice in the world."

"Marissa thinks she recognizes the name but can't remember from where. I'm wondering if that's Marissa's connection to these other victims—a court case. No one has mentioned a homicide in our victims' pasts, so perhaps they were involved in a nonfatal case."

"A rape?"

"I can't imagine what else our department would be involved in. Fatals, sexual assault, and missing persons, that's it. If it were drugs or DUI, Toxicology would be in court, not us. But the only way to search is to go through the index of each ledger, year by year. Can you do that?"

Tony stared as if she'd asked him to rip out a fingernail. "Did I ever tell you I'm allergic to dust?"

"Tony! Come on! I need you."

As usual, direct confrontation confused him. "Okay, I'll check the ledgers. Alexander, huh?"

"Thank you."

Evelyn taped Kelly Alexander's clothing and quickly searched the acetate sheets. More blue fibers, similar to the ones from the parking garage in Marissa's attack, turned up. Three blond hairs, too sandy to be Kelly's, stuck to her shirt.

To Evelyn's surprise, the acid phosphatase test on Kelly's underwear came up negative. She had not been raped. Had he been rushed, interrupted by Giardino? Didn't feel secure in an office instead of a home? Or had the injury Kelly inflicted put him right out of the mood?

Evelyn turned the alternate light source on the items, finding only two streaks of crayon and a shiny spot on the left shoulder. She pressed it to the gold plate for FTIR analysis, leaving a thin streak for the machine to analyze.

She noted the results without surprise—the same oil found on Grace Markham, the stuff that didn't match anything. The black streaks on the floor were almost pure carbon. As in Frances Duarte's apartment, she would have suspected herself of carelessness with the black powder processing, but she had collected the carpet fibers before pulling out the fingerprint brushes.

She picked up the picture on its strange paper. The artist still refused to sign his work. His pictures had also grown more detailed. Did that have significance? Hell, did *any* of it have significance?

Remembering what Henry Taylor had done, she switched the alternative light source back on and flooded the paper with ultraviolet light. Nothing happened, except the lime green headlights on the car glowed even brighter. She turned the paper over.

In regular light, the reverse surface had no markings. Under the blue UV light, however, a series of red letters sprang to life, clear and sharp as a filet knife. Evelyn nearly dropped the paper in shock.

Reversed print read "od Care Center" across one corner, in a fourteen-point Times font. Underneath that, "ng ter."

This was not the first time Evelyn had seen a pattern emerge under UV when it remained invisible in regular light. She did not know exactly why the letters fluoresced, nor, at the moment, did she care. At one time this piece of paper had been pressed against something with "od Care Center" printed on it, and that was all that mattered. It seemed like her first real clue in three days.

She called David to tell him, but he had switched the phone to voice mail—probably to interview witnesses without interruption. She didn't bother dialing Riley; he'd have done the same thing.

Considering that the letters appeared on a child's drawing, Evelyn assumed they belonged in the name of a day-care center. She pulled the yellow pages from the secretary's desk and had another shock, this one at the sheer number of such places listed for the area. In ten minutes she had fifteen possibilities ending in "od," with none of them listed specifically as "——od Care Center." This could take forever, and she didn't have that much time.

Tony shuffled out of the evidence closet. "Nothing. I don't find a Kelly Alexander listed anywhere."

Evelyn's shoulders slumped. "Crap. I thought if—"

"Anything else? 'Cause I gotta go." Then he remembered who had been named supervisor and reworded. "I'm going. Don't forget to *not* put in for overtime for this."

"Mmm."

He swung several of his chins at the phone book. "What's that? Calling for takeout?"

She switched on the UV light and showed him the letters. "I'm assuming it's a day-care center. Maybe if I can find this kid, they can tell me why all these dead adults have his pictures at their crime scenes."

"What's the letters underneath?"

She showed him "ng ter" again.

"Long term."

"Very good."

"I play Scrabble a lot," he preened. "But what is long-term day care? You drop off a baby and then pick him up when he turns twenty-one? I'd have had kids if I knew that was an option."

She slumped onto a stool. "You're right. What an idiot I am."

"I'm glad to hear you finally admit it."

Evelyn held her forehead in one palm as if it hurt. "The kid isn't in day care. He's in a hospital, or a medical facility."

"He's sick."

"Or injured. Or disabled. Or he's perfectly healthy and *visits* someone in a care facility." She pulled the phone book closer. "I'm not even sure what to look under."

"Good luck," Tony said, picking up his briefcase. "And good night."

THE NURSE at the front desk listened carefully to Evelyn's introduction, perhaps because she had flashed an impotent but official-looking county ID. Evelyn concluded with "This is going to sound strange, but do you have any children here?"

"Children?" The nurse asked around the wad of gum in her mouth. "As patients?"

"Yes."

She glanced at the hallway, where an older nurse's aide draped a sweater around the shoulders of a frail man in a wheelchair. "Greenwood is a long-term care facility. Most of our patients are elderly."

"I know, but aren't some disabled? They might be younger?"

"No," she insisted. "No kids."

"What about this?" Evelyn pulled out the latest picture. "Have you seen this picture or pictures similar to it?"

The woman shook her head and explained: "We use markers here. Crayons are too easy to eat."

Evelyn thanked the woman for her time and returned to the car. Convalescent-care centers almost outnumbered day-care centers, and facilities had a positive jones for names ending in "od." Greenwood, Brynwood, even something called Elvenwood. Most were nursing homes for the elderly, and it seemed unlikely that they might have a child as a patient. But she did not want to eliminate them out of hand and risk missing her target. Of course, Marissa would be home and unprotected and probably murdered before Evelyn could canvas every place, and Riley and David could not help. They were tied up questioning everyone involved in Kelly Alexander's life, which, especially in the past few weeks, had been extremely active.

She needed to think.

The second rape victim, the one in Parma, had always felt that she knew the man. She had also been the only victim attacked in a single-family home instead of an apartment building. She fell out of his pattern—why?

Because she was special, Evelyn thought. He varied his MO for her because she was not a random choice. He knew her, and he probably knew her house if he felt comfortable enough to enter it. He probably lived nearby.

She started her car, watching the windshield wipers push the rain out of their way. He might have lived across town and known the teacher from his child's school or a social organization or just saw her in Tower City and followed her home for all I know, Evelyn thought, but just for the sake of argument, let's say he lived around there. His kid is now in convalescent care. Wouldn't he pick one close to home, easy to visit, bring his kid fresh paper and crayons?

Evelyn picked up the phone book she had pilfered from the lab and ran her finger down the addresses. Parma listed only two facilities, Corinthian and Brynwood. She set the book aside and pulled out of the lot.

The route took her past Parmatown Mall, where Evelyn had shopped for shoes and clothing all her life. The basement of May Co. had had the only hot-pretzel stand she knew of in the days before microwaves and the expansion of the frozen snack aisle. She thought of this as her stomach rumbled.

Brynwood Care Center had a small but lovingly appointed lobby, complete with a Pergo floor and antique furniture. Evelyn approached the three girls hanging around the front desk and explained where she worked, and that she needed to find a very young patient.

"I can't give out any personal information." The girl seated at the desk wore a cardigan sweater buttoned tightly over a white blouse. The other two girls wore scrubs.

One of them added, "And we don't have any kids here."

"Do you have crayons?"

They began to look concerned, as if perhaps they should call the security guard. Evelyn pulled out the picture left near Kelly Alexander and held it up.

"Does this look at all familiar? Do you have any patients who draw like this?"

The one behind the desk squinted at it. "That looks like any kid on the planet would have—"

"Craig." One of the girls in scrubs said it; the other nodded her agreement.

"Who?"

"He's in B301. He draws all the time. Stuff like that."

Evelyn stared, making the girl nervous, but she couldn't help it.

"I mean, I can't be sure it's his—"

"No, no, that's fine. I'd be glad of any help. Can I talk to him, please?"

"I don't know—" the receptionist began.

"I'll be happy to talk to your director first, get permission."

"But Mrs. Ellis is at dinner right now, and she really hates to be disturbed—"

"And she won't let you do anything anyway," the talkative aide in scrubs continued. "She'd tell us not to breathe if she could get away with it. Come on, if you can make it quick, you can be gone before she does her evening rounds. It isn't going to do you any good anyway."

She turned, and Evelyn left the other two in the dust before they could protest. "Why won't it do me any good?"

"Because Craig can't talk." She held open a heavy metal door with a red placard Evelyn didn't take the time to read. They passed a brightly lit gathering area, where patients watched a trivia show, some with interest, some with glazed eyes. "Didn't I see you on the news? Outside the building where that rich lady got killed?"

"Is Craig too young to talk?"

"He's too disabled. Here's his room."

Evelyn followed her in as her eyes adjusted to the dimmed lighting. Miniblinds kept out the depressing afternoon rain. Craig's roommate slumbered, snoring from a toothless mouth, in the bed nearer the door. A bulletin board on the left held more drawings. Evelyn stepped past the divider curtain.

Craig was not a child.

CRAIG SINCLAIR HAD PASSED HIS TWENTY-SECOND birthday the week before. He had smooth skin, short black hair, and calm brown eyes, now turned toward the slivers of light from the window. He lay completely still, unconcerned by their entrance.

Evelyn turned to the pictures pinned to the board, felt the paper. It seemed identical. She turned on the overhead light and observed the scenes of rounded automobiles and stick figures, sometimes inside the cars or watching from a house.

Craig now looked at her. The light must have disturbed him.

"How . . . what is his condition?" she whispered to the nurse.

"He retained some motor skills." The young woman spoke with professional clarity. "He can draw, as you see, he can feed himself a little. No speech, no control of bodily functions. Generally easygoing."

Evelyn moved closer. He could not respond, but she couldn't act as if he were not a human being either. "Hi, Craig. My name is Evelyn."

Not the slightest muscle twitched in his face, though his eyes had followed her when she moved.

"I'm interested in your pictures. They're very nice."

No reaction.

She had no idea where to go from there. Speaking to an actual child racked her nerves, much less a man who now had less than the mental capacity of one. "Is it okay if I look at your crayons? I won't take them. I just want to look at them."

No reaction.

A nightstand sat next to the bed, and a small wardrobe had been tucked into the corner. The top of it had been filled with two football trophies, a teddy bear, and a dust-covered video game joystick, the remains of a former life. "Where are his supplies?"

"In the activity room. Every patient has their own stuff in a little locker."

"Can we go there?"

The girl twirled her ponytail. This was turning into more of a project than she had bargained for, but curiosity battled the caution on her face. "Sure, I guess."

"Bye, Craig. It was nice to meet you. I might be back."

His gaze switched back to the window, either dismissing her or simply losing interest.

Outside, Evelyn trotted to keep up with her guide. "What happened to him?"

"Car accident, I guess. I'm not really sure. Come on, we'll take the stairs, they're always working on that stinking elevator. Activities are on the second floor."

Evelyn followed her into the stairwell with a fluttery feeling, remembering the last time, flying down the steps after someone who turned around and nearly killed her. "How long has he been like that?"

"About two years, I think. He moved into that room right about the time I started working here, but he could have been in a different room before that, so I don't know."

"Does his father come and visit him a lot?"

"He doesn't have a father. His mother comes all time." They emerged into a lower hallway and crossed it to a wide, bright room filled with tables and chairs. Boxes and plastic crates lined the walls on each side. The aide pulled down a milk crate with "Sinclair, Craig" written in marker on its edge. "Here's his stuff."

Evelyn excavated the crate, filled with construction paper, paintbrushes, paints, a coloring book, pieces of yarn, and a bottle of glue. She also found a slender shoe box full of crayons and a roll of paper similar to her items of evidence. "Does Brynwood provide this stuff?"

"The paints and the construction paper. Families bring in the extra stuff."

"Did his mother give him this?" Evelyn held up the roll.

"Dunno."

"Does she come in every night? Will she be here soon?"

"Usually about this time, but she's out of town this week. She told me that last week so we'd know, in case Craig got agitated or something, missing her." The girl sat on the table, propping her feet on a chair. "It's sad, though."

"What is?" Hell, what *wasn't* sad about an incapacitated, otherwise healthy young man?

"He won't miss her. He doesn't notice if she comes or not. She should know that, but I guess she convinces herself that he's aware of more than he's really aware of, you know what I mean?"

"And you're sure he has no father?"

"No." But she drew out the vowel, the way Marissa had.

"It's very important. I wish I were at liberty to tell you *how* important it is."

"I think his parents are divorced. The day I started here, Mrs. Ellis was orienting me, and Craig's mother stalked into the office and ripped Mrs. Ellis up one side and down the other. I guess she found a man in Craig's room. Mrs. Ellis shooed me out, but I heard Craig's mom screaming about a court order and parental rights and he was not *ever* to be allowed here. I remember it because it was the first—and not the last, let me tell you!—family fight I saw here, and because I've never seen anyone yell at Mrs. Ellis and live."

Evelyn ripped a piece of paper off the roll and began to mark it with samples from the crayon box, trying to choose colors similar to those used in the drawings left by the victims. "So his father is out there somewhere but not allowed to visit?"

"Yeah . . ." The aide glanced around the room and, finding it empty except for them, went on in a conspiratorial tone. "But I see a guy with him sometimes, after Mrs. Ellis's rounds, when normal visiting hours are over. I assume it's his father. I don't know how he gets in there, because the receptionist wouldn't let him in and all the other doors are locked."

"What does he look like?"

"I dunno. I just get a glimpse of him—just sort of tall, not real heavy."

"Is he white?"

"Yeah."

"What color is his hair?"

The girl screwed her face up, trying to remember. "Maybe light brown?"

"How does he dress?"

"Slouchy clothes. Dark colors, when I saw him."

"And you've never asked him who he is?"

"No. It's always, like, the middle of the night and I'm doing something else. Then when I go back, he's gone. But he leaves the paper and crayons and sometimes chocolate bars for Craig."

"And you've never reported this?"

"I'm not the security guard."

Evelyn raised an eyebrow. The girl flushed even as her jaw tightened into a stubborn line. "When my parents split, my mother spent three years trying to turn my sister and me against our dad. I figure this guy's got a right to visit his son whether Mrs. Sinclair likes it or not. Craig never seemed upset or agitated about it, and hasn't he got the right to see his father?"

"That's a good point," Evelyn said, replacing the milk crate in its assigned space. "Will Craig ever get better? Is there any chance he will improve?"

The aide shook her head, whipping the ponytail around her freckled face.

"He can't learn, or even make limited progress?" Evelyn pressed, her heart sinking. What must it be like, to have every avenue of your life closed off forever?

"I asked the doctor that once. He said to let Mrs. Sinclair think whatever gives her comfort, but there's no chance. Craig might live another fifty years and he won't change one bit. It's pretty sad, if you ask me—at least the old people here got to live their lives first. He didn't have much of one. You know," she added, as if the thought had just occurred to her, "I think he's only a few years older than me."

Evelyn let the girl have a moment or two to thank her lucky stars that she hadn't been disabled and bedridden before she turned old enough to drink, and then said, "I promise I will not tell anyone what you've told me or that you took me to see Craig. But I really have to talk to Mrs. Sinclair."

The aide guided her back into the hallway. "I can't give you her number, if that's what you're asking. Anyway, she's not home."

"But I— Well. Hmm." The girl was right. Riley and David might have to get a warrant simply to find out the woman's phone number. Or they could just wait for her to come visit her son. "When is she getting back?"

"Maybe tomorrow? I'm not sure. She said a week." The aide delivered Evelyn to the front desk and squared her shoulders, as if she had completed a difficult task.

"Mrs. Ellis is going to kick your butt," the receptionist told the aide.

"Only if some bitch rats me out." The aide fixed her coworker with a gaze like cast iron. "And who would do that?"

RILEY, WHERE'S DAVID? I TRIED HIS NEXTEL AND HIS
pager, but he hasn't called back."

"He said he had to go out for a minute." Crackles over
the transmission blanked out every other letter of his words, but
Evelyn made out the gist. "I assumed he was getting our usual order
over at Barrister's. Why?"

"I've located our artist." She summed up what she had learned
in the past half hour, including the name of Craig's mother.

"And where is she?"

"In Cancún," she repeated—shouting, as if that would help.
"Her first vacation in five years, according to the care center staff.
She should be back tomorrow."

"And you think this mysterious father figure is our killer?"

"I'm following his trail and it led me here. I don't understand it
any more than you do, but there we are. I've already approached the
indomitable Mrs. Ellis, who told me to go pound sand. Or is that
salt? Salt would be more appropriate in this case."

"Evelyn, are you losing it?"

"Lost it years ago," she admitted. "She says she can't divulge any
patient information, period. I need you to get a search warrant. I
also need you to put someone on Craig Sinclair's room. His father

will almost certainly come back to visit. If he's planning on killing someone else, he'll need another picture."

"And we're basing all this on a drawing by a mentally, um, challenged young man who can't speak?"

"It's not a drawing. It's the killer's calling card. It's his testimony to us."

"What does it mean?"

"I haven't the slightest idea."

"It will be tough to get a judge excited about that," the detective warned.

"This woman knows everything we need to know about this killer. I *know* it. All we have to do is ask, but we can't because we can't find her."

"How about the phone book?" he joked.

Evelyn slapped the copy sitting in her passenger's seat. "Guess what? She's not listed. I called every initial and female name under Sinclair in the phone book."

"And we haven't run across anyone named Sinclair in this investigation. At least I haven't. I'll check all the apartment building employee lists from the three homicides again, but it really doesn't ring a bell."

"Not just who actually works in the building, Riley—it could be someone who works for the realty companies that own the apartments."

"The salt mine owns their own building . . . I think. Okay, check them all for a guy named Sinclair."

"I hate to say it, but it's possible that won't help. Mrs. Sinclair could have changed back to her maiden name after the divorce. None of the nurses know her first name, and Mrs. Ellis wouldn't tell me. On the phone I just asked for Craig's mother. Maybe some of the Sinclairs I called are relatives, but she told them not to give out any information about her."

If Mrs. Sinclair went to the trouble of changing her son's name as well, plus banned her ex from the care center, she *really* did not want any contact with him. On the other hand, the husband's name might be Sinclair and she simply wasn't listed in the phone book. Evelyn favored the first theory. This sounded like a very bitter divorce.

"We'll do what we can," Riley promised. "But Craig's mom will probably return from sunnier climes by the time we could get a warrant signed anyway. By the way, Robert is busting Marissa out of medical prison as we speak."

"What?"

"The swelling has gone down and she's healthy otherwise. She's being discharged."

"What about the guard?" Marissa would return to the supposedly high-security Riviere, right where Grace Markham had been brutally murdered at her own kitchen table. Evelyn wished current medical insurance allowed for longer hospital stays . . . but then, the hospital hadn't been any safer, had it? Her face burned where the killer had struck her.

"We'll put a policewoman in the apartment with them. The two kids weren't happy about it, of course. They *are* almost newlyweds."

"Good."

"But I don't know how long we can keep her there. Two days at the most, our sergeant says."

Craig's mother would have returned by then, and at least their killer would have a name. It might not make him any easier to catch, of course, but Evelyn would feel a lot better.

He's just a man, David had said. Not magic.

Though he seemed to appear and disappear as if he were. He got in and out of the Riviere. He got in and out of Brynwood. He got in and out of the salt mine, leaving his messages, his testimony—

"I have an idea," she said.

"What?"

"Never mind, you won't like it. Good luck with the warrant."

She hung up, pulled out a card, and dialed the number printed on it.

It took a moment to go through. She studied the building in front of her, wondering how Craig's sad, doting father meshed with the murderer and rapist she'd been chasing. Was it the same man? How did his crimes relate to Craig?

The line clicked. "Clio Helms."

"Ms. Helms? It's Evelyn James. I have a favor to ask."

T HE PLAIN DEALER BUILDING HAD BEEN AT THE COR-
ner of East Eighteenth and Superior for as long as Evelyn
could remember. She parked in a Cleveland State student lot
off Payne and hiked through a light drizzle to the glass double
doors. The receptionist had gone home for the day, but Evelyn's escort waited by the empty desk.

Ten minutes later she stood in a room filled with reporters'
desks from end to end, broken up by filing cabinets, blue recycling
containers, and a coffeemaker. It resembled the homicide unit in
both lack of decor and presence of clutter. The reporters even favored worn blazers, like the cops.

The newspaper offices, however, had more paper. *Lots* more. In
the modern world of PCs, Internet, and e-mail, every desk seemed
walled in with two-foot stacks of files, pads, and sheets of paper.
Some had started piles on the floor. If a strong wind hit the room,
the resulting mess would be irreversible.

"You mentioned the Archive before," Evelyn said without pre-
amble.

Clio Helms, her twenty-something-year-old skin still dewy fresh
well past dinnertime, sat back to gaze at her guest. Her desk chair
had been upholstered in a 1970s orange, and the stuffing escaped

from its shackles at points; the scratched desk sat in the very middle of the room, to be buffeted by every passerby; Clio's desk organizer consisted of a series of small cardboard boxes, but the reporter smiled as if the seller had just lowered the price on an item she wanted. And in a way, Evelyn had.

"And I get an interview?"

"After the arrest. And I still can't give out any nonsanctioned information. I mean, I won't be able to tell you things that the cops and the prosecutors are holding back in preparation for trial. But I can explain the forensic techniques I used—without specifics, of course."

Clio nodded with mock solemnity. "Of course."

"That's the best I can do."

"I understand perfectly," she purred, a cat with one paw on the canary's tail. Evelyn would have to watch every word, to think not twice but three times before speaking around this woman, or the ME would be dangling her job over the precipice. He could forgive any mistake except bad publicity, and losing this case because Evelyn had talked too much would result in very bad publicity indeed.

"So what are we searching for?"

"Something to connect the three victims." The victims' names and the assumption that they shared the same murderer had already been published, so Evelyn felt safe with this tack. "I'd like to find mentions of them intersecting, being in the same place at the same time."

"This must be serendipity." Clio bounced up, pulling a delicate pink sweater from the back of her chair—no elbow-patched tweed blazers for her. "I had been planning to do the very same thing, but between the salt mine disaster and that fire on the East Side, I haven't had time."

"I hope you didn't have other plans for tonight."

"Tonight, hmm." The reporter pushed the button for the elevator. "Tonight was supposed to be the assistant to the mayor's press secretary. Six-two, works out, is a Big Brother, likes dogs."

"Sorry."

"Don't worry. He'll wait."

The Archive Department took up half of one massive floor. Most of it contained floor-to-ceiling files, but five computer monitors lined one long table.

"How long ago are we talking?" Clio asked.

The rapes had begun four years ago, as far as they knew. Grace had married three years ago. Craig might have been hurt two years ago, according to the nurse's aide, but it could have been longer than that. "Four years."

"Wow." Clio settled herself in a metal chair in front of the first monitor. "I hope you've had dinner. There's a vending machine down the hall if you haven't."

Evelyn sat down and tried David again while they waited for the monitor to warm up. She got only a buzzing noise.

"You might not get any reception in here. The walls are pretty thick. So we're looking for any mention of Kelly Alexander, Grace Markham, and Frances Duarte, together or separately. Anyone else?"

"No."

"You're sure?" the reporter pressed.

No way could she mention Craig Sinclair. If his name popped up, she'd cross that bridge when she came to it. "Nope."

Clio typed the names, her fingers flying in a blur. Evelyn noticed a large scar on the back of her left hand, the healed tissue standing out in a jagged line. That must have bled a lot. She said nothing, not wanting to like Clio Helms any more than she could already help. The Simpson trial had made most forensic technicians quite paranoid.

"Okay. May, four years ago. Rock and Roll Hall of Fame Summer Festival Committee . . ."

An hour and a half and two stale granola bars later, Clio sipped a diet cola and asked, "How did you get into this line of work, anyway?"

"I watched a lot of cop shows when I was a kid."

"So why not become a cop?"

"I don't like people. Wait, that didn't come out right—remember I haven't had a decent night's sleep all week. I couldn't deal with stressed-out human beings day in, day out. I *did* like science, so it was a natural compromise."

"But you can deal with dead bodies?"

"They're quiet. Crap—that's not going to wind up in the Sunday magazine, is it?"

"I should be so lucky, to see my byline there." At Evelyn's frown, the girl reassured her. "Relax. I'm not out to 'get' you. I'm just curious. How do you cope with seeing death, violent death, up close and personal?" She ignored her monitor, turning to the forensic scientist. "Doesn't it ever get to you?"

Evelyn answered honestly. "Not yet."

"How is that possible?"

"You don't think about it."

"It's that simple?"

"It's that simple. There's no point in me standing there and weeping over a life cut short. It won't do the victims or their families any good, and it certainly won't help me. I think about what tests I have to do, what evidence I have to collect, what paperwork I have to fill out, and maybe what to make for dinner."

"You just turn your feelings off?"

"Yeah, pretty much. You learn to do that early on, or you get into another line of work."

"Then turn them back on when you go home at night?"

Did she? Or had they been in sleep mode for so long that they might stay that way? Could that be why she wanted David close but not too close?

Maybe he was right. Maybe she made excuses and put off decisions because she didn't want to face either living constantly with the sharp emotions he aroused in her or enduring the pain of losing him. Feelings were more comfortable at a distance, locked up in a little box at the back of her mind.

"I have a problem with that," Clio continued, flicking through electronic pages. "When I'm writing certain stories, I go home and neglect everyone, my parents, my boyfriend, my dog. Here's another one—October 2006. 'Heiress involved in accident.'"

Evelyn abandoned her thoughts with relief. "What was that?"

"'Kelly Alexander, heiress to the Alexander salt mine, was involved in a two-car accident at Euclid and East Ninth late Saturday night while returning home from a fund-raising event. The driver of the other car was injured. Police have not ruled out alcohol as a factor, nor determined who was at fault.' Period. That's pretty lame," Clio critiqued. "No follow-up on the salt mine angle? Who wrote this?"

"Does it say who the other driver was?"

"No. Let's go on. A week later: 'Kelly Alexander was arraigned in common pleas court this morning on a charge of DUI. She pled not guilty, stating that she was not the driver of the car. A trial date has been set for November twentieth.' Okay, next. December eleventh—guess it got delayed. 'Heiress found not guilty of DUI. A jury returned a not-guilty verdict in thirty minutes in the case of salt mine owner Kelly Alexander. Members interviewed afterward said that blood on the steering wheel proved Alexander to be the driver of the vehicle, despite her assertion that she was not, but still her blood alcohol level was not sufficient for a DUI charge. Also, the other driver, Craig Sinclair, had possibly run a red light and caused the accident. Alexander, the daughter of salt mine owner' . . . blah blah blah, the typical bio."

"I don't believe it," Evelyn said. Kelly had hit Craig, and now Craig's father left a picture of a car next to her corpse.

"Me neither. This is buried in State and Local. It should have been on page one."

"Who else was in the car?"

"You know what I think? We had an interim editor at the time who had worked in the Legal Department, and the guy was a real candy-ass. Afraid of his own shadow, much less a lawsuit from one of the richest men in Ohio. What was that?"

"If Kelly said she wasn't the driver, she must have blamed someone else in the car with her."

Clio nodded, tossing curls to and fro. "No passengers are mentioned. Hey, maybe this is where she, what did you say, 'intersected' with Marissa? Wouldn't Marissa have testified in the trial?"

"Not DUI—that would be the Toxicology Department." A tremor ran through Evelyn's stomach . . . Did this killer have another ME staff member on his hit list?

She needed to get into Toxicology's records, but that wouldn't be any easier than getting patient information from Mrs. Ellis, and besides, everyone in that department had gone home for the day.

The blood on the steering wheel—that could have been sent for DNA, to Marissa.

"So you think this Craig Sinclair is taking his revenge on the woman who hit him two years ago?"

"I don't know." That was true enough; she couldn't see how Craig could take revenge on anyone. But his protective mother? His mysterious father? Her heart began to pound. "I'd like to know who else was in that car."

"And besides, if Marissa verified that Kelly *was* the driver, why would the victim be mad at her?" Clio shook her head. "I like it, but it's kind of far-fetched."

"You're right there." Evelyn sat back, feigning disappointment, willing her body to stay still when it wanted to dash from the room. "I'll check it out, but let's go on. Next story?"

FINDING DAVID'S CAR IN HER DRIVEWAY FILLED HER with conflicting surges of adrenaline. Had something happened to Angel? Marissa? Or had he come to say good-bye, to tell her that love wasn't going to be enough?

Angel, seated at the kitchen table, looked up from her books. "About time you got home."

"I was—"

"Yeah. Working." But she spoke without malice and seemed amused. "*We* were eating. David made gumbo."

The detective emerged from the refrigerator with a brick of cheese and seemed to be suppressing a grin himself.

"Gumbo?" Evelyn shook off her wet coat and left her shoes by the door. "Where does a midwestern boy learn to cook gumbo?"

"Ah, just one of the many mysteries of my past."

"It's not bad," Angel admitted. "Well, once he got done telling me all sorts of gross stories about drunk-driving accidents, anyway."

"I could add one of my own tonight," Evelyn said, thinking of Craig Sinclair's damaged body. "But perhaps you've had enough."

"Definitely enough."

David set a steaming bowl in front of her. It smelled so good that she forgave them both for the fun they were having at her surprise. "Thanks."

"It's all part of my master plan to make myself indispensable."

"It's working."

"Where *have* you been, anyway?"

Halfway through the list of what Evelyn had learned from Clio Helms, Angel yawned and collected her books. "It's almost midnight and I'm going to bed, so keep it down."

"Actually," her mother told her, "David and I have to go out."

FACE-TO-FACE interviewing often revealed much more than a voice on the phone. Besides, Evelyn planned to go straight on to work and find out if or how Marissa had become involved with Kelly Alexander's DUI trial.

The night doorman buzzed the Quinn residence only after examining David's badge and ID like a jeweler with the Hope diamond. Markham's voice bellowed over the electronic speaker.

"What the hell do you want now? Do you know what time it is?"

"It's twelve forty-five," David informed him with a sort of relish. "We need to ask you a few questions."

"Go away."

"You're a material witness who has still not been cleared in the murder of his wife, Markham. I can place you in temporary custody if I want to."

Inside the elevator, Evelyn asked, "Could you really? Take him into custody?"

"I'm not sure. Probably not, but to screw with him, it would be worth the risk."

Markham did not look as suave in the wee hours as he did during the day, and he did not seem to try to. He and Barbara stood cross-armed in their foyer, refusing to let Evelyn and David any farther into the apartment.

"The car accident?" William Markham asked after David explained their purpose. "What the hell are you asking about that for?"

"We'll take up less of your time if you just answer the questions, sir. Do you remember a car accident in which Kelly Alexander was charged with DUI about two years ago?"

"Hell, yeah. She said Grace was driving."

"What?"

"They were coming home from some fund-raising thing . . . the kids' hospital—"

"Butterfly Babies?" Evelyn asked.

He nodded. "They'd all been drinking, but they'd had a full meal too, Grace said. Kelly T-boned some kid at East Ninth, and she was worried about bad publicity for the mine—all Kelly cares about is that stupid mine, believe me—and when the cops got her on the Breathalyzer, she panicked and told them Grace was driving. It wasn't much of a defense—she was sitting in the driver's seat when the damn cop arrived, and it was her car."

"She tried to pin it on Grace?" asked Barbara, who seemed to be hearing this story for the first time.

"For about ten minutes. She gave Grace this song and dance that she thought Grace hadn't drunk anything, so she couldn't be charged—which was a lie, they were all drinking and Kelly knew it. The judge threw it out anyway—Kelly blew under a point-eight alcohol level, and the other guy ran a red light."

"Did Grace get angry about it?"

"She was pretty ticked, yeah. Of course she wouldn't admit it to *me*, since I'd been telling her for years what a bitch Kelly Alexander is. She'd be civil to Kelly in public, but they stopped hanging together after that." He yawned, setting off a chain reaction in the foyer. "Oh hell, you can come in. Babs, honey, do we have any coffee?"

"Certainly. Right in the cabinet over the pot."

He scowled, whirled, and they followed him to the kitchen. To

Evelyn's surprise, he made enough coffee for all four of them, and even poured.

"So the case went to trial." Where, perhaps, Marissa presented evidence. Evelyn accepted a cup from Markham with a grateful smile. "Did Grace have to testify?"

"I think so. I'm not completely sure . . . I had a big project going on at the time and Grace didn't say much about it. She knew what I thought of Kelly Alexander."

And after a year of marriage, she probably knew how much sympathy to expect from you, Evelyn thought. "Who was in the other car?"

"I don't know, some guy who got hurt. That's the only reason it went to trial, Grace said—because his family raised such a fuss."

"One guy or two guys?" Could Sinclair's father have been in the car with him? Maybe have been driving?

"I don't know. Grace only mentioned one."

"Do you remember his name?"

He looked at her as if she must be mad. "Of course not."

Just because his wife had nearly been charged with critically injuring a very young man, that was no reason for the incident to stick in his mind. "Only Grace and Kelly were in their car?"

"Yeah. I wasn't, if that's what you're thinking— Wait, that Frances chick was there too. The one that just got killed."

"Frances Duarte?"

"Yeah. They always went to those kids' hospital things together."

Evelyn shook her head. "These three particular women wind up dead in the past week, and it never occurred to you to mention this accident to anyone? Not even the cops investigating your wife's murder? Everyone has a right to be self-centered, but you abuse the privilege."

"You think this is about the accident?"

"Don't you?"

"Why would I? That was two years ago. Hell, *I'm* a more likely connection than that."

"You?"

"Me." For the first time, a touch of guilt registered on his face. "I'm building a high-rise in the Flats and I live in a high-rise in the Flats. Kelly put a factory smack in the middle of primo real estate, and Frances helped her. That was the connection between us all that crossed my mind. That's why I wouldn't stay in that apartment."

"Hell of a way to protest urban development," Evelyn said.

"It sounded insane to me too. Then I got to thinking about all that money missing from the hospital Grace used to raise funds for and figured that's a whole lot more motive than development on the east bank. Certainly more than some car accident."

Money over a young man's life. Sure. "You mean the missing fifteen million at Butterfly Babies?"

Markham pursed his lips as if to whistle. "That much, huh?"

"Did Grace suspect Mark Sargeant?"

"Who?"

"The capital campaign chair?"

"Don't know him. Grace didn't mention it at all. I saw the story in the paper, like I said."

"And you didn't mention that to us either," David pointed out.

"You got so interested in Barbara and me that I thought I'd keep my theories to myself."

David sighed. "Back to this accident. Did Kelly try to pin it on Frances when Grace didn't pan out?"

"Nah. Kelly was tighter with Frances than Grace, and—and something else." He concentrated, then snapped his fingers as another memory came back to him. "That was it. Frances drank way more than Kelly and Grace. Even though she was older, she always put more away than they did. I think that was another reason Grace dropped her."

Perhaps Frances's investment had salved a guilty conscience,

Evelyn thought. Frances blamed herself, not Kelly, for the accident because the two younger women had been drinking just to keep her company.

"I asked Kelly if anyone was hurt in the accident, and she said no," David said. "No, wait, she said *Grace* wasn't hurt. She never mentioned this other driver."

"She forgot about it?" Evelyn asked in disbelief.

"From her hesitation, I doubt it. She remembered, all right, she just didn't want to raise that specter again. She already had enough attention from the media with the mine disaster."

"That's Kel," her ex-fiancé said bitterly. "She never thought of anything besides herself. Her and that damn mine."

"OKAY," David said in the confines of Evelyn's Ford Tempo. Raindrops fell in a wayward pattern; flashes of lightning framed the tall buildings against the inky sky. "I'm convinced. Craig Sinclair's father is killing the women from the car that crippled him. But if his motive is revenge, than why rape?"

"Because he likes to rape. We've already established that. Besides, what better way to express hate, contempt, and ultimate power?" She thought a moment longer, twirling her Egyptian mummy key chain. "That's why he straps them up in a sitting position. It's like they're in a car. On top of that, we found Frances just sitting, but Grace and Kelly both had their hands out in front of them, as if holding a steering wheel. Maybe this guy really doesn't know who was driving, Grace or Kelly."

"Marissa proved that the driver was Kelly—and yet he still seems to have a beef with Marissa."

"Maybe he thought Grace drove and she got off scot-free."

"They both got off."

A flash of lightning split the sky. Grace tensed, waiting for the following thunder. "Because they weren't over the alcohol limit."

"Maybe he's just nuts."

"Blood alcohol content is a Toxicology Department analysis. What if one of our toxicologists is next on his list? What if I've been running around looking for this guy all week and his next victim works on my floor?"

"Don't panic. We'll do a head count in the morning."

"God, David!"

"Well, what choice do we have? Do you really want to call every one of your coworkers in the middle of the night just to ask if they're still alive?"

She said nothing, just worried, thinking that the killer had left a picture of sad people around a car at Kelly's murder scene—the crux of his project. Did that mean he had finished, that he had no other victims lined up? "Is he done now that he got the three women from the car, or is he going to move on to the toxicologist, the cop who wrote the report, the jury members who let Kelly go? Is he going to go back to Marissa and finish the job?"

"I don't know, hon." David let one hand fall to her head, tucked her hair behind an ear. "She's got an armed guard with her tonight. We just have to have some faith. In the meantime, we have to find Craig Sinclair's father."

"I know where to pick up his trail."

"Evelyn?"

"What?"

"*Now* you're going to say 'to the Batcave,' aren't you?"

EVELYN RAN THE FTIR SPECTRUM OF CRAIG SINCLAIR'S crayons against the samples from the drawings and the victims' clothing while David made phone calls. The compositions were identical for most of the crayons used in the drawings and similar for the samples from the clothing. Perhaps after the father used the crayons to draw on the victims' clothing, he hadn't returned them to his son.

Thunder rumbled past the building. "I can't believe it's still raining," David said.

"Lake effect."

"I thought that caused snow."

"Any precipitation. The water stays warmer than the land and condenses the moisture in the cold air over it. We blame lake effect for everything. Any luck?" she added as the printer issued color graphs of her spectra.

"Not so far. You wouldn't believe how many airlines have regular flights from Cancún."

"It's a popular spot." The dirty areas on Kelly Alexander's office carpeting had been fouled by carbon dust, similar to the dirt found in Frances Duarte's apartment. The two samples were not identical, however—the carbon from Kelly's office had been contaminated with particles of salt. Probably every surface in the building developed a microscopic coating of salt, as air circulated through the mine and the huge loads of broken boulders were brought to the surface.

She slid the tapings of Kelly Alexander's clothing under the stereomicroscope. They immediately revealed two things: that Kelly had a Siamese cat and that her turquoise shirt had been composed of silk and rayon. Evelyn also found three unusual fibers, very straight and clear. They looked almost like hairs without medullas. "Kevlar."

"What?"

"There's some Kevlar fibers on Kelly's shirt."

David frowned. "From one of us? Riley and I weren't wearing bulletproof vests, and the patrol guys shouldn't have been in there."

Detective Womack would also have routine contact with protective gear, but who would wear such a heavy garment to murder a slender, unarmed woman? "It doesn't have to have come from a bulletproof vest. Pathologists wear Kevlar gloves underneath the latex, to protect themselves from accidents. Scalpels can slip, even the bone saw can bounce up unexpectedly. Mechanics wear Kevlar gloves too, especially around moving parts or sharp parts. Kevlar can't be cut and it doesn't conduct electricity."

"How do you know so much about mechanics?"

"I used to be married to one."

He rubbed one eye. "Sorry I asked. What about— Hello, is this Continental?"

Evelyn took a break to get a diet cola from the staff kitchen; only a copious amount of caffeine would get her through the rest of the day, or night, or whatever the hell it was. She had crayons, carbon dust, and Kevlar. And oil on a mesh strap. Where did that take her?

"Found her." David tossed the phone back in its cradle with a triumphant dunk shot. "She's on a red-eye from Miami. She'll touch down in forty-five minutes, unless this thunderstorm holds them up. I'm going to pull Riley out of bed and form a welcoming committee. Want to come?"

"No, I'll stay here. The answer's here somewhere, I know it."

"All right."

He kissed her, and she grasped the lapel of his jacket to keep him close. "I suppose you think you can cook one meal and chat up my daughter and you can breeze right into my household?"

"Yep."

"You're right."

He kissed her again, taking a little more time with it, and left.

Evelyn stood at the window to watch him drive away in the pouring rain, feeling the damp settling into her bones. She went to the closet to get her lab coat, more for warmth than for cleanliness.

Not that the coat was clean anyway. A streak of oil still stained the bottom hem.

The streak of oil she'd picked up at the salt mine on the day of the explosion—the same building where Kelly Alexander had been murdered three days later.

As long shots went, it wasn't the worst she'd tried. She pulled out her gold-plated slide and transferred some of the oil to its shiny surface. The FTIR waited, warmed up, cooled down, and got ready to go.

The sample nearly matched the smear found on Grace Markham's arm. It had slightly more silica and of course the ubiquitous salt, but otherwise, the spectra were the same.

Evelyn had dirtied her lab coat when she spilled the bottle at the salt mine. The man there had said it was cable oil for the elevator.

As if on cue, the elevator in the hallway rumbled open its doors. Perhaps David had returned. She couldn't think who else would be there at that hour.

She moved across the lab to the door. The lights were on in the room and the door had glass panels, so she had no chance of remaining unseen. But the door also locked automatically, so she didn't feel too nervous. Until she thought of all of Grace Markham's security features.

If her luck had changed, the newcomer would be one of her coworkers from the Toxicology Department. If it had not—

Through the glass panels she saw a man's huge back, shoulders straining the seams of a flannel shirt, and wispy brown hair caught in a long ponytail.

She burst out of the lab door. "Ed! Am I glad to see you!"

He did not seem the least bit glad to see her. "What are you doing here?"

"I came in early. Listen, I have a question—"

He unlocked his laboratory door, stamping his hand on the wall for the lights. "Three in the morning is not early, it's ridiculous."

"Then why are you here?"

"I am remarkably dedicated."

She followed him in. "Listen, I have a question—"

"I also have neighbors prone to insomnia. They deal with their wakefulness by watching TV." He deposited his lunch in a small refrigerator next to his desk, locked it with a hasp and a padlock, and dropped the key into his pocket. "They never choose tender romances or sound tracks with gentle music, no, they are addicted to action adventure themes replete with car chases, explosions, and a great deal of shooting. All in surround sound."

"You have my sympathy. I wanted to know—"

"You want to know about the sample of grease you gave me the other day, and yes, I have characterized it further. It's most likely used in—"

"Elevators?"

Evelyn would never have made such a blunder if she hadn't been so very sleep-deprived. The stout scientist puffed up like a blowfish, agitated and lethal.

"If you already know all about your little glob of lubricant, then *why did you waste my time*? It's difficult enough doing the most with the least in the time-honored tradition of all government workers, but then when I do agree to wear my fingers to the nub a little more purely as a favor to a friend—"

We're friends? Evelyn wondered. Then she realized that, given Ed's temperament, appearance, and amount of time spent at work, she might very well be the closest thing he had. Which was downright pathetic. "I'm so sorry. Your data is still important, vitally so."

He threw himself into a task chair and faced his computer, stonily watching the screen come back to life.

"My conclusion is just an inductive guess," she went on. "I need the scientific proof."

The ponytail gave an irritated little shake.

"And I'm still really baffled by this. Listen: I had the elevator guy at Grace Markham's apartment take two samples from the top of the elevator, and they don't match the smear I gave you." She explained, to his back, where she had picked up the oil on her lab coat. "Does that mean that the sample on Grace had to come from the salt mine, or can there be more than one type of oil used in the mechanics of an elevator?"

Silence. The set of his back managed to convey his utter lack of interest in her difficulties.

"Marissa is still in danger, Ed. This guy is too determined to stop. And she's sitting right where Grace Markham sat, like a fish in a barrel."

A short pause, then finally: "Of course more than one type of oil would be used. Heavy machinery doesn't work on WD-40."

She pulled up a chair.

"Different lubricants would appear at different spots. To put it in layman's terms"—he made the words sound like an expletive—"imagine your car. The oil added to the engine to lubricate the cylinders is not the same as the heavy grease added to the wheel bearings or the thin pink fluid used in the transmission."

"So depending on where he took the samples from, I might get more than one result."

"You might have ten distinct lubricants used in one machined process. And that's not even considering contaminants, which could vary greatly from one mechanism to another. You let someone else collect your samples?"

She didn't care for criticism of her technique from a guy who never left the lab, but she let it slide. "Would it be the same for all elevators?"

"I doubt every elevator in the country buys exactly the same brand of oil, though if they do, I'd get some of that manufacturer's stock. In this case, it's a product called Vitalube. But the chemical composition wouldn't vary too greatly from brand to brand. Unless you have a petroleum-based versus a synthetic, of course. The synthetics would show up as a quite different composition."

"I'll have to get a sample of the cable oil used at the Riviere to make sure, but for the moment I'll assume that, since Grace Markham had a smear of cable oil on her arm, and since the elevator opens directly into her apartment, the killer used the elevator to make entry."

"Bravo," Ed said, without inflection. "Truly brilliant."

"Sarcasm is not becoming in a man of your stature, Ed." The elevator man in Grace's building had been named Jack. What about the man at the salt mine? And hadn't he said something about carbon? Carbon brushes, that was it. They could be the source of carbon that the killer tracked across the carpeting.

Also, they both wore green uniforms, when neither the salt mine workers nor the Riviere employees wore uniforms at all. What did that mean?

We wasted all that time trying to find employees that the Riviere and Gold Coast had in common, she thought, when the elevator repairmen don't technically work for the building at all. The same elevator company could easily service a number of buildings, though that did not guarantee the same repairman would go to all of them. "Do you think only an elevator repairman would be able to do that, get in and out through the elevator?"

"I would not know from personal experience. Thanks to my parents and a decent education, I have been spared a life of manual labor."

"Your best guess?"

"I've seen articles that say children in New York City ride the tops of elevator cars as a dare."

So it could be anyone with a little pluck and a vague knowledge of mechanics. Like the building manager, or Gerard, though he had demurred from joining her on the roof and a fear of heights would have kept him out of an elevator shaft. She tried to find a question that would eliminate some possibilities but came up empty. Besides, as soon as Mrs. Sinclair provided a name and description for her husband, finding the killer should be as easy as taking a drive to his house.

But would he be home?

"One other thing, Ed. This guy has it in for Marissa."

He deigned to glance at her. "You're positive he wants her, specifically? Do you know who your killer is?"

"Yes and no. If we've located the right motive—and I'm going to assume we have—then we will know who he is very shortly. Can you look up a DUI case for me?"

He gave a heavy sigh but moved himself over to the Digital terminal. The Toxicology Department had always been slightly ahead of Trace in modernizing and systematizing their analyses and results, partially because of Tony's reluctance to change, but also because of the nature of the work. Ninety-eight percent of the Toxicology Department's work was to analyze blood, urine, and gastric contents. The Trace Department, by contrast, might analyze blood spatter on a wall, gunshot residue on a victim's shirt, or a pollen spore. Their daily tasks were too unpredictable to regiment successfully.

Kelly Alexander's name brought up a nonfatal case folder. Two samples had been submitted—a blood sample from Kelly Alexander and a swab of blood from the steering wheel. The second sample had been submitted to the Trace Department for DNA analysis. Evelyn wondered if this roundabout submission explained why no one had indexed Kelly Alexander's name in their daybook.

"Her blood alcohol content did, indeed, register below a point oh-six. I did the analysis myself."

"Did you testify?"

He clicked the cursor to bring up another screen. "No notation of it here. It probably didn't go to trial."

"No, it did. Marissa testified, and I bet she presented your blood alcohol results."

"Why would Marissa be presenting a toxicology report? That's like the flower girl tossing the bridal bouquet. That's like the bus boy flambéing the cherries jubilee—"

"Watch it there, bub."

"Besides, I doubt any defense attorney would stand for it. They barely let you guys present each other's results. They'd never let us cross departments."

"The defense wouldn't object in this case. Marissa had good news for them—the woman wasn't legally intoxicated. At the same time, all the prosecution had left was the DNA proof that Kelly had driven the car and lied about it, so they wanted Marissa to testify. No point dragging you out to the Justice Center just to clear the DUI charge. She probably read your report into evidence. And for that, Craig Sinclair's father wants her dead, and he isn't going to stop until she is. So don't complain, Ed. She kept you off his hit list."

D AVID BROWSED THE C GATES NEWSSTAND AT
Cleveland Hopkins Airport, not for reading material but to
keep himself awake while waiting for the plane from Miami.
Craig's mother—first name Joan—had left the beachfront city more
than four hours before, but violent lightning over northern Ohio had
kept the plane circling. Riley snoozed in a seat by the assigned gate.
The Cleveland police officer assigned to airport detail paced around
him in wide circles.

In the midst of picturing what he thought would happen to a
plane struck by lightning in midair, David remembered that Evelyn
wanted him to move in with her, and a warm flush began in his belly
and spread out. He might have pushed her a little, and he had no
doubt that Angel's approval had been and would continue to be vital, but what the hell, he'd take his breaks anyplace he could find
them.

A Continental gate agent suddenly scurried into Gate C-17, and
David followed. The lightning must have let up long enough to allow the plane to land before it ran out of gas.

The Cleveland police officer explained to the gate agent how
they needed to find a woman and had nothing but a grainy DMV
photo to go by. She called the plane and had the flight attendant

bring Joan Sinclair forward before a crush of departing passengers could block her in. The gate agent disappeared down the Jetway and shortly returned with their object in tow.

The dark-haired woman looked both dog-tired—she had spent the entire night on airplanes—and healthily tan. Clevelanders in spring resort to sitting on a curb during their lunch hour with their faces tilted to the sky, letting the UV rays work on their winter white skin. A few late-life wrinkles were an acceptable price to pay. Joan Sinclair positively glowed.

She dropped a bulging black canvas tote bag with "Mexico" in tie-dyed, sunny letters at their feet and said, "What?"

"Joan Sinclair?"

"Yeah. What is it? Is Craig okay?"

"Craig is fine," David assured her. "At least—"

Her eyes narrowed at his hesitation. "There's no change, is that what you mean?"

"Yes. We're here about your husband."

Joan Sinclair hefted the tote bag onto her five-foot-three frame with visible effort. "Whatever my *ex*-husband has done, it isn't my problem." She turned to follow her fellow passengers making a bee-line for baggage claim.

Riley stuck his arm out. "You can spare us a couple minutes. It takes forever to get all that luggage off these planes."

"Get your hands off me! I've got nothing to do with him. I've been flying all night, and I just had to land in the middle of a damn thunderstorm. Leave me alone."

"Three women are dead," David said. "And one barely escaped."

She dropped the bag again and stared at him with wide eyes. He took her elbow and guided her into a molded chair as her knees slowly gave way. Riley got the bag.

"No." One hand covering her mouth, she spoke through her fingers. "No way. He's no killer."

"We believe he is, ma'am. Now, we could be wrong, but we need to talk to him to clear this up. We don't want anyone to get hurt, but—"

"He's a lot of things. Mostly a lying, cheating, jerkish son of a bitch, a crappy father, and I'll wish to my dying day that I never set eyes on him, but he's not some kind of psycho."

"Ms. Sinclair, what is your husband's name?"

"*Ex*-husband."

"Sorry," David said through gritted teeth. "Ex-husband."

"John Tufts."

David waited for bells to ring. They remained stubbornly silent. "When your son was hurt—"

"I left him before that! What the hell kind of father— All he ever taught Craig to do was tinker with electronics and read *Playboy*. At *ten*. He—" She stopped, kneading her temples with long, thin fingers. "He loved Craig, as much as he's capable of loving anyone— which, believe me, isn't much. But he had no clue about what was and was not appropriate to discuss with a child."

She stopped, causing David to prompt, "Was he ever violent?"

"No—not exactly. When we first got married, things were fine. He was calm and funny. Then after a few years, after Craig was born, he was calm most of the time but started blowing up about little things, like if I bought the wrong brand of butter. He lost interest in me entirely—in every way." She looked up at the two men listening to her, blushed, and turned her gaze to the wide windows. Her eyes followed the lights of a jet taxiing to the runway, backlit by a sheet of lightning that bounced across the low-hanging clouds. "I sound like an idiot, but it happened slowly. He stopped going to family parties or out with friends. He talked mostly to Craig or stayed in the basement, tinkering with things or watching TV. He'd watch the local news obsessively for a while and then it would be nothing but old sitcoms for a while and then back to the news. Oh, and I wasn't permitted down there; he put a padlock on the door. I don't know why—after I threw him out I broke it, and there wasn't anything down there but the TV and some tools. Wire, duct tape. Normal stuff."

"You asked him to leave?" David asked gently.

"Oh, yeah." The woman gazed with disdain at her own reflection in the black windows. "I went to get his lunch pail out of his work van—he couldn't be bothered to do it himself and I didn't want it molding in there all weekend. In his cup holder, he had some jewelry that wasn't mine. Dainty gold necklaces, one with a floating heart. I realized why he'd lost interest in me."

"You thought he was having an affair." David wondered if those partners had still been willing ones at that point in the man's history. Had the divorce pushed him over the brink to rape, or had there been earlier attacks not linked to him? And what pushed him from rape to murder—did it take him two years to catch up with the three women, to find a way into their secured homes? "When was this?"

"It will be six years next month." Joan Sinclair's gaze alternated from one detective to the other. "As much disgust as I felt for him, I felt three times that for myself, that I had been so blind. I went back in the house, told him to leave, and called a lawyer."

"You got custody."

"Complete custody. I changed my name back and Craig's too, and applied to terminate his parental rights on the grounds that he was a total pervert. My lawyer told me it wouldn't work, but then he got on the stand and blamed his screwing around on work stress or some baloney like that and said he needed to discuss this with his son so Craig would know what the real world was like. The more he talked, the weirder he sounded. He gave the *judge* the creeps. Plus there were some complaints in his employment file—which, gee, he'd never mentioned to me—and when it was over, the judge gave me full custody and told him not to come near us until he'd had a thorough psychological evaluation."

"Did he?"

"He ignored the restraining order right and left. He didn't want it to apply to him, so in his mind it didn't. The cops told him time and time again, threatened him with jail. That's what made the judge finalize the custody order. I finally moved, unlisted my phone, and gave my job and my family strict instructions not to tell anyone anything about me, ever, no matter what kind of song and dance he gave."

"But he came to see Craig after the accident?"

Her mouth twisted in an irritated grimace. "Showed up at the convalescent center. I don't know how he found out Craig was even in an accident, much less where he was. He even came to the trial of that rich bitch that destroyed my boy, but I couldn't do much about that."

"About her trial?"

"About him being there. I stopped him from coming to the care center, I told him the cops would be waiting for him next time he pulled into the lot, but I couldn't do anything about a trial in a public courtroom. I didn't want to make a fuss, not there. I thought that bitch's attorney would use it against us, say Craig was from a dysfunctional family . . . Which of course he was, but that didn't make it okay for her to walk just because she had money. But I wasn't going to let him sit next to Craig's hospital bed and whisper all his sick thoughts into my child's ear. Don't look at me like that," she warned Riley. "You think I'm vindictive. I don't care. Craig is my responsibility, not John."

"I don't think that, ma'am." Riley spoke with unusual solemnity, or perhaps simple exhaustion. "In light of recent events, you may have been right all along. More right than you realize."

She blinked at him, as if recalling how the conversation had begun. "What do you think he's done now? You think he killed somebody?"

David hesitated. "Ma'am—now keep in mind we can't be sure about this, yet—we believe your ex-husband may be responsible for a series of rapes over the past four years."

She went still. Then in one movement she stood, swept up her overloaded tote bag in one hand, and strode off toward baggage claim.

David hurried to keep pace with her. He didn't mind walking; it would keep the blood flowing. "Ma'am, I know that must be an upsetting thought."

"You don't have any *idea* what it feels like, for a woman to hear that." She would not look at him. Riley paced along on her other side but said nothing.

"I'm sorry to have to hit you with this, when I'm sure you're tired from your trip. But—"

"You're wrong. You have to be wrong."

"Look, ma'am—"

"He's crazy, but not that crazy."

"Joan." He took one elbow in a firm grip and stopped, whirling her in a ninety-degree arc. The tote bag swung and nearly took him out. "It's not your fault."

Nothing moved in her face for a moment; then it began to crumble. "Yes, it is. I should have known. I should have followed him, figured out *exactly* what he was doing, I should have forced him to go to a shrink, I should have slit his throat in the middle of the night if it could have prevented this."

"It's not your fault," he repeated. "Why don't you sit down?"

"I don't want to sit down! I want to go back in time and kill the bastard the minute he walked into my geometry class in high school, that's what I want to do!"

"Joan, where can we find him?"

"I don't know."

Riley stood between her and baggage claim. "Ms. Sinclair—"

"There's nothing I would like to do more than get him behind bars," she insisted. "Maybe then I could take an easy breath. But I don't know where he is. I haven't seen him since the trial."

The older cop flipped open a notebook. "What's the last known address?" He wrote it down in careful letters as she spoke, raising her voice over the hum of a transport cart going by. Then he asked, "What does he do for a living?"

Joan Sinclair scratched one cheek, where her tan had already begun to peel. "He works on elevators."

"Where?"

"I don't know, now. He got fired from his old job about the time I said good-bye, because of those complaints at work." The lines around her eyes softened just a bit. "The only thing he'd talk to Craig about, besides sex, was mechanics. Craig rebuilt that engine in his car, the one he drove that night. I sure as hell hope that's the *only* characteristic he's inherited from his father."

EVELYN LEFT ED TO EAT HIS BREAKFAST AMONG THE compressed-air tanks and returned to the lab. Tony had been annoyingly efficient for once and had locked his office, cutting her off from the computer with Internet access. She picked up the phone book and turned to Elevators—Parts and Service. To her surprise they had twenty-four-hour service centers, no doubt a comfort to riders stuck between floors in the middle of the night.

David would, no doubt, find out Craig's father's name, address, and occupation as soon as Mrs. Sinclair stepped off the plane, but just in case the flight got diverted, or Mrs. Sinclair didn't know her husband's current whereabouts, or she had downed one too many margaritas and missed her flight from Cancún . . . Evelyn pulled the telephone toward her.

There were only nine companies, but halfway down the list she found E-tech, the name embroidered on Jack's shirt at the Riviere. She could not remember if the man at the salt mine had had a logo on his, but the color had been the same.

"Hello," a young woman answered, sounding entirely too perky for the wee hours. Evelyn wondered if the customer service department might be in India—where it would be lunchtime—but the girl's accent sounded purely midwestern.

"Hi. I'm calling about the Riviere apartment building in down-town Cleveland."

"What is your customer number?"

"No, I don't work for the Riviere. I want to know who you have working there."

Even over the phone line, the girl's silence sounded baffled.

"I mean if someone got stuck or something, what's the name of the guy you send there to get them out?"

"You're stuck in the elevator? I'll have to page the mechanic on call."

"No, I'm not stuck. I'm saying if someone were— Look, you employ the man who fixes and maintains the elevator in the Riviere apartment building in Cleveland, Ohio, right?"

"I really can't tell without the customer number."

"Can't you look it up by the name of the building?"

Silence again. "I suppose I could *try*."

"Thank you."

"But we don't usually do it that way. We usually have a customer number."

"Just this once. Please."

It took ten minutes of listening to the girl breathe into the phone, to pages flipped with impatience, and a keyboard tapped at a rate of perhaps ten words per minute, but finally the operator said, "Yes. We have one elevator at the Riviere—on West Tenth Street?"

"That's it."

"Wow. I never knew you could do that, look it up by the name. Peggy, did you know you can look up jobs by the name of the building?"

"Now, what is the name of the guy who works for you at the Riviere?"

"—yeah, I didn't know that either. I'm sorry, what did you ask? Who is our regular mechanic there?"

"Yes."

"I wouldn't know. You'd have to call the local office. Why do you want to know? Do you have a complaint?"

Lightning crossed the sky in a hissing crack, and the overhead lights flickered. Great, Evelyn thought. That's all we need, a three-story building full of dead people and no power. "No, no complaint. I need to know who works in the building. Who do you call if someone gets stuck?"

"Are you stuck?"

"No! But if someone were—"

"Then it would be the guy on call."

On call. She and Marissa rotated weekend calls, coming in on Saturday and Sunday mornings if a homicide or suicide victim had to be autopsied that day. "So that might not be the guy who's there every day?"

"Well, he wouldn't be there every day anyway. The building would be on the regular mechanic's route. He probably comes in every week or two to do maintenance, or if the building calls with a problem."

"And that wouldn't necessarily be the same guy you call if some-one is stuck?"

"Right, that's whoever is on call. This week it's John Tufts. I'll page him. What elevator are you stuck in?"

"I'm not stuck!"

"Then what do you need service for?"

"I don't need service. I just wanted to know the name of the guy. Look, never mind. I'll call the local office in the morning."

"You don't need immediate service, then? I can cancel the page?"

"Yes, cancel it."

"Okay. Anything else I can do for you?"

"No." Evelyn rubbed her forehead with a sore palm. "Thank you."

"Thanks for using E-tech!"

"Wait!"

"What?"

"How do the repairmen get into the buildings? I mean, if some-one was stuck—"

"Are you—"

"No, I'm not stuck! But if someone was and it was late at night, how could they get into the building?"

"Peg, get this. Now she wants to know— Oh, sorry. Um, let me think. Any place that would call for twenty-four-hour service would be a place like a hospital or a hotel, and they would have a doorman or a lobby open twenty-four hours."

"What if it didn't?"

"It depends on what kind of facility it is. They might have a key to the maintenance unit, or at least the public areas so they can get to the maintenance area. Or we might have to wake the building super up. Why are you asking all this? Are you sure you don't have a complaint?"

"What about from the roof?"

"Ma'am," the girl said wearily, "machine rooms are usually on the roof. If you see a guy walking on the roof of your building, there's nothing wrong with that."

"They would have keys to those rooms?"

"Of course. So they can get in and fix the elevator."

From the roof. Evelyn pondered this so long that the girl let an impatient *huff* out into the receiver, then asked if there would be anything else.

"No, I don't think so. Thank you."

"Thanks for using E-tech. Peggy, you won't believe this one—"

"Wait!"

Across the line, she could hear the gears turning in the girl's mind. Pretend you didn't hear her, and hang up . . . Professionalism won out. "Yes?"

"Does your company also service Gold Coast Apartments in Lakewood, Ohio?"

Sigh. The novelty of looking up a job by the building name had worn off in no uncertain terms. "Let me check." After several more minutes of page turning and keyboard tapping, she said, "No."

"No? You're sure?"

"Yes, ma'am. Will there be anything else?"

"Metro General Hospital."

"We have a lot of hospitals," she admitted. "Let me see . . . yes. No."

"No?"

"We have the service and passenger elevators in the new wing only. So it depends which elevator you're talking about, whether it would be ours or not."

Close enough. An E-tech guy still had opportunity to become familiar with the hospital and its exits. "How about the Alexander salt mine on Front Street, in Cleveland?"

"A what?"

"A salt mine."

"They get salt from mines? I always thought they, like, evaporated it out of seawater or something like that."

"Do you have it?"

Long pause. "Yes. We have two mechanics assigned there, John Shea and Mike Yugama."

So the two green uniforms she'd noted had come from the same company. The same men didn't work at both Grace's building and the salt mine, but both could have visited either place during their on-call rotation.

But then, so could any of the elevator mechanics. "How many men do you have working for you in the Cleveland area?"

"I don't know," the girl snapped. "Probably about thirty."

Still, it narrowed down the suspect pool. "Thank you."

Click. Not even a "Thank you for using E-tech."

Evelyn rubbed absently at the healing abrasion on her palm. The evidence pointed to a mechanic or maintenance man, someone who

knew the back ways of a large facility, ways to get in and out without catching the attention of its occupants. Elevator men would also
be familiar with the roof access doors.

David would learn all this, very shortly, from Craig's mother,
but Evelyn couldn't keep her restless mind from pursuing it as well.
Grace's elevator repairman—Jack, which could be a nickname for either of the two Johns mentioned—had told her right off that he
could have gotten into Grace's apartment. Why hadn't she listened?
He'd also said he wasn't working in the building that day, but he
could have lied. Had anyone verified that? Even if he hadn't killed
Grace, any one of his coworkers could have. Any one of them could
get in and out of the Riviere without being seen—through the roof
or, if they could get into the building, up the back staircase.

Evelyn pictured what she could remember of the top of the
elevator—after all, she'd been trying *not* to look at it at the time.
From the machine room, the killer could have jumped out of the controller to move the car to the right floor, riding on the top—he
couldn't get down the shaft without a ladder, unless he actually slid
down the cable . . . which would leave cable grease on his hands and
clothing. Perhaps that was how Grace got that smear on her arm.

Then through the hatch into the top and into the apartment.
But how would the doors open without the code?

Tenants entered the code when they got into the elevator at the
lobby. Once the elevator reached the right floor, the doors opened
automatically. The killer could leave after the murder by doing the
same thing in reverse, if he left the hatch ajar so it could be opened
from inside the elevator. He'd kill Grace Markham, call the elevator,
get in it, and climb up and through. There would be no chance of
finding another tenant in the car when he went to leave, and the elevator would simply arrive at the lobby apparently empty. Justin or
one of the other doormen might notice that, but they might not.

The killer knew Grace, would have stalked her, riding on top of
the elevator and listening to his potential victim. People discussed

anything in elevators, believing that they were alone. Grace and William could have spoken of the upcoming pregnancy, the safe combination she could never remember, what time he had to leave for work.

And now Marissa had gone home, to her apartment, which this man, determined to kill her, could enter and leave at will.

Robert is there, Evelyn reminded herself. And an armed guard.

But he attacked her with me sleeping right beside her bed. He is not afraid of other people. And he may not know there's an officer with her, he might take the chance that Robert would be working another late shift at the hospital.

Light flooded the lab from another crack of lightning; the bright sheen temporarily overpowered the indoor bulbs. Evelyn had no reason to believe Marissa might be in danger—

Screw that. She had *every* reason to believe it.

She called David on a Nextel connection tinged with static, but she could make out most of his words. "We're taking her statement now. Craig's father is named Tufts, John Tufts."

Her throat burned where he had choked her, her skin electric with recognition. "That's him. That's the guy who services Grace's elevators. That's how he got in. Does he go by Jack?"

David's voice disappeared into muffled tones. Either the signal had faded or he had turned away to talk to another person. Then: "She says his friends call him Jack."

"What's the name of the cop you have in Marissa's apartment? We've got to warn her that this guy can get in any time he wants."

"She's armed, Evelyn. And she's going to notice if some strange guy suddenly pops out of the elevator."

"You're not getting this, David! He's *good* at it. He could disable the lights in the elevator car, turn off the bell. He maintains those doors, he knows how quiet they are or aren't. He could do it."

"Okay, I get your point. The cop on night duty is Connie Seraviso. I don't have her Nextel number, but I can get it from Dispatch."

"Thanks. I'd rather call her radio than the apartment phone, just in case there's nothing wrong and Marissa is finally getting a decent night's sleep."

"Unlike the rest of us. Here's the car, Ms. Sinclair. Watch your head. Evelyn, I—"

A crackle, then nothing.

The signal had faded. Perhaps lightning had hit a radio tower. She tried to call him back and got only a buzzing noise. Before she had a plan in mind, she moved down the stairs, out the back door, and unlocked her Tempo. The number for Cleveland PD Dispatch refused to come up in her weary brain, and she finally called 911 to be connected. The young woman on duty recognized Evelyn's voice and gave her Connie Seraviso's phone number without argument.

She pushed one tiny, glowing button at a time while peering through her windshield, the wipers going at maximum speed against the driving rain. The wipers lost, and she navigated by the few streetlights and traffic lights still operating. Euclid Avenue seemed to stretch all the way to Indiana.

The cop's phone gave a busy signal. All this modern technology, Evelyn thought, and no one put call waiting on these damn things? Who would the woman be talking to at this time of night? A boyfriend, also stuck working the night shift, and bored?

Perhaps David, she hoped. Maybe David got through.

She splashed to a stop in front of Playhouse Square, saw no one around, and started to drive through the red light. She nearly hit a very wet man with an overfull grocery cart. He shook his fist at her. "Like I don't have enough problems!" he shouted over the thunder.

"I'm sorry, I'm sorry, I'm sorry," she said aloud for the next three blocks, unsure if she spoke to the man or her friend who might already be dead, trussed up at her own kitchen table as if testifying before a jury about the woman who destroyed Craig Sinclair's life.

W HEN SHE DARED TAKE HER EYES OFF THE ROAD, Evelyn dialed Marissa's home phone with her cell phone. The number hadn't been programmed into her Nextel, and she couldn't do it from memory.

No answer. No busy signal, no nothing. She dialed the number and simply nothing happened. She refused to hang up until the obnoxious beeping began, telling her that the call had not been completed and that was that. Were the apartment's phones out? Had Evelyn's cell service gone out? Had Jack cut the wires?

David would have officers heading to John Tufts's address. He'd soon be in custody and Marissa would be safe. Except—what if John Tufts wasn't at home? Knowing the identity of the killer did not solve her every worry. Until they actually had him in cuffs, he remained free to kill.

She zigzagged around Public Square and headed into the Flats, down the steep hill that she always avoided like hell in the winter, when the roads were icy. They weren't much better now. As she was turning left at the bottom, the back end of the Tempo fishtailed and a rear wheel hit the curb. She hoped she hadn't bent the axle. She couldn't afford another car, and Angel would be needing her own soon . . .

The night doorman—what was his name, Leroy?—looked up in

surprise as the soaked forensic scientist burst into the lobby. No, the elevator man wasn't there, and no one had reported any problems. Ring the Tenneyson apartment? But it's the middle of the night!

He relented when Evelyn reached over the counter, ready to pick up the phone herself. He dialed the number—helpful, since Evelyn didn't know it—and she heaved a sigh of relief when he spoke.

"Hello, is this Ms. Gonzalez? No? Well, Officer, I have a lady down here who insists—"

Now she did rip the phone from his hands, albeit with a hasty smile and a thank-you, and found herself talking to Officer Connie Seraviso, very much alive and more than happy to give Evelyn the code to come up and fill her in.

"Thank you," she said again to the doorman. "Sorry if I startled you."

"Oh, that's all right," he assured her, discreetly drying off his receiver with a tissue. "Hell of a storm out there, huh? I heard a boom like something took out the Terminal Tower. The lights even flickered. Um—you want a towel or something?"

Evelyn said no, bade him good night, and entered the elevator, punching Marissa's floor code onto the little white buttons. The doors closed off her view of the lobby just as one more flash of lightning illuminated her Tempo, parked at an angle on the wrong side of the street. Oh well, she doubted traffic cops would be out in this weather. She just hoped no one slid into it in the pelting rain.

She opened her Nextel and found David's number on the glowing green screen. To her surprise, he answered.

"David? I'm in the Riviere to check on Marissa, but I just talked to the cop, and they seem to be okay. Where are you?"

She listened, got no response, and looked at the screen to see that the call had ended. The signal had probably faded almost instantly—amazing that she'd gotten a signal at all. She had no idea if David had heard a word she said, but she'd try again when she got into Marissa's apartment and could stand by a window. Or she'd just use the landline.

Marissa lived on the seventh floor. The elevator had just passed four when the lights went out.

Evelyn stopped breathing.

A roll of thunder like an atomic bomb rattled the building. The darkness closed in on her like a wet blanket, cutting off her air, enveloping her limbs.

Calm down. The power must have gone out. If the killer had stopped the car somehow, the lights would still be on, wouldn't they? And no sound emanated from anywhere, as if not only the elevator motor but every fan, refrigerator, and watercooler in the building had stopped running. The tenants were asleep and wouldn't notice, or stir. The doorman had just told her the lights had flickered. No big deal.

But Jack had, what was it again—the controller? Wires and circuit boards and switches. He controlled every single thing about this elevator. He could turn out the lights if he wanted to. If he wanted to stop her from warning Marissa, from cutting off his secret access.

The answering service girl had asked if she should cancel the call to the on-call repairman—John Tufts. John Tufts was Craig Sinclair's father.

Cancel the call? Did that mean she had already paged him? Did he call back, only to be treated to the story of the crazy lady who called wanting to know if E-tech serviced all these jobs—and get this, she had only the names of these buildings, not the customer numbers.

If Jack knew she was on his trail . . . But why would he not have come to the ME's office? Granted, not too many people, even killers, wanted to break into a morgue, but its security hardly compared with the Riviere's.

But he wasn't familiar with the ME's office, and he liked to work in familiar surroundings. No doubt if they reinvestigated four of the five rapes, they would find that E-tech held the service contracts for the elevators in all four buildings. The home in Parma, of course, sat right across the street from his own. He hadn't attacked the three women from the accident until he found them in buildings he could get comfortable with. He needed to feel secure before he attacked.

She heard a sound from above, a faint thump, perhaps residual thunder or a cable swinging to rest after its abrupt stop. Other than that, dead silence.

He might have gotten the call from the E-tech line, left his home—to which David and Riley were speeding—and come to the Riviere to finish his work. He could have entered from the roof, jumping from the building next door and unlocking (or having left open) the stairwell door. Opened the elevator door with the key, brought the elevator up, and gotten onto the top of it.

After he got into the shaft, it could work just as she suspected— he opened the doors of a dark elevator into the quiet Tenneyson apartment, where Officer Seraviso perhaps watched TV or chatted with her boyfriend, unaware that an intruder had slipped out of the metal box. Except that Officer Seraviso now expected Evelyn to arrive. Jack would not find the complacent victims to which he'd become accustomed.

Another thump, or rather a sliding sound. Evelyn gripped the handrail and stared hard into the absolute darkness. Her hand went to her Nextel. She probably wouldn't get a call through, but she could try.

It's my imagination, she told herself. He's not here. He's not.

A definite click sounded over her head. The residual effect of cooling machinery? Or the sound of the ceiling hatch opening?

She took her hand off the Nextel. Even if it worked, the green glow would illuminate her. Without it, Jack couldn't see in the dark any better than she could.

He's just a man, David had told her. Not magic.

He's also a brutal, ruthless killer. And rapist.

She moved as silently as she could to the other side of the car. Her wet Reeboks betrayed her with a small *squish*.

She put her back against the corner, gripping the handrails on both sides.

Cloth, in the absence of other sound, is noisy. She wondered if Jack wore his hooded blue nylon jacket. If so, it must be jersey knit, the back of her mind coolly noted. Tightly woven nylon would swish a lot more.

The front of her mind wanted to curl into a ball and sob.

A brush—possibly a foot against the hatch jamb. Another brush, maybe a calf. She could see with her mind, if not her eyes, his legs slipping into the car. In another second he'd drop down and there would be just the two of them, in a very small space, from which she could not possibly escape. Even if she screamed enough to wake a tenant— and she doubted he'd give her that chance—no one would be able to get to them. They'd assume she'd gotten stuck in the elevator and become hysterical. Then who would they call? The elevator man?

She fought back a giggle of panic.

Remembering the wiry Jack, she knew she could not defeat him in hand-to-hand combat. He was strong and, more important, crazy. She had nothing except a Nextel she didn't dare use.

Wait. Perhaps she had one chance.

Without giving herself time to second-guess, she rushed forward with arms swept wide and embraced his lower legs with all her strength.

He was not a figment of her imagination. Rock-hard calves clothed in long pants writhed against her stomach, heavy boots trying to kick without sufficient clearance.

He had to be hanging on to the hatch frame. He had nothing else to grasp for support on the way down, so if he let go, his upper body would fall to the floor full force. She doubted that would harm him in any significant way, but what the hell, it was all she had.

At least it confused him. He wiggled, twisting his legs, forcing her to move around the elevator. She had grabbed him from behind; his heels dug into her abdomen.

Finally he gave up and let go. Directly beneath him, she abruptly took on his full weight. It dropped her to her knees, sending jarring pain through the injured one. His upper body landed somewhere in the darkness, but with his hands to break the fall, it had probably been easier on him than on her.

Still, she hung on. Restraining his legs left him nothing but his arms, and they were facing away from her. Shifting her weight to her right hip, she swung her left leg out and kicked him in the back. This was her injured knee, so the kick lacked strength, but she felt a pang of satisfaction when she heard him grunt.

He twisted to one side. If he could sit up, he'd knock her block off, so she rested all her weight against his calves to keep him from turning over. It wasn't enough. With one convulsive move, he bucked her off enough to free one leg. Then a fist connected with her chin, snapping her head back. She let go.

S HE COULD HEAR HIM BREATHING, AND NO DOUBT HE could hear her. Evelyn crouched on the floor, instinctively feeling that he would stand and expect her to do the same. She did not move.

Then she heard the air part in front of her as he aimed a vicious kick in her direction. She grabbed his calf, stood, and kicked back, trying for the groin and managing only a glancing blow off what felt like a hip or a thigh. His leg slid from her sweaty grasp. She prepared to duck.

No blows came, and he made a huffing sound, as if bent over. She couldn't have hurt him.

Suddenly she remembered Kelly Alexander's office, the red liquid on her community service award. Kelly had drawn blood—probably in the thigh. Not enough to incapacitate, obviously, but enough to hurt, enough to make him pause.

Kick, a martial arts enthusiast had told her once. Pound for pound, a woman's legs are as strong as a man's. *Kick.*

She kicked.

He had been bent slightly forward, so that her foot caught him on the chin—or at least something high and solid—and she heard a loud snap and a thud as he went down.

Please, she prayed, tell me I've broken the bastard's neck.

Silence. He did not move.

She knew she should feel for his neck, find a pulse, see if he remained conscious, but she could not bring herself to touch him. Her mind had not yet accepted that he had come into the elevator—only her animal instincts knew how to respond. Sometimes boxing up all your feelings *could* be helpful.

He might be unconscious, he might be waiting for her to come closer. After all, he had plenty of time. She had nowhere to go.

Except up through the hatch. With a whimper of fear—it meant giving up the darkness, and she was pretty damn sure she didn't want to see what was in the elevator with her—she opened her Nextel. The glow of the screen showed a dark form on the floor, which did not move. Then she aimed it upward. The hatch was still open, a darker square in a dark square, right over his body.

She put the flipped-open top of the phone in her mouth, aimed upward to illuminate her goal. Then she put the foot under her good knee on the man's turned hip and pushed off him as hard as she could, stretching her arms up to the hole in the ceiling.

The fingers of her right hand caught the edge of the hatch opening, the metal biting into her skin as her left hand knocked against the ceiling of the elevator, trying to find the opposite side of the frame. The backlight from the Nextel screen reached its ten-second mark and automatically turned off, plunging her back into pitch. Her sweaty fingers also reached their limit, and she fell to the floor, landing partially on the still-unmoving man. She stumbled, rolled onto her side, and pushed up with her arms, moving with the lightning speed of panic. She had dropped the Nextel.

He was going to wake up. He was going to wake up any split second now, and when he did, she had no defenses. She should tie his arms, but she had nothing to tie them with, no belt, no purse strap. Removing her shoelaces would take too long, time she would rather spend *getting out of the damn elevator.*

Her hands swept over the floor in her search, touching his pants, his jacket, even his hair, and each contact made her shudder with revulsion. Just as she considered giving up, she touched the little black plastic brick.

She stood up, used her foot to make sure the man's body still lay on its side, felt for the hip bones— Was that a spasm? Was he alive? Was he about to move, get up? She opened the Nextel, clenched the open lid between her teeth, located the hatch in the ceiling. Then she took a bounding step and used her good knee to push off. She pushed the man, the tight space, the memory of his victims out of her mind and focused on that small, dark square in the ceiling.

Over her own breathing, she heard a grunt from the floor. It didn't mean he was conscious. She'd probably compressed his lungs a bit in her launch.

Her fingers caught the frame neatly on both sides. Now she just had to pull herself through it.

Yeah, right.

Her legs, swinging in the air, had never felt heavier, pulling her damp fingers off the smooth metal and back into the pit. But she could reach the wall and plant the sole of one foot there long enough to stabilize herself, to pull hard enough with one hand to thrust the other one into the darkness above the elevator. Unfortunately, no handholds presented themselves, and her hand swung wildly in the void.

The fingers of her other hand began to slip. Her feet again swung loose.

Then her right hand brushed a metal bar and she clutched at it. Not meant to be a handle, the flat, perforated piece dug into her fingers, but at least it didn't move. She pulled her arms up with muscles she didn't know she had, and hoped she'd never have to use again.

She moved her shoulders into the hatch, her legs still deadweight and flailing uselessly. Once she'd raised herself enough that her arms could push down instead of pull up, she knew she had it. She'd make it. With one last burst, she moved her hips into the roof space and rammed her forehead into something very big and very hard. She chipped a tooth on her Nextel, its screen now dark, and it clattered to the roof.

Sitting on the hatch frame, she could let go of the braces. One hand to her head felt wet warmth while the other hand traced the obstacle—the crossbeam across the center of the elevator top. The handle of the bucket, to which the cables attached.

Forgot about that.

Something touched her left foot, just the merest wisp of contact. Before she could even snatch it away, two hands closed over her ankle and pulled.

She grabbed for anything she could find, which happened to be the same uncomfortable piece of metal, and one of the cables stretching up from the center of the crossbeam. Its diameter fit comfortably in her hand. Unfortunately, it had been covered with oil.

She kicked at his hands with her right foot, banging her knee on the hatch frame as she tried for leverage. His fingers loosened for a minute, then renewed. He must have been bending his knees and hanging his entire body weight on her foot, wrenching the knee until pain shot up past her hip.

Her fingers on the cable began to slide. The cables hung in the center of the elevator roof. Anytime one moved around on top of the car and needed to steady oneself, say, if the car were moving, the cables would be a natural handhold. Perhaps right before dropping through the hatch to surprise Grace Markham in her own apartment.

She kicked again, hitting his wrist. Then she gave up and pulled her right leg out of the hatch. With her foot braced on the car roof and both arms anchored, she got her left leg, with Jack's entire body swinging from it, to clear the hatch. She screamed a bit at the pain in her left knee.

With both feet on the car roof, she released one hand and

grabbed the hatch cover. Jack had already freed one hand to close on the hatch frame. In another instant he'd shoot himself through the hole, onto the car top. He did this all the time.

She slammed the cover shut.

He gave a strangled yell as the cover hit the wrist of one hand and the fingers of the other. With her free foot, Evelyn stomped on the heavy cover.

He let go, slipping down into the elevator. She sat on the hatch cover and heard him bellow in anger or pain.

The hatch could be opened only from the roof, not the inside of the car. Unless he had lied about that. So she planted her butt on the hatch and hoped he didn't have a gun.

You hate the dark, a voice in the back of her head pondered. You hate heavy machinery, you hate enclosed spaces, and you have a love-hate relationship with heights. Yet you just climbed into an elevator shaft to get away from this guy.

Yeah, well. Go figure.

She felt a weak thump under her buttocks. He was jumping, trying to get the hatch open, but with it closed, there was nothing to grab on to. Her fingers explored the edge of the cover and found a latching mechanism. After the car had remained quiet for a moment or two, she lifted herself up one inch and tugged slightly. The cover didn't budge. Jack had told the truth about it.

She was safe. He couldn't get to her.

But she couldn't get out.

Gingerly—her knee aching and her heart pounding hard enough to bruise her ribs, she stood up. The elevator did not move, did not bob up and down. With fingers outstretched and no desire to cave in her forehead again, she explored her cage.

If she hiked over the crossbeam, she could reach the front half of the elevator roof, which seemed relatively unobstructed. Reaching out showed her a rough concrete wall—they must have been stuck between floors. She moved around the edge, counterclockwise. Apparently Jack had also been truthful about the lack of rung ladders in elevator shafts. There was no way up except the oil-covered cable.

At the back of the elevator, the roof had a slight lip, which caught her toe. Her hands, skimming the wall, suddenly dropped off into nothingness, a great black hole into which her body began to tilt.

She crouched and grabbed the edge of the car top, letting gravity bring her to rest. The shaft in which the counterweight rode up and down—she had nearly fallen into it.

A tap on the hatch cover reminded her that Jack had not given up.

With no way to climb out, she decided to start screaming. The tenants of the Riviere would not appreciate the early wake-up, and they wouldn't be able to open their elevator doors to help her, but at least they could call the fire department or the elevator company. Eventually they would get her out, while Jack remained locked up for the cops to come and arrest.

She opened her mouth.

A rumbling sound echoed down the shaft, and a whirring response came from the controls on the car top. The faintest light appeared through cracks approximately six feet above her, where a tenant must have left a lamp burning in an apartment before turning in.

The power had come back on.

The elevator began to move downward.

Being on top of an elevator in a dark shaft was bad enough. Being on top of a moving elevator in a dark shaft was enough to make her sob in terror. She wrapped both arms around the crossbeam and buried her face in her shoulder, hanging on with every usable muscle she had left.

After about two floors she realized that it really wasn't that bad. The car moved smoothly; so long as she didn't get caught between the moving car and the wall, she had nothing to fear. It slid to a stop at, she assumed, the lobby. At the edge of the car top, a mechanism moved to the side, and she could see the marble floor through the tiny crack. The doors had opened.

If Jack had any sense at all, he would leave, run now before the police arrived.

"Leroy!" she shouted, as loud as she could. "Call the police! Call the police!"

Hearing a disembodied voice might confuse the doorman, but with luck he would at least investigate. She had to pray that he would not try to stop Jack—why should he? He knew the man.

Nothing happened. No sound came from the lobby. Was Leroy there, or was he off seeing to the power failure? Perhaps the building had a generator he had started—her struggle in the dark had seemed like hours, but it couldn't have been more than ten minutes.

She kept her eye on the lobby floor. Jack did not exit. Instead she heard the faint tinkle of keys on a ring, then a beep. The doors closed.

The elevator began to move upward.

She clutched the crossbeam more tightly. Was he heading for Marissa's apartment? He had a job to finish, and she now believed that he could change or find out the codes for each apartment. He'd told her so the first day.

She would shout as soon as the elevator stopped. The armed police officer already expected her to show up and would be waiting. Evelyn could warn her before Jack left the elevator car.

An ominous sound built up behind her, a demon roaring down the shaft on a collision course. Just as she opened her mouth to scream, it whooshed past, disappearing down a rabbit hole of pitch dark. The counterweight. It had passed the elevator, which meant they had gone past the approximate midpoint of the shaft. They had passed Marissa's floor.

They just kept going up.

The shaft ended somewhere up there in the dark. Evelyn could not see it. What was at the top of an elevator shaft?

She tried to remember the machine room. The motor, with the cables looped over its heavy wheel, disappearing through the floor into the shaft. Under that, the elevator car, where the doors opened into the room.

A concrete ceiling. That was what was at the top of an elevator shaft. A flat, hard ceiling that the car top fitted up against without room for human beings, because why would a human being be there—

The end of the shaft came into view.

The dimmest of lights, sneaking between the cracks of the machine room door, removed just enough shadow for her to see her demise, to see the death she now hurtled toward, which would leave her body a smashed, bloody mess—

She screamed.

37

AND THE ELEVATOR ROLLED TO A SMOOTH HALT.
Her body was not smashed between two hard surfaces but had a roomy two-foot space to move around in, provided she did it on hands and knees.

The mechanism at the edge slid to the side again as the doors opened. This time Jack did get out.

I'm still safe. He still can't get up through the hatch.

But she was sure he'd have another way to get to her.

The doors, after waiting the appropriate time, slid closed. For a moment, all was still. Then the elevator began to move down.

Go to the lobby, she prayed. Get to the lobby, and when the doors open I can jump down through the hatch and get out, after I flip the emergency stop button. I'll use the desk phone to call the police, and in the meantime, if I see Jack, I'll run like hell. Marissa will be all right. He can't get to her without the elevator.

The car stopped, level with the machine room floor. A shadow crossed over the light at the doors' edges.

Then she heard a scratching noise, like a metallic rodent finding its way through a maze.

Or a key.

The doors began to slide open.

Jack stood, a silhouette against the bright machine room lights. "I didn't particularly want to kill you, Evelyn. I thought maybe you'd understand, having a child of your own."

She pushed her voice out, a wavering squeak. "I know why you're doing this."

"Of course you do. You know because you went to the home they've got my boy locked up in. You went to see my *son*!" He leaned into the dark space, and she automatically shrank back, nearly stepping into the counterweight shaft again. Her foot slipped off the car top, but she grabbed a rail—now she could see it.

"You really should have left him out of it," he added.

"Why Marissa?"

"She let that bitch go."

"She reported the facts, which weren't under her control. How can you hold that against her?"

"It wasn't true! Kelly Alexander's daddy paid for those results. He could afford anything to keep the salt mine out of the papers."

"Then why didn't you kill him?"

He stepped onto the car top, stopped. "What?"

"I notice your hit list of justifiable homicides doesn't seem to have any men on it. What about the cop that said the accident was your son's fault? What about Kelly's defense attorney, who got her off? What about the judge who let her go without punishment? You haven't been riding the elevators in their apartment buildings, have you? Strapping them into chairs so they look like they're sitting in a car?"

She didn't speak to save her life or even to postpone her death, since antagonizing him would hardly help. But she'd be damned if she didn't shatter the vigilante-for-justice persona.

"Why use the safety harness for a murder weapon? Using your own equipment turned you on?"

"We always have to wear the harness when we're working in the shaft. It's a safety thing," he added primly. He stepped over the crossbeam and grabbed the front of her shirt with one hand, nearly lifting her off her feet. With the other, he blocked the kicks she aimed at his groin. She swung a little wider, remembering his damaged thigh, but faster than thought he moved to the other side of the beam so that it protected him instead of her.

He pulled. She made a fist and socked him on the jaw as hard as she could. She thought the impact broke one of her knuckles, but it didn't seem to faze him, so she stretched out her fingers for his eyes instead. But he jerked his head back so she couldn't reach them.

The doors were almost closed, shutting off the light.

Her thighs hit the crossbeam, and she bent her knees, curling her body around it like a gymnast around a parallel bar. She grabbed for a handhold with her left hand, catching the oily cables. With her right, she continued to scratch and punch at him.

He stopped the door with one foot, pushing it back a foot or so. Then he yanked her so hard that the beam across her midriff forced the breath out of her, and she sagged for a moment, scraping her face on the large buttons on the front side of the crossbeam.

Three days before, she and Jack had reversed positions; she'd stood in the machine room while he stood on the car top to collect oil samples for her—samples he knew wouldn't match the oil found on Grace, the oil used specifically for the cables. The buttons on the crossbeam had clear labels—the red one said Stop, and two black ones read Up and Down.

Jack reached under the crossbeam and grabbed her legs out from under her. Now only one elbow hooked around the crossbeam kept her on top of the elevator.

Her body stretched in midair, horizontally, as a man with twice her weight and strength did his best to drag her onto his killing ground. Her right arm screamed under the pressure. Her left hand found the buttons. She pressed Up.

The car began to move, slowly.

Jack's force flagged. "What are you doing?"

Her finger slipped off the button, and the elevator stopped. She pressed again, held it.

Jack's grip slid down her body to her ankles, so that he now stood safely outside the elevator. Her calves spanned the threshold. If the elevator continued to move, she would amputate both feet.

"You're a rapist, Jack," she gasped out. "Not some kind of loving father or rebellious citizen. You're a sick corruption of organic molecules."

He lunged, got the top of her pants in his grip, and pulled. But then he went slack, his legs without leverage, dangling beneath them in the open elevator doorway. His grasp slid to her knees.

She flexed her legs and drew her feet out of the doorway, to bring Jack farther in with her. In the next moment, the top of the car approaching the top of the door opening like a guillotine to its lunette, he let go.

And she held on.

S HE RELEASED THE UP BUTTON TO GRASP HIS SANDY blond hair. Then she hitched her right shoulder closer to the crossbeam so she could wrap her arm around it and reach the button with her fingers.

Unfortunately she pushed the first button her index finger could find, the Down one. The motion pointed out her error.

Jack pulled against her hand. His foot banged against the now-closing door.

Her middle finger found the Up button. The car reversed direction.

Jack wiggled, striking at her arm with both fists, but with his lower body dangling, he had no leverage. He could not see the approaching threshold, but he worked with these machines every day. He had to know what would happen.

He changed tactics and began to climb onto the car top. Now she locked her left elbow and held her arm stiff, trying to keep him out. All he had to do was get to the Stop button and she would die.

Both his hands grasped her shirtsleeve, his legs flailing, trying to pull himself into the safe space.

"You bitch!"

In the next instant, the top of the door opening met his back, just above his waist. The car kept moving upward.

His scream filled the shaft, filled her head, filled every brain cell down to the nucleus until her chromosomes vibrated with the awful thunder of it. She let go of the button, let go of his hair to clasp her hands over her ears. Stop, why wouldn't he stop?

Slowly it dawned on her that he had stopped, as soon as the doorjamb cut off the lower half of his body. After that, the screams were all hers.

She could still feel his fingers on her arm . . . In horror she realized that they *were* still on her arm, and she shook them off, her hand and arm thrashing against metal and concrete until spots of pain convinced her to stop.

She curled into a ball and stayed there, the cement ceiling of the elevator shaft pressing against the back of her neck, the metallic smell of blood already penetrating past her knees to her face. She had to move, she had to face it, she had to get out of there.

In a minute.

At least she'd have a moment of darkness before she had to face what she'd done. Gingerly, she lifted her head—or rather, lowered her knees, her head couldn't go any farther—and turned it away from the body, toward the controls. The Down button. That was all she needed.

She went to push it, but her right arm was stuck. She had forgotten, from her last trip to the top of the shaft, that the crossbeam ended flush with the ceiling. Another inch and she would have crushed her shoulder.

She pushed the Down button with her left hand and snaked her right arm back over to rest against her body. If it hurt, she couldn't feel it. She couldn't feel much of anything except a desire to get out of the machine room without seeing the thing that used to be a man.

But that would not be possible.

A peek at the light told her that the door remained stationary with about a foot clearance. His lower body must have blocked it. She did not level the car but stopped a foot above the machine room floor, having no desire to further mutilate the dead flesh that lay there.

Some sort of dark object lay on the car top, and it had flooded the area with some sort of dark liquid.

She would have to move if she didn't want to stay there permanently.

Don't think about it. Don't think about what your mind is seeing—the open, red gore, the splash of blood on your pants, the wetness soaking into your shoes. Stand up. Turn. Push the door open farther. Step to the edge. Jump.

Her Reeboks made a squishing sound when she landed on the gray concrete floor.

Leave.

The shoeprints faded out after four flights.

You're spreading a crime scene, leaving a trail of biohazard throughout a residential building.

Yes.

You need to get your camera, start documenting.

Yes, I know.

Your arm hurts. Your shoulders hurt. You're going to wake up tomorrow morning and not be able to move.

Yes.

You need to call David. But the Nextel is still up there on the car top and you're not going to get it.

No.

She entered the ground-floor hallway, turned to the left, and went out into the alley.

It's still raining.

Isn't that great?

She lifted her face to the pelting drops and let them soak her clothes, soak the blood and the tissue and the flecks of bone from the fabric. High up, between the buildings, lightning stretched across the sky with its accompanying thunder. The alleyway, though, became illuminated by red and blue lights.

"Evelyn!"

David's arms encircled her. "Are you all right? Is he here? I got your message. Officer Seraviso said you called but never made it up to the apartment. Are you all right?"

"I'm great," she said, just as her knees went out entirely and she sagged against him.

Clio Helms materialized in front of her, for once not looking perfect as the rain plastered her hair into an unflattering mat. Her face, however, glowed with excitement. "What's going on? We heard you on the police scanner, and your boyfriend here sounded panicked. Did you get the guy? Evelyn? You okay?"

"Peachy."

"Get out of the way," David ordered. "She needs to sit down."

"She *is* okay, isn't she?"

"Don't know yet."

"I'm peachy," Evelyn repeated. She was still alive, after all, and so was Marissa. "And I'm never getting in an elevator again."

"Glad to hear it," Clio said, looping one of Evelyn's arms around her own neck. She and David supported Evelyn between them to the end of the alley, where an ambulance had just pulled up.

"Seriously. I'll take the stairs."

"They're good exercise," the reporter agreed. "There's Channel Fifteen, and I know the *Sun Star* guy always has his scanner on. You remember our deal, right?"

"Yeah," Evelyn said, collapsing on the bumper. "You've got your story."

The reporter straightened, a smile of sheer triumph breaking through the worry on her face. "Cool."

I T'S JUST A LITTLE SHOCK," THE PARAMEDIC TOLD David. "She's coming out of it. Be sure to keep her warm."

"Has anyone checked on Craig Sinclair?" Evelyn asked. "If Jack thought his plan was falling apart—"

David wrapped a fresh blanket around her shivering body. "He's fine. I got hold of the nurses right after you called me. You know, it actually crossed my mind that maybe Craig was faking his disability and sneaking out of the center at night to exact his revenge."

"Nobody would fake living like that. Not for two years."

"It would be the perfect alibi."

"Jack came to work one day and saw Grace Markham. Even if she saw him, she might not have recognized him. You never look at someone in uniform; you just see the uniform and accept that they belong there, that they're not a threat. And then he realized he was probably the only person in the world who could get to her. He told me so, the first day. He was that confident."

"But first, a practice run," David said. "Frances."

"E-tech doesn't service that building."

"His old company did. The one that fired him over sexual harassment complaints right about the time of his divorce. He would have known that building inside and out."

"So he killed Frances, his first job having graduated from rape to murder. Then Grace. He meant to save Kelly—the driver—for last. He probably wanted her to make the connection, to make her think he was coming for her, believing she wouldn't ask for protection and let the media rehash the accident."

"It worked," David said, wiping rain from his forehead. "I think the accident weighed on her mind, but she didn't want the story to resurface in the middle of the mine disaster. Now we'll never be able to ask her. You know, you'd be warmer if we sat inside the ambulance, or even inside my car."

"I like the rain."

"Since when?"

"Since I got covered in someone else's blood."

He tucked a lock of sodden hair behind her ear. "Maybe this is the wrong time for this. On the other hand, maybe it's exactly the right time. I have something I'd like to give you."

Her eyebrows lifted. "Coffee?"

"This." He pulled a small box from his pocket and pressed it into her hand. Raindrops immediately spotted the velvet covering, and patrol car lights reflected in the spots.

She had just gotten her heartbeat under control too.

"I bought it before I came to your house last night, but we never had a chance to talk."

The square-cut diamond seemed impossibly big. The platinum warmed quickly, once on her hand.

"I know you said you didn't want to get married again, but I hope you'll change your mind."

Clio Helms approached, holding out a foam cup. "Here, drink this, it's hot. The medic said you— Holy shit, is that an engagement ring?"

Evelyn couldn't speak.

"Yes," David said.

The lithe reporter turned, her voice penetrating the rain, the sirens, and the chaos. "Paul! I need a photographer over here *right now!*"

ACKNOWLEDGMENTS

Most of my thanks go to my husband, Russ, who provided not only all the technical knowledge but the germ of the plot as well. I'd also like to thank our friend Danny, who shared his experiences of working in the salt mine; Ciba Jones; and critique partners Sharon and Sheri. And, as always, the friendly folks from the Trace Evidence Department during the second half of the 1990s—Linda, Sharon, Kay, Dihann, Jim, Bernie, and Dr. Balraj; Elaine and Stephanie at the Elaine Koster Agency; and my mother, Florence.